DECEBAL
TRIUMPHANT

Book One in the Rome - Dacia Wars Series
85 – 99 A.D.

Peter Jaksa

Attention Publishing

CHICAGO, ILLINOIS

Peter Jaksa/Attention Publishing
30 North Michigan Avenue, Suite 908
Chicago, IL 60602
www.addcenters.com

Publisher's Note: This is a work of fiction. Names, characters, places, and incidents are a product of the author's imagination. Locales and public names are sometimes used for atmospheric purposes. Any resemblance to actual people, living or dead, or to businesses, companies, events, institutions, or locales is completely coincidental.

Decebal Triumphant / Peter Jaksa. -- 1st ed.
ISBN 978-1-7349923-2-8

For Jonel, my brother

And for Anna W.
who will always sing with the angels

Contents

Chapter 1

THE MASSACRE IN THE SNOW

Roman province of Moesia, December 85 AD

The snowfall drifted in the morning breeze and covered the frozen ground with a fresh blanket of pure white. The Dacian army filled the flat and narrow valley, from the craggy hills in the north to the thick pine forest in the south. Men and horses stood and shivered, warm breath misting in the winter air.

Even as they endured the cold and snow the soldiers stirred with excitement. All eyes turned towards the east, where the Roman legion was deploying for battle. The soldiers knew that they were about to fight the fight of their lives.

King Duras of Dacia rode his black stallion slowly and calmly along the front line so that his troops could see him. At his side rode his nephew and commander of the army, the thirty year old General Diurpaneus. More and more of the soldiers were calling the young general Decebal. It was a title given to honor his bravery and military leadership. The General rode tall in the saddle, straight backed and proud astride a great chestnut warhorse.

Behind them rode a warrior carrying the draco flag on a long wooden pole. The draco was the ancient symbol of Dacia, a flowing cloth pennant with the head of a wolf and body of a dragon. Behind the draco came the cavalry of the King's Royal Guard.

The men cheered loudly as the King and his escort neared their sections. They banged their swords and spear shafts against their round shields. Their shouts and clamor filled the valley.

King Duras turned his elegant, graying head toward Decebal and gave the younger man a bemused smile.

"Are they cheering for me, Nephew? Or for you?"

Decebal smiled back. In moments of tension his uncle often took a light and joking tone. Few things in life created more tension than preparing to fight a Roman legion.

"They are cheering for Dacia, Sire. And all men know that you are the strength of Dacia."

"Hah!" King Duras grunted. "I am the monarch of Dacia, Nephew. But every soldier in our lines knows who leads them."

The tone of resentment in his uncle's voice, mild as it was, caught Decebal by surprise. The King was aging, soon to be sixty-three. That was old for any man and very old for a king. Duras ruled Dacia for the past fifteen years and was respected by his people as a fair and just monarch. So why this hint of jealousy now?

"We both lead, each in our own way," Decebal said evenly, then decided to change the subject. He looked towards the Roman army to the east. "Governor Sabinus is positioning his legion for attack."

"So he is," King Duras agreed. "You will follow the strategy that we discussed?"

"Yes, Sire."

"Is the cavalry in place? Drilgisa and the infantry?"

"Everything is in place," Decebal reassured him.

"Good," King Duras said. "You planned a solid strategy, now go and make it work! The battle is in your hands."

"Yes, Sire," Decebal acknowledged respectfully. "I shall celebrate with you after the battle, Uncle. Zamolxis watches over us and will bring us victory this day."

The King watched his general ride away, the chestnut horse's hooves kicking up clumps of snow. All jealousy was washed away by a strong surge of pride. His nephew was only thirty years old yet he was already Dacia's best battlefield commander since the days of King Burebista.

Burebista had been a contemporary of the great Julius Caesar, one hundred and fifty years ago. Dacia was a unified and mighty nation then, a nation of warriors strong enough to concern Rome and the legendary Caesar. He prayed that Dacia would be that strong again. If Zamolxis willed it, it would be so, but who knew the will of the gods?

Gaius Oppius Sabinus was a former consul of Rome, a Senator of Rome, and a friend of Emperor Domitian. He was now appointed governor of the rich Roman province of Moesia, which was located north of Macedonia and south of the Danubius River.

It was recognized by all that the Danubius River was the northern frontier of the Roman Empire. This Dacian incursion south across the Danubius was a military threat to be taken seriously. For weeks now they attacked and razed a number of Roman forts and camps in Moesia. Sabinus and Domitian and the Senate of Rome all agreed that the barbarian nations north of the river had to be held in check, otherwise it would only encourage wider rebellions against Rome.

From horseback Oppius Sabinus reviewed the magnificent array of his troops. They stretched out across the width of the valley, facing the Dacian lines. His legionnaires were veterans, none better. They had marched for a week through cold and mud for this moment. Now they were grim, determined, and ready for battle.

The core of his army was the veteran Legio V Macedonica. It was manned by five thousand and two hundred foot soldiers and one hundred and twenty cavalry. Sabinus also had command over one thousand auxiliary troops, recruited from local Moesian tribesmen. Although the Moesians were related to the Dacians, with a common language and sharing many cultural traditions, under Roman rule they fought for Rome. Their homes and families were hostage.

In the distance the Dacian troops stood and waited. Few were in armor, Sabinus observed, and very few on horse. They waited and clearly invited him to attack. Very well, he would oblige them. He had the advantage in numbers, six thousand against what looked like the Dacians' four thousand, and he had an advantage in the quality of fighting men. There was no disputing that Roman legions were the finest military in the world. It was time to show these barbarians why that was so.

General Decebal fought in the middle of the Dacian line because a leader best inspired his men by leading from the front. He was a head taller than most men. Broad chested and muscular in the arms and legs, exceptionally well trained and experienced from over a decade of military service, he was a strong and skilled warrior as well as a gifted military strategist.

Like most Dacians Decebal wore little armor. A coat of steel mail covered a thick woolen shirt. He wore a steel helmet, rounded on top, lined with leather. From underneath the helmet spilled black hair that fell down the back of his neck. Like most Dacians he wore white woolen breeches against the cold.

To Decebal's right on the line was his younger brother Diegis. Five years younger and two inches shorter, he was otherwise as strongly built as his brother. Diegis was armed with a sica, the razor sharp Dacian sword with a curved tip, and a round shield. The Dacian shield was made of oak wood and covered in front with a sheet of copper. This made the shield strong yet also light enough to be used as a weapon in battering down enemy warriors.

To Decebal's left stood Buri, a small giant of a man who also served as the General's bodyguard. Buri was as tall as Decebal but much thicker and stronger. He took up as much space on the line as two ordinary men. His long reddish brown hair and bushy beard gave him a fierce appearance. Normally even tempered, in battle Buri was a ferocious fighter and the equal of any three other men. He carried a shield on his thick left arm as if it were a toy. Buri was armed with a long handled battle axe.

General Decebal surveyed the Roman line across from him. Over the years he studied Roman military tactics, and he had a good idea of what to expect. If Governor Sabinus followed standard tactics his legion would march in tight formation to within pilus throwing range. They would then unleash a thick volley of these throwing spears at his men, and follow immediately with a ferocious charge against the Dacian line.

Often this tactic was enough to frighten and scatter the enemy, which was then ripe for slaughter. These tactics had worked well in Gaul, Germania, Africa, and many other places where Rome's armies were sent to conquer. Governor Sabinus, Decebal knew, was first and foremost an aristocratic politician and not some type of innovative military genius. There was every reason to expect him to follow standard Roman tactics.

General Decebal however had no intention at all of fighting on the Romans' terms. He had other plans entirely.

Oppius Sabinus turned to his tribune, Titus Lucullus. "Titus! On my command, sound the advance."

Sabinus drew his sword and raised it to point towards the enemy line. He held his arm still for a heartbeat, then slashed down so that the sword pointed at the ground.

"Advance!" Titus shouted the command.

Thousands of Roman army boots shuffled forward in unison. The men were quiet but disciplined and determined, doing what their training taught them to do. They knew from many past battles what was expected of them. Their steady, rhythmic advance trampled the freshly fallen snow into the ground.

"Hold steady!" Decebal shouted to his troops. His order was repeated by officers up and down the line. "Hold steady! Hold steady!"

Dacian soldiers stirred impatiently, chafing at being held back in the face of the advancing legionnaires. They were eager to charge the enemy, excited to begin the fight. No one felt the cold now.

"Hold steady!" Decebal repeated. "Let them come to us!"

"The Romans are drawing within pilus range, Brother," Diegis pointed out.

"I am aware of their range," Decebal replied calmly. "I want to draw them closer."

Every legionnaire carried a pilus, the light Roman throwing spear. It was hurled at the enemy at the start of the battle and was deadly efficient. As every soldier knew, blocking or dodging one spear is easy. A swarm of spears cannot be dodged.

"Hold on to your shield, the spears will start flying," Decebal said to his brother.

"At least I have enough sense to carry a shield!" Diegis replied with a grin. "Unlike you, Brother!"

"Buri is my shield," Decebal said with a sideways glance at the large man on his left.

Decebal carried no shield because he was fighting with a falx. This was the two-handed Dacian weapon shaped like the sica but with a much longer handle and blade. That gave it a longer reach and more striking power. It was a weapon that Roman legionnaires would come to dread fighting against.

Some legionnaires were now close enough to where they could throw the pilus and reach the Dacian line. Close enough to see the misting breaths and facial features of individual soldiers.

Decebal turned to his left and shouted an order down the line. "Retreat slowly, in formation!" He turned to his right and did the same. "Retreat slowly, in formation!"

The soldiers shuffled backwards one step at a time towards the west, away from the advancing Romans.

"I don't like to retreat," Diegis growled, eyes blazing. "We can't kill Romans if we retreat."

"Patience, Brother," Decebal replied. "Do you trust me?"

"You know I do."

"Show patience then and set an example for the men. We fight like the wolf, not the boar."

"The Dacians are retreating!" Titus Lucullus exclaimed in surprise. "They're not even putting up a fight."

"They're afraid to face Roman armor directly," Governor Sabinus judged. His tone of disdain reflected his low opinion of barbarian armies. He expected them to run in the face of superior forces. These barbarians lacked the character and the training of Roman soldiers.

The Dacians refused to engage and so both armies drifted further west. From the pine covered hills on the Roman left some Dacian archers were shooting at the passing formations of legionnaires. They were not a serious threat to his flank but could not be allowed to harass the troops so brazenly.

Sabinus beckoned towards his commander of cavalry, Antonius Trebonius.

Trebonius rode closer. "Sir!"

"Take fifty cavalry and clear out those damn archers in the trees."

"Immediately, sir," Trebonius replied with a grin and rode off to dispatch his horsemen. Cavalry going after archers were like foxes chasing rabbits. Very slow rabbits, at that.

The unexpected Dacian retreat took the Roman officers by surprise because this was not how barbarians fought. The young tribune Titus Lucullus felt strangely unsettled. He cleared his throat before he spoke.

"Governor Sabinus, a word if I may?"

"Yes, Titus?"

"Our left flank is being exposed to attack from the pine woods, where those archers are. Should we deploy the Tenth Cohort reserve to guard the tree line? As a precaution, sir."

Sabinus frowned, but he knew that Lucullus had a point. "They don't seem inclined to fight us at all, Titus, much less attack. But yes, as a precaution, send the Tenth Cohort to guard against the tree line."

"Yes, sir," Lucullus acknowledged and turned to a messenger with orders. He wanted the five hundred men of the reserve cohort in a defensive position quickly.

The Roman cavalry dispatched by Trebonius were running down the Dacian archers and chasing them into the woods. The infantry front line was advancing and meeting no resistance. The Dacians would soon be backed up against a hill to their rear, and would be forced to either stand and fight or scatter and run. The battle was being won almost too easily.

And then everything happened all at once.

"Sir!"

One of the Governor's cavalry guards sounded the alarm, pointing east towards the Roman rear. A column of smoke was rising thick and black against the gray sky from the area where the baggage carts and supply wagons were positioned.

Now distant cries of a besieged camp came from that direction. Men shouting and yelling, women screaming, the sharp sound of metal clashing against metal, the drumming of many horses' hooves on the frozen soil.

A rider approached in a hurry from the direction of the rear camp. The man shouted for directions and was pointed straight to the command post. He pulled up in front of Sabinus and saluted.

"Report!" The Governor demanded sharply.

"Dacian cavalry to our rear, sir! They are swarming over the camp. The rear guard is overwhelmed, sir." The rider paused to catch a quick breath.

"How many cavalry? Speak up you fool!"

"Hundreds, sir. Perhaps three or four hundred."

Sabinus' face went rigid.

From the south, on his left, the fifty Roman cavalry that had chased the archers were now riding fast out of the pine woods. They were no longer fighting, but escaping. Behind them a thick swarm of Dacian infantry emerged from the tree line. They were walking fast but not running. They paid no attention to the cavalry but headed straight for the exposed left flank of the Roman legion.

This was the flank attack that Titus Lucullus cautioned against. Too late to stop it now with the Tenth Cohort. With a growing sense of alarm Titus made a quick estimate of the Dacian forces coming out of the woods. Five hundred men, a thousand, fifteen hundred. And soldiers were still emerging from the trees.

To the west, where the two main armies faced each other a spear's throw apart, the Dacian forces stopped retreating.

"Halt and deploy for attack!" General Decebal shouted.

The new orders were met with cheers from his men. Warriors hated to retreat. Now the battle would finally begin and they would take the fight to the Romans.

The column of smoke rising from behind the Roman position was the signal from General Sinna and his Dacian cavalry that they were attacking the Roman camp. The cavalry had been concealed behind hills to the north, and they attacked exactly on time.

From the south, two thousand Dacian foot soldiers swarmed out of the pine forest where they had been in hiding overnight. They were led by General Drilgisa, a fierce veteran warrior. They closed in fast on the nearest Roman units that now had to turn to face them.

"In formation, forward!" Decebal shouted. "At a fast walk! Do not run! Maintain formation!" He led his army towards the Roman legion as a fast moving but organized force. A mad disorganized rush would be reckless and playing into the Romans' hands.

"Behind me!" Buri shouted. He stepped in front of Decebal just as the first Roman spears flew at them. A pilus struck his shield, another landed in front of him inches from his foot, many other spears flew overhead to strike the men further back.

Some spears hit the ground or were stopped by shields, but many found unprotected faces, necks, and legs. The soldier next to Diegis cried out sharply with pain as a pilus plunged into his unprotected thigh. He staggered and fell forward, and bright red blood gushed out over the blanket of freshly fallen snow.

Roman officers shouted orders and positioned their men to meet the two attacks coming at them from different directions. The Romans were now the ones fighting a defensive battle. Dacian troops closed in with speed and discipline.

"Attack! Find gaps!" Decebal shouted.

The front line Dacians with falxes attacked first, and the battle became a game of stealth. The legionnaires were armored and better protected, but heavier and less mobile. The Dacians had the reach advantage of the falx over the much shorter Roman gladius. They were quicker in darting in to attack, then pulling back out of reach of the gladius. The fight took on a look of wolves attacking porcupines.

Decebal came face to face with a tall red-headed Roman. He thrust the two-handed falx at the Roman's face, staying out of reach of the soldier's sword. The legionnaire raised his shield and blocked the blow. Decebal's falx did not hit hard because the main force of the blow was directed in a swift downward move in front of the Roman's shield. The falx flashed low and found a knee, thrusting forward hard to cut through muscle and sinew. The legionnaire grunted sharply with pain and slumped to the ground on his one good knee.

Diegis jumped at the kneeling Roman and plunged his sica into the man's exposed neck, between breastplate and helmet. A spray of blood splashed over both of them. Diegis jumped back swiftly to avoid a sword heading for his belly.

Buri swung his battle axe one-handed and smashed his shield against Roman shields to drive men back. The strength and ferocity of his attack made soldiers back away out of his reach.

Beside him Decebal fought a legionnaire who was skilled with shield and sword, blocking every falx blow thrown at him. Decebal again had the much longer reach advantage and the Roman's sword could not find him.

"Buri!" Decebal shouted. "Hook!"

Buri knew exactly what that meant, they had practiced the hook and pull hundreds of times. He stepped towards the legionnaire with his shield blocking the man's sword arm. He reached out with his right arm until the axe head hooked over the top of the Roman's shield, then gave a powerful tug. The legionnaire struggled to keep his balance as his shield was pulled forward and lower. In the blink of an eye Decebal's falx slashed over the top of the shield and took the man in the face. The soldier dropped to the ground like a stone.

All around the edges of the battlefield Dacians and Romans were screaming, bleeding, and dying. The Romans were outnumbered, outmaneuvered, and slowly giving ground. They were being pushed back towards the east.

Dacian cavalry now attacked the legion from the east, the Roman rear. Some circled around the Roman right flank to attack from the north. For the most part the cavalry did not fight with spears or swords, but with bows as horse archers. They rode in close, fired their arrows with great accuracy at short range, and then quickly rode away. Their horses were smaller but quicker than the bigger horses of the Roman cavalry. The horse archers were elusive and lethal.

When infantry was attacked in this manner, from the flanks or from the rear, they were not able to protect themselves with their shields. The legionnaires fighting against Dacian infantry had little defense against the horse archers.

"Push them back!" Decebal yelled. "Attack the gaps!"

"That's what we are doing!" Diegis yelled back, his voice hoarse with excitement. He turned quickly to give assistance to a Dacian soldier pressing forward into the Roman line.

A Roman rushed at Decebal, shield out front and gladius in his right hand poised for attack. Decebal took a quick step to his right, away from the legionnaire's sword hand. His falx lashed out low then pulled back sharply, like swinging a scythe. The curved tip of the blade caught the Roman across the left calf, cutting through muscle and sinew to the bone. Like cutting down a stalk of corn, he thought to himself.

The wounded legionnaire staggered and fell. A Dacian pounced on him with a sica to hack him to death. Blood flowed over the frozen ground to turn more snow crimson.

"We have them now!" Diegis whooped and raised his bloodstained sword in triumph. He was fully caught up in the wild thrill of battle.

"Not yet!" Decebal replied. "They are not breaking and the battle is not yet won. Mind that you don't get careless and get killed at this late stage, Brother!"

He looked past the battlefield towards a low hill from where a group of Roman cavalry watched the battle. That was the Roman command post, and that was where he would find Governor Sabinus.

"The legion is being cut to pieces," Titus Lucullus said. The battle was only a few hours old but it was going very badly. The Dacians had the advantage in numbers and position. If the legion did not retreat it would soon be enveloped. Envelopment, being surrounded on all sides, would lead to annihilation.

Oppius Sabinus watched in silence from his saddle. His mind was reeling. The prospect of defeat was too humiliating to consider. How was he to explain this to the Senate and the Emperor? He must find a way to turn the tide of battle or everything was lost.

"Titus!"

"Sir!"

"Send in the Tenth Cohort reserve and the cavalry reserves. We must take control of this battle."

Lucullus grimaced, then swallowed hard. "The legion is being overrun, sir. We must retreat."

"Nonsense!" Sabinus protested. "We will fight our way out of this!"

"With due respect sir, we must think of saving the men." Titus scanned the battlefield quickly, a look of quiet resignation on his face. "The battle cannot be won, sir. We must retreat now or else lose the legion."

Governor Sabinus turned on him in fury. "Are you disobeying my order? I will have you charged with cowardice and treason!"

To their right a detachment of Dacian cavalry and infantry were engaged in a fierce battle with the Governor's personal guard. More Dacian troops were streaming in their direction.

"Send in the reserves!" Sabinus commanded, his anger rising. He raised his sword and with his knees urged his horse forward towards a Dacian soldier who had just speared the stallion of a Roman cavalry officer. The Dacian noticed Sabinus too late, tried to duck, and took a sword blow to the head that knocked off his helmet and threw him to the ground. Sabinus' horse, trained for battle, reared up and then smashed down with a hoof to crush the man's chest.

Suddenly everything was chaos. A Dacian cavalryman rushed Sabinus from the left, lunging with his spear. Sabinus parried the spear with his sword and steered his horse away. A Dacian footman grabbed his right leg to drag the Governor off his horse. Sabinus turned and swung his sword in a downward arc, slashing across the man's shoulder. The Dacian staggered back and fell.

A Dacian with a falx cut at the horse's left hind leg. The animal screamed in pain and bolted forward. Sabinus lost his hold in the saddle and fell hard on his left side. He was stunned for a moment, then stood and faced two Dacians in front of him. His vision was blurry and time seemed to be moving very slowly.

"Sir, we must retreat now!" Titus shouted while also fighting off a Dacian spearman. He could not tell if the Governor heard him, then had to turn his horse swiftly to fight off a Dacian cavalryman.

Oppius Sabinus first sensed, then felt, the sharp curved tip of the falx as it pressed lightly against the front of his throat just under his helmet strap. The metal felt very cold against his skin. He could not see the Dacian behind him who was holding the falx, but heard the man shouting a command that he did not understand. His right hand tightened around the hilt of his sword. This was an outrage! He was a Governor of Rome. He would not be commanded so by a barbarian. The man shouted again. Sabinus opened his mouth to protest but no sound came. The Dacian soldier gave the falx a hard tug and the blade cut deep.

Titus Lucullus watched Governor Gaius Oppius Sabinus fall on his back, where he died quickly in a spreading pool of blood. He knew then that the battle was over. More Dacians were climbing the hill to assault the command post, which was now indefensible. He urged his horse to the rear towards a group of legionnaires who guarded the legion's Eagle and also the signal corps.

Tribune Titus Lucullus, now commander of the legion, gave the only order that could be given.

"Sound the retreat!" Lucullus commanded.

At the sound of bugle signals the men of Legio V Macedonica began to retreat in formation. They were too well disciplined to scatter and run, which would have invited a slaughter. The forward units moved backwards slowly while fighting a defensive battle to keep the still attacking Dacians off them. The Dacian horse archers kept attacking and harassing the retreating troops. There were few Roman cavalry left to counter them and those were now also retreating.

General Decebal looked over the sprawling battlefield, covered with Dacian and Roman bodies. He saw that the battle was won, and that his men were bloodied and near exhaustion. He made a quick decision not to pursue the retreating survivors. The battle was over.

The Romans avoided annihilation but in so doing left behind their dead and wounded. For them the only goal now was survival. Of the proud veterans of Legio V Macedonica perhaps two in five were now walking away. The rest were dead, wounded, or captured.

By midafternoon the snow flurries stopped. The sky grew brighter, here and there showing patches of blue. The field was still and quiet except for the moans and screams of the wounded and dying. The wounded were carried to the rear of the Dacian lines, where the field surgeons waited.

Prisoners were disarmed, stripped of weapons and armor down to their tunics and boots. The men stood and shivered and waited to learn their fate. Horses from the Roman cavalry were herded towards the Dacian camp.

"A good victory," Diegis said solemnly. His clothes were stained with blood, and he had a cut on his left cheek where a sword tip had just missed his eye. He felt tired and sobered by the scale of the slaughter. Buri, standing close by, looked the same.

"Yes, Brother, a good victory," Decebal agreed. "You fought well. You too, Buri."

The big man grunted and waved away the compliment, which made Decebal smile. Buri was a man of few words and ill at ease with receiving compliments.

"You are dismissed, Buri. Go back to camp and find a meal. We shall talk later, my friend."

As Buri walked away a dozen Dacian soldiers approached from the opposite direction. Four of them carried the body of Governor Oppius Sabinus.

Decebal held up a hand and the soldiers stopped. Sabinus was still dressed in full armor and uniform. The body of an army commander was not to be looted. Decebal looked down at his enemy, the corpse now so drained of blood the skin was almost as white as the snow. This was the nobleman, the former consul of Rome, sent to put down the Dacians.

"Take him to the King," Decebal ordered, motioning towards the hill where the royal party waited. "Treat the body of the Governor with dignity."

General Drilgisa approached leading a group of a hundred or so Moesian prisoners. He was a handsome man of thirty-two who at the moment looked like a bloody horror. As a child he had been a Roman slave, then was bought and rescued from slavery by a wealthy Dacian trader who raised him as his own son. Drilgisa never talked of his childhood but carried an intense hatred for all things Roman.

"Did you take all these men prisoner yourself, General Drilgisa?" Decebal joked. "Or did you need some help to capture them?"

Drilgisa laughed. "These fine Moesian lads wish to join us. As you can tell by their clean and unbloodied clothes, they didn't put up much of a fight when we approached them. They want to fight Rome, not serve Rome."

Decebal looked the crowd over and saw that Drilgisa was right. These were frightened men who a short while ago expected to be killed, but now dared ask to be given a new life.

"If I allow you to live in Dacia, will you fight for Dacia?" he asked the crowd in a loud voice. "Will you serve Dacia?"

One of the men, a twenty year old with long black hair and a wispy mustache, took a step forward.

"I swear loyalty to you and to Dacia, Lord," he began in a voice thick with emotion. "I have no family or land in Moesia. I don't wish to go back to live under Roman rule."

"And the rest of you?" Decebal asked, his eyes scanning the group. Every man in the crowd swore his loyalty. They were finally free of Roman control.

"I welcome you, my Moesian brothers!" Decebal raised his voice so all the men could hear him well. "We share a common language and customs. We fight the same enemies. And I promise you that one day, as allies, we will free all of Moesia from the tyranny of Rome!"

The Moesians gave a loud cheer. This was more than they had hoped for.

A young man standing beside Drilgisa could no longer contain his curiosity. "Are you General Diurpaneus?"

Drilgisa turned and cuffed him lightly across the back of the head.

"Boy, did your mother never let you off the farm? This is General Decebal. He just defeated a Roman army, then to be generous he just gave you your life and your freedom. Address him properly!"

Decebal held up a hand. "No need to upbraid the boy, he is simply curious. Yes, lad, I am General Diurpaneus. Some stubborn soldiers like General Drilgisa here insist on calling me General Decebal."

One of the older Moesians nodded his head. "The name suits you, General. Even more so after today."

Drilgisa pointed the Moesian soldiers towards the Dacian camp to the west. "Men, listen up! Go that way. They will take your names and provide you with water and bread."

"Very well done, Drilgisa," Decebal said, watching the Moesians walk away. "We need to recruit every Moesian we can. We are going to need every ally for what is coming."

"Aye, we will," Drilgisa agreed. He nodded towards the crowd of Roman prisoners, shivering in the cold. "And what do we do with them?"

"We'll ransom them or exchange them. If they are badly maimed and can no longer fight we will release them. Better to let the Romans feed them than us."

Drilgisa frowned. "Better to cut their throats now, I tell you. If you let them go now we'll have to fight them again later."

"Then we will defeat them again later."

Drilgisa turned to Decebal so sharply that Diegis stepped to his brother's side.

"It is a mistake to let the Romans live! Remember that I said this, Decebal."

"I will remember." Decebal paused and took a breath. He looked Drilgisa in the eye and spoke in a calm and measured tone. "General Drilgisa, there is no finer infantry commander than you. You have a talent, and I must say a passion for killing Romans. Even so, we will not execute these prisoners. This is my command."

"As you command, then," Drilgisa replied, anger cooling. He had spoken his mind and there was no room for argument. Decebal was the highest ranking general and acknowledged leader of the army. Drilgisa nodded a farewell to each of the men, then turned and walked away.

Diegis looked at his brother and gave a shrug. Drilgisa's hate for Romans was legendary. No one quite understood it.

"Come with me, Diegis, we need to see the King. Also I am hungry and the royal table has the best food."

That made Diegis smile. "Where you lead, Brother, I follow."

Chapter 2

SARMIZEGETUSA

Roman province of Moesia, December 85 AD

*K*ing Duras sat at a table on the hill from which he had watched the battle. The High Priest Vezina, his closest advisor, sat opposite the King. No one knew quite how old the tall, thin, silver-haired Vezina was. Before serving as advisor to King Duras he had been High Priest and advisor to his older brother King Scorilo. His long white hair falling down to his shoulders, and long white beard, made him look ancient and wise.

King Duras wore a long sheep-skin coat against the cold. Vezina wore the same over the blue robes, embroidered with silver and gold thread, of the High Priest of Zamolxis. Both wore the lambs-fur cap on their heads, the pilati, which was a symbol of Dacian nobility.

The King and High Priest were talking as they gazed at the body of Governor Sabinus, laid out on a blanket some distance away. A man with a spear stood guard near the corpse to chase away any carrion birds that might wander too close.

The soldiers of the Royal Guard stood respectfully as Decebal and Diegis washed themselves at a water basin. The two brothers were well respected, in part because they were Dacian royalty. Along with their two sisters, Dochia and Tanidela, they were the children of King Scorilo, the monarch prior to Duras. Dochia was the oldest of the four siblings, Tanidela the youngest.

Even more importantly than their royal bloodline, the brothers were respected for their courage as warriors and for their fairness. They took the same risks they would ask any other soldier to take. Nothing created stronger bonds of loyalty from the common soldiers.

The brothers found room on the benches placed on either side of the table. Servants brought trays of food and a pitcher of water. The food was simple but hearty, mutton and fowl roasted with vegetables and spices, and loaves of bread.

King Duras looked very pleased, and for good reason. He just watched his army rout a veteran Roman legion. His mood was much more relaxed post-battle than it had been prior to the fight.

"You brought us a great victory today, Nephew," Duras said in compliment to Decebal.

Decebal acknowledged the praise with a nod. "The men fought very well, Sire. They showed courage and discipline."

"You are being much too modest. Yes, the men fought very well, and that is the mark of a well-trained army."

The High Priest echoed the King. "Much of the credit belongs to you, Decebal. If we fought the Romans like barbarians, wild men running and smashing against their lines, we would have lost this battle. Instead you used their arrogance against them. Well done, General."

Decebal dug into his food with relish. "Arrogance is a dangerous thing and it can easily be exploited. Is that what you are telling me, Vezina?"

The question made the priest laugh. Decebal had long ago learned all the lessons that Vezina had to offer. A High Priest of Zamolxis was a highly trained scholar, well versed in history, science, and military tactics. When it came to military strategy at least, this student had surpassed his teacher.

"Indeed, arrogance in battle is often fatal," Vezina agreed.

King Duras frowned as he glanced over at the body of the dead governor. "I have one question, Nephew."

"Yes, Uncle?"

"How did Governor Sabinus come to be killed?"

Decebal shook his head with regret. "He fought and died in battle. So I was told."

Diegis paused from taking hungry bites from a leg of mutton. "Sabinus put up a fight when our men attacked his command post. One of our boys nearly took his head off with a falx."

"Most unusual behavior for a Roman noble," Vezina said lightly. "They usually expect to be ransomed for a small fortune. Most often their wealthy families pay the ransom."

King Duras turned to him irritably. "This is no joke! He was the governor of Moesia. He was a consul of Rome just last year. I wished to speak with him."

"Yes, Sire," Vezina said with a nod. "Emperor Domitian will also not be happy. He will consider the destruction of his legion and the killing of the governor as a terrible insult to Rome."

The King had no love for Rome or Caesar, and this comment pleased him. "No doubt Domitian will blow his top like Vesuvius when news of this reaches Rome."

Vezina continued. "He won't be the only one. The Senate of Rome will not be happy, and they will blame Domitian for this defeat. They have no love for him, only contempt."

"Good, let them fight against each other," Diegis said with a laugh.

"This will bring Domitian here," Decebal declared between bites of food. "He will bring a larger army."

King Duras raised an eyebrow. "Why do you believe Domitian himself will come? Roman emperors do not travel with their legions. Not since the days of Augustus in any case."

Decebal pushed his plate away, his mood turning somber. "What we know about Emperor Domitian, thanks mostly to your informers Vezina, is that he is arrogant and vain. He must also prove himself as a military leader, in order to live up to what his father and brother accomplished. His hold on power in Rome may depend on it."

Vezina thought for a moment. "You make a good point. His father Vespasian was a very accomplished general, which is precisely why he was made emperor. He conquered Judea after the Jewish rebellion. His brother Titus did the same, he sieged and captured Jerusalem."

"Titus was a good emperor for Rome," King Duras said, "while he lasted."

"Yes, Titus was an admired emperor but he died young," Vezina continued. "It is said that he died under questionable circumstances and that his brother aided in his death."

Diegis raised an eyebrow. "Domitian killed his brother? Is that so?"

"Romans are overly fond of assassinating their rulers," King Duras said with a frown. "Family ties are no shield."

"The important point to ponder," Vezina said, turning towards Decebal, "is that you are correct, General. Compared to his illustrious father and his brother, Domitian is seen as a weak emperor. He still needs to prove himself. His war against the Chatti in Germania a few years ago earned him scorn, not respect."

Decebal acknowledged with a nod. "And that is why, after what happened here today, Emperor Domitian must seek revenge. To do so he must come with a larger army. Governor Sabinus did not travel with artillery because the weather was rain and snow and the roads were rivers of mud. The next Roman army will come during their war season, in the summer. They will bring more legions and also artillery and more cavalry."

"Then we must be ready," King Duras declared. "No matter what they bring or however many of them there are."

"We'll be ready," Decebal said firmly, "but we must start to prepare now. We cannot be lax or overconfident." He glanced at the High Priest with a smile. "Overconfidence, I hear, is just as dangerous as arrogance. Isn't that so?"

Vezina gave him a solemn nod. "Indeed. They are two sides of the same coin, and both will get you killed."

Sarmizegetusa, Dacia, January 86 AD

The army marched from Moesia into Dacia across the frozen Ister River, which the Romans called the Danubius. They followed the northern bank of the Ister and made their way heading west, then turned north into the heart of Dacia. They marched through snowy mountain valleys and narrow forest roads towards the capital, the holy city of Sarmizegetusa.

The mountain roads to Sarmizegetusa were guarded by a series of stone walled forts. An army seeking to reach the capital would have to fight an arduous campaign and suffer heavy casualties. For a long time no army had even tried.

Many Dacian cities and forts were built high in the mountains for obvious defensive reasons. Show me a city built on the plains and near a river, the father of Decebal often said, and I'll show you a fat easy target for the next army that marches by. We should not make things easy for our enemies, King Scorilo insisted. He was following a strategic policy that was established by other kings a long time ago, even before the time of Burebista.

Sarmizegetusa itself was built into the side of a mountain. One side faced a steep, high cliff. Another side was protected in part by another cliff that dropped sharply and could not be climbed. The city was protected by stone walls thirty feet high and nine feet thick. On top of the walls were battlements and towers made from limestone and the hard volcanic rock andesite, which made it easy for archers and spearmen to fight off any attackers. Massive gates made of thick wood reinforced with iron guarded the main entrance.

Inside its walls Sarmizegetusa was a large sprawling complex. Houses for the civilian population were built on a series of wide and flat terraces carved into the mountain, each terrace a little higher than the one below. Higher up was the royal palace. Highest of all were the sacred areas, including the Holy Temple of Zamolxis. The temples were always built on the highest ground by Dacian tradition, so as to be closest to Zamolxis.

A large complex of water pipes brought fresh water for drinking and bathing from streams higher up the mountain. A system of sewer pipes kept the city clean. Large granaries, barns, and animal pens kept the city stocked with food. Orchards and gardens grew enough fruits and vegetables to feed the city population.

Cavalry scouts rode ahead to alert the city of the army's arrival. The soldiers received an enthusiastic homecoming celebration after a long and tiring march. King Duras and General Decebal rode in front of the column, up the mountain road lined with ancient trees. They passed through the city gates to the cheers of the sentries manning the walls. The people of the city came out in the cold and lined the streets to greet and cheer their King, and also their sons, husbands, fathers, and brothers.

The Royal Guard marched to the palace to escort the King and his entourage home. Up the road and higher up the mountain was the Holy Temple of Zamolxis, where Vezina and his priests lived. The soldiers gratefully went to their homes and their waiting families.

It was dusk by the time Decebal arrived at his family quarters in the royal palace. His son Cotiso waited outside the main entrance, eager to be the first to greet his father. The twelve year old was taller than most boys his age but still very thin and wiry. He had his mother's light brown hair and his father's dark brown eyes.

Cotiso was the son of Decebal's first wife, Tyra, who died from a fever six years ago. Cotiso was six years old then and took the loss of his mother very hard. Decebal married his new wife, Andrada, two years later. They were now the parents of two daughters. Andrada was twenty-four years old and too young to be treated by Cotiso as his mother, but he took pride in his role as older brother.

"Welcome home, Tata," the son said with pride and affection and held out his hand. He would be a man soon, he thought, and it no longer felt proper to embrace his father in public.

"Hello, Son. I am happy to see you." Decebal shook his hand, then put an arm around Cotiso's shoulders and led him inside. "Have you been looking after your sisters?"

"Yes, Tata," the boy answered in a serious tone. "Adila is just now learning to talk. She really likes to talk and never stops!" he laughed. "Zia is quieter but she is very smart."

"And your mother Andrada? Are you treating her with respect?"

Cotiso frowned. "I like Lady Andrada but she is not my mother. And yes, of course I am treating her with respect."

"She is your mother in spirit, Son. Will you try and treat her in that manner?"

"Yes, Tata," Cotiso replied. His father was a fierce champion of family loyalty. Any show of disrespect or disloyalty was simply not tolerated.

Andrada and the girls were playing in the large room where the family spent most of their time. Rugs covered the stone floor and tapestries hung on the walls, which made the room very colorful and kept it warm in winter. Three year old Zia was on the floor with her mother playing with a wooden toy horse and farm wagon. The toy wagon was carting real carrots and onions from an imaginary farm to an imaginary market. One year old Adila was repeating words with the help of her aunt Dochia, the older sister of Decebal.

Andrada looked up first when her husband and stepson entered the room. Her blue eyes brightened and her lips widened into a smile.

"Zia, look who is here!"

"Tata!" Zia had not seen her father in several months, and she jumped up and ran across the room into his arms. Adila looked up at the excitement but did not remember this tall man who hugged her sister and kissed her cheeks.

Dochia picked up Adila and carried her to the door. "Adila, this is your father. Give your Tata a kiss."

The toddler drew back, a little confused and frightened by all the commotion. Decebal laughed, then took her in his other arm and kissed her cheek.

"My daughters, you are both growing so fast!" He kissed each on the cheek again, then bent down from the waist and gently sat them down on a soft couch. "And every day you look more and more like your beautiful mother."

Zia giggled. Both girls had their mother's lustrous black hair and big blue eyes.

"Welcome home, Brother," Dochia greeted Decebal with a hug. She was a stout woman of average height, with brown hair and hazel eyes. She was older than Decebal by two years.

"It's good to see you, Sister," he replied. "You look well."

"Welcome home," Andrada said, finally embracing her husband.

He drew her in a tight embrace. "I am happy to be home, Wife. Very happy indeed."

"Good," she replied. "Now let's have dinner, and then you must tell me about everything that happened. I hear many stories but you can't always believe stories."

Dinner began with a pot of hot lentil soup and freshly baked bread. Dacia was famous for its wheat fields and abundant wheat crops, and bread was a staple with every meal all year round. Dochia ladled the thick soup into a large wooden bowl for her brother and brought it to him at the dining table. The rich aromas of the soup and of bread fresh out of the oven made Decebal realize that he was famished. For many weeks his diet had been mostly hard bread and cheeses, with occasional venison or wild boar. He attacked this food with gusto.

Seated around the table were Andrada, Cotiso, his sister Dochia, Zia who could barely reach the table top while seated on a cushion, and a servant who held Adila and fed her with a tiny spoon. The talk among the women was about things that happened that day, and plans for the next day. It was a very normal and peaceful scene, but in that moment it made Decebal's heart ache.

This was why he fought and led men to their deaths, he thought. This was why he risked his life every time he went into battle and never gave it a second thought. This was why the Roman aggression had to be stopped at Dacia's border. Simply so that his family could live free, and feel safe and secure to sit around the table, share the news and gossip of the day, and enjoy their lentil soup and freshly baked bread.

"Husband, you seem far away," Andrada said.

"Do I?" Decebal asked. "I was simply thinking how much I missed having a meal with all of you."

That made Andrada smile. "That is nice to hear. Now that the war is over you should be home for many more meals."

"Is the fighting really over?" Dochia asked. Beyond the usual worry about the security of Dacia she always felt an older sister's concern for his personal safety. This last military campaign took longer than anticipated and, as always, those who waited at home waited in a state of worry.

"Yes, Sister. For now the fighting is over," Decebal replied. "The Romans will not attack us until summer or perhaps not until next year. It takes time to prepare for war and Dacia is a long distance from Rome."

"But they will attack us, you expect?"

Andrada turned to her and answered instead. "Of that we can be sure. Besides Germania, we are their next frontier to conquer."

"What is conquer?" Zia asked her mother.

"It's something that grown-ups do when they can't get along with their neighbors," Andrada said, using a napkin to wipe soup from her daughter's chin.

Decebal laughed. "That is as good an explanation as any!"

"The Romans are not our neighbors, nor do they wish to be our neighbors," Dochia said.

"No, Sister, they are not. The Moesians are our neighbors. So are the Sarmatians, the Celts, and the Bastarnae. The Romans are the invaders and enslavers of our neighbors."

Dochia sighed. "I am afraid that you are right. King Duras told me that Rome once made plans to invade Dacia during the reign of King Burebista."

"Is that right?" Andrada asked, curious.

"Yes," Decebal said. "Shortly before he was assassinated Julius Caesar moved six legions to Macedonia, with plans to lead them to invade Dacia. When he was killed in Rome those plans were never carried out."

"How awful if he had carried them out," Dochia said.

"Fortunately," Decebal said with a smile, "as King Duras likes to say, the Romans are overly fond of assassinating their rulers."

A servant walked in with a tray of pastries of different shapes and sizes. Some had a filling of fruit preserves, cheese, or chopped nuts, and some were coated with honey. Dacia had an abundance of wheat, honey, and fruit orchards. Pastries were never out of season and were mandatory for all special occasions.

"Here, have one of these," Andrada picked out a fruit filled pastry. "You love apricots and this was the last of our apricot preserves. We won't get any more until summer."

"Thank you," Decebal said. He looked at Zia and gave her a wink. "I think I'll have two!"

His daughter's laugh made him feel like he was finally at home.

After the evening meal the couple retired to their sleeping quarters. Now Decebal could be fully relaxed. Andrada was young, but wise beyond her years. She was a student of healing and medicinal plants, and also of astronomy and mathematics. She had a very practical mind, as did Decebal, and was often the best counsel he could rely on.

She stretched out on her side next to him and placed a hand on his chest. "Something troubles you, Husband."

He caressed her back slowly as he gathered his thoughts.

"My uncle the King grows old."

She looked into his eyes. "This we know. What else?"

"Old men sometimes grow jealous of younger men. I fear that my uncle grows not only jealous but," he paused for a moment to find the right word, "also resentful."

"No," Andrada said and slowly shook her head. "He loves you like a son. The son he never had. You know this."

"Yes, I know. I am also a threat to his authority, or perhaps he may fear that is so. The men look to me as their leader in military matters, not to the King."

"Why should he fear you? When your father King Scorilo died you accepted King Duras as your king. You were only fifteen years old then, much too young to be king, but now you are the best man to follow King Duras. Everyone says so."

"That would be the most practical solution," Decebal agreed. "We shall see."

"We shall see, my foot!" Andrada exclaimed with emphasis. "You are the best man for the succession. Diegis would be a good monarch in time perhaps, but you are older and wiser. And you have the loyalty of the army. They recognize you as their military leader because that is precisely what you are!"

"Ah, the army." Decebal smiled. "Do you know what they call me now?"

"Yes, I heard. They call you Decebal. They wish to honor you."

"Do you like it?" he asked curiously.

"Decebal," she said the name slowly to sound it out. "Decebal, the brave. Decebal, the strong. Decebal, the force. Hmmm."

"It has a ring of vanity to it," he protested mildly.

Andrada looked into his eyes again, her expression serious.

"No, it's a good name. It suits you. It's a good name for a general."
She paused for a heartbeat. "It's a good name for a king."

"Enough talk of succession," he said impatiently.

"Why?"

"Because plans and plots about crowns leads to cut throats in the middle of the night."

"Pah!" Andrada frowned. "No throats will be cut. You are not a threat to Duras and he loves you like a son. There will be no power struggles and no assassinations."

"I think not, but Duras may still fear it. He needs reassurance, perhaps."

She smiled. "I could talk to him, perhaps."

"You will do no such thing."

"I am only teasing, Husband. But tell me this. Will you now have two names? Diurpaneus and Decebal?"

"No," he replied. "Dacians don't need two names."

"And why not? Romans have three. Often five or six."

"I am not a Roman," he growled. He paused in thought.

Andrada gazed at him patiently. "I sense a decision forming. Yes?"

"Yes. Very well, then. I shall call myself Decebal. If the people wish it there must be a good reason. Let it be so."

Andrada raised her eyebrows. "So Diurpaneus is no more?"

He nodded. "Diurpaneus is no more."

"Farewell to Diurpaneus then. I was fond of him."

He smiled at her sentimentality. "I am still the same man."

"Decebal," she addressed him with his new name. "The brave. The strong. The force of Dacia."

"If Zamolxis wills it."

"Good," Andrada proclaimed. A mischievous smile flickered across her lips. "This should make King Duras feel more reassured!"

Chapter 3

THE EMPEROR DOMITIAN

Rome, Spring 86 AD

*E*mperor Titus Flavius Domitianus, also called Domitian, was not pleased with the progress of his sculpture. This was a bust of the Imperial head and shoulders, slowly and meticulously taking shape step by step as it was sculpted in thick clay by the renowned sculptor Dimitros of Rhodes.

The clay bust would be reproduced in bronze and placed in many prominent locations in Rome's public buildings. The Emperor wished for all citizens of Rome, and indeed all the people of the civilized world, to admire and love the ruler of the world. He gave himself the titles of dominus et deus, master and god. His public images of course were required to reflect those divine qualities.

Standing next to the sculpture was Domitian's valet, Parthenius, holding up a large mirror. Standing next to Parthenius was the royal poet, Marcus Valerius Martialis, who would become more commonly known as Martial. Both Parthenius and Martial knew how particular Domitian was about his image. The artist Dimitros was just now learning first-hand.

The Emperor shifted his gaze back and forth from his image in the mirror to the clay sculpture. He frowned.

"The eyebrows are too large, Dimitros. The neck should be thicker, and the chin more prominent. The shoulders should be bigger. And the hair." Domitian scratched his chin irritably. "The hair does not look right."

Dimitros looked at the bust, then at the Emperor. In his eyes they were a perfect match. One did not, however, make that observation and disagree with royalty.

Domitian was a young emperor, five months shy of his thirty-fifth birthday. He was a man of medium height, with curly brown hair that was receding in front and on top and leaving a bald spot. His neck was thin, the same with his wiry arms and legs that were the product of a lifetime of leisure and the avoidance of strenuous work. He was also a lover of good food and fine wines, and consequently developed a bit of a pot belly. Thankfully that part of his physique would not be included in the sculpture.

"Yes, Caesar," Dimitros acknowledged with a small bow. "I will be happy to make these improvements."

"Good, good. We are creating art here, not pottery! Every detail must be perfect. Isn't that so, Marcus?"

"Indeed, Caesar," Martial agreed. "The statuary are works of art no less than my poetry." He motioned for Dimitros to stay where he was. "If you might excuse us, Caesar, I will stay with Dimitros and further discuss our art."

Domitian nodded his approval. He turned and walked briskly out of the room, followed by Parthenius carrying the large mirror.

"Genius must be catered to," Martial said with a smile.

Dimitros let out a sigh. "I agree. Royal genius most of all. I must confess however, there is something I do not understand."

Martial raised an eyebrow.

"The hair." Dimitros gestured at his statue. "How is the hair not right?"

Martial laughed easily. "We are creating art, my dear Dimitros. Art should not imitate reality too closely. The problem with the hair," he gestured at the statue, "is that it's not there."

"Your meaning is that I should add hair to where there is no hair?"

"Exactly. The Emperor is very sensitive about his bald spots. He believes that it makes him look less manly. So, add hair!"

"I see," the sculptor said with no enthusiasm.

"Come now, Dimitros. We are artists and we know what people like. The Emperor does not want his statue to look like his image in the mirror. He wants it to look the way he wants people to see him."

"Certainly," Dimitros conceded.

"All artists lie," Martial said with a smile. He turned to walk away, then looked back over his shoulder with a grin on his face. "Poets most of all!"

The Emperor Domitian never served in the military. He liked to wear a military uniform however, even while doing official business in the royal palace. He wore the uniform for this occasion, reclining on a couch with a silver goblet of wine in his hand as he listened to the prefect of the Praetorian Guard. Cornelius Fuscus had been a general under the previous emperors Nero and Vespasian, but Domitian was the one now dressed in military gear. Military tunic. Military cloak. Military boots.

Domitian wore the uniform because he wanted his soldiers to feel like he was one of them. Nothing was more important, he knew, than the support of the army. For that reason after becoming emperor he substantially increased the soldiers' pay. That did much to raise his popularity within the army ranks.

Even more strategically, Domitian doubled the salaries of the Praetorian Guard. The life of an emperor depended quite literally on the loyalty of his Praetorian Guard, the palace troops protecting him and his family. He was also attentive to building ties with the Guard's commander, Fuscus. They often shared wine and discussed politics. A very important part of Cornelius Fuscus' job was to keep track of the Emperor's political rivals and enemies.

"Agricola is keeping very quiet," Fuscus said. He took a sip of wine, then smirked. "The poor man is afraid to leave his house! He receives very few visitors."

Gnaeus Julius Agricola was the best known and most admired general in the Roman army. For many years he had been military commander in Brittania, where he won a series of victories fighting the tribes of Scots in the northern part of the island. He was close to conquering the entire island when Domitian recalled him back to Rome, along with a substantial part of his army.

Publically it was explained that the Emperor needed the legions for his future campaigns against Dacia and the perpetually hostile Germanic tribes along the Rhine. Privately it was also understood that Agricola's growing popularity made him a political threat to the Emperor. Domitian's political rivals were suppressed in a variety of ways. Many were exiled or executed. General Agricola knew this well, hence his very low public profile since returning to Rome. It was best for his fortune and health to not draw attention to himself.

"Agricola served us well in Brittania," Domitian said and raised his wine goblet in a toast, "but his time is over."

"You don't plan to include him in the Dacian campaign, Caesar?"

"No, I do not," the Emperor replied dismissively. He looked Fuscus in the eye. "I need a commander I can trust implicitly when we invade Dacia. I can think of no better man than you, Cornelius."

This decision was not completely unexpected to Fuscus, yet it still pleased him enormously. He had not commanded an army since the death of Emperor Vespasian. Now, at the age of forty-nine, he was being handed a prime opportunity to earn honor and riches. The general who conquered Dacia would earn enormous prestige. What drove Cornelius Fuscus' ambition was a strong thirst for recognition and also for wealth. Agricola might have the reputation for military genius, but Fuscus had something better. He had Domitian's trust.

"I am honored, Caesar," Fuscus said in a solemn tone. "I am ready, and so are the men. When do we leave?"

"Make preparations to march within two weeks. You will travel at the head of the Praetorian legion. Once in Moesia you will command five legions. I will join you there soon."

"With five legions I can cut through Dacia like a scythe through a wheat field, Caesar."

Domitian smiled at the General's confident tone. "We must avenge the defeat of Oppius Sabinus. That is a stain on Rome's honor that must be removed."

"Of course, Caesar." Fuscus drained his wine goblet and stood up to leave. "I will get to work on the preparations immediately."

Domitian nodded approvingly. "I know that you will not let me down, Cornelius. We shall achieve great things together."

As Fuscus departed a regally proud and elegantly dressed woman entered the room. The Empress Domitia Longina sat on the couch opposite her husband. A bountiful head of curly red hair framed her beautiful face. Her hair was one of the things that drew Domitian to her. He forced her first husband, Aelius Lamia, to divorce her so that she could become his wife.

"So it is Fuscus, not Agricola?" she asked with mild surprise.

"I know what to expect from Fuscus. I trust Cornelius and he will do what I ask."

She nodded in acknowledgement. "Indeed, he owes you both his fortune and his honor. But remember, Husband," the Empress paused for a beat, "you also trusted Oppius Sabinus when you sent him to Moesia. There are many in the Senate who still blame you for that decision."

"Sabinus was a senator of consular rank!" the Emperor protested irritably. "He was eminently qualified to be Governor of Moesia."

"Yes, he was," Domitia agreed, her green eyes bright and sparkling with intelligence. "Many of those now criticizing the choice would have welcomed the opportunity if offered to them, even though less qualified than Gaius Oppius."

Domitian scowled and went to re-fill his wine goblet. He filled it half-way with wine, then filled the rest with water. Romans did not drink wine undiluted. That was only for barbarians and for those who wished to get drunk quickly.

"Sabinus was careless," the Emperor said. "He went up against the Dacians with one reinforced legion. We will attack Dacia with five legions. We will not be careless or outmanned."

"We, Husband?"

"Yes." Domitian was amused by her surprise. "I shall go at the head of the army. And why not? Julius Caesar did it. Augustus did it, at times. It is time for Caesar to lead armies again, not sit back and let others take the glory."

Domitia laughed her gaily laugh. "You will earn plenty of glory, no doubt. Although I rather think the glory would come easier with Agricola than with Fuscus."

"No matter. The glory will belong to Caesar."

"And what," she asked with a mild frown, "am I to do here while you are gaining glory killing barbarians in Dacia?"

"Whatever you wish, my dear, as always. When have you ever been able to sit around and be bored?"

Chapter 4

THE CHILDREN OF ZAMOLXIS

Sarmizegetusa, Summer 86 AD

C oncern about the military buildup of Roman forces in Moesia led King Duras to call for a meeting of his war council. General Decebal sat on his right, the High Priest Vezina on his left. Sinna was a general in the cavalry, Drilgisa in the infantry. They listened attentively to a report from Tsiru, the veteran captain of the cavalry scouts. Short in stature and slim in build, the cavalryman could stay in the saddle for days on end and often did. He had just returned from a scouting mission in Moesia.

"There are six legions headquartered at Naissus," Tsiru explained. "The new army commander is General Cornelius Fuscus."

Vezina raised an eyebrow, mildly surprised. "Fuscus? He is the commander of the Praetorian Guard. He was a general under Nero and Vespasian, but he has not commanded an army for many years. Are you certain of this information?"

"Yes, Your Holiness," Tsiru answered. "General Fuscus marched from Rome at the head of Legio V Alaudae, the Praetorian legion."

"The Praetorian legion, eh? Domitian is sending his best," Decebal said, impressed. "The Praetorians are the best trained, best armed, and best paid soldiers in the Roman army."

Tsiru continued. "Emperor Domitian is also with the army. He does not go out with the troops but relies on his generals instead for all military matters."

"So why is the Emperor there?" King Duras wondered.

"I don't know, Sire." Tsiru cleared his throat. "What we hear is that the Emperor stays in camp in his imperial tent. And that he is well supplied with wine, food, and his harem."

Vezina chuckled. "The Emperor is there to enjoy himself. And also no doubt to take credit for what his generals accomplish."

"Royalty has its privileges," Drilgisa laughed. He caught himself and glanced at the King with an embarrassed look. "I do not mean you, Sire."

King Duras waved his hand dismissively to show that he was not offended. General Drilgisa was as tough a soldier as there lived but he was always respectful of the King's dignity and authority.

Vezina turned to Decebal. "You were right, the Emperor came here in search of personal glory. He fights the ghosts of his illustrious predecessors Vespasian and Titus."

"Chasing ghosts is a tricky business," Decebal said. "Domitian wants to give the appearance of being a strong military leader. He creates an illusion."

"I think the same, Nephew. And only weak leaders have a need for creating illusions," King Duras said scornfully. He turned back to Tsiru. "How are the Romans attacking us?"

"With three or four cohorts, Sire. Two thousand men, give or take. They attack our forts in Moesia and Banat on the south bank of the Ister. We put up some resistance, then withdraw further west." Tsiru bowed towards the King apologetically. "Our forts in Banat are small and protected by palisades and earthworks. We cannot fight and win against the Roman numbers, Sire."

The King nodded his acknowledgement. "Nor are you expected to. Give some resistance but don't sacrifice our men needlessly."

"So how do we fight the Romans, then?" Drilgisa asked. He turned his head towards Decebal. All others did the same.

"We fight them on our terms, the time and place of our choosing," Decebal declared. "Always on our terms. We'll fight them in the mountains, not on the plains of Banat and Moesia."

"Exactly so," Vezina said. "Rome's armies have been successful for two hundred years because they dictate the terms of battle. No one can match the Roman legions fighting on open ground."

"That is their strategic advantage," Decebal continued. "It is what Roman legions are designed for and that is how they win."

"What, then?" Sinna asked. "My cavalry is most effective in open ground."

"We must draw them to us, General Sinna. We fight them in the mountains. Your cavalry will be less effective but more importantly so will their infantry."

"What if they don't come to us and fight us in the mountains?" Sinna asked again.

"They will," Decebal declared. "Emperor Domitian and General Fuscus are not in Moesia with six legions to clean up forts along the Ister. They are here to invade Dacia. That requires that they come to us. Sooner or later, they will."

"So we wait," Drilgisa said.

Decebal smiled. "In war, my friend, patience is a virtue."

The Holy Temple of Zamolxis was located on the highest terrace of Sarmizegetusa, the part of the city closest to the heavens. It was built with stone and intricately decorated woodwork. The inside walls were painted with colorful geometric designs and nature scenes.

The temple was built in a round shape to symbolize the sun, as were all Dacian temples. The outer walls were ringed by eight great pillars of stone that held up the temple roof. The pillars were covered with thin gold plate, with intricate designs carved into the gold. On a bright day the sunlight shining off the gold pillars dazzled everyone in the temple's vicinity.

The temples of the Dacian people reflected their culture. Dacians loved color, far beyond the simple elegant splendor of gold and silver. Color played a prominent role in many areas of life. It decorated their homes, their temples, and the exquisitely detailed jewelry made with precious metals and gemstones.

Their ceremonial clothing was richly embroidered with threads of various colors, particularly clothing worn on religious occasions and special events such as weddings. Almost every home had a vegetable garden and also a flower garden. In springtime and summer the land was in colorful bloom everywhere the eye turned.

Decebal found Vezina sitting on a patch of grass in front of the Holy Temple. He was teaching a group of twenty children, from six to twelve years of age. They sat attentively in a semi-circle in front of him. Teaching was done through discussion, asking and answering questions. This was how Dacian children learned since the ancient days of Zamolxis.

Following in the footsteps of their founder, the priests of Zamolxis were highly educated teachers and trained healers. They taught many subjects including ethics, history, mathematics, herbal medicine, and astronomy. They also performed the many religious ceremonies for festivals that were held throughout the year, and presided over the many other ceremonies such as marriage and funeral rites.

"What are you smiling about?" Andrada asked, coming up from behind Decebal. Her medical clinic was located down the road on the next terrace, in a small building not far from the royal palace.

He inclined his head towards the group of children engaged in a discussion with their teacher. "That was me, about twenty years ago. Listening to Vezina and asking all my silly questions."

"Ah, yes. That was me too, fifteen years ago," she said wistfully. "Soon we should bring Zia to the lessons. She is curious about every little thing and has a love for learning."

"She will have no better teacher than you."

Andrada shook her head. "The more teachers the better. She will learn from us and from the priests. Also it will be good for her to learn alongside other children."

A curly haired, green-eyed seven year old boy raised his hand to get the teacher's attention.

"Yes, Tarbus?" Vezina acknowledged him. He recognized the boy as Buri's son.

"Is it true that Zamolxis once walked in these mountains?"

"Yes, he did. Many hundreds of years ago."

The boy looked puzzled. "But how can a god walk on the Earth?"

"Before Zamolxis became a god he was a man, like any other man," Vezina explained patiently. "He was born in these mountains and walked amongst us. That was six hundred years ago, a very long time ago in the history of Dacia. When Zamolxis became a priest he travelled to the corners of the world to learn all the knowledge of the world."

"He went to Babylon and Egypt, and he studied with Pythagoras," an older girl said proudly.

"That is so," Vezina continued. "Zamolxis travelled to Egypt, and Persia, Greece, and even Italia. For many years he served as a disciple of the great Pythagoras, the father of philosophy and mathematics. He learned all that Pythagoras had to teach. When Zamolxis returned to Dacia from his travels around the world he became our first High Priest. After he died Zamolxis was re-born as a god to watch over the people of Dacia. Today his spirit lives in the holy mountain Kogaion."

Another girl raised her hand. "My brother says that Zamolxis turns into the Great Wolf and hunts in the mountains. Is this true?"

Vezina shook his head. "No, child, that is not true. The legends tell us that a long time ago a great army of our enemies came to invade Dacia. Zamolxis turned one of his priests into the Great White Wolf. The wolf killed hundreds of the enemy and helped Dacia win the war. That is why we honor and worship the Great White Wolf."

"Why don't we have a statue of Zamolxis?" a boy asked. "Romans have many statues of their gods. I want to see what Zamolxis looks like." Several of the other children nodded their heads in agreement.

"Because, my child, Zamolxis wants us to worship his spirit, not his image. That is why we don't have pictures or statues of our god. It would be unholy."

The little boy looked unconvinced. "I like to look at pictures and statues," he said. Another question crossed his mind. "Does Zamolxis want us to kill the Romans?"

"Ah, that is a very good question," Vezina said. He looked over to the edge of the group where Decebal and Andrada were standing. "Perhaps General Decebal would care to answer that question?"

Decebal walked over and sat down by the High Priest, so that he would not tower over the children. He had their rapt attention, as Vezina knew would happen.

"Zamolxis teaches us to get along with each other, and with all our neighbors. However," Decebal paused for effect, "he also teaches us that we must kill our enemies. It is the sacred duty of every Dacian, every man and woman, to kill our enemies."

"Who is our enemy?" a little girl asked, looking a little worried.

"Our enemy is anyone who tries to take away our freedom or our land. Our people have lived in these mountains and valleys for many years, since the beginning of time. Dacia has never been defeated by our enemies. We must always fight to protect our land and freedom."

"Is Rome our enemy?"

"Yes," Decebal answered in a calm but serious tone. "At this time Rome is our enemy. They invade and conquer many of our neighbors. They kill many people or sell them into slavery. They take treasures and wealth from other people and send it back to Rome."

"Will they come to Dacia?" a girl with strawberry-blond hair asked in a small voice. She overheard her parents discussing this and it frightened her. Romans were almost as scary as strigoi, evil spirits of dead people who wandered in the night.

"They may try to invade us," Decebal replied. "If they do then we must fight them and kill them. This is why your fathers and brothers are training as soldiers and preparing for war." Decebal saw the frightened look on the girl's face, who seemed close to crying. "Do not worry child, you will be safe. If the Romans come we will fight them and stop them."

"Do you promise?" the girl asked.

Decebal paused. "What is your name, my child?"

"Salia."

"Yes, Salia, I promise," Decebal said in a solemn tone. "We will do whatever we need to do to keep you safe."

"Why do the Romans do this? They should leave us alone!" the curly haired Tarbus said with passion.

"Because this is what Romans do," Vezina replied. "Why does a swarm of locusts invade a field of wheat? Because that is what locusts do. The Romans are very greedy for the land and the treasure of other people."

"The Romans are big thieves!" yelled a boy from the back row.

"Yes, they are," Vezina said. "They also believe that their gods want Rome to rule all the people of the world. That is nonsense of course, but it gives them an excuse for what they do."

"When I am older I will kill all the Romans!" Tarbus declared.

Decebal smiled and shook his head. "No, my brave boy, we must not kill all the Romans. We only kill the Romans who attack us and wish to enslave us. Those Romans are our enemies."

Vezina stood up and clapped his hands once to get their attention. "That is all for today, children. Off with you now to your homes and your noonday meal! We meet again tomorrow. Here on this spot if the weather is good, or inside the temple if it rains."

Each of the older children had responsibility to watch over one of the younger children. The older ones now took charge to guide their younger siblings and friends home.

"The children worry," Andrada said, watching them drift away. "They don't like to hear about the Romans."

Decebal gave a small shrug. "Ah, they will be fine I think. Children need to know the truth, otherwise how will they grow into honest and wise adults?"

"That is so," Vezina agreed. "The truth is that we are at war with Rome. The truth is also that when they invade Dacia we will throw them back. We have a great deal of experience fighting off locusts."

"You men always sound so certain," Andrada exclaimed.

"Yes, my lady, we do," Decebal replied. "And we must always be certain. On the day we believe in our hearts that we will be defeated, on that day we are already defeated."

She reached out to touch his arm. "Then I pray, Husband, that day never comes."

Chapter 5

WAR PLANNING

Naissus, Moesia, Summer 86 AD

*G*eneral Cornelius Fuscus took off his dusty riding cape and handed it to a servant before entering the Emperor's tent. It was late summer and the spring mud of the Moesian roads was now dried clay and dust under the feet of his legions. Riding was not much better since it kicked up even larger clouds of dust. Roman engineers were building miles of good solid Roman roads, the best in the world by everyone's measure, but the going was slow in the summer heat.

A sentry opened the tent flap and Cornelius ducked inside. It was shady and cooler in the tent. Air vents allowed the free flow of air when a breeze stirred up. A table in the middle of the tent held a large map and two jars, one of water and one of wine. Against one wall was the Emperor's bed, piled with silk cushions, on which one concubine napped and another sat with a small fan that she used to cool herself. They were both elegantly beautiful and dressed in some thin silky material that only the nobility could afford.

Domitian stood behind the table studying the map. He looked up when Fuscus entered. The Emperor was in a good mood. He had put aside his military uniform and wore only a light tunic.

"Ah! Cornelius! I have been waiting for you."

Fuscus raised his right arm stiffly in front of him and snapped the Roman salute. "Hail, Caesar!"

"How was your journey from Banat? Here," Domitian gestured to the jars and silver goblets on the table, "have some wine. You must be parched from your ride."

"Thank you. I am thirsty." Fuscus poured himself a goblet of water and drained it. Then he poured himself another drink, half wine and half water. "We cleared the Dacians out of Singidunum."

"Excellent," Domitian said with satisfaction. Singidunum was a good sized city and a major hub for transportation and trade south of the Danubius.

"We drove the barbarians out of Roman territory, back to their forests and sheep pastures in Dacia. Only some scattered parties of cavalry scouts remain."

The concubine who had been sleeping woke up and drowsily looked around to get her bearings. Domitian gestured politely to the entrance, and both women stood up and obediently walked briskly out of the tent.

Domitian clasped Fuscus on the shoulder. "Well done, Cornelius. Well done! You have managed this campaign very well."

Fuscus acknowledged the praise and poured himself more wine. "The next step, Emperor, is the invasion of Dacia proper. That is why we brought the legions here."

"I am fully aware of why we are here, Cornelius."

"Of course, Caesar. I would not think to question your judgment. I wonder, however, about our schedule for the invasion of Dacia?"

Domitian poured himself more wine. "I have spoken with Gallus, Pegasus, and Flavinus. You know them, and they know this area well. They advise bringing in two or three more legions, and recruiting more Iazygi cavalry." The Emperor paused and looked at Fuscus to gage his reaction.

Cornelius was not pleased, but kept a straight face. Rubrius Gallus had extensive experience fighting against the Sarmatian tribes in the region. Quintus Pegasus and Marcus Pompeius Flavinus had both been governors of Dalmatia. Each of them knew the local area well and had a great deal of experience fighting the local tribes. The Iazygi were a tribe with a long history of hostility and military conflicts with Dacia. They were eager to ally themselves with Rome against Dacia, and Roman commanders welcomed them because Roman armies depended on local tribes to supply them with horses and cavalry.

"That would be a wise strategy if we wish to be cautious," Fuscus said thoughtfully. "It would delay the invasion. We will lose the good weather."

"Do you have other thoughts in mind, Cornelius?"

"Yes, Caesar. We have six legions here at present. We should leave one legion in Moesia to keep the peace, and attack with five legions across the Danubius into Dacia. I will take Legio V Alaudae and lead the attack."

"And how do you propose to cross five legions over the Danubius in summer? The barbarians only cross in winter when the river is good and frozen."

"The barbarians don't have Roman engineers," Fuscus snorted. "We will build a boat bridge across the river. I have already scouted an excellent location in Banat. In two months I can be marching on Sarmizegetusa."

The Emperor was impressed by his general's enthusiasm. "That is a bold plan, Cornelius. I applaud your initiative. It will require a large number of boats and a large number of engineers."

"It will, Caesar. I have already seen to the preliminary planning. The boats can be assembled in a week. I have the engineers required. I need only your order to proceed."

Domitian became quiet and paused to think, his eyes distant. Fuscus felt his hopes sinking. The Emperor did not look convinced, his enthusiasm ebbing. Cornelius waited for the "but" that he knew was coming.

"The invasion must wait for now, I think." Domitian took a sip from his silver goblet, savoring the fine wine. "I am leaving for Rome tomorrow. There are matters there I must attend to, trouble in the Senate again. My enemies grow bolder and more active when I am not in Rome."

Fuscus did not show his deep disappointment. "Yes, Caesar. With both of us here I am not surprised that the trouble-makers in Rome are stirring up dissent."

Domitian scowled. "I will attend to the troublemakers in Rome, Cornelius. You will stay here and keep the peace, and continue with preparations for the invasion."

There was no arguing with Domitian once he made up his mind. Indeed the Emperor considered that an egregious sign of disloyalty. The gods save us from foolish and arrogant royalty, Cornelius thought, and wisely kept the thought to himself.

"As you command, Caesar," Fuscus said. "I will stay and continue the preparations here."

"Good," Domitian proclaimed. "Building a boat bridge across the Danubius is an excellent idea. Work out the details and be ready to do so on short notice. We will invade Dacia when time and conditions are right."

It occurred to Fuscus that the Emperor was not against invading Dacia, in fact he seemed eager for it. The problem was that Domitian did not want the invasion to proceed while he was in Rome. That would deprive Caesar of credit for the victory.

"Of course, Caesar," Cornelius said. "Everything will be ready for the invasion, on short order. I will wait for your command."

Mountains of southern Dacia, Late Summer 86 AD

General Decebal completed his inspection of troops in the mountain camps and was satisfied with the soldiers' readiness. Diegis, Drilgisa, and Buri walked with him. Everywhere they went they were greeted with swordsmen, spearmen, and archers in good spirits. This was an important part of their mission in touring the camps. After strategy planning, Decebal's most important job was to inspire confidence and hope in the men. There was no better way than to walk among them and talk with them.

King Duras and Vezina waited outside the command tent. They were too old to be walking up and down the mountain slopes visiting the soldiers in their camps. Even so, the King always preferred the fresh outside air to the stuffiness of a tent. He liked to look at green trees and a blue sky. It lifted his mood and made him feel alive.

"How are the men?" the Kind asked as Decebal and Drilgisa joined him and the High Priest.

"The men are in good spirits, Sire," Decebal said. "As well as we could wish for."

"They are eager to face the enemy," Drilgisa added. "Most did not fight in Moesia and are eager to prove themselves in battle."

"What is our current strength?" Duras asked. "I see that more troops joined us today."

Decebal took a moment to think. "One-thousand infantry and five-hundred archers joined us today. As well as another hundred or so cavalry." He glanced at Vezina. "You are keeping the tally, Vezina."

Vezina took out a parchment from the sleeve of his robe and turned to address the King. "In total, Sire, eight thousand infantry, three thousand archers, nine-hundred and fifty cavalry."

"We need more men," King Duras said.

"More infantry will arrive within two weeks, Uncle," Decebal told him. "They also bring extra supplies to feed the army for another two months."

"I wish the Romans would come," Drilgisa exclaimed. "The men are ready and eager now. Warriors grow stale from waiting."

King Duras frowned. "The Romans will attack with twenty-five thousand men, General Drilgisa. Are you prepared to fight that army now?"

"We will be prepared, Sire," Drilgisa replied confidently.

Decebal nodded. "We should have enough men to fight the fight that we want to fight."

"It is always better to have too many troops than not enough," Vezina said, "but I fear that will never be the case in our war with the Romans. They bring in troops from across the empire when engaged in a major war."

"That is true," Decebal agreed. "Which is why trying to fight them with brute force fails against Roman armies."

The King shook his head, frustrated. "Even the Germans can't beat them with brute force. And we are not as many as the Germans." He turned to address Decebal. "Send out scouts and regular patrols. We must know where the Romans are and what they're doing."

"I have already given the orders, Sire," Decebal said. "We will not be caught by surprise."

Rome, Late Summer 86 AD

In Rome the atmosphere was tense. The Emperor's sour and cynical mood was directed against the senators who had been stirring up opposition while he was in Moesia. They were not happy with the higher taxes imposed on the wealthy Roman citizens. Grumbling about taxes was to be expected however, and that did not upset the Emperor. The more serious crime was to challenge or even question Caesar's laws, because that was considered atheism.

Domitian was both Lord and God, as Martial so often described and praised him in his poems. To question Caesar's judgment was to question his divinity. Men and women were exiled and sometimes executed for that crime.

"You hear everything that goes on, my dear," the Emperor said to the Empress Domitia Longina as they relaxed after dinner. "Who among the Senate and the nobles have been vocal against me?"

Domitia carefully adjusted the folds of her thin and elegant dress. Naming names was the same as a sentence of treason against those accused of disloyalty.

"People are too fearful to name names. I hear grumblings." She looked at him with sympathy. "Greedy nobles who resent you taking their wealth, plus the usual rabble of Stoic philosophers who wish to abolish the monarchy."

"Abolish the monarchy!" Domitian cried. "Where would Rome be without Caesar? Rome is Caesar, and Caesar is Rome."

"Of course you are correct, Caesar," she replied with a smile.

"My father, the Divine Vespasian, twice found it necessary to throw these damnable philosophers out of Rome." Domitian gulped down some of his wine. "I will need to follow his example, and soon."

Domitia nodded in silent agreement. The efforts of Vespasian did not stop the Stoic movement and their philosophy of a simple and frugal life. Still, they challenged the authority of Caesar. So did the Christians, who were rapidly growing in number in Rome. Like Nero, Domitian despised Christians.

"What is the Senate grumbling about now?" the Emperor asked. "Besides money, of course!"

"Of course," the Empress smiled. "High taxes and the high costs of your games and building projects. As usual."

"They should be thanking me for my building projects. I am the greatest builder in Rome since Nero. How can I be Caesar," he asked, his voice rising, "and not build great works worthy of Caesar?"

"Indeed. Small minds cannot think like you do, Caesar." Domitia looked out the window at the fading light. "I think nobles from the ancient families are resentful and jealous. You diminish their power by appointing your friends and supporters to high positions. The old Roman nobility is very resentful of having their power and influence diminished."

"When I was younger, while my father was Emperor, those fools detested me. I was laughed at and ridiculed." Domitian sneered. "Who is laughing now?"

The Empress looked sympathetic but kept her silence.

"Tomorrow there will be posted a list of senators to be sent into exile," he said with satisfaction. "Only five this time, not so many, but it will send a message. I must show a firm hand while I am in Rome or they only grow bolder."

"Five of the wealthier senators I assume?" Domitia asked, no trace of irony in her voice. There was no such thing as a poor senator since high wealth was one of the requirements for office, but some families were immensely wealthy.

"Of course wealthy senators," the Emperor replied. "Two birds with one stone and all that. The treasury needs the money."

Domitia changed the subject. "How goes the campaign along the Danubius?"

"Things are in place. Fuscus grows impatient, he is eager to attack Dacia. I must leave soon to re-join him."

"So Cornelius is still your man?"

"He is," Domitian said with a firm voice. "I know that you advised for Agricola, but Fuscus is very able."

Domitia raised her elegant wine goblet. "To Cornelius Fuscus then, may he find glory and wealth in Dacia!"

Naissus, Moesia, September 86 AD

General Cornelius Fuscus sat outside his command tent in Naissus and watched the sun slowly sink below the horizon. The evening air was turning nippy. The General was in a sour mood, as he had been for many weeks while waiting for orders from Rome. When the weather turned cold campaign season would end, and the invasion of Dacia would have to wait until the next year. Perhaps he would still lead the military campaign then. Or perhaps not. He took a deep breath and made an effort to push aside dark and dangerous thoughts.

Riders were approaching in a hurry on the road from the west, standing out against the red setting sun. As they drew closer Fuscus saw that some slumped in their saddles or rode with difficulty.

"Sir, wounded men approaching," Sextus Capito called out. He was Fuscus' second in command, a battle tested veteran with a deep scar across the left side of his forehead. Over the years Capito became Fuscus' most trusted aide, even before Cornelius won favor with the Emperor.

There were a dozen riders in the returning party of cavalry scouts. Capito walked out to meet them as they dismounted. The badly wounded were led away to the medical tent. Sextus returned with one rider who was dusty and dirty but did not appear to be injured.

"Report!" Fuscus ordered.

The soldier saluted sharply. "Lucius Gavius, sir!"

"What happened to you Gavius?"

"Our patrol was ambushed by enemy cavalry. Horse archers, sir. We fought them off but suffered casualties. They rode off towards the west, sir."

"Did you capture any prisoners?"

"No live prisoners, sir," Gavius replied, knowing that Fuscus would be disappointed with the answer.

"Did you identify the enemy?" Capito asked.

Gavius looked uncertain. "Sarmatians or Dacians, sir. I could not be sure. The horses were not in the Sarmatian style horse armor, but Sarmatian scouts do not armor their horses. It weighs the animals down too much, sir."

Capito looked at Fuscus and raised an eyebrow. Both were asking themselves the same question in their minds.

"Is it likely they were Dacians? Think, man," Fuscus insisted.

"Yes, they could have been Dacians," the soldier answered. He paused, then added, "I did not notice tattoos on them, sir."

"How are tattoos important?" Cornelius asked.

"Sarmatians often wear tattoos, but the Dacian scouts never have them," Gavius explained. "It is just one of those things I notice, sir."

"Very well. Dismissed," Fuscus said.

Gavius saluted, turned, and briskly walked away.

"Dacians, Sarmatians, they often fight together," Capito said.

"You heard the man. No tattoos!" Cornelius said with a smile. "They were most likely Dacians then."

"You are eager to initiate the Dacian campaign, General," Sextus observed, stating the obvious. "So am I. So are the men."

Fuscus grimaced. "We sit here waiting for word from Rome, and we keep losing more men. I don't like it, Sextus."

Capito smiled. "This is the third cavalry ambush in the past week. Are the Dacians launching an offensive, sir?"

"It appears so to me," General Fuscus replied. He made a quick tactical decision, then suddenly felt better than he had in months. Too much time had already gone to waste. No more.

"Muster the troops, Sextus. The time has come to take action and counter these Dacian attacks."

Chapter 6

A ROYAL BETRAYAL

Banat, Autumn 86 AD

Even at its narrowest span the river Danubius, called the Ister by the barbarians, was a daunting body of water. It was far too wide and deep to build a conventional bridge across it. The solution was to build a pontoon bridge on top of a long line of boats stretching from one river bank to the other. The Roman engineers lashed the boats together with thick ropes, then built a timber framework on top of the boats. Thick planks were nailed on top of the timber frames to build the floor of the bridge and provide smooth and solid footing.

General Fuscus ordered the bridge be made wide enough to allow soldiers to march four abreast across it, with a margin of safety. His army was composed of five legions, or twenty-six thousand fighting men. He also had another twenty thousand support personnel to transport, plus supply wagons and baggage carts.

Cavalry horses were walked across the bridge in single file, with a hood placed over their heads so the animals would not get spooked and panic. The bridge was strong enough to allow wheeled artillery, the ballistae and catapults, to be pulled across by mules and oxen. The bridge was a marvel of Roman engineering.

It took a number of days to move the army across to the Dacian side on the north bank of the river. The crossing was unopposed, and indeed there was no sign of any Dacian military in sight other than a small number of cavalry scouts who stayed at a cautious distance. General Fuscus did not expect to see any Dacians in force until his army was well inside Dacia. Decebalus would not meet him on open ground. And if he did, Fuscus would crush him.

The Romans were on a wide plain in the river valley. To the north was the mountain range that protected Dacia's southern frontier. The way through the mountains and into the heart of Dacia was a very narrow mountain pass approximately eight miles long. The entrance to the pass was guarded by a Dacian fortified city called Tapae.

"We will be ready to march north tomorrow, General," Sextus Capito announced. "The men are eager to go."

"No more eager than I am, Sextus," Fuscus replied. "We march at first light. I am tired of sitting around and wasting time."

Capito smiled. "Now we make the rules. As it should be."

"Why, Sextus, do be careful not to hint at insubordination," Fuscus chided him good naturedly. "Caesar has long ears. Even so, yes this is why we came here."

"Do we siege Tapae?" Capito asked.

"I will make a decision when I see their fortifications first hand. In any case it will not take five legions to siege a fort."

"That is true, General," Capito agreed. "We should push on into Dacia before the weather turns."

The fortified city of Tapae barred its gates, manned its walls, and prepared to resist the invaders. The walls of Dacian forts and cities were made of stone, not the earthworks and timber palisades that were common in Gaul and Germania. An outer stone wall was backed with a thick inner wall of earth and gravel, reinforced with timber support, then followed by an inner stone wall. The walls could not be burned down, and they could withstand a pounding from battering rams and the boulders hurled by ballistae. The city was well supplied with food to withstand a long siege.

The Romans surrounded the city on three sides. The northern side of the city was built flush against a mountainside. They began the siege with an artillery bombardment with ballistae and scorpions. The defenders took cover behind the stone ramparts. Dacian archers could not match the range of the Roman siege engines, they could only shelter in place. They would wait for the enemy to come to them.

General Fuscus and Sextus Capito made an assessment of the city defenders on the walls. These were archers and spearmen for the most part. Almost none were wearing any armor. Surprisingly there were more than a few women manning the walls alongside the men. This was a civilian defense force, not Dacian military.

"How many are defending the walls, Sextus?"

"Between seven and eight hundred, sir."

Cornelius nodded. "Seven or eight hundred civilians, it looks like. Even so they are well defended. If we assault the walls directly it will cost us many casualties."

"I agree, sir," Sextus replied. "We should pound them with artillery instead."

"Continue the attack, Sextus."

After a day of artillery attacks it became clear that the walls were too strong and little damage was being done. General Fuscus made a quick decision.

"I will take the army and march north tomorrow. You will remain here and siege the city with four cohorts. Their siege equipment and supply wagons stay with you."

Capito tried not to show his disappointment. Two thousand men were enough to press a long siege but not enough to assault the walls of a strongly fortified city.

"Yes, sir. We may be here a long time, General. Most likely we'll have to starve the bastards out."

"You are in charge here now. Use the strategy you think best. If you need to starve them out, then starve them out."

"Understood, sir." Capito looked Fuscus in the eye. "All the same, I would rather march north with you, sir."

"Come now, Sextus, you will share in the plunder from Dacia," Fuscus assured him as if reading Capito's mind. "For now I need you here for this important job. You will take Tapae and hold it until my return. This is the main route into Dacia and it must be guarded."

"Of course. I understand my mission, sir. I will follow your orders exactly, as always."

"I march tomorrow," Fuscus continued. "Legio V Alaudae will be in the vanguard. The going will be slow, I'm sure. There are no good roads heading north through the mountains because the Dacians are no road builders."

"Give them a deer path through the woods and they're happy, eh," Capito said with a grin.

"No matter what the roads are like, I want to push the attack hard." The summer weather was gone, and Fuscus silently cursed the Emperor for delaying so long.

Sextus nodded. "Good fortune, sir. I will manage the siege here."

Rome, Autumn 86 AD

In Rome the Emperor Domitian was in a dark and dangerous mood. Rumors of a plot against him turned out to be accurate. He found it necessary to execute four senators for treason and confiscate their property. He exiled another eleven wealthy nobles and confiscated their properties as well. That provided a small financial cushion for the imperial treasury.

Domitian gazed over the cool placid waters of a large fountain in his gardens when Martial approached. The royal poet was very good at judging the Emperor's moods and lifting his spirits when those moods grew dark.

Martial smiled and bowed. "My Lord and my God, I rejoice to see you again," he said with practiced sincerity. Martial was renowned for his talents for both poetry and flattery, and took pride in both. What was poetry after all, the poet judged, but the art of uplifting the human spirit?

"I wish that I could rejoice, Marcus," Domitian said grimly. "These are unfortunate times."

"Indeed, Caesar," the poet agreed. "Yet Rome still rejoices to see Caesar dispatch the traitors, some to their graves and some to the far corners of the Empire."

"Are there still murmurs of treason?" Domitian asked.

"No, Caesar," Martial assured him. "The people of Rome worship you. You are the greatest commander of the Earth and the parent of the world."

The Emperor frowned. "One traitor remains. You have witnessed his interrogation?"

"Yes, Lord. Under torture he has confessed to all the crimes he is accused of." Martial paused, a look of distaste on his face. "The man is as profane as he is reckless. He has bragged in public –"

The poet stopped, looking embarrassed. Domitian gave him a sharp look.

"Bragged in public about what?"

Martial looked down at the gleaming marble stones around the fountain. "I would rather die than cause you pain, my Lord," he said.

"You will tell me, Marcus. I command it."

"The man has bragged," he said with a scowl, "about the Empress' talents in oral satisfaction."

Domitian gave a painful grimace. He did not doubt the reports were true. He allowed himself a thin smile, then turned towards a doorway and beckoned with his right hand.

Four Praetorian Guards escorted the Empress Domitia Longina and her two closest handmaidens. The handmaidens, loyal servants for many years, looked pale and terrified. Domitia held her head up and maintained her regal composure. She was a Roman noble and the daughter of a famous Roman general. Come what may, she would not be cowed.

"Come, my dear," Domitian beckoned her toward a chair beside him. "Sit with me. I want you to be a witness."

"A witness to what, Caesar?" she asked warily.

Instead of answering Domitian beckoned to a doorway on the opposite side of the garden. A soldier emerged leading a man by a rope tied around the man's neck. The man's hands were tied behind his back. Three other soldiers followed, each carrying a heavy club.

The Empress gasped and the color drained from her beautiful face. The beaten and bloodied prisoner was Paris, the most famous actor in Rome. Considered to be the most handsome man in the city, his battered body was now covered with cuts, burns, and bruises. His fingernails and toenails had been ripped away. His nose was a bloody pulp, and his cut and swollen lips and eye sockets disfigured his face. Domitia felt her stomach turn and struggled to hold back a strong urge to vomit.

"Do you have any last words for your lover, my dear?" Domitian asked, his voice sad but surprisingly gentle.

The Empress stared straight ahead but did not reply. Domitian sighed, then turned and nodded to one of the men holding a club.

The soldier reared back and hit Paris with a vicious blow across his upper back. The actor staggered and fell to his knees. Another man kicked him hard in the ribs and knocked him over on his side. All three clubs started raining hard blows on every part of the fallen man's body. Hands still tied behind his back, Paris was helpless to resist or to protect himself against the falling clubs. He drew his knees up to his chest and resigned himself to his death. Blood streaming from his head soon flowed over the marble stones.

Horrified, Domitia tried to stand but was held firmly in place by two of the guards. She was also a prisoner, she realized. She fixed her gaze at a distant spot on the horizon, no longer willing to watch the brutality unfolding in front of her. The actor Paris stopped moving, then soon after stopped breathing. Her foolish star-crossed lover was mercifully dead.

"Take him away," Domitian commanded. "Do not burn him. Throw his body to the dogs."

Domitia Longina turned sideways to face him, her face pale but still composed. "And what of me, Caesar? I am equally guilty."

Domitian stood up from his chair and looked down at her. "Yes, my dear, you are equally guilty. You will not, however, face the same punishment." His face turned sad. "You are exiled from Rome. You will leave today."

"As you command, Caesar," the Empress replied, her voice numb. To a Roman noble being exiled from Rome was equal to a sentence of death. "And my servants?" she asked.

Domitian turned towards the two women with contempt. "These two were no doubt complicit in your betrayal. For their crime they shall lose their heads."

One of the women lowered her face to her hands and began to sob. The other looked pleadingly at the Empress, but there was no hope for salvation there. They were quickly rushed away by their guards.

"As you command, Caesar," Domitia Longina repeated. She was resigned to her fate, her heart as cold as ice.

Mountains of southern Dacia, Autumn 86 AD

Tsiru, captain of the cavalry scouts, found King Duras and General Decebal reviewing battle plans. The High Priest Vezina, Drilgisa, and Diegis joined them to hear his report.

"What news of Tapae?" the King asked.

"The city is under siege, Sire. The Romans attack with artillery but not infantry. This news is from yesterday."

"Tapae can withstand an artillery attack for weeks," Duras said.

Decebal gave a nod. "Months, or longer if need be. They are well supplied with food and their water comes from wells within the city. Did the Romans not storm the walls, Tsiru?"

"Not as of yesterday, General. What we do know today is that General Fuscus is marching north with four legions."

Drilgisa gave a grin. "Eager bastard, isn't he?"

"Eager or not, he badly outnumbers us in infantry," Decebal said. "Our cavalry might be their equal, but we have nothing to counter their artillery."

"So we must negate their artillery," Vezina said. "That can be done in a narrow mountain pass where they have no room to maneuver."

"We should have our own artillery," Diegis said. "It gives them too big an advantage."

"I agree, Brother," Decebal replied. "And we will, in time. But not in this battle."

King Duras became impatient. "We must stop them here, now, at Tapae!" he declared. "I don't want to hear any more talk of artillery or future battles!"

"We will stop them, Sire," Decebal assured him.

The King's anger was understandable. This was the first army to attack on Dacian soil in many years, and they all felt the urgent need to stop it. This was a fight for Dacia's survival.

Chapter 7

FIRST BATTLE OF TAPAE

Tapae, Dacia, Autumn 86 AD

*T*he mountain pass north of Tapae became muddy as the weather turned wet. On both sides of the pass heavily wooded slopes angled up the mountainside. The terrain was too narrow to allow travel in large formations so the legionnaires marched six men abreast. This was the standard Roman marching formation, but it stretched out the army across miles of muddy road and provided no room for maneuvering.

The column moved slowly, for in the back were the baggage carts and the heavy wheeled artillery pulled by oxen. The oxen plodded along at a pace of two miles per hour at best. After half a day's march the army made slow progress and was still within the pass.

General Fuscus rode in front with the Legio V Alaudae. This was the legion of the Praetorian Guard, the Emperor's legion. They were the elite units of the Roman army, best armed, best trained, and best paid. While Emperor Domitian paid legionnaires twelve gold coins per year, the men of the Praetorian Guard were paid double. They were privileged and took great pride in that fact.

Riding just ahead of Fuscus was a unit of cavalry. Behind him came the standards bearers who proudly carried the imperial flags and the legion's golden Eagle. The Eagle glittered brightly on top of its pole when rays of afternoon sunshine cut through between the trees. Drummers beat a slow and steady marching cadence. Behind the standard bearers marched units of legionnaires, stretching back for miles.

General Fuscus was unhappy with the pace of the march, but that was nothing unusual. The army always marched too slow. There was no way to make the oxen and other pack animals go any faster.

Fuscus was not concerned about threats of enemy activity here in this narrow and limited terrain. He found himself becoming irritated however with the lack of reports from his forward scouts. He called to the officer in charge of cavalry, Metellus Varro, who rode up to join the General.

"Your scouting party is late, Varro," Fuscus complained.

"Yes, sir," Metellus replied. "I was thinking the same, General." The lead scouts worked in teams of six. The last detail to go out was slow to report back. "I'll see that it doesn't happen again, sir."

"See to it," Fuscus said impatiently. "Send out another party."

Varro urged his horse towards the front to give orders, then saw that the riders at the front were stopped. There was a slight bend in the road just ahead and Varro hurried forward to investigate. Now the entire column came to a halt, section by section, as each trailing unit was blocked from advancing further.

"No delays!" General Fuscus yelled and urged his horse forward to catch up with Varro.

"We are blocked, sir," Varro explained.

Fuscus reached the bend, looked up the road, and cursed under his breath. In front of them, blocking the pass completely, was a solid mass of Dacian cavalry and infantry. At the very front was a tall rider on a big chestnut horse. This rider motioned to a bugler, who then blew a very loud piercing note on his bugle that echoed up the sides of the mountain and down the length of the pass. A second very loud bugle call followed immediately.

The bugle signal brought on a swarm of arrows and spears that rained down on the Roman column. The attack came from the tree lines on both sides of the pass and from higher up the wooded slopes. Up and down the length of the column men and horses were hit and fell bleeding and screaming.

Fuscus urged his horse back down the trail, leaving Varro in charge of the cavalry. He was furious with the scout units for failing to provide him with advance warning of the enemy, but dealing with them and with Varro would have to wait. First he had to organize his infantry to repulse this attack. The enemy showed a boldness that he did not expect, but that did not worry him. Fuscus was confident that he had the far superior army.

"Testudo!" centurions yelled the familiar command, although the men did not need to be told and were already taking defensive action. They bunched closely together and raised their shields above their heads in the testudo, or tortoise, formation. The overlapped shields sheltered them from the rain of arrows and spears coming down from the trees. Their safety was short lived.

"Kill them!" Drilgisa shouted. He yelled a blood-curdling battle cry as he ran down the slope towards the now disorganized Roman column. Thousands of Dacian infantry shouted their battle cries and howled like wolves as they ran downhill with him, brandishing spears, falxes, swords, and axes. They crashed violently into the unprepared and overwhelmed Roman troops.

The legionnaires fought back desperately but everything was in chaos. The Roman column was stretched out too far and too thinly. They were under attack from two directions, both the western and eastern mountain slopes. The massed numbers and downhill run momentum of the attackers overwhelmed the defenders where the column was thinnest.

Drilgisa reached the column on the run and buried his spear into the side of a Roman soldier who was looking elsewhere and never saw him coming. He stepped back and drew his sica, the Dacian sword with the curved tip, and rushed forward to attack another man. That

Roman was holding off a spearman with his shield while also fighting to fend off Drilgisa with his gladius. In this section of the line Dacian attackers outnumbered Roman defenders by three to one.

The Dacian sica was lighter than the Roman sword and well suited for slashing as well as stabbing. Drilgisa stepped to his left to dodge a lunge from the gladius, then slashed the razor sharp sica across the side of the Roman's exposed neck. The blade cut deep and Drilgisa was sprayed with blood. The legionnaire dropped to the ground without uttering a sound.

"To me!" a Roman officer shouted, trying to organize a defense. "Gather to me!"

Thirty legionnaires formed a square around the centurion. Now they could better protect themselves against the onrushing Dacians. The ground in front and behind them on the road was momentarily empty, then filled with swarming Dacian infantry. The legionnaires found themselves surrounded. Fighting desperately to hold off the infantry attackers, they had no defense against the Dacian archers shooting down at them from higher up the mountain slopes. At short distances of twenty or thirty paces the archers found easy targets that were not protected by legionnaire armor.

Diegis led a large group of infantry down the wooded slopes and came up behind the rear of the Roman column. Their mission was to cut off the Roman retreat and keep the legions penned up in the mountain pass. The Roman rear guard, a cohort of infantry and a small number of cavalry, was there to protect the baggage train and the army's supplies. They were not intended to fight a major battle. Now, very suddenly, they found themselves in a fight with waves of screaming Dacians coming down from the forests on either side of the mountain pass.

The captain of the Roman cavalry unit quickly realized the army was involved in a major battle and not simply a raid on his supply train. Dacians were attacking from both sides and gathering at his rear. He turned to a group of ten riders and shouted an order.

"Get word to Tapae and Capito! Now! Ride!"

The horsemen took off heading south at a gallop. Diegis and a line of Dacians blocked the way, armed with spears and falxes.

"Form a line! Spears in the ground!" Diegis yelled. He knelt down on one knee and planted the butt of his spear into the dirt, the spear pointing up and angled forward. Others lined up with him and did the same. They knew that horses would not charge a wall of spikes unless they were in complete panic. The picket line of spears worked, or at least it worked most of the time.

The Roman cavalry charged straight at them, the horses gathering speed with every stride. Diegis gritted his teeth and held his ground. At the last second the four horses in front tried to turn away from the wall of spears. The horses behind crashed into them. Two of the front horses fell sideways on top of the Dacian spearmen, crushing some of them. Four horses in the back pulled up, and they and their riders fell to spears and falxes. Four of the riders jumped over the fallen horses or found gaps in the Dacian spear line. Archers took down two of the fleeing riders.

Diegis got to his feet and watched as the remaining two Romans galloped away towards Tapae, the horses' hooves throwing up clumps of mud. He had no cavalry and they could not be caught. No matter now. He turned his attention instead to the Dacians still streaming down out of the trees.

"Form a line here!" Diegis shouted. "Give them no retreat!"

At the northern end of the mountain pass, the Dacian end, General Decebal approached the fierce battle on foot. Buri walked beside him, always alert for any threats. The ground was covered with the bodies of dead and dying men, Romans and Dacians. Pools of blood formed on the wet and muddy soil.

The Roman troops converged into groups that grew smaller and smaller. Dacian cavalry rode into the pass and joined the battle. The horse archers added their deadly accurate shooting to the archers on the mountain slopes. The beleaguered legionnaires fell one and two men at a time. There was no shelter and no place for them to escape the Dacian assaults.

Decebal noticed a group of legionnaires just ahead putting up a fierce struggle. The Roman imperial flag and the golden Eagle, the military standard of Legio V Alaudae, was raised over their heads. The soldier holding up the Eagle fell with an arrow through his neck. Another legionnaire swiftly snatched up the pole before the Eagle could tumble into the mud. These men would fight to the last man to protect their legion standard.

Decebal locked eyes with a man in the center of the group who was being shielded by those around him. He knew that look in the man's eyes. It was the look of pride that came with high authority.

"Cease fighting!" Decebal shouted to the Dacians around him, raising his sword over his head to get their attention. "Stop fighting! I wish to talk!"

The Dacian soldiers halted their attack and took a few cautious steps back. The Romans also stopped fighting, glad for the respite to catch their breath, but watched the Dacians warily.

"Are you General Cornelius Fuscus?" Decebal directed his question to the proud Roman in the middle of the group.

Fuscus took a step forward. "I am. Are you General Decebalus?"

"I am General Decebal," he replied in an even tone. The two men stood silently for a moment, taking each other's measure.

Decebal gestured at the battle going on further down the pass. "Your position is lost, General Fuscus. Your army is cut to pieces and surrounded. Enough blood has been spilled. Do you yield, General?"

Fuscus raised his chin ever so slightly, a proud and defiant look. "I do not yield. Roman generals do not yield." Many of the legionnaires standing nearby grinned or shouted their approval.

"I offer the chance to save your men," Decebal continued. "They will be prisoners but not corpses. You will be ransomed and set free, as befits your title."

Fuscus snorted a short, scornful laugh. "I am not a nobleman and have no wealthy family to pay ransom. As for my men," he gestured at those around him, "they fight for Rome and for honor."

Decebal heard the stubborn pride and resolve in the man's voice. He made one last try. "Be reasonable, Fuscus. This is an offer that I regret I could not make to Governor Oppius Sabinus. He was killed in battle before we could talk."

Fuscus gave a grim smile. "Ah, I see. This is an offer that Sabinus would have accepted." He shook his head. "I am not Sabinus."

Decebal nodded, knowing that discussion failed. "Very well, then, General. Now we finish the battle." He pointed his sword forward.

"Attack!"

Dacian soldiers shouted battle cries and moved in again for the assault. The Romans steeled themselves in defensive positions and the battle was on again, even more fiercely now than before. General Fuscus stepped forward to lend his shield and sword to the fight.

A Roman soldier made a dash for Decebal, who was fighting only a few steps away. The man roared as he charged, determined to take out the Dacian leader. Decebal blocked the gladius with his shield, then raised his sica and slashed down with an overhead swing aimed at the Roman's head. In a quick motion the legionnaire raised his shield and blocked the blow.

Buri, standing on Decebal's left, swung his sharp battle ax in a downward arc and sliced off the legionnaire's sword arm at the shoulder. The man fell back in agony and shock.

Cornelius Fuscus fought with desperate energy. He knocked a spear aside with his shield, then stepped forward to drive his gladius deep into the Dacian's belly. He gave the sword a sharp twist so that it would not stick in the man's guts as he pulled it out. An arrow hit high on the right side of his chest and bounced off his plate armor.

"Fuscus!"

The shout came from Cornelius' left, and he turned to see Decebal making his way towards him. He smiled, very gratified to accept this challenge. He waved the nearby legionnaires away.

"Decebalus is my fight! Clear some room!"

By unspoken agreement common to all soldiers, Dacian soldiers and Roman legionnaires stopped fighting and took several steps back. This was now a duel of honor between two generals and army commanders. It was a sacred rite of battle that every soldier there understood and accepted.

Fuscus braced himself and waited calmly. He carried the large Roman shield called the scutum on his left arm. His right hand gripped the leather covered hilt of his gladius, the weapon so familiar from so many hours of training and countless battles that it felt like a natural extension of his arm. He wore the sturdy Roman helmet, and the most modern Roman plate armor to protect his torso.

Decebal fought with a sica, the Dacian sword. On his left arm he carried the round Dacian shield, smaller and lighter than the scutum, made of oak wood covered with copper. He wore mail armor, older and less effective than the Roman plate armor. On his head he wore the round steel helmet of the Dacian infantry.

Both were exceptionally well trained and experienced soldiers. Both had killed dozens of lesser men in the frenzy of battle. This fight was not driven by fury and frenzy however. Each man represented his nation, and this was a fight for pride and honor.

Fuscus stood with his gladius at his side, inviting attack. Decebal took a quick step forward and stabbed at the Roman's face, but Fuscus easily blocked the blow with his shield. He counter-attacked by stabbing low with the gladius at Decebal's leg. Decebal parried with the sica to knock the gladius aside. The gladius was heavier and sturdier, the sica lighter and much more maneuverable.

Both men circled, looking for an opening. Decebal made a feint to his right but Fuscus held firm and did not react. He took a quick stab at Decebal's face. The Dacian raised his shield to block the sword and moved in to his left, slashing up with the sica at Fuscus' sword hand. The curved tip of the sica caught the side of Fuscus' right hand and drew blood.

Fuscus took a step back. The cut on his sword hand was not very deep but it was bleeding steadily. He could still grasp the gladius firmly, but knew that in short time his hand and the leather hilt of his sword would be slick with his own blood. It was better to finish the fight quickly. The Dacian was younger and faster, so he had to beat him with power.

Fuscus attacked aggressively with a series of short, quick stabbing moves. Decebal gave ground and retreated. His right foot slipped in the mud, and he dipped low and almost fell to his knee. Fuscus lunged forward and stabbed down with the gladius towards Decebal's exposed neck. Instinctively the Dacian's round shield flashed up to block the sword tip, and in one swift motion Decebal sprang up to his feet and moved to Fuscus' left.

Quick as a blink the sica slashed across the unprotected back of Fuscus' left thigh. The Roman turned and stabbed wildly with his gladius but Decebal had already stepped back out of reach.

Fuscus staggered back a step on his injured leg. The cut on his thigh hurt with a burning pain and was bleeding heavily down his leg. Now Decebal had him at his mercy. Cornelius was fighting on one leg and with a wounded sword hand.

"Yield, General," Decebal urged in a quiet but firm voice. "I do not wish to kill you or more of your men. This battle is already settled."

"Go to Hades," Fuscus spat bitterly. His honor would not allow him to give in. He lunged forward with the tip of the gladius aimed at Decebal's guts. The Dacian took a quick sideways step and easily dodged the sword thrust. Fuscus stumbled by and almost fell, and Decebal chopped down hard with the sharp blade of the sica across the back of the Roman's neck. Fuscus fell face forward to the muddy ground and did not move again. A pool of blood quickly formed around his head.

Decebal turned towards the now disheartened Roman troops who watched the fight. He pointed his blood stained sword at them.

"Yield and live!"

A dozen legionnaires had no fight left in them, and they put down their arms and surrendered. The others defiantly moved back down the pass where other Roman troops continued fighting for their lives. Dacian infantry and cavalry fell on the retreating soldiers like wolves on sheep. The Dacians could taste and smell victory now, and that drove them to an even greater fighting frenzy.

Some legionnaires rallied to the small group defending the legion flag and their golden Eagle. Many fell under a barrage of arrows from Dacian horse archers who had them surrounded. At close range the archers easily found the spots not protected by shields and armor. The Romans knew they were fighting a losing battle, falling one by one, but refused to give up. Finally Dacian infantry moved in to beat down the last defenders.

Buri saw that a dead legionnaire still held onto the bloodied pole on which was mounted the legion's Eagle standard. He pulled it away from the dead man's hands, raised the pole up to the sky, and stared at it in wonder.

Decebal was still standing near the body of Cornelius Fuscus when Buri, surrounded by several other Dacian soldiers, walked towards him proudly carrying the captured Eagle. It was a solemn occasion because all the men understood the significance of this moment in the history of Dacia's wars with Rome.

"The Eagle of Legio V Alaudae is yours by conquest, General," Buri said with a touch of awe in his voice. Decebal took the standard and gazed up at the golden Eagle. Of all the battles he had fought in his long life as a warrior, this was his proudest moment. The elite Roman legion of the Praetorian Guard was no more.

Diegis was fighting a protracted battle against the remaining Roman troops retreating south, stragglers seeking to escape towards the city of Tapae. His own Dacian forces were thinning out and getting tired. Dusk was approaching. Two long sharp notes from a Dacian bugle echoed on the mountainsides. There was a pause, then three more. That was the signal to end hostilities.

"Enough!" Diegis yelled to his men. "Cease fighting unless you are attacked! Secure the supply wagons!"

Wounded and exhausted legionnaires put down their weapons and surrendered. The battle was over and there was no escape. The prisoners were rounded up into small groups and put under guard.

As dusk fell Dacian soldiers began to enthusiastically go through the treasures, weapons, food, and other materials in the very long line of Roman supply wagons that stretched for half a mile. Supplies that were intended to provision twenty thousand Roman fighting men and another ten thousand people in support roles were now captured Dacian loot.

Decebal rode up with a troop of Dacian cavalry. Buri rode beside him. They left the captured Eagle with King Duras and the royal party at the northern end of the pass.

Decebal dismounted, walked up to Diegis, and lifted him off his feet in a tight bear hug. "Well done, Brother! We did it! We broke this Roman army."

"Broke it entirely," Diegis said with a grin. "Now put me down!" He motioned at the line of wagons. "All their material is ours. Food, weapons, supplies. It will take them many months to resupply."

"Much longer than that," Decebal said. "We have destroyed the equal of two legions and captured thousands of men. There will not be another attack by Rome for a long time."

Hearing that made Buri happy. "I hope so, Decebal. Maybe now I can plant my crops and tend my orchards for one full season?"

"I think so, Buri," Decebal assured him. "You have earned that right as much as any man. More than most."

"What now?" Diegis wondered.

"Now we secure the prisoners and supplies. And, you know that artillery you were wishing for, Brother?" Decebal asked with a grin.

"We have it now," Diegis grinned back.

Decebal swept his hand over the long line of supply wagons and wheeled artillery. "We have it now, along with the Roman engineers to maintain it. Find the engineers among the prisoners and make certain they are treated well."

"I will be happy to. I would like an education in Roman artillery, myself."

"In two days we meet in Tapae. The King wishes to see that the city is secure, and to give the army a celebration."

"A celebration well earned," Diegis said.

"Yes, well earned," Decebal agreed. "And also hard earned. We have suffered many losses to gain this victory, Diegis. But for the Romans, this is a disaster."

Chapter 8

THE NEW KING

Tapae, Dacia, Autumn 86 AD

*F*ollowing the defeat of General Cornelius Fuscus, Sextus Capito abandoned the siege of Tapae. He led the troops under his command south to the Danubius River. They marched back to the boat bridge, harassed intermittently along the way by Dacian horse archers. His men and the legionnaires who were survivors of the battle considered themselves fortunate to escape the fate of their general.

Little damage was done to the city of Tapae. The Romans never stormed the walls and so the defenders suffered few casualties. After Capito's army departed the people of Tapae threw open the city gates and joyously welcomed King Duras and the Dacian army.

The victory celebration in the city was a magnificent feast, making use of the local food supply and the captured Roman goods. Oxen, sheep, pork, geese, and chickens were roasted richly coated with spices. There was no shortage of vegetables and fruit. The women of Tapae baked basket after basket of flaky Dacian pastries made with butter, honey, fruit fillings, nuts, and various types of cheeses.

While the adults worked on preparing for the celebration, the children played games and competed in races and athletic contests. The evening would be given to singing and dancing. Dacian tradition was rich in songs and dances to fit every occasion. Celebrating a big military victory called for reciting epic songs and stories. New songs would be created to describe the victory at Tapae.

Two hours before sunset, following the orders of King Duras, the army and the townspeople gathered on a large grassy field outside the city. There were too many people to fit inside the city walls. A wooden platform was raised in front of the city wall so that all could see and hear the King. A throne rested in the middle of the platform. The Dacian flags and colorful banners fluttered in the afternoon breeze. The draco wolf-head banner flew high behind the platform.

King Duras, General Decebal, the High Priest Vezina, and Diegis sat on the platform watching the happy crowd gather. Vezina had gathered information from the scouts and provided updates for the royal party.

"The Romans are retreating back into Banat. Once across the Ister they will dismantle their boat bridge, I am sure. They don't want us chasing after them," Vezina said. "Clever bit of engineering, that boat bridge."

King Duras nodded. "When the Romans are not destroying they can be very efficient builders. I will credit them that."

"They are beaten for the time being," Vezina continued. "How I wish I was in Moesia when news of this reaches the Emperor."

"Domitian is in Moesia?" Decebal asked, surprised.

"Yes, he returned to Moesia recently," Vezina replied. "He is in Naissus with one legion."

King Duras laughed. "He wanted to take credit for General Fuscus' victory in Dacia, eh?"

"Most likely, Sire," Decebal said. He was pleased to see that the King had a twinkle in his eye and was in an unusually good mood. It was good to see the old man happy.

"Will you address the people, Uncle?" Diegis asked.

"Yes, Nephew. I will," the King replied.

"On what message?" Diegis asked. "This is a momentous occasion in the history of Dacia. Songs will be sung, and your words will be remembered, Uncle."

"I will speak about this and that, Nephew. This and that," Duras said with a smile.

Diegis glanced at Decebal, seated next to the King. Decebal gave a small shrug and looked out over the crowd. People were settled in and in a talkative, festive mood.

"Let us begin, Your Holiness," the King said to Vezina.

The High Priest stood and walked to the front of the platform. He raised both arms high over his head to get the crowd's attention. As people noticed him their talk quieted down.

"People of Dacia! Children of Zamolxis!" Vezina spoke in a loud and clear voice that carried to the back of the crowd. "We celebrate a great victory here today over the armies of Rome! We are thankful to the heroes who fought this battle! We are grateful for the heroes who gave their lives to win this battle, and we rejoice with them because at this moment they are also celebrating in the heavenly kingdom of Zamolxis!"

There were no cheers or shouts of victory. The solemn moment deserved respectful silence.

"People of Dacia! Children of Zamolxis! We are thankful to our King, who prepared our army for battle and won this victory!" Vezina paused for a moment. "Now let us welcome our King! King Duras!"

The crowd immediately came to life. Duras stood up from his throne to the sound of loud cheers that became louder by the second, and walked to stand beside the High Priest. Vezina bowed to the King, then went back to take his seat besides Decebal and Diegis.

Duras basked in the cheering of the crowd. He allowed them some time to celebrate the moment. Every person there would remember this day until their dying day. After a while the King raised his hands for silence.

"People of Dacia!" King Duras spoke in a loud voice that was still strong at his age. "Dacia has won a great victory here at Tapae! This victory will be remembered for a hundred years!"

The enthusiastic cheering resumed. After a short while the King raised his arm again to quiet them.

"This is a victory very hard fought, over a powerful enemy!" The King's tone was solemn, not boastful. "This is a great battle won, but I tell you now, there will be many more hard battles to come! Rome is a powerful enemy, and it is a vengeful enemy!"

The crowd grew quieter. What was the King saying?

"I have the honor to serve Dacia as your monarch. Truthfully, my people, no man may hold a greater honor!" King Duras paused for a breath. "Now it is my honor to give you a gift! A gift that will keep Dacia strong! Strong and secure in the days to come!"

Decebal turned his head and caught Vezina's eye. The High Priest gave him a pleasant smile and focused his attention back to the King.

King Duras turned away from the crowd and walked back to stand beside his throne.

"General Decebal and Your Holiness, you will join me here," Duras instructed the sitting men.

They did so, Vezina with perfect calm poise and Decebal looking puzzled. Duras put his hand on Decebal's shoulder.

"Sit on the throne, General Decebal," the King commanded.

"Sire," Decebal began. Then words failed him.

"Do as I say, Nephew," Duras said, his voice strong and resolved.

Decebal turned to face the crowd and then sat down on the throne. He looked out over the vast colorful array of people, his army and also the citizens of Tapae. Vezina stood on one side of the throne, the King on the other. Some people in the crowd now understood and excited murmurs began to spread.

King Duras reached up with both hands and took the crown off his head. Moving slowly and with a solemn dignity he placed it on the head of Decebal. Duras turned to face the crowd that waited with hushed breath in anticipation.

"People of Dacia! I give you your new king!" He calmly motioned for Decebal to stand.

"King Decebal!"

The excited crowd stood and erupted with cheers, shouting at the top of their lungs. Diegis leaped to his feet as well. People shouted, clapped their hands, and stamped their feet. This coronation was not expected but it was met with enthusiastic popular approval.

Duras and Vezina led the newly crowned King Decebal to the front of the stand to acknowledge the crowd's joyful affirmation. The sound of their cheers and shouts built up to a crescendo that swelled out and filled the valley.

"Decebal!"

"Decebal!"

"Decebal!"

"Decebal!"

Sarmizegetusa, Spring 87 AD

King Decebal gazed out the window from his throne room. It was a simple joy each spring to watch the Earth come back to life. Trees and shrubs were budding new leaves, and after a dormant winter the grass turned into a rich green color. The tall, majestic maple tree in the courtyard was growing a crown of new leaves. Newly born lambs and colts frolicked in the fields.

Decebal and his uncle Duras were engaged in casual conversation when Vezina walked in the room. The tall, thin High Priest was in an obvious good mood. He gave them an amused smile.

"News from Rome?" Duras asked. "I know that look on your face, Vezina. What has happened?"

"Much news from Rome," Vezina began. "The Emperor Domitian has returned to Rome and declared a great victory over Dacia."

Decebal gave him a puzzled look. "What great victory over Dacia?"

"Ah! A perfectly good question, Sire. That is the Emperor's story to the Senate and people of Rome, that he has won a great victory over Dacia. Not only that, but Domitian also persuaded the Senate to give him a triumph. Actually, a double triumph!"

"A triumph? For what?" Decebal asked. A Roman triumph was awarded by the Senate of Rome to celebrate great military victories. It included a lavish parade through the streets of Rome and a great public feast, all at great expense for the state treasury.

"What has Domitian done to earn a double triumph?" Duras asked, equally surprised.

"In part he celebrates his war against the Chatti tribes, some four years ago, in Germania. He also celebrates the victories of Cornelius Fuscus last year to re-capture the Roman forts south of the Ister. Of course the Emperor takes the credit for himself. His poets are singing his praises as a military hero."

Decebal leaned back in his chair and laughed. "A military hero! He stayed in his tent with his mistresses and his jugs of wine while Fuscus did all the fighting!"

"And what do you hear about the loss of General Fuscus and his army?" Duras wondered.

Vezina chuckled. "The Emperor Domitian would like to pretend that the battle of Tapae never happened. The Senate likewise also considers it an embarrassment for Rome. It is not a topic for public discussion, so everyone pretends it does not exist."

Duras frowned, his face showing his disgust. "This Emperor is a liar and a fraud. He has no real accomplishments of his own, so he invents pretend victories."

"He seems to have a talent for that," Decebal said. "You once told us, Vezina, how Domitian once returned from a failed campaign in Germania without prisoners or captured loot. But he still celebrated a triumph using slaves in his parade dressed up as German prisoners?"

"I remember that," Duras said. "He used furniture and treasures borrowed from the royal warehouses to pretend that it was captured loot from Germania. The man is an utter fraud!"

"Ah, but there is more I have to tell you," Vezina continued, still amused. "The Emperor presented the Senate with a letter from you, King Decebal, signed by you, pledging loyalty to Rome and agreeing not to pursue any further hostile actions against the Roman Empire."

"What?" Decebal asked, astonished. "I wrote no such letter!"

Duras shook his head and chuckled.

"Apparently there are some in the Senate who believe the letter to be legitimate, and some who do not," Vezina explained.

"No doubt we can divide those men into two camps, those who seek favor with Domitian and those who do not," said Decebal.

"Exactly so, Sire. Many senators treat the letter as a farce but are afraid to say so in public. Their scorn for the Emperor is expressed only in private and behind closed doors. In public they remain silent."

"It would be dangerous for any Roman to call Domitian a liar," Duras said. "They risk losing their necks. It is always this way, it seems, between Roman dictators and the Roman Senate."

"Ah, but there may yet be a few stout necks left among them!" Vezina continued. "The Emperor wanted to be granted the title of Dacicus. In other words, the conqueror of Dacia. The Senate refused his request."

"The gall of the man!" Duras spat, his face turning red.

Decebal laughed again. "Uncle, this is comedy not tragedy. The man is desperate for recognition but all he does is bring more scorn on himself."

"He is still Emperor of Rome!" Duras said, no longer in a laughing mood. "He may act the fool but he is still dangerous."

Decebal nodded. "Of course you are right, Uncle. I understand that we must take him seriously. He represents Rome, and Rome will always be dangerous."

"Always dangerous is correct, Sire," Vezina said. "Which is why we continue to prepare for the next attack."

"That work of preparation never stops," the King said. "We are training infantry and cavalry. We are breeding more horses and will purchase more from the Sarmatians. The Roman engineers that we captured at Tapae teach our men to use and maintain the artillery."

"Very good," Duras said. "We shall need all of them, and more."

Decebal sat back and became thoughtful. "Domitian is humiliated but must pretend that he has won. That explains his little farce with the Senate."

"A farce that only shows his failure and his weakness," Duras said.

"Indeed, Uncle. What is more important than Domitian's pride, however, is that Rome also has been humiliated. This will make them even more hostile towards Dacia."

Vezina stroked his long white beard. "Beware the wounded beast. The Romans will lick their wounds then come for us again."

"So we prepare for war, and we stay on the alert," Decebal said. "Uncle, you will help me negotiate more alliances with our neighbors. Rome is a threat to them as much as to us."

"Yes they are," Duras agreed. "Let's start with Chief Attalu of the Marcomanni and Prince Davi of the Roxolani. Your victory at Tapae has encouraged our neighbors to increase their resistance to Rome. They have seen that Rome's armies can be beaten."

Decebal turned to the High Priest and chief advisor to the King. "And, Vezina? Your mission is somewhat different."

"Yes, Sire?"

"Hire more spies."

Chapter 9

CALM BEFORE THE STORM

Rome, Spring 88 AD

O ne year later the Emperor Domitian was still making preparations for the next Dacian war. His new army commander, General Tettius Julianus, had served as a governor of Moesia. He was familiar with the territory and the tribes of the Danubius River region, including the allies and enemies of Dacia.

Julianus was also a hard-nosed, no-nonsense commander. Some compared him to the legendary general Gaius Marius, the uncle of Julius Caesar, who modernized the Roman army and saved Rome from destruction more than once. After the rash military leadership of Cornelius Fuscus, Tettius Julianus was exactly the kind of tough and disciplined commander the Emperor wanted in charge of the army that would invade Dacia.

Domitian stood in his palace gardens talking with Senator Marcus Paullus, his biggest political supporter in the Senate, when General Julianus arrived exactly at the appointed time. Walking at his side was a soldier who looked vaguely familiar to Domitian. The man was trim and fit, in his thirties, black hair and pale gray eyes.

"I will leave you to your military business now, Caesar," the flabby Senator Paullus said, taking his leave. "The money for the games will be appropriated at the next meeting of the Senate."

"I trust that they will, Marcus," Domitian said. "You never fail to deliver what you promise."

"I treasure your trust as always, Caesar," Paullus said. He nodded a greeting to Julianus on his way out.

"New games, Caesar?" Tettius asked with genuine interest.

The Emperor was loved by the common people for the lavish games he produced to entertain the citizens of Rome. He was hated by the Senate for the lavish expenses these required, but expenses were unavoidable. Caesar would not allow high costs to lessen the quality of his games.

"Ten days of games, Tettius!" Domitian beamed. "Chariot races, gladiators, including female gladiators and midget gladiators. People get tired of the same old thing. And we'll round up some Christians to feed the lions, that always gets a good reaction. You must come as my guest to see the games. And who is this?"

"Caesar, this is my senior tribune," Julianus said. "Titus Lucullus."

Titus straightened his back and saluted smartly. "Hail, Caesar!"

Domitian eyed him curiously. "Why do you look familiar? I can't place you, Lucullus."

"I served with Governor Oppius Sabinus in Moesia, Caesar," Titus explained.

"Ah, yes. Poor Sabinus. He was outfoxed by Decebalus and it cost him his head. Is that not so?"

"Yes, Caesar, that is so," Lucullus answered, some sadness in his eyes. He had respected Sabinus despite the man's stubbornness and aristocratic arrogance. Aristocracy and arrogance went together, he knew, and Oppius Sabinus was no different than most men of his social rank.

Domitian raised an eyebrow. "And do you believe you can serve Julianus better than you served Sabinus?"

Titus' face reddened. "Yes, Caesar. I will do my duty to the utmost of my ability."

Julianus intervened. "Lucullus is an excellent strategic planner, Caesar. He knows Moesia and Banat well, and knows the local tribes and their chieftains. He also knows King Decebalus better than most, and once faced him in battle."

The Emperor looked unimpressed. "Very well, then. I trust that your next battle against Decebalus will go better than the last batle, eh, Lucullus?"

"Yes, Caesar."

Domitian pointed to two benches beneath a poplar shade tree. "Come, sit, and tell me how you plan to defeat this barbarian king who bloodied Rome twice even before he became a king."

"We are assembling nine legions in Banat, Caesar," Julianus began once they were seated. "Legio V Flavia Felix is marching west from Dalmatia. Legio VI Victrix and Legio XIII Gemina are marching east from Germania."

"Are we weakening Germania too much for the sake of the Dacian war?" Domitian asked. "There are those in the Senate who still blame me for losing northern Britannia in order to provide more legions for Fuscus."

Tettius shook his head. "No, I do not think so, Caesar. The troops in Germania will keep the peace there."

"I don't need you to think, Julianus! I need you to be sure!" The Emperor turned to Titus. "And what do you think, Lucullus?"

"I agree with the General, Caesar. The Germanic tribes are always restless and we must keep an eye on them. However I believe that nine legions are necessary for the invasion of Dacia."

"Very well. I like to see that you actually use your brain, and do not immediately tell me what you think I want to hear."

Titus did not know how to respond to that, so wisely kept quiet.

"Thanks to Caesar's negotiations," Julianus cut in, "we also have the use of one thousand Iazygi horse." The Iazygi tribes often became allies of Rome against Dacia.

"Ah, excellent news!" Domitian exclaimed, very pleased with this development. Rome was famed for its infantry, not cavalry. Cavalry was expensive to train and maintain. Horses broke down when they had to travel over long distances. For economic and logistical reasons it was much better to recruit cavalry from among local tribes allied with Rome.

"The attack should commence in the summer, once our troops are in place," Julianus said.

"The sooner the better," Domitian replied forcefully. "Dacia must be punished, and you must retrieve the legion standards lost by Fuscus." The Emperor's face turned grim. "That humiliation cannot stand."

"Yes, Caesar. It will be done," Tettius declared. Conquering Dacia was just as important to him as it was to Domitian. "We cross the Danubius in good weather and take Sarmizegetusa within two months, before the weather turns cold. We cannot fight in those mountains in winter."

"And how will you cross the Danubius, Tettius?"

"Via a boat bridge, the same as Fuscus. That was one thing that Cornelius did very well. We still have the boats and the engineers in the area and they can be assembled on short notice."

"Pity that Cornelius was not nearly as good a general as he was an engineer. Don't fail me like he did, Julianus."

"I will not fail, Caesar," Julianus vowed.

"Good. Make sure of it, Tettius. I want to see Decebalus marching in chains down the streets of Rome in my next triumph parade."

"It will be done, Caesar," the General promised.

The meeting was over. The two soldiers stood and turned to walk away.

"Lucullus!" the Emperor called out abruptly, causing them to pause and turn back to him.

"Yes, Caesar?"

"Tell me, Titus, since you know Dacia well. Is it true that the streets of Sarmizegetusa are paved with gold?"

Lucullus was taken aback. Surely the Emperor was not serious?

"I expect that is an exaggeration, Caesar. However it is true that Dacia is a wealthy land. They are rich in grain and in livestock. Their mountains are very rich in minerals, and they have been mining those mountains for hundreds of years. It is common knowledge that Decebalus possesses large amounts of gold and silver."

"Ah, an honest answer!" Domitian smiled. "I know those things are true, Lucullus. But answer me this, why has no one taken those treasures before now?"

"Some have tried. None succeeded."

"Evidently so." Domitian gave both men a hard look. "Now listen well, this is my command to both of you. Bring me those treasures of Dacian gold and silver."

"Yes, Caesar," Tettius replied dutifully.

"This is imperative, Julianus!" Domitian said. "It is imperative. The state treasury is near empty, as are the public grain bins. We must buy more grain and must pay our legions. Whatever the cost, bring me the Dacian gold."

When he was finally alone Domitian took a long walk through his palace gardens. He was happiest in moments like this, when he could be alone with his thoughts. He, and only he, was fully aware of the great burden carried by Caesar, the ruler of the world. He carried the heaviest burden of any man in the Roman Empire.

Maintaining Rome's vast empire was monstrously expensive. The state treasury was always near empty. Paying the army was ruinous, yet the army must be paid or the Empire would crumble. The Divine Augustus, in his great wisdom, reduced the total number of Rome's legions by half, and still military expenses were monstrous.

He simply did not have enough legions to handle all of Rome's military campaigns, which made it necessary to move them around like so many pieces on a game board. Every time he had to do that he received more criticism from fools in the Senate. Brittania won and then given away, they carped. The fools could not understand that Dacia and Germania were more important.

The Emperor firmly believed that he was ruling no different than his predecessors, including Titus, Vespasian, and the other emperors before them. For over two hundred years Rome's rulers knew that two things must be done. The army must be paid, and the common people must be provided with bread and games. Those two things were essential to the survival of the rulers, and indeed the survival of the state.

Domitian was bitterly aware that thus far in his rule as Caesar he showed little talent for military success. That galled him to no end. The memories of his father Vespasian and his brother Titus burned in the pit of his stomach like sulfur. They were celebrated for their many military victories. He was scorned for his struggles fighting against Germania, and now Dacia. The conquest of Dacia would put an end to those pains. He would pay any price, sacrifice anything, to achieve that end.

His most natural talent, Domitian knew very well, was in creating the most inventive games and entertainments for the people. He had a genius for it. Gladiator fights including men, women, dwarves, people of all colors enslaved from all corners of the world, brought to Rome for the Emperor's games. Recreated infantry battles. Cavalry battles. Sea battles. Hunts involving hundreds of wild beasts. The public execution of Christians and other criminals.

Blaming the Christians for many of Rome's ills was a brilliant idea, following in the footsteps of Emperor Nero. The Colosseum crowd cheered wildly when Christians were put in the arena with hungry lions and other wild beasts. The people were happiest when blood flowed, and the more blood the better. It distracted them from their problems and worries. It distracted Caesar as well from the heavy burdens of ruling the world.

It weighed heavily on Domitian's mind that the Empress Domitia Longina was still exiled on the island of Pandateria. She lived out a lonely existence with a few loyal servants and a small contingent of guards. Some senators were advising Domitian to bring her back to Rome, but Domitian's pride would not allow her that satisfaction.

The Emperor turned a corner and glimpsed a vision of loveliness under the bright sun. His niece Julia Flavia, the only daughter of his brother Titus, sat on a stone bench reading a book. Julia was twenty-four years old and married to Titus Flavius Sabinus, brother to the consul Flavius Clemens. She was slim, with light blue eyes and curly blond hair that shone like gold in the bright sun.

Julia heard his approach and looked up with a shy smile.

"What are you reading, Niece?" Domitian asked and sat on the bench beside her.

She held up the book. "The epigrams of Marcus Valerius Martialis, Caesar. He sings your praises most admirably."

The Emperor laughed. "As well he should, and not only because I pay him well. He calls me his lord and god, and he is most sincere in his worship of me."

"All Romans are sincere in their worship of Caesar," Julia said, and believed it to be true. Domitian was emperor and also divine. He was a god.

"Ah, I must have you talk to my enemies in the Senate!" Domitian exclaimed with feigned excitement. "If you would turn your charm on them perhaps it will save me the trouble of having to exile or kill them, eh?"

Julia heard the tension in his voice that belied the humor in his words. "There are no loyal Romans who are your enemies, Caesar," she reassured him.

Domitian leaned closer and looked into her pale blue eyes. Julia was lovely, and she could see into his soul. He took her hand and squeezed it gently between his two hands. "But let us not talk politics, my dear."

Julia lowered her eyes shyly. She was taken aback by the Emperor's sudden attention. She was not alarmed, just confused that the usually aloof Uncle Domitian was taking such a personal interest in her.

"Tell me," Domitian continued in a pleasant voice, "how goes your marriage to Titus Flavius?"

Sarmizegetusa, Summer 88 AD

Andrada watched her daughters running around on the grass. They were chasing each other in a game of tag with several other children their age. Three year old Adila could not keep up with five year old Zia, but she was determined to try. The sisters liked each other but both were also very competitive. In quieter times the older Zia would teach her sister new words or new games to play.

Their father, the King, was absent again. He was often gone on trips to attend to military or political matters. Dacia was building new forts and strengthening the existing forts on its borders and in the mountains. Walls needed to be built and repaired. Troops in the infantry, cavalry, and archery units needed to be trained. Vast amounts of supplies and equipment needed to be stored where they would most likely be needed.

After the battle of Tapae a sizable number of Roman deserters, over two hundred, had joined the Dacian forces. Decebal paid them much better, and unlike Rome he paid the soldiers regularly. These deserters proved to be very valuable in teaching Dacian soldiers how to fight the Roman legionnaires. The training never stopped and King Decebal supervised and reviewed all his troops.

There had been no large scale military clashes for a year and a half after the battle of Tapae, but there was no mistaking that Dacia was at war. The Dacian leadership knew that Rome was preparing a very large military campaign. They made every effort to make sure that neither the army nor the people became careless and complacent.

Andrada's reverie was interrupted by the sound of Adila crying. The child was on the ground, sniffling, while her older sister tried to help her up. Their friend Tarbus also tried to comfort Adila.

"Tarbus pushed me!" Adila complained between sobs. She had a mild grass burn on her left knee caused by her fall.

"He did not!" Zia explained. "You ran into each other. He did not mean to push you."

"Come here, my brave girl," Andrada held out her arms. She peered down to examine Adila's knee. "That does not look bad. We'll wash it with clean water and your knee will be good as new."

"He pushed me!" the girl persisted, wanting to convince them that she was right.

"Hush now, Adila. Tarbus is a good boy. He would not try to hurt you. It was a little accident, that's all."

Before the child could complain again their attention was drawn to seven riders approaching. Six of them were dressed in military gear.

Zia jumped up excitedly. "Is that Tata coming home?"

Adila stopped sobbing and followed her gaze. Andrada noticed the female figure in the middle of the group and shook her head. "No, it is not your Tata. It's your aunt Tanidela."

The riders pulled up. Tanidela dismounted, then thanked and dismissed her escort. They bowed to her from the saddle and left, leading her horse to the stables.

"Auntie! Auntie!" The girls ran to their young aunt, who went to one knee and gathered both in a big hug. She had not seen the girls for months.

Tanidela was the younger sister of Decebal and Diegis. She was twenty-three years old, with light brown hair and striking green eyes. Her light, comfortable riding clothes accented her slender figure.

As Andrada walked up to greet her, Tanidela stood and gave her a small bow. "My Queen, it is good to see you again," she said with a relaxed smile.

"My Queen, my foot," Andrada said with a laugh. "Family does not bow to family. Not to me, anyway. How are you, Sister?"

Andrada was three years older than her sister-in-law. They had always treated each other as sisters.

"I am very tired, so tired of riding," she replied. She reached down to tussle the hair of her nieces. "But I am very happy to be home and see you all again."

"Do you bring any news?" Andrada asked. Tanidela knew exactly what news she was waiting for.

"Yes. I left my brothers at Pelendava. From there they were going to Tapae."

Andrada took in a sharp breath.

"What is it, Mama?" Zia looked up, anxiety in her voice.

Andrada smiled down at the girls. "Nothing for you to worry about, my darling. Now let's take Auntie inside and welcome her home. She must be dying for a bath, I think."

"Yes!" Tanidela cried, then took the girls by the hand and walked them towards the palace entrance. "A bath is exactly what I need, then a good meal. I'm so hungry I could eat a small horse!" That made both girls giggle.

Andrada walked behind them, but her mind was already with her husband. Pelendava was a fort in the southern mountains of Dacia. Tapae was the first line of defense against enemies crossing the Ister north into Dacia. The only reason for Decebal taking the army there was because the Romans were preparing their invasion there. The war with Rome was about to be renewed.

Chapter 10

THE SIEGE

Banat, Autumn 88 AD

G eneral Tettius Julianus watched impatiently as the last of the heavy artillery pieces were pulled by teams of oxen across the boat bridge. He would be going up against well defended walled forts and cities. Artillery and other siege equipment including ballistae, scorpions, and battering rams, were essential to the army's success. Producing enough of these weapons to properly arm nine legions was hugely expensive. The Emperor protested, but Julianus would not accept no for an answer.

Now all that remained was to bring the remainder of the baggage train and supplies across the river. The supply wagons were lighter than the siege machinery and the work would go much faster. Even so, a large army required a vast amount of supplies to travel through enemy territory. It always took longer to move than he would have liked.

"Two more days should do it, Titus?" Julianus asked his tribune. Lucullus was in charge of planning transport because he had a good mind for numbers and organization.

"Yes, sir," Titus replied. "No more than two days, and we'll have the entire army on the north side of the river."

"Well done, Titus. Without you this army would move like a snail."

Lucullus ventured a smile. "A very large snail, General. They are not known for speed."

"Indeed not. Nevertheless, we will have to drag this army halfway across Dacia to reach Sarmizegetusa. And we will will have to crush anything that stands in the way."

"Yes, sir. Tapae will be a good test. Its walls are as strong as any of their strongest forts."

"Small matter how strong it is, Titus. We will take the city, and then go through the mountains, and we will do it properly," Tettius said. "Fuscus was impatient. We will not travel blind, and we will not leave an enemy in our rear."

"No, sir," Lucullus agreed. This old man was no fool. Unlike, Titus thought, so many other Roman nobles who fancied themselves as military geniuses. He kept that last thought to himself.

Tapae, Dacia, Autumn 88 AD

King Decebal, High Priest Vezina, and Diegis were seated in a house inside the walls of Tapae. Tsiru, the captain of the cavalry scouts, made his report.

"We count nine legions, at full strength, with full complements of artillery and siege engines, Sire. They look well organized and are marching at good pace."

Vezina nodded. "This is what we expected. Led by General Tettius Julianus, who used to be governor of Moesia. He is a superior general and a sly old fox."

"How many cavalry?" Decebal asked.

"Best count, around two thousand, Sire. And just as we expected the Iazygi are in the Roman camp again. They make up the bulk of their cavalry," Tsiru said with a look of distaste on his face. Over the years he fought several battles against Iazygi horsemen, who were considered traitors for siding with Rome.

"Well done, Tsiru," Decebal said. "You are dismissed."

"Yes, Sire." Tsiru turned and left the room. He had more scouts coming in and his work was never done.

"That's a lot of cavalry," Diegis observed.

Decebal waved it off. "We will not fight them on open ground. But yes, that is a lot of cavalry and their mobility will cause us problems even in the mountains."

Vezina leaned forward, worry lines forming on his forehead. "Tapae cannot stand against an army this size. The question is how long the city can hold out."

"I will stay here and organize the city defenses," Diegis said. "We can hold off the Romans for a week, perhaps two, while you mobilize the army in the mountains, Brother. There are more troops arriving every day."

The King shook his head. "No, you cannot remain here. I need you and Drilgisa with the infantry." That was understood to be an order and not a suggestion.

"I will stay and organize the city's defenses," Vezina cut in. "The first job is to evacuate the children and those women who can't fight. That must begin today."

That took Diegis by surprise. "You?"

"My son," Vezina explained patiently, "priests of Zamolxis have managed military campaigns for hundreds of years. Were you not paying attention to my lessons when you were a boy?"

"He was paying attention to the girls," Decebal said with a grin. "Very well, Vezina, you stay and defend the city. Give us one week to allow for the reserves to arrive."

"We will hold them off for one week," the High Priest replied.

"Listen well, Vezina," Decebal continued. "One week! After that you find an escape route through the mountain. You know the tunnel escape routes better than any of us."

"Indeed, Sire, I designed the best ones," Vezina acknowledged. "We will hold the city for one week. And following that, poof! I shall disappear in a puff of smoke, leaving the Romans to ask, where did he go?"

Diegis grinned. "Make it work, Vezina. If the Romans capture you that puff of smoke will be from the fire they set under your feet with you tied to a stake."

"Oh, ho!" Vezina cried with a laugh. "Another lesson you evidently missed, youngster, was the one about respecting your elders!"

"This meeting is concluded," Decebal declared. "Diegis, you will help Vezina organize the evacuation of children and noncombatant women who are able to travel. Have them escorted to Argidava, it may be a while before they can return here."

"Yes, Sire," Diegis acknowledged.

Decebal stood and turned for the door. "We have no time to waste. There are nine Roman legions heading this way, our army is still arriving day by day and we have a great deal of work to do."

The bombardment of Tapae with siege artillery began the next day at dawn. Ballistae launching large stones, some weighing upwards of one hundred pounds, battered the western wall and the main gate of the city. The stone walls were very thick and could not be brought down by artillery. The purpose of the attack was to weaken Tapae's defenses on the walls, cause damage inside the city, and demoralize its inhabitants. Scorpions launched bolts from hundreds of feet away with enough range to hit some of the men standing guard on top of the city walls.

The walls were defended by three hundred Dacian infantry plus the civilian population that was old enough and fit enough to fight. More than two hundred women, armed with bows and spears, also manned the defenses. Men and women held equal responsibility for defending their land and their families.

Vezina, dressed in plain civilian clothes, looked out from the top of the battlement built over the main gate. Outside the walls a sea of Roman legions and their camps stretched out as far as the eye could see. In all his years he had never seen an army even close in size to this Roman army.

His defenders had a few of the smaller scorpions captured from the army of Cornelius Fuscus in the first battle of Tapae. Vezina had these placed on top of the wall, however they were no match for the number of Roman artillery or the range of the larger machines. The Dacians' scorpions would be more effective later when the attackers came to storm the walls.

"Will they attack today, Your Holiness?" asked a sentry standing next to the High Priest.

"No, not today," Vezina replied. "They are building ladders and siege towers. Tomorrow perhaps or the day after."

Vezina and the soldier ducked involuntarily as a large boulder launched from a ballista flew over their heads. The rock crashed into a house behind them with a loud noise and collapsed the roof in.

A number of people inside the city died from being crushed by boulders and pierced by bolts. The bolts were shot from ballistae and scorpions hundreds of yards away. They travelled too fast for the eye to follow, and the victims never saw them coming.

The soldier standing near Vezina pointed to four construction sites at the front of the Roman lines. "Those siege towers are going up quickly."

"They are," Vezina agreed. "The Romans brought the materials with them. That way they can assemble the towers on site quickly."

"These bastards mean business," the soldier grimaced. "No time to waste, eh?"

Vezina turned to the man and clasped him on the shoulder. "We mean business, too. When they approach with their towers we'll set them on fire. When they bring a battering ram to our gates we'll crush them under a pile of boulders and burn it with fire arrows and scalding oils."

The soldier grunted in agreement. They both knew, however, that the odds were heavily against them. They would put up resistance to give King Decebal and the army time to organize a defense in the mountains north of the city. That was their mission, and it had to be done whatever the cost.

Mountains north of Tapae, Autumn 88 AD

"Permission to lead a raiding party against the Roman camp, Sire?" Sinna asked the King in the war council meeting. They were gathered in a clearing in the woods, along with Drilgisa and Diegis.

Decebal gave it thought for only a few moments. "You have my permission. Don't let the Romans get too comfortable on Dacian soil. Horse archers, hit and run."

"Yes, Sire. I'll take three hundred horse and hit them in two or three locations. If I see the right opportunity I'll take out some of their artillery crews."

"Hit and run, Sinna," Decebal cautioned. "Don't get too ambitious and get cut off and trapped."

"Understood, Sire."

Decebal turned to Diegis. "How many new arrivals today?"

"Three thousand infantry and almost a hundred cavalry. Which gives us fifteen thousand infantry in total. Six hundred cavalry or thereabouts."

"Five hundred and eighty cavalry," Sinna added.

Decebal became thoughtful. "Julianus is attacking Tapae with one legion. That leaves eight legions to move against us. That is roughly forty thousand men. Once Tapae falls he will have the large part of another legion at his command."

"Which means," Drilgisa said, "that we must hold off an army of forty thousand with our fifteen thousand."

The officers became quiet as they considered those numbers. It was true that defenders held an advantage in battle, but there was no winning against overwhelming numbers.

"Within ten days we will be reinforced by another ten thousand, infantry and archers combined," Diegis said.

"Julianus will not wait ten days to attack north," Decebal declared. "Even if Tapae holds out that long he will want to attack us sooner. And anyway, Tapae cannot hold out that long."

"Why not surprise them and attack?" Drilgisa asked, his black eyes twinkling. "Give them something they don't expect, eh?"

"We do not attack fixed Roman positions, Drilgisa. You know that," Decebal said with exasperation. "Every day the Romans march, and every evening they build fortifications to protect their troops. Even when there is no enemy anywhere in sight. Every day!"

"Of course you are right, Sire," Drilgisa conceded with a small shrug. "I am being over eager."

Decebal waved off the apology. "There is a time to be eager and a time for sound strategy. This is a time for sound strategy. We are badly outnumbered."

"The men are in defensive positions on the mountain," Diegis pointed out. "What further strategy do you propose?"

Decebal paused to gather his thoughts. "Julianus will not repeat the mistakes of Fuscus. He won't march in column straight into the lion's jaws."

"No, he will not," Drilgisa agreed. "I have command of the west slope, Diegis has command of the east. We can counter a broader Roman attack."

"That is exactly what we must do, Drilgisa. Julianus will attack on the road through the pass and along his flanks through the forest. So we must beat back a broader attack than what Cornelius Fuscus tried, even though we have fewer men."

"We will be spread out very thin," Sinna observed.

Decebal looked at each of the men around him. "We have no other choice, my brothers. We must fight a defensive battle in the pass and in the forest on the lower mountain slopes. Give ground when you must, but don't let the Romans break through. Keep your messengers close at hand and communicate smartly, and don't let them outflank you."

"And you will defend the pass, Brother?" Diegis asked.

"Yes. I will take five thousand infantry plus Sinna and the cavalry, and stop the Romans from advancing north through the pass. The passage is narrow which is to our advantage."

Drilgisa frowned. "With eight legions Julianus will chew you up."

"He may, but not without paying a heavy price. Remember, we fight a defensive battle and give ground in retreat when we must."

"We need our reserves to reach us, and soon," Diegis exclaimed.

"If Zamolxis wills it, it will be so," Decebal said.

"If the bastards marched faster, it would help," Drilgisa blurted out. He got a sharp look from the King and threw up his hands. "Ah, forgive me, brothers, I am impatient today."

"You are always impatient, Drilgisa. You will feel better after you kill a few Romans. You will get your chance very soon."

Chapter 11

FLIGHT FOR LIFE

Tapae, Dacia, Autumn 88 AD

*J*n the morning on the second day of the siege of Tapae the Roman siege artillery stopped their bombardment. Titus Lucullus rode up close to the main gate under a flag of truce. He stopped his horse when he was within shouting distance but still made a poor target for a good archer with no regard for a truce flag.

Titus looked up at the parapet above the gate where a lone elderly man stood calmly and watched his approach. The man was tall and thin, with a long white beard, and clad in plain civilian clothes.

"People of Tapae! General Tettius Julianus offers you terms for peace!" Lucullus shouted up at the defenders, but he knew that his main audience was the lone, tall figure standing above the gate.

"Surrender the city now and all inside will be spared! Children, women, and men!" Titus paused briefly. "You have one hour to accept this offer!"

The elderly man on the wall spoke with a surprisingly clear and strong voice. It was a voice of authority. "Dacians do not surrender to slavery, Roman!"

"Listen to me well! Surrender the city or all will die! This is the word of General Tettius Julianus!" Titus did not honestly expect to convince them, but an effort had to be made. It would prevent a needless slaughter and save many Roman lives that would perish in an assault against the well defended walls.

"We are not afraid to die, Roman! Our souls are immortal!" came the strong reply. "Dacians choose death over slavery! It has always been so!"

That defiant statement from the old man drew loud cheers from the defenders on the walls. He inspired them to greater defiance.

"You have one hour to open the gates and surrender! One hour!"

The old man did not reply, but simply turned and walked away. Lucullus turned his horse around and rode back towards the Roman lines. He paid no attention to the insults and jeers coming from the Dacian defenders on the walls.

General Julianus waited for him by one of the siege towers.

"How many defenders on the walls, by your estimate, Titus?" the General asked.

"No more than eight hundred, sir," Lucullus replied.

"That seems right," Julianus agreed. "And I see many civilians with spears and bows. And more than a few women among them."

"Yes, sir. Dacian women are taught to fight alongside the men. They are not as effective fighters as the men of course, but some can be deadly enough. They make good archers, and some can handle a spear well enough to kill."

"What is this about not being afraid to die?" Tettius asked with open scorn. "That sounds like barbarian nonsense."

"Sir, to them it is not nonsense," Titus explained. "Their religion of Zamolxis is based on the immortality of the soul. They believe that when their Earthly body dies their spirits go to the realm of Zamolxis and their souls live there forever."

"Rubbish," Julianus said dismissively.

"That may be so, sir, but with my own eyes I have watched Dacian soldiers laughing even as they are dying, because to them death in battle means immortality." Titus shrugged. "It makes many of them damnable fanatical fighters."

"They die just the same," Julianus spat. He turned his gaze to the city walls. "They will not surrender, then?"

"No, sir, they will not surrender."

"Pity, that," Julianus replied. "It will further delay us, and I don't want any more delays."

"No, sir. I will give orders to resume the attack."

"Good. Let's make these Dacians happy and send them to their gods," the General said grimly.

"Our men will be happy to do exactly that, General."

"And, Titus?"

"Sir?"

"Give the command. When we get inside the walls, no mercy."

At mid-morning on the second day of the siege of Tapae orders were given that the walls of the city be stormed. Earlier a ram had been sent against the city gate but did very little damage before it was set on fire by the defenders on the wall. Any siege engine that came close to the walls was met with buckets of flaming oil and fire arrows.

Neither the sturdy city gate nor the thick walls could be breached, General Julianus decided, so the only way into the city was over the top of the walls. This required sending many brave men to certain death climbing up ladders while arrows, spears, rocks, and buckets of burning liquids rained down on their heads. Those who reached the top faced determined defenders fighting desperately with spears, axes, falxes, and swords.

Titus Lucullus watched the four siege towers being towed towards the walls. The tall wooden structures were protected by metal facings, but even so fire arrows found open wood and started fires that had to be put out with buckets of water carried in the towers. Once they were close enough to the wall the towers would drop their ramps across the top of the wall and discharge dozens of legionnaires very quickly. That was not as good as a breach in the wall, but still very highly effective.

"Archers!" Vezina shouted. "Line up here. Rain fire on that tower and turn it into a burning pyre!"

Thirty archers lined up quickly along the section of the wall where the High Priest directed them. Half of them were women, one a girl no older than thirteen. Many women of Dacia practiced with the bow from a young age and were as accurate as the men.

Shooting down at legionnaires climbing up ladders was an easy kill. There were always unprotected places on faces, necks, and legs. Providing cross-fire on attackers a short distance down the walls was easier than picking off squirrels in a tree. What made the venture more tricky of course was that some of the Roman squirrels on the ground fired arrows back.

The front sections of the fire arrows were wrapped tightly with wool, soaked in oil, and set alight from a torch carried by fire bearers. The thirty archers poured fire into the oncoming siege tower. More archers rained arrows on the men pulling the ropes to tow the tower forward. The closer the tower approached the easier it became to find weak spots and openings. More fires were set than could be put out. The smoke became so thick that the legionnaires inside had to climb out and abandon it.

"Well done, my warriors!" Vezina praised them. "Well done!"

An arrow whistled by very close to his head. His archers directed their arrows towards a group of Roman archers on the ground. The Romans made much better targets and were taking heavier losses. After a short while they pulled away, out of range of the archers on the walls.

As dusk approached more than two hundred Dacian defenders were killed or wounded. Three times that many attackers were killed or wounded on the Roman side. The defenders had the advantage of cover behind stone ramparts, and of fighting off attackers who had to climb to reach them. The attackers had the advantage of numbers.

This was a contest, Vezina knew, that would ultimately be won by numbers.

Of the four Roman siege towers, two were burning wrecks and two others were damaged and immobilized. The attack would have to be finished the hard way, by men on ladders. By dusk the attack stalled. The legionnaires retreated for the night to re-group and re-supply.

Vezina made a tour inside the city walls to assess the damage. Even more importantly he needed to encourage the warriors, both men and women, who had fought to the point of exhaustion. The city's garrison was reduced by almost a third, half of the casualties dead and half wounded. To make matters worse, those casualties included many of the front line warriors who took the greatest risks and did the heaviest fighting.

Tapae survived a brutal attack for the better part of a day. The Romans would be back tomorrow, in greater numbers than today. They were building many more ladders, and they would send many hundreds of men.

A young woman with a very pretty face and long black hair stepped in front of Vezina to get his attention. He stopped, startled to find his path blocked.

"Excuse me, Your Holiness, but you must rest," the woman said.

The High Priest paused. He was not only very tired but also, he just realized, famished. There had been no time for food since early morning. A small group of people were gathered by the wall passing around food and a pitcher of water. The young woman took the priest by the arm and led him there.

"Thank you, my child," Vezina said. "I am very hungry. And what is your name?"

"Andrada," the young woman replied.

"Ah, Andrada," he smiled. "I know another woman by that name. You remind me of her."

She took it as a compliment to be compared to the Queen, and smiled back. "Here, you must have some food."

Someone had brought out trays of bread, cheese, and fruit. And also, Vezina was gratified to see, a tray of pastries. When Dacian women worried, they baked.

The people around him were considerate and gave him time to eat in peace. Finally one middle aged man could not contain his curiosity any longer.

"Forgive my asking, Your Holiness, but why are you not at the side of our King?"

Vezina finished off a pastry with a cherry filling and brushed away some crumbs. "King Decebal is gathering our army in the mountains to stop the Romans from marching into Dacia. What we are doing here," he gestured around him at the Dacian defenders, "is giving him time to get the army ready. The King appointed me to lead the defense of Tapae."

"Then we die for a good cause," the young Andrada declared.

Vezina looked at her and felt his heart breaking. "We fight for a good cause, my child," he said. "Did you fight today?"

"No," she replied, shaking her head. "I am a healer. I patch up the wounded and heal the sick."

"Ah, very good. Just like our Queen Andrada. That is equally as important as fighting."

"When the Romans come inside the city I will fight," the young woman continued. "And if I cannot fight I will climb to the top of the wall and jump to my death." She paused, the look on her face sad but determined. "I will not be a slave."

Vezina reached out with two fingers and gently touched her on the forehead. "May Zamolxis keep you, my child."

"And you also," she replied.

"And now I must go and finish my rounds," the High Priest said, bidding them farewell. "Tomorrow we must fight again, just as hard as we did today. Fight for our freedom, my children. That is always our most just cause."

By mid-afternoon the following day the defenders on the wall were too few to fill in all the gaps. Legionnaires were gathering in small groups on the ramparts and driving the defenders off the walls. The Dacians fought a desperate battle but were badly outnumbered, and soon all knew that the city was lost.

Vezina felt agonized. Decebal had asked for the defense of Tapae to hold out for a week, but he had only managed to give him three days. It could not be otherwise. The size of the Roman army was simply too overwhelming, the number of the forces sent against him too many to fight off. He did not agonize for himself, but for worry over the readiness of the Dacian army in the mountains.

There was nothing more to be done for the city's defense. Roman soldiers were now gathering in the streets and chaos and slaughter began. No mercy was shown to a city that refused to surrender to a Roman army. That policy was meant to encourage other cities, in other places, to surrender.

Vezina walked quickly to the northern part of the city, the section built against the side of the mountain. He gathered people with him as he went.

"Come with me!" he commanded some and encouraged others. "This way! Come with me! This way!"

He entered an old barn on the edge of the city, built against the mountainside. The small crowd followed him in. In a corner of the barn he moved an old bench, found the axe hidden underneath, and gave it to a broad chested man.

"Remove those boards!" he commanded, pointing to the barn wall behind the bench. "Hurry!"

The boards broke and fell away after a few powerful strokes of the axe because behind them was hollow space. A dark opening emerged, tall enough and wide enough for two people to walk through. This was a tunnel that went deep into the mountain and emerged further north into the woods.

Vezina opened a nearby barrel and spilled out a pile of torches on the dry ground. Someone gathered a bit of straw, flint and metal were produced, and very quickly they had a small fire for lighting the torches.

"Go!" Vezina said to the people in front. "This will take you into the forest! Our army will find you! Go now! Hurry, and don't stop!"

As people lit their torches and filed into the tunnel the High Priest went back to the barn entrance. People were running up and down the street in panic.

"This way!" the old man beckoned to them, standing outside the barn door. "This way to safety! Hurry!"

They came singly and in small groups, and were quickly steered to the escape route. Cries of panic and screams of pain were drawing closer. There was no more fighting to be done now, only straight slaughter of those who could not defend themselves.

A man and a woman came running down the street, each leading two children by the hand. Vezina guided the panicked couple and their children into the barn. "This way! There is a tunnel in the back! Light a torch and go! Hurry!"

I should go, he thought to himself. It is too dangerous and there is nothing more to be done. Rapid footsteps were coming around the corner and Vezina hesitated. These would be the last.

Six men turned the corner and immediately spotted him. They wore the uniforms of Roman legionnaires. Vezina had to make a fast decision, that instant. To enter the barn was impossible, it would lead the soldiers to the tunnel and those who escaped would be hunted down. He turned quickly, heading down the street in a direction away from the approaching legionnaires, and ran. He was the rabbit leading the hounds away.

The six legionnaires came after him, each carrying a gladius stained with blood. They were not running but walking rapidly. The city was theirs now and the old man had nowhere to run.

Vezina did not know where he was running, he just ran. He turned a corner, saw an open door leading into a house, and ducked inside. He ran to the back and emerged into a small vegetable garden. His heart was beating fast enough to burst out of his chest and he stopped to catch his breath. He heard no footsteps coming after him. A solitary old man was not worth pursuing by six legionnaires, or so he hoped.

Vezina was now three or four streets away from the barn and the escape tunnel, and in the frenzy of his escape he had lost his sense of direction. He knew only that he must reach the tunnel. People were still screaming and dying, and Roman soldiers were on every street. He heard a noise coming from inside the house, footsteps, then quickly and silently moved to the garden of the house next door.

The back door was unlatched and Vezina entered the house. He stopped, momentarily shocked. Three bodies were lying on the floor in a large pool of blood, an older woman, a younger woman, and an older man. They had died clinging to each other, the stab wounds on each body the work of a Roman gladius.

He turned to leave, then heard footsteps approaching from the garden. His escape path was blocked.

The High Priest dressed in plain clothes sat down in the pool of blood next to the three dead bodies. He stretched out flat on his back for two heartbeats to let the blood soak into his clothes and his hair, then turned over on his stomach. The approaching footsteps from the garden entered the room. Vezina closed his eyes peacefully and stilled his breath. He waited.

"The city is cleared out," Titus Lucullus informed Tettius Julianus. The general was sitting at a table outside his command tent. The final attack on the city walls had been brutal and very costly for the Roman attackers.

"Prisoners?" Julianus asked.

"A small number of young women for the slave market. It appears that most women and children were evacuated prior to our attack." He paused to pour a cup of water and drank it thirstily.

"Did you manage to capture any military officers?" Julianus asked impatiently. Women and children were not his concern. He needed information about the Dacian army.

"All defenders were put to the sword." Lucullus reported. "The fighters did not allow themselves to be captured, sir, not even the women. If we did not kill them they killed themselves. A knife across the throat, quick and efficient. Many women simply jumped off the high walls to their death."

The General nodded his understanding. "You were right, Titus. They fight like fanatics. I have seen this battle fever before, when I was in Germania. In the open field it works to our advantage because they rush us like crazed men. Here," he gestured toward the city, "when they defend city walls it works to their advantage."

"There are many more forts like this one, General, as you know. They all have stone walls and will be defended just as ferociously."

"I am aware of that, Titus," Tettius Julianus said patiently. "And we will clear them out one by one in our march to Sarmizegetusa."

Lucullus straightened up. "Apologies if I spoke out of line, sir."

Julianus waved the apology away. "Always feel free to speak your mind, Lucullus, or you would be no use to me as tribune."

"Yes, General. Thank you, sir."

"I understand that you are unhappy with our losses here, Titus, and they are heavy. However, know that you did a good job in taking the city so quickly. We cannot delay the attack against Decebalus, so a frontal attack against the city walls had to be done."

"Understood, sir."

"Secure the city with a small guard detail. There is no resistance left. Tomorrow we launch the main attack. Get me some prisoners that I can interrogate, Titus. Preferably of officer rank."

"Yes, sir." Lucullus knew that was more than a suggestion.

"That old man," Julianus wondered, "the one on the city wall. He was their spokesman. Any sign of him?"

"We did not find him," Titus replied. "He is most likely killed. However..."

"However what, Titus?"

"We found an escape tunnel hidden inside a barn, sir. It goes into the mountain and no doubt comes out somewhere in the woods on the eastern slope."

"Had the tunnel been used?" Julianus scowled, not pleased with this latest news.

"Yes, sir. We discovered the tunnel quickly but people had already fled through it. I do not know if the old man was one of them."

"A pity if he was. He would be a useful prisoner."

"Indeed, sir. I ordered the tunnel blocked with stone and timber, and guards are posted at the entrance," Lucullus explained. "It will not be used as an escape again."

Vezina did not move from his spot on the blood covered floor until darkness fell. Occasional patrols of Roman legionnaires came by at random times. To Roman eyes he must appear as just one more corpse in a city of thousands of freshly killed corpses.

He was very thirsty and his throat was parched, but there was no remedy for that now. He stayed as quiet and unmoving as the three actual corpses in the small room. He listened to the silence and breathed in the smell of death.

While Vezina waited he planned his escape in the night. It was very likely the Roman clean-up details would carry off these bodies the next day. He had one chance for escape, tonight. If there was no opportunity for escape then he must take his own life.

Becoming a prisoner to the Romans was not an option because he was too well informed about Dacian military matters. A Roman army carried a torture detail for interrogating prisoners, and Vezina's high status would not protect him when General Julianus decided he wanted high level information. Perhaps Diegis had been right, he took too great a risk by staying in Tapae. He pushed the thought out of his mind. Only one thing mattered now. Escape.

As darkness fell the city grew quieter. The legionnaires would be in their camps, eating their meals and cleaning their weapons. There was no priority to guard a city of corpses. Any plunder that was worth taking had already been looted away. For a short while he was alone, or so he hoped.

In late evening, when it was fully dark, Vezina finally moved into action. He sat up slowly and stretched his arms and legs, working out the painful stiffness. His clothes were stiff with dried blood. There was no sound coming from outside the house. He took off his sandals because walking barefoot on the stone paved streets would be much less noisy.

He needed to avoid the streets so he went out the door that led to the garden in the back. He was thankful that it was a crescent moon, which shined little light on the building and the streets around him. The only fires were off in the distance, closer to the walls. He walked slowly, always staying in the deep shadows along the walls of houses and other buildings. Stealth was more important than speed.

Vezina thought it very likely that the escape tunnel hidden in the barn had been discovered by now. If so it would be guarded. Going there would be walking into a trap.

He headed instead to a different part of the city, several streets away, that was also built against the side of the mountain. There was more open space here, with trees and shrubbery. He crouched in the shadow of a house and carefully watched a clump of trees some one hundred paces away. That was his immediate destination. He could see no movement in the trees, and no movement in the street.

He would have to leave cover and expose himself over that short distance, but there was no other choice. He headed for the trees, walking swiftly in his bare feet, taking every caution to avoid making noise, eyes and ears alert for any movement or noise. He reached the trees and ducked behind an elm tree. He paused to catch his breath.

Vezina would have to find his next destination from memory, in the dark. No moonlight penetrated the tree foliage and the darkness was near complete. He walked towards the mountain side, holding both hands out in front to make sure he did not walk into any objects or low branches.

A sudden noise to his right made Vezina freeze in his tracks. Something was moving through the trees, fast, and coming straight towards him. His heart pounding wildly, Vezina turned towards the threat and crouched into a defensive position, his hands balled up into fists. Something bumped against his right leg, and he felt a large wet tongue licking his right hand. Then the dog stopped licking and barked loudly.

It was a friendly bark, not an aggressive one, but it carried far in the still night air and made Vezina's blood go cold. He reached down and found the dog's back, and stroked it gently to calm the animal.

"Shhhh," he whispered soothingly. "Shhh. No noise."

The dog was panting softly. Somehow it had escaped the killing, and no doubt it was hungry and afraid. Whoever took care of it was long dead. Vezina had nothing to give it.

"Shhh," he repeated. "Come with me." He tried to guide the dog in the direction in which he had been heading. It was not far to go, but he could barely see in the dark and the going was slow. The dog was following him, still panting but thankfully not barking.

Just ahead the trees cleared and Vezina saw moonlight shining off a rocky surface. He made out the large oak tree on the edge of the copse, and the thick shrubbery growing behind it. He made his way through the tall shrubbery, now being able to see better in the dim moonlight, and found the wooden boards blocking the hole dug into the mountainside. The entrance to the tunnel was smaller than the tunnel itself, for better concealment, and he would have to get down on hands and knees to enter.

This was a much smaller tunnel than the one in the barn, narrow and barely tall enough for an adult. A tall adult would have to crouch or duck his or her head. It was however a way to leave the city and escape into the woods.

Vezina cleared the wooden boards away from the entrance. The tunnel was completely dark, pitch black. He had no torch and no way to make fire. He would have to guide his way forward and navigate the tunnel by touch alone. The passage was narrow enough so that there was no possibility of getting turned around. There was nowhere to go except forward. He would suffer some scrapes and bruises in the dark, small price to pay for escaping with his life.

The friendly dog sat panting and watching him as he worked. In the dim moonlight he could now see that it was a medium sized, brownish dog of mixed breed. Vezina reached down and stroked its head.

"I can do nothing for you now. You will not follow me into a dark tunnel, so go! Go and find a way out." He tried to wave the dog away. It took a step back but would not leave.

The High Priest of Zamolxis got down on his hands and knees and entered the tunnel. Once inside he had room to stand, but thought it wise to stay crouched low. He put his left hand straight out in front and the right hand on the side of the tunnel wall, and took small and careful steps forward. Behind him the dog barked a few times. That did not matter now. All that mattered was the next step forward in the dark. All that mattered was survival.

Chapter 12

SECOND BATTLE OF TAPAE

Tapae, Dacia, Autumn 88 AD

*T*he Dacians built a wide and high barrier of felled trees and earthen works to block the mountain pass north of Tapae. The barrier was as tall as a man. An army moving north though the pass would have to climb and fight over this obstacle. King Decebal, along with eight thousand infantry and a thousand cavalry, would defend this choke point.

Some distance behind this barrier Decebal placed a battery of scorpions. These were manned by Dacian soldiers who had been trained by Roman engineers. The scorpions were powerful enough to launch bolts several hundred yards away, over the log and earthen barrier, to hit the advancing Roman troops.

Diegis and Drilgisa each commanded armies of roughly seven thousand men on either flank, positioned on the lower mountain slopes above the pass. Their mission was to harass the legions moving north and protect against flank attacks. Though outnumbered, the soldiers had confidence in their leaders and in their tactics.

This was home ground for the Dacians and they knew the terrain well. They could move faster than the Romans, conceal themselves better, and choose the best locations for ambush attacks. The Romans would have to explore their way forward slowly, via probing attacks, as they advanced into Dacian territory.

King Decebal was talking with Tsiru when Diegis walked up to join them. The newly arrived reserve troops were positioned in place and given their orders. Now they waited for the Romans to arrive.

"Any news from Tapae?" Diegis asked Decebal.

The King nodded to Tsiru instead. The chief of scouts collected all information from all the scouts and also from people arriving from the city.

"As best we know, one cohort of legionnaires is camped inside the city," Tsiru reported.

"Is that all?" Diegis asked. "How do they plan to pacify the locals and defend the city with just five hundred men?"

"There are no more locals," Decebal said.

It took a heartbeat for the meaning to sink in. "Bastards!" Diegis spat, furious.

"Some young women were taken for slavery. The rest of the people were put to the sword," Tsiru explained. "Some escaped, around three hundred, through tunnels. We are interviewing as many of them as we can now."

"And Vezina? Any word?"

Tsiru shook his head. "No word. We know that he organized the city defense, then led the escapes when the city fell. He was last seen directing people to a tunnel. The Romans were pillaging inside the city by then."

Diegis swore. "I warned the old man not to get captured." He turned to the King. "It should have been me who stayed to defend the city."

"No," Decebal replied with finality. "You are more important here commanding the army. Vezina knew the risks and accepted them. He may be dead by now, or captured, or he may still be free. He is very resourceful, as you know."

"How resourceful must one be to escape an entire Roman army?" Diegis asked skeptically.

Decebal gave him a hard look. "As resourceful as necessary. Now let's focus on the Roman attack that is coming. Can I depend on you, Brother?"

Diegis calmed down. "Of course. What do we know of the Roman positions?"

"General Julianus seems eager to press the attack. The main force is advancing through the pass," Decebal explained. "He will hit us with his artillery, soften defenses, then bring in infantry."

"And while he hits you, we will hit him back," Diegis said. "It won't be as easy for him as he expects."

"We don't know what he expects, Diegis. We only know that he's no fool, so stick to our strategy as we planned."

"Understood. I told you, you can count on me."

A Dacian bugle call echoed twice on the mountainside.

Decebal looked up. "The battle begins," he said, reaching for his sword. "Zamolxis be with you."

The three men hurried to their command posts.

Roman scorpions and ballistae battered the improvised Dacian wall. Men ducked behind solid cover to avoid the barrage of bolts and small boulders hurled at them. Some unlucky ones were caught in the open and cut down by bolts that struck with tremendous speed. A bolt from a scorpion could travel eight hundred feet, and an enemy soldier never saw it coming.

The Dacian scorpions returned the artillery fire. They were fewer in number than the Roman machines, and the Dacian crews were not as skilled as the Roman soldiers, but still the Dacians scored some hits and inflicted casualties on the attackers.

Roman infantry waited patiently for their artillery to do its work. After a period of bombardment they would storm the Dacian wall. They were supported on each side of the pass by troops that advanced slowly through the trees. There would be no Dacian surprise attacks from the forest this time.

Farther up the mountain slope Drilgisa and fifty of his men waited in ambush position, hidden by thick shrubbery. Beneath them was an open expanse of trees through which the Romans would advance. These Dacians were skilled hunters in mountain terrain, and the same skills of concealment and stalking applied to hunting deer or men.

Drilgisa allowed the legionnaires to draw even with his position. There were seventy or eighty men in the group, what the Romans called a century. They advanced with the confidence of soldiers who expected to easily defeat whatever enemies came at them.

Without uttering a single word Drilgisa motioned to the men around him then jumped out and rushed at the nearest enemy. His men ran immediately behind him, each having picked out a Roman target to attack. The Dacians had the advantage of surprise and the momentum from attacking downhill.

The nearest Romans had no warning and were put down easily. The others turned and braced themselves to take on the onrushing attackers. There was no room for the legionnaires to maneuver as a group on the sloping and tree-filled ground, so all the fighting was one on one and every man for himself.

The battle was fierce and ended quickly. Fifteen legionaries fell to sica and spear, and nine Dacians fell to the gladius. Reinforcements came up quickly to support the Roman front line. Two more Dacians fell, one to an archer and one stabbed in the gut.

"Back!" Drilgisa yelled a sharp command, seeing that his men were quickly being outnumbered. The Dacian soldiers melted back into the shrubbery and the trees, then rapidly moved further west on a prearranged route.

A centurion shouted orders to his men. The wounded men were carried back towards the Roman camp, but his orders were to keep advancing. His group of sixty remaining legionnaires moved forward again, but cautiously, unfamiliar with the terrain and with no idea of what dangers waited for them further ahead.

"Wood and earth barricades don't stop a Roman legion," Julianus said. His artillery and archers had forced the Dacian defenders at the top of the wall to take cover. "Send in the infantry, Titus."

"Yes, sir!" Lucullus signaled to a tribune, who then gave the order to his men to advance. With the Roman artillery attack paused for the time being so they would not hit their own men, the Dacian archers and spearmen reappeared on the wall. Legionnaires marched to the barrier in the testudo formation, overlapping shields over their heads to protect against arrows and spears.

The Romans targeted select areas of the barrier so they could overwhelm the defenders. Spears and falxes beat them back, but a stream of legionnaire reinforcements pressed on. The battle on the Dacian wall continued for the better part of the day. By late afternoon Roman infantry gained a foothold in some sections and legionnaires stormed over the barrier. Now they could attack the defenders on the wall from behind.

Dacian bugles sounded the retreat. The defenders abandoned their makeshift wall and moved further north to establish a defensive line besides their artillery. The scorpions fired bolts at close range at the attackers. The Roman attack slowed, then stopped for the time being. Dusk was approaching.

"Dismantle that rubbish!" General Julianus ordered from atop his horse, looking scornfully at the abandoned Dacian wall.

"Immediately, sir," Titus Lucullus replied. He turned to a group of nearby soldiers. "You men! Clear away that barricade and clear the road. Be quick about it!"

The legionnaires put down their shields and hopped to the task. Some sections of the wall were built with full sized tree trunks and needed many men to move them. Engineers with tools could finish the job more efficiently, but engineers were too valuable to be put to work under enemy fire.

A scout rode up behind the commanders and saluted the General.

"Report!" Tettius commanded.

"We are getting ambush attacks on both flanks, sir," the cavalry scout reported. "The enemy skirmishes and then withdraws. Our men continue to advance steadily, sir."

"Casualties?" Titus asked.

"Under six hundred, sir."

"Very well," Julianus said and dismissed the scout. He turned to Lucullus. "Decebalus is willing to give ground slowly. He wants to use delaying tactics."

"Yes, sir," Titus agreed. "We should not assume he will continue doing so, however. The man has surprised us before."

"He has never fought me before, Titus. I will drive him off these mountains."

"Yes, sir."

"Press the attack, Lucullus. We must not slow down. By staying on the offensive we keep Decebalus on the defensive."

"Of course, sir. Our men have orders to keep advancing."

They steered their horses to the side of the pass to allow a large troop of legionnaires to move forward. After they cleared away this obstacle the army would advance in force. The Dacians might slow them down but the attack would not be stopped.

Centurion Sextus Asprenas led his men through the trees at a slow walk, all eyes alert for a Dacian ambush. They were sixty men moving in a line, twelve men across and five men deep. The terrain was a moderate slope, a good distance from the pass below, and here the forest was peaceful and quiet. Birds cried out to each other, but grew silent as the men approached.

Somewhere to their right a woodpecker suddenly started making a racket, digging into a tree trunk in search of insects. It startled a few of the younger men. The legionnaires had not encountered any Dacian forces yet but knew the enemy was close.

From their left came a crack of timber breaking, and a tree fell right across their path. Here was the ambush, Sextus thought. No sooner had he finished the thought when a shower of arrows and javelins rained down on his men from in front of his position and further up the mountainside.

"Formation!" Asprenas yelled, although his men were already bunching up into groups to interlock their shields against the hail of arrows and spears. Still no Dacians showed themselves.

"Hold formation!" Sextus commanded. He expected a rush of spearmen and swordsman at any moment, running downhill at them to break their lines. His men bunched closer together as the rain of arrows continued.

The attack came not from spearmen but from another falling tree that had been pre-cut almost all the way through and positioned to fall precisely on their position. Sextus cursed himself for falling into a trap. Legionnaires rushed to scatter out of their tight formation but many were crushed under the weight of the large falling tree trunk.

In the confusion that followed the Dacian infantry attacked. They did not come only from the upper slopes but from every direction. The sixty legionnaires were swarmed by twice as many Dacian spearmen and swordsmen armed with the sica. Asprenas took the whistle that hung around his neck and blew it loudly. If he did not get reinforcements quickly his men were doomed.

The Dacians seemed to fight with a strange battle joy, with no fear for their own safety. Some of them were laughing. The legionnaires fought desperately to survive while the Dacians fought to kill. In this kind of battle, Sextus knew, the aggressor fought with more energy and abandon and had the advantage.

Roman reinforcements were fast to arrive but not before half of Sextus' men were on the ground, many dead and some wounded. The Dacian captain shouted an order and his men dispersed quickly into the surrounding woods. No Romans chased them, wary of further traps and ambushes.

King Decebal rode his chestnut stallion to the medical area in the rear of the Dacian lines. Buri rode beside him on a grey mare. Hundreds of wounded men were being placed on wagons to be transported north to the mountain fort of Singidava. After four days of bloody fighting the casualties for both the Dacians and the Romans were in the thousands. The Romans were gaining ground but their progress was slowing.

Drilgisa sat on a bench outside the medical tent, getting his left shoulder bandaged. Blood soaked through the bandages. Decebal and Buri dismounted and joined him.

"Archer, I hear?" Decebal asked.

Drilgisa grimaced from the pain as the surgeon tied the bandages tightly. "Damned Roman archer, may he rot in Hades. I never even saw him. Bastard put an arrow into my shoulder." Drilgisa winced again, then broke into a grin. "He was aiming for my head no doubt, but I was on the move and he missed."

Decebal looked at the doctor and raised an inquiring eyebrow.

"It's a clean wound high on the shoulder," the doctor said. "No bone or cartilage damage. I cleaned the wound and applied a salve." He paused to look his patient in the eye. "General Drilgisa will keep the bandage clean and change it daily. He should be good as new in a few weeks."

Drilgisa shrugged. "Yes, of course I will change it," he agreed.

"I trust that you will, if you wish to fight again," the doctor said. "Keep the bandage moist with vinegar water. Come back tomorrow to have it changed." He gave a curt bow in the direction of the King, then left to look after the next patient

"You will not do any fighting for a while," Decebal told him. "The battle has slowed in any case. General Julianus will advance one mile at a time, while we ambush him and take bites out of his carcass. He has already lost some two thousand men."

"And so have we," Drilgisa said grimly.

"And so have we," Decebal replied.

"But he will advance and think he is winning," Drilgisa added.

"He will think so, yes," Decebal agreed. "He took Tapae and now he pushes us back. He will find that he has to fight through fifteen more forts like Tapae before he gets to Sarmizegetusa."

"They will never reach Sarmizegetusa!" Buri growled.

"No, Buri, they will not," Decebal said.

A familiar voice shouted to them from a distance. "Hey! Look what I found!" Diegis called out as he approached. He was grinning from ear to ear.

Walking beside him, slowly and somewhat stiffly, was a familiar tall and thin figure. Decebal started laughing and jumped up to greet them.

"Vezina! I am glad to see you. We did not know if you were alive or dead."

"Sire." Vezina gave the King a small bow, and seemed to falter on his feet. Diegis took him by the arm and guided him to a seat on the bench besides Drilgisa.

"Welcome back," Drilgisa greeted him happily, ignoring the pain in his shoulder.

"Forgive me, Sire," Vezina began. "I have not slept for two days. I've had no food and very little water until I reached Diegis' troops."

Decebal looked at him with concern. The old man was completely exhausted. He had a cut high on his forehead that was turning into a large scab. He was dressed in plain clothes that were covered with dried blood.

"Are you injured?" Decebal asked, indicating the blood soaked clothes. "What happened to you?"

Vezina shook his head. "Not my blood, Sire. I had to hide among fresh corpses and pretend that I was dead to avoid capture."

"Always the clever one," Diegis smiled. He expressed the sense of relief that they all felt.

"So you were almost captured?" Decebal asked.

"A very close call, Sire. A Roman patrol walked right past me and mistook me for just another corpse." He paused and let out a sigh. "Tapae was full of corpses by then."

"What happened to your head, Your Holiness?" this question came from the doctor who walked over to join them.

"Oh, that," Vezina reached towards his forehead but did not touch the scab. "I hit my head against the wall of the tunnel. After hiding all day I sneaked out during the night and made my way to one of the small tunnels that the Romans had not yet discovered. I had no torch, so had to feel my way through the dark by touching the walls step by step."

"None of that matters now," the King said and clasped Vezina on the shoulder. "What matters is that you are safe and Dacia rejoices at your return."

"Thank you, Sire," Vezina replied. "There were moments when I doubted that I would ever make it back."

Chapter 13

STALEMATE

Southern Dacian mountains, November 88 AD

T he twenty legionnaires in the foraging party approached the house on the edge of the woods with caution. It was not a proper house by Roman standards but more like a large round hut. The walls were made of packed earth and the steep, sloping roof was made of thatch. There was only one entrance, a low wooden door, and one small window. This simple dwelling most likely housed a shepherd and his family. There were no signs of people around.

The centurion in charge of the search party was in a sour mood. The weather was turning colder. It had to be November by now. Food supplies were low and rations were lowered again. An even bigger problem was the lack of hay and other forage for the horses and pack animals. The animals were getting thinner every week, and there was no hope of them lasting through the winter under these conditions.

"Search the property for food and forage!" the centurion ordered. There would be nothing else of value they might find in this hovel. In any case food and forage were more useful than gold or silver at this point in the campaign. They could not eat gold nor feed it to their animals, and there was nothing to be purchased with it.

The centurion noticed a well on the other side of the house and made his way towards it. As he got closer the telltale smell told him that it was not right. He looked over the stone edge and peered down into the well anyway, and at the bottom saw the rotting carcass of a sheep floating in the dark water. The well was deliberately poisoned to deprive the Romans of drinking water, as were nearly all the wells they came across.

"Damned barbarians," the soldier growled.

When Dacians retreated they left a wasteland behind. Whatever food and other supplies could not be carried away were burned. Barns full of grain were turned into smoky ruins. Horses, mules, goats, and sheep were herded away, but the slower oxen and cattle were sometimes slaughtered and left to rot in the fields.

The Dacian hut was deserted. That was fortunate for the shepherd and his family because Dacian civilians who were captured often paid for their resistance with a gladius through their guts. The Romans were getting hungrier, and hunger made them mean.

There was no food to be had around the hut and nothing else of use. What had once been three haystacks in the near distance were now charred ashes blowing in the breeze. The centurion ordered that the thatched roof be torn down. It made poor fodder for the animals but it contained some straw and was thus better than nothing. They loaded the thatch on the backs of six mules brought for this purpose, then slowly made their way back up the mountain.

King Decebal sat eating his noonday meal when Buri calmly got his attention and nodded in the direction of the Roman legionnaires coming up the mountain trail.

"Here comes more of them," Drilgisa said, biting into a ripe pear. He used the back of his hand to wipe pear juice from his chin.

The group of five legionnaires were still wearing their armor but were unarmed. They were escorted by half a dozen Dacian soldiers armed with spears and swords. They were Roman deserters.

While his shoulder was still healing Drilgisa was put in charge of handling deserters. It was necessary and important work. He tossed away the pear core as he stood up and walked a short distance to face the approaching group. The Roman soldiers stopped and stood stiffly at attention before him.

"Which one of you is the leader?" Drilgisa asked. In every mutiny there was always a leader.

"I am, sir," one of the older men spoke up promptly. "Legionnaire Cassius Danillo, Legio VI Victrix."

Drilgisa looked him up and down. Danillo looked every part the well trained Roman soldier, a seasoned veteran. He was exceptionally fit from years of marching, training, and fighting.

"You are no longer a legionnaire, Danillo, and you are no longer a member of Legio VI Victrix. As of now you are only my prisoner."

"Yes, sir!" Cassius snapped to attention. "I would prefer however to be your ally rather than your prisoner. As would these men with me, sir."

"Tell me why you wish to change sides," Drilgisa said evenly.

Danillo looked mildly surprised by the question, as if the reasons were obvious. "The men have no food and don't get paid, sir. Every man knows that King Decebalus pays his soldiers well." He paused and looked Drilgisa in the eye, one veteran to another. "A soldier should get paid for his work, sir."

"Indeed, soldier," Drilgisa replied with a nod.

"General! Bring those men over here." The order came from King Decebal. He remained seated and continued eating his meal as the men approached him.

"You said that you served with VI Victrix, Danillo?"

"Yes, sir. We were stationed in Germania until this past summer, then marched to Dacia to serve under General Julianus."

"And how do you find Dacia so far, Cassius?" Drilgisa could not suppress a smile.

"Cold, hungry, and deadly, General."

"For the past few weeks," Decebal continued, "we see a stream of Roman defectors such as yourselves. Tell me, how is the spirit of the men in General Julianus' army? Does he still hold the loyalty of his soldiers?"

Danillo paused to gather his thoughts. "General Julianus is not the problem, sir. I, all of us," he gestured at the other Romans, "would gladly fight for General Julianus. However the spirit of the men is not good under present conditions, sir. The men are not supplied and not being paid."

Decebal nodded. "I see. Very well, here is my offer. For serving in the Dacian army you will be paid twice the salary that Rome pays you. And you will be paid in Dacian gold."

Every Roman grinned at hearing that. They all knew that Dacian gold coins were only made with pure gold and were more valuable than the coins of neighboring nations, including Roman coins. Twice their old salary meant two gold coins per month instead of one. And unlike their Roman paymaster, this Dacian king would pay when payment was due. This was why they made the difficult decision to switch sides.

Danillo again spoke for all of them. "Thank you, sir. We will give our oath in writing. We understand that our lives are forfeit if we break that oath."

Decebal nodded in acceptance. "Serve Dacia well and you will have a new life here. Betray Dacia and you will be immediately executed. Understood?"

Every soldier voiced his agreement. They were in the Dacian army now and there was no turning back. Their lives were in the hands of King Decebal.

"Dismissed," the King said, and watched the Dacian guards lead the Romans away.

"We are getting a lot of them," Buri exclaimed. "Are they starving over there?"

"No, not starving. At least not yet. How many so far, Drilgisa?"

"I need to check the lists for an exact number but I would say close to three hundred deserters so far. And Buri is right, things are not good for them and likely getting worse. Food rations are low and their animals are dying, so the men tell me."

Decebal paused and looked up at the sky, an old habit when he needed to think and make a decision. "Perhaps it is time to have a talk with General Julianus."

"I'll go," Drilgisa volunteered with a glint in his eye. "I'd like to stand in front of that Roman bastard and look him in the eye."

"No, my friend," Decebal shook his head. "Not you."

Roman camp, Dacian mountains, November 88 AD

General Tettius Julianus was listening to unit reports from one of the junior tribunes when Titus Lucullus entered the command tent.

"Sir, we have visitors," Titus announced, a surprised look on his face. "A delegation from King Decebalus has arrived. Two men. They are waiting outside."

"A delegation? What do they want?"

"I don't know, sir," Titus replied. "They insist on speaking to you only." He paused for a beat and smiled. "It appears to be a very highly placed delegation."

Tettius scowled impatiently and followed Lucullus outside. It was the middle of November and the weather turned chilly. The general wrapped his red winter cloak tightly around his shoulders.

Lucullus had placed two benches outside the tent. On the far bench sat two men in well fashioned civilian clothes that marked them as Dacian nobility. Neither carried a weapon, those being left with their horses.

The younger man was built like a warrior, in his late twenties, with short brown hair and hazel eyes. His eyes showed only curiosity, no fear. The other was a very large man in his thirties, with reddish brown hair and green eyes. He looked very much like a simple farmer uncomfortably dressed for a formal occasion.

"General Tettius Julianus, may I present General Diegis, brother to King Decebalus of Dacia. And this," Lucullus gestured towards the big man, "is Buri, advisor to King Decebalus. They come on a mission from the King."

"What is this mission?" Julianus asked. He'd already had a bad morning and was in no mood for political talks.

Diegis spoke for the Dacians. His tone was respectful but firm. "King Decebal proposes a truce between the armies of Dacia and the armies of Rome."

"A truce?" Julianus asked indifferently. "I understand the benefit of a truce for the armies of Dacia. We are driving you further back across the mountains every week. But tell me, General Diegis, what is the benefit of a truce for Rome?"

Diegis expected the question and kept a calm expression on his face as he gave his answer. "The benefit for Rome, General Julianus, is that your army can withdraw to your camps in Moesia before winter hits without having Dacian raiding parties killing more of your men every step of the way. Should you not withdraw from Dacia before the heavy snows fall, you will starve and freeze in these mountains while we kill more of your men every day."

Julianus' face hardened at this brazen response. Titus gave Diegis a stern look and a very small shake of his head. Don't antagonize the general, the look said.

Rather than replying to Diegis, Tettius addressed Buri instead. "Why does your king send a pup to negotiate his treaties? Where is your High Priest and royal advisor, Vezina?"

Buri looked uncomfortable but said nothing.

"I speak for Dacia, General Julianus, so address your questions to me," Diegis said, his voice firm but polite. "To answer your second question, the High Priest Vezina narrowly escaped from the jaws of Rome once already. You had him trapped inside Tapae but he gave your soldiers the slip. One close call was enough for him, we decided."

Titus' eyes widened just a bit. He had wondered what happened to the tall thin man standing on top of Tapae's walls who spoke about Dacian immortality. That the man was Vezina himself was rather astonishing to him.

If Julianus was surprised he did not show it. "You did not answer my first question, young pup," he growled.

Diegis nodded. "To answer your first question, over the past three years this young pup has commanded infantry attacks that killed or wounded roughly two thousand Roman soldiers." He said it as a calm declaration of fact, not a boast.

The two legionnaires standing guard bristled and turned towards Diegis with hostile looks on their faces, ready to reach for the hilts of their swords. Buri tensed up but remained seated. Lucullus waved down the guards, and they stood at attention again.

"Enough of this negotiation," Julianus declared. "You are trying my patience, young pup, but I will grant that you have some bite to you to match your bark."

"And what is your answer to King Decebal, General Julianus?"

Julianus stood up from the bench. "You may tell your King that I have decided to march east and then south, not north. That will take my army to Moesia and not to Sarmizegetusa. This concludes our discussion."

Diegis nodded, pleased with the answer. Buri looked relieved that there was no bloodshed. Julianus turned away and walked back to his tent. He looked authoritative and composed, but there was a certain weariness in his step.

"These men who brought you here will now escort you out of the Roman camp," Lucullus told the Dacians as he gestured to the small group of guards. "Farewell, Diegis and Buri."

"Thank you, Titus," Diegis said. "And farewell."

Lucullus watched the Dacians leave, feeling frustrated and very disappointed. This was the end of the Dacian invasion for this year. He returned to the command tent where Julianus waited for him.

"That was a waste of time," Tettius declared irritably.

"It was, sir," Lucullus agreed. "We gave them what they asked for, which is exactly what we already decided to do anyway. This will make our withdrawal to Moesia for the winter easier and also prevent additional casualties."

"Decebalus will consider it a victory, no doubt."

Titus gave a small shrug. "He may do so. This is still the correct tactical decision, sir."

"The obvious tactical decision," Julianus admitted. "It is too late in the season to press our attack further. We must wait until spring, or perhaps early summer. We certainly can't wait out the winter here."

"Yes, sir," Titus acknowledged. "I believe the Emperor will see the sound reasoning behind your strategy."

Julianus looked unconvinced. "Perhaps so. Caesar is not the most patient or forgiving of men."

"He will still want Dacia conquered," Lucullus said. "And very clearly he still wants Dacia's gold. That will be unchanged next year."

"We shall see what next year brings. However, I do have one premonition about the future, Titus."

"What is that, sir?"

"That only one of us will get to see Sarmizegetusa," Julianus said with a sad smile. "And I do not think it will be me."

Chapter 14

Rebels And Traitors

Sarmizegetusa, January 89 AD

*E*arly in January King Decebal and the High Priest Vezina returned home. The army of General Tettius Julianus was retreating east along the Ister River. Dacian cavalry were following the Romans at a distance and sending back regular scouting reports.

Most of the Dacian troops, led by Diegis and Drilgisa, quartered in the many forts stretched out along the roads leading to the capital. Unlike the Roman army, the Dacian troops were well supplied to last out the winter.

Decebal sent no word ahead to announce his arrival, but once his travelling party entered the city word spread very quickly that the king was back. It was always a joyous occasion for the city because it made things feel right. A king belonged at home with his people, not on some far off battlefield.

The reception Decebal received when he entered the royal palace was even more joyful. Four year old Adila flew across the room and jumped into his arms, followed right behind by her older sister Zia. Family reunions with their father was always an exciting time for them because he was away so often for weeks and months at a time. They pulled him down to sit on a couch and smothered his face with kisses.

"Welcome home, Husband," Andrada said, sitting down beside him. She would let the girls have their time with their father first. The two of them would have their own reunion later. For now she was simply content and relieved that he returned alive and unharmed from yet another war.

"I am happy to be home. You look well, my love."

"They keep me busy," she smiled. "Adila is always asking to do something, and Zia is raising cats."

"Tata, Zia has three kittens but she won't give me one!" Adila said with a pout.

"Get your own kittens!" Zia told her.

Andrada rolled her eyes. "See what I mean?"

"Daughters, don't argue," Decebal said sternly but without anger. "You are both princesses of Dacia, and princesses don't argue."

"But she has three, it's not fair!" Adila complained. "If I have three I share, like Mama says."

"I found them in the barn so they're mine," Zia insisted. "Anyway kittens are not like cookies!"

"Zia, Adila, stop!" their mother laughed. "Your Tata just got home from the war, he doesn't want to hear you argue about kittens!"

That made Decebal smile. "About that, my dear, I must disagree. Listening to my daughters argue about kittens is what I have been looking forward to for the past few weeks."

After the evening meal Decebal went to see his uncle, the former king Duras, at his living quarters in the royal palace. Duras was too old and frail to travel on military campaigns any longer. His mind was still very sharp however. Decebal trusted his judgment and valued his wealth of knowledge.

Duras sat on a chair in front of the fireplace, wrapped in a blanket. The fireplace gave heat and light for reading, both appreciated by the old man. These days he felt the winter chill in the marrow of his bones.

"Welcome, Nephew." Duras put aside the book scroll he had been reading. Whatever Decebal's age or title, to Duras he would always be first and foremost his nephew.

"Hello, Uncle. You are looking well," Decebal said.

Duras smiled. "Vezina was here a short while ago, and he told me the same lie."

"It is no lie." Decebal pulled up a chair to sit by his uncle's side. "What book are you reading, Uncle?"

"A history of the life of King Burebista." He picked up the scroll and handed it to Decebal. "I have read it three times and it has no more lessons to teach me. It is yours now."

"Thank you, Uncle. No doubt the great man has many lessons for me to ponder as well."

"He was a great king and made Dacia a powerful nation. Dacia was much larger and powerful then. The kingdom of King Burebista also included the lands of Moesia and Pannonia." Duras gave a sad sigh. "In the end he made a terrible mistake, and it undid all his great works."

"Do you mean allowing the Dacian nobles to betray him?"

"Yes. He made them very wealthy and powerful, and in turn the ingrates became jealous of his power and resented being ruled by one king."

Decebal knew the history. "The nobles arranged to have King Burebista assassinated, then broke up Dacia into four smaller parts. What is the lesson there for us, Uncle?"

"The first and most important lesson, Nephew, is to not allow yourself to get assassinated."

Decebal laughed. "And the second lesson?"

"The second important lesson," Duras continued in a serious tone, "is that Dacia must never be divided again. The kingdom must have a strong king to keep us united."

"I agree completely, Uncle. I am working every day to unite all the tribes of Dacia, and also the tribes neighboring Dacia. If we do not unite Rome will devour us piece by piece."

"Exactly so," Duras said. "And it is no simple thing to hold so many different tribes together."

"It must be done, Uncle. We do not have an army half as large as the one that was led by King Burebista."

Duras nodded. "True. Burebista had a larger kingdom and many more men. So you must be more resourceful than Burebista."

"I understand. Dacia must be resourceful."

Duras held out his hands towards the fire to warm them. "Vezina tells me that he almost lost his life at Tapae."

"Yes. He outsmarted the Romans and escaped the siege, however. He is more resourceful than any of us."

"Oh, I have no doubt," Duras said. "Sometimes he thinks he can do the impossible."

"Nothing is impossible, Uncle. Sometimes the impossible is even necessary. A king must always find a way, isn't that what you keep telling me?"

"Yes," Duras said. "Dacia is fortunate that somehow King Decebal always finds a way."

Decebal looked down at the book scroll in his hands. "Sometimes too much is expected of me, Uncle. Even King Burebista could not always find a way. He trusted the wrong people, and in the end he was betrayed."

"Yes, he was. This is why we must learn from history. Learn from Burebista and do not repeat his mistakes."

King Decebal gave Duras a warm smile and stood up to leave. "Thank you for the kingly lessons, Uncle. I shall do my utmost to avoid being assassinated. And I shall work hard at building alliances and keeping Dacia strong."

Duras gave him a nod. "Those are good lessons for any king to keep in mind. There is however a third lesson that the history of Burebista teaches us."

"And what is that, Uncle?"

"Beware of greedy and jealous nobles."

Later in the evening, in their sleeping quarters, the King and Queen finally had time for uninterrupted conversation.

Andrada asked the foremost question troubling her mind. "Are the Romans truly not coming back?"

"Not this winter, certainly. Julianus seems content to destroy some of our smaller forts and settlements during his retreat but that is the limit of his aggression. He will quarter his troops in Moesia where he can be supplied for the winter."

"And then? When winter ends?"

Decebal stroked her long black hair slowly and absentmindedly. "Then we shall see how ambitious Emperor Domitian is feeling next year."

"He sent nine legions against Dacia with General Julianus. Nine legions! I would call that ambitious."

"Yes, my dear, very ambitious. And we made them pay a heavy price for their ambition."

"Yes," Andrada said, but found no real joy in the Romans' losses. "And what of the price we paid?"

"Too many, as usual."

"Always too many," she reflected. "How long can Dacia do this, Husband?"

He heard the worry in her voice and turned to look into her eyes. "For as long as necessary. As many times as we are threatened."

Andrada sighed. "I know. We do not have a choice."

"The only choice is freedom or slavery. I choose freedom. For me, for you, and for them. This is why I fight."

"For them? Do you mean the girls?"

"Yes, for our children most of all, but also for all the others."

"Ah!" Andrada exclaimed. "The King speaks."

"Yes, my love. It is one duty I can never escape."

She gave him a serious look. "Do you wish to?"

"No," he replied without hesitation. "I think that I was born to be king. It is the destiny Zamolxis chose for me."

"It's funny," she said, "but I have no such thoughts about being queen. I was simply me, enjoying my simple life. And then I married you!"

Decebal laughed. "Perhaps that is the destiny Zamolxis chose for you, Andrada."

She shook her head dismissively. "Who knows what the gods want. Sometimes I pray to them, but I don't know if they hear me."

"What do you pray for?" he asked.

"I prayed that you would defeat the Romans. I prayed that you would return safely to us."

Decebal reached out and softly touched her cheek. "Then Zamolxis heard you."

Rome, January 89 AD

Emperor Domitian was agonizing over multiple political and military challenges. In Dacia his army under Tettius Julianus retreated to Moesia for the winter. This was something they planned to avoid, but now those plans had to be abandoned.

The Dacians were a better organized, more determined, and more formidable military foe than Domitian had bargained for. He had badly underestimated Decebalus three times. Sabinus lost one legion. Fuscus lost the better part of four legions in a campaign that was too shameful to even talk about. Julianus went in with nine legions. He lost almost two legions before retreating to Moesia. So it would take more than nine legions, and perhaps a better general.

Domitian shook his head angrily, then pushed the Dacia problem out of his mind. The more pressing problem at the moment was a revolt in Germania. His general Antoninus Saturninus, the Governor of Germania Superior, had gone rogue and declared himself in open opposition to the Emperor. He had the support of his legions and also made allies with the powerful Chatti tribes. The Chatti were one of the largest of the Germanic tribes, and Domitian had personally led a war against them before the Dacian wars. Along with Saturninus they were inflicting heavy losses on army units loyal to the Emperor. The situation in Germania was bad and getting worse.

Domitian put aside a letter he was writing when his close political ally, the corpulent and affable Senator Marcus Paullus, entered his study. Paullus was always in a good mood when summoned to meet with the Emperor.

"Hail, Caesar," Paullus greeted him, extending his right arm in the Roman salute.

Domitian gestured to a couch beside his desk. "Sit down, Marcus. We have much to discuss."

"This Saturninus' business is a nasty affair, Caesar. The man must be insane!"

"Does he have any support in the Senate, Marcus?"

"No one dares come out publically in his support, of course. Even so I would say that very few senators support the traitor. Saturninus' position is weak. What he hopes to achieve is absurd."

Domitian gave him an impatient frown. "What does he hope to achieve?"

"If he becomes powerful enough in Germania and gathers more support in Rome, he will declare himself emperor and march on Rome."

Domitian smiled thinly and shook his head in disdain.

"As I said, Caesar," Paullus assured him, "the poor man is insane. He will never win enough support to march on Rome."

Domitian became quiet, deep in troubled thought. "What will it require to strengthen my own support in the Senate, Marcus?"

Paullus had his answer prepared because he spent considerable time thinking about it. Caesar's problems with the Senate were an ongoing concern. Many detested him. He hated them and, when an opportunity came along, he punished them.

"The best stratagem at this time, Caesar, is to form an alliance with Marcus Nerva."

"Nerva?" Domitian scowled. "Nerva is an old woman."

Paullus nodded amiably. "That he may be, Caesar, but he is also a master diplomat with a very shrewd political mind. He takes no sides, but brings enemies together and makes peace. And, in addition to that," Marcus paused to emphasize the point, "he served your father the Divine Vespasian well as an advisor."

Domitian made a quick practical decision. "Very well, Marcus, have a talk with Nerva. Make him promises. If he is able to suppress the opposition against me in the Senate then I will make him my co-consul next year."

Marcus was pleased, and also impressed. "A very generous offer, Caesar. I think he will be agreeable."

"But more importantly, Paullus, Saturninus must be stopped now. He cannot be allowed to build his strength. The Chatti are attacking us along the Rhine in the west, and the Sarmatians are attacking us in Moesia in the east."

"A difficult situation, Caesar," Paullus acknowledged. "Our armies are already stretched too thin in the northern provinces."

Domitian slammed his fist down in frustration against the desk top, scattering his writing supplies. "I don't have enough legions to respond to all these attacks!"

"We don't have the money to pay for additional legions, Caesar." Paullus again acknowledged what Domitian already knew. "The only solution is to relocate them."

Domitian frowned. "I know that, and I have already made some decisions."

"Of course. And you must tell me how I may assist Caesar in these matters."

Domitian leaned back in his chair and looked the senator in the eye. "You will be my emissary and my ambassador, Marcus."

"I am always at your service, Caesar."

"Julianus is stalled. I am taking away four of his legions and will take them to Germania to deal with the problems there. He will still have enough troops in Moesia to deal with the Sarmatian problem."

"I understand, Caesar. However, four legions is half his army. How is he to pursue the invasion of Dacia?"

"He will not," the Emperor said firmly. "You, Marcus, will go to Dacia. You will serve as my envoy and speak with King Decebalus."

Now this was a real surprise. "Speak with Decebalus, Caesar?"

"Yes!" Domitian exclaimed impatiently. "We must make peace with Dacia while we beat back the rebellions in Germania and Moesia. You will negotiate a peace treaty with King Decebalus."

"Of course, Caesar," Paullus declared, as if the answer had been obvious all along.

"The situation is perilous, Marcus." Domitian's voice turned cold. "Do not fail me."

Paullus bowed to him. "On my life, Caesar, I will not fail you."

"We must put down the traitor Saturninus and do it quickly. In addition to the legions from Julianus I am sending troops from Spain to Germania."

"Yes, Caesar. Might I ask, whom are you sending from Spain?"

"A young general, a Spaniard. He commands the new legion VII Gemina," Domitian explained. "His name is Marcus Trajanus. His men call him Trajan."

After his meeting with Marcus Paullus the Emperor summoned his niece, Julia Flavia. The young woman came in and politely accepted the invitation to sit on the Emperor's couch. She wore the black veil of a woman newly widowed.

Domitian walked over and sat beside her. "How are you, my dear?"

Julia looked up, her pale blue eyes misty with emotion. "I am in mourning, Caesar. Otherwise I am well."

"Tell me, Julia," the Emperor continued. "Do you understand the reason why Titus Sabinus was executed for treason? I wish for you to comprehend fully."

"Yes, Caesar," she replied quietly. "My husband was conspiring with the traitor Antoninus Saturninus." She paused, eyes brimming with tears.

"No, you mustn't cry for him," Domitian urged. "My people in the Senate found proof that he was a traitor to Rome. You however are not complicit in his betrayal. I hold you completely innocent, Julia."

"I am grateful, Caesar." She looked up at him. "I knew nothing of any plots against you. Forgive my asking, but what evidence did you find against Titus?"

Domitian shook his head patiently. "I cannot tell you that, it would mean revealing state secrets."

Julia nodded sadly. "I understand."

"Now you must forget this entire dreadful affair. We shall not speak of it again because I know that it will only upset you."

"As you wish, Caesar."

Domitian looked into her eyes. "From now on, my dear, you will stay here in the palace with me. I will take care of you as you should be taken care of."

Julia paused briefly, surprised, then nodded her head softly.

"Yes, Caesar."

Chapter 15

THE SPANISH GENERAL

Moguntiacum, Germania, February 89 AD

*N*ear the end of February General Marcus Ulpius Trajanus arrived in Germania to find that the revolt of Governor Antoninus Saturninus had already been squashed. The hero of the campaign was General Aulus Maximus, who defeated Saturninus' army before the armies of Emperor Domitian and General Trajan even got there. He was helped by an astonishing stroke of good fortune that soon became part of Roman legend.

Even though he arrived too late to join the battle, Trajan would earn the Emperor's gratitude for the speed in which he brought his troops from southern Spain to Germania. He pushed his men through the mountain ranges, through snow and winter weather. They followed him loyally through every hardship and adversity.

General Trajan had a well-earned reputation for being liked and admired by his men. He showed his men that he was one of them by acting and living like one of them. As army commander he showed a rare combination of being in command without being arrogant. He was a master tactician who invited his officers to share in planning strategy. He was a fair leader who also possessed an iron will when it became necessary.

To those who did not know him well Trajan was an enigma. He carried no pretentions of nobility because there was no history of it in his background. His family came from very humble origins, a town in southern Spain that had been settled by retired Roman army veterans from the wars in Africa. There were no noblemen among them. The Trajanus family became very wealthy by growing olives and exporting olive oil to Rome. One of his relatives was also smart and industrious enough to build a factory for manufacturing the thousands of clay amphorae needed every year for transporting the region's olive oil to Rome.

His father, Traianus, was a general for Emperor Vespasian in the Judean campaign. He was later awarded a triumph in Rome for his victory against the Parthians. Traianus earned Vespasian's trust and admiration, and with the Emperor's support went on to rise to the Senate of Rome and later elected to the office of Consul of Rome. Thus it was that the Trajanus family and the Flavian family became closely allied.

Trajan arrived at Moguntiacum in late afternoon. Senior military men were often amazed to learn that he marched alongside his men, refusing a horse or a carriage. Already tall and strongly built at thirty-two years of age, he was exceptionally fit from the long marches.

The new arrival from Spain was directed to the Emperor's tent where a group of highly ranked officers gathered. The only person Trajan recognized was Domitian himself, although he had not seen the Emperor for a number of years. He walked over and presented himself.

"Hail Caesar! I came as fast as winter conditions permitted."

Domitian clasped him on the shoulder, a friendly smile on his face. He had been drinking wine for a while and was in a good mood.

"I commend you for the speed you made, Trajanus. I wish all my generals could be so mobile!" He turned to the heavy-set middle-aged man standing next to him. "This is Aulus Maximus, who defeated the traitor Saturninus. He saved us the time and trouble of dealing with the wretch ourselves!"

"Congratulations, General," Trajan offered, genuinely impressed. "To defeat the legions of Saturninus and also the tribesmen of the Chatti is a formidable victory."

Maximus acknowledged the compliment with a modest nod of his head. "Saturninus put up a good fight. As for the Chatti, they never joined the battle."

Trajan was surprised. "Never made it to the fight? How so?"

Domitian chortled loudly. "Tell him, Aulus!"

It was obvious that Maximus had already told the story many times. It was also clear that he enjoyed telling it again, particularly in front of the Emperor.

"Near the end of January I marched on Saturninus' camp. He was waiting for the Chatti army to join his forces. Together they would have outnumbered me three to one."

"Poor Saturninus!" Domitian laughed again. "If he had not died he would still be waiting for the Chatti! Isn't that right, Aulus?"

"Indeed, Caesar," Maximus grinned.

Trajan sipped his wine and waited patiently. Maximus and the Emperor were enjoying themselves, putting on a show.

Aulus continued. "I attacked with three legions and Saturninus had no choice but to fight. The Chatti," he paused and smiled, "were trapped on the other side of the Rhine."

Marcus raised an eyebrow. "In what way were they trapped?"

"An early thaw!" Domitian exclaimed gleefully. "The ice melted! The Rhine thawed out in January! Can you fathom that?"

Trajan slowly shook his head. "It is difficult to fathom, Caesar. The fortunes of war take unexpected turns."

Domitian waved his comment away. "Fortunes of war, nonsense! This was an act of Mars himself. The god of war intervened to keep the barbarians on their side of the river and allowed Maximus to bring the traitor to justice!"

Maximus humbly agreed. "Yes, Caesar. I was only an instrument in the hands of Mars."

"We are all in the hands of the gods," Trajan said thoughtfully.

Domitian gave Marcus a sly look. "You forget yourself, Trajanus. Caesar is also a god."

"As I said, Caesar, we are all in the hands of the gods. Are we not all in the hands of Caesar?" Trajan asked with a pleasant smile.

"Well said!" Maximus said with a laugh. "We are all in the hands of Caesar. And that includes the wretched prisoners we took from among the traitor's men." He turned to Domitian. "Their punishment will be executed tomorrow, if that is the wish of Caesar."

Domitian nodded his assent. "The sooner the better, Aulus. Make an example of them." He turned to Trajan again. "You arrived just in time to witness Caesar's justice, Trajanus. Come now, have more wine! This is a happy occasion."

At noon the next day, the winter sun high and bright in a clear blue sky, the legions were assembled to witness the Emperor's justice. Twenty of Governor Saturninus' captured officers were placed on display before the assembled troops, who felt only scorn for them. They were traitors who rebelled against Caesar and fought against fellow Romans. They rightfully deserved whatever punishment was coming to them.

The twenty prisoners were lined up behind four large logs that had been stripped of all branches. Their humiliation began when they were stripped naked, forced to kneel on the frozen ground, and had their hands shackled and chained to the log in front of them. Off to one side was a good sized fire burning charcoal. It was tended by a blacksmith with a pair of hand bellows, and four guards.

The Emperor Domitian, his armor shining brightly under the noonday sun, rode his horse slowly in front of the prisoners. He looked at each of their faces for a brief moment, placing them in his memory. Some of the prisoners looked up at him but most kept their eyes glued to the ground. They were doomed men resigned to their fates.

Domitian sat high in the saddle and addressed the troops in a loud voice. His words were repeated down the lines so that those further away could follow along.

"These men," the Emperor shouted, pointing at the prisoners, "are traitors to Rome! They are worse than scum! They are worse than the barbarian Germans they call their allies!"

The men in the front rows jeered and booed the traitors. The men in the rows behind them joined in.

"These men turned against the people of Rome! They turned against the legions of Rome! They turned against Caesar, the Father of Rome!"

The jeering grew louder and angrier. The soldiers wanted blood.

"These men are a wretched abomination in the eyes of the gods! What shall be their punishment?"

"Kill them! Kill them!" many in the ranks yelled.

"This is the punishment for treason!" Domitian screamed. "The punishment for traitors! I give them iron and fire!"

The blacksmith, accompanied by the four guards, walked to the first prisoner kneeling naked in the snow. He held a large pair of metal tongs in his hands, and the tongs held a long thin iron rod that glowed red hot even in the bright sun.

The four guards each took hold of one of the man's arms or legs to keep him immobilized. The legionnaires watching from the front lines yelled their approval. Some jeered loudly, some laughed.

The Emperor rode his horse to where Trajan and Maximus were waiting, and dismounted to stand beside them. The first prisoner screamed as the red hot iron was inserted into his private parts.

"A fitting punishment, don't you think?" Domitian asked.

"A punishment fit for traitors, Caesar," Maximus answered.

Trajan nodded his head but stayed silent. He understood the need for the punishment but was sickened by the brutality. Men behaved badly in the past, they would do so again in the future, and the brutal punishments of Caesars did not seem to make any difference.

Domitian watched as the first prisoner finally went silent and died. The blacksmith went back to his fire to get a new iron rod for the next prisoner.

"Trajanus?"

"Yes, Caesar?"

"Now that you brought your legion here, let's put them to work. I am told the men have not been bloodied and need some seasoning."

"That is correct, Caesar. Legio VII Gemina is a new legion and the men have not yet had a chance to distinguish themselves."

"Very well, here is your opportunity. I need you here Trajanus, not in Spain. You will take VII Gemina plus two more legions and press a campaign against the Chatti. Also the Suebi Marcomanni, who broke their treaty with Rome when I was fighting Decebalus."

Trajan was pleased. This is what he had been waiting for. "I am honored by this opportunity, Caesar."

"Good. These barbarians are all too willing to break their treaties with Rome, it simply cannot be tolerated." He paused as the next prisoner screamed in agony. "Punish the Chatti and the Marcomanni, Trajanus. Do not fail me."

"I never fail, Caesar." Trajan said it humbly, as a simple statement of fact, and believed it completely.

Chapter 16

THE WHEEL OF LIFE

Sarmizegetusa, April 89 AD

$\mathcal{T}$he large dining hall in the royal palace at Sarmizegetusa was filled with children's shouts. The celebration was for the princess Zia, eldest daughter of King Decebal and Queen Andrada, in recognition of her sixth birthday. It seemed to Decebal that every young child in the city was invited to this lively celebration. More than that, it seemed that every child had something to say, something to ask for, or something to cry and complain about.

Four year old Adila, the younger daughter, was just as excited as her sister. She spotted her father entering the banquet room and left her friends to run and give him a big hug. Most of the children shyly kept their distance from the King.

"Tata!" Adila shouted joyfully. "Uncle Diegis says the Romans are coming here!"

Decebal laughed. "He is just teasing you. Only a few Romans are coming and they only want to talk, not fight."

Adila made a face. "I knew he was teasing because he had this silly smile."

Her mother Andrada overheard and came over. "Oh, Diegis is smiling a lot these days."

"What do you mean?" Decebal asked.

She nodded her head towards the near wall. "Look for yourself. He's over there."

Diegis was deep in conversation with a beautiful young woman. They seemed to be in their own world and hardly aware of dozens of children running around the room.

"I know that look," Decebal said. "So my brother has a new friend?"

"More than a friend, I would say. They are becoming inseparable."

"Ah. It's about time, I suppose," he exclaimed. "Diegis is no longer a young man and it's time he settled down."

"That's what we all tell him," she laughed. "He gets sick of hearing it. But this," she gestured at the couple, "is not because of me or your sisters."

"Hmmm, that sounds serious. When Diegis makes an important decision it is only because he strongly believes in it. Let me go and say hello and meet his friend. "

As Decebal approached the couple Diegis looked up, startled. The young woman gave a curt bow before the King.

"Hello, Brother," Decebal greeted him.

"Hello, Brother," Diegis replied pleasantly. "This is Mirela. And Mirela, this is – "

Her easy laugh interrupted him. "I know who the King is, silly," she chided him. "Sire," she said and bowed again.

"Welcome to our home, Mirela," Decebal said with a warm smile. The young woman was no older than seventeen, of medium height, with long light brown hair hanging down her back. She had unusual, striking amber-brown eyes. She seemed to radiate charm and poise. Diegis was obviously enchanted. Was she also enchanted with him?

"Diegis, you must bring Mirela around to share our evening meal," Decebal told him.

"Of course. We shall join you this evening." He looked at Mirela, who smiled and nodded her assent. She was suddenly grabbed by her left hand and pulled away by Zia , who wanted her to join a game.

"Excuse me, Sire, I am needed elsewhere!" she laughed, looking back over her shoulder.

"Mirela," Decebal wondered. "The name means – "

"It means timeless," Diegis replied.

"Ah, yes," Decebal acknowledged. "She is a timeless beauty. And you, my brother, look smitten."

"She will be my wife," Diegis said simply.

"Then I am happy for you," Decebal replied. "It is time you started a family."

"That's what our sisters keep telling me," Diegis laughed. "Also Andrada, as well. But no matter, I did not need convincing. Mirela is reason enough."

"That is the best reason of all to marry."

"I just heard word from Tsiru," Diegis said, changing the subject. Tsiru was the head of Dacian cavalry scouts.

"Yes?"

"The Roman envoys are perhaps a week away. Their ambassador rides in a carriage so it slows them down."

"Ah, I see. You must expect that, Diegis. Roman nobility demand a life of ease and luxury. So, a week then. I am curiuos to hear what this ambassador has to say. I believe the Emperor honestly seeks a treaty."

"Is Domitian still in Germania?"

"Vezina believes so. Domitian put down the rebellion there, and now fights the Chatti again." Decebal stopped to help a child up who had fallen at his feet. "Off you go! And be more careful, boy!"

"The Romans will be fighting the Germans until the end of time," Diegis said.

"Very likely so. No matter how aggressive the Romans get, there are simply too many Germans to kill them all."

"I wish I could say the same about us," Diegis said in a somber tone. "The numbers do not work in our favor."

"Indeed. So we'll just have to outsmart and out-fight the bastards instead, eh?"

After a while Decebal left the lively but noisy birthday celebration and wandered outside into the courtyard. He was looking for Cotiso and found him practicing his sword craft with Drilgisa. The sounds of their wooden practice swords filled the cool air.

The boy was fifteen years old and growing into a man. At his age Decebal had been a soldier. Cotiso had grown taller but was still thin as a reed. He had his mother's thin build and, Decebal feared, would never fill out with muscle. Well, then, if he was not going to be a strong soldier he would be a fast and skilled one. He would find no better teacher than Drilgisa.

"High blow, block with your shield," Drilgisa said. "Low blow you parry with your sword. You must do so without thinking."

He stepped forward and stabbed high at Cotiso's neck. The boy raised his shield to block the sword and immediately countered by stabbing at Drilgisa's forward leg with his own wooden sword.

"Yes! That's the way," Drilgisa encouraged him.

Cotiso cut his sword swiftly through the air, trying to confuse his opponent. Drilgisa frowned.

"Don't waste your energy! In battle men get tired quickly. Tired men become slow and careless, and then they die." He took a step forward and stabbed at Cotiso's thigh, which the youngster parried easily with his sword. "Every move you make should have a purpose, to attack or to defend! Everything else is wasted energy."

"Yes, sir," Cotiso agreed. He dodged a stabbing move toward his sword hand, then swiftly moved sideways and stabbed his sword at Drilgisa's side. It was blocked by the older man's shield, but Drilgisa grinned with approval.

"Good! You are lighter and faster than a legionnaire. Your sica is lighter and gives you more options, you can slash with it as well as stab. His gladius is heavier and good mostly for stabbing. Move and find openings! Then attack!"

Cotiso gave a shout and jumped into the air, swinging his sword overhand for a blow at Drilgisa's head. The warrior blocked the blow easily with his shield and hit Cotiso in the face with the hilt of his sword. The blow sent the boy sprawling and he landed on the ground on his back. A small trickle of blood ran from one nostril.

King Decebal walked up and stood over him. "What lesson did General Drilgisa just teach you, Son?"

Cotiso quickly scrambled to his feet, a sheepish expression on his face. "Never jump. That was stupid of me."

"Yes it was stupid," Drilgisa said. "You have no balance when you jump! You can't change direction when you jump! In a real battle I would have smashed you hard in the face, not the little tap I gave you just now. You would be dazed and an easy kill." He paused and gave him a hard look. "But you knew this. So why did you jump?"

"I got too excited," Cotiso said with a shrug. "A foolish mistake."

"Foolish mistakes get you killed in battle, boy!" Drilgisa shouted. "A warrior does not make foolish mistakes. I never want to see that again, not even in practice, not even in jest!"

"Yes, sir," Cotiso said. "It will not happen again."

"Every single thing General Drilgisa teaches you could save your life one day," Decebal told him. "Every little thing. So listen carefully, and remember."

"Yes, Tata. I understand."

Decebal gave him a slap on the back. "Good. Did you attend your sister's birthday celebration?"

"I went for a time. It got too noisy so I asked General Drilgisa for a lesson."

"Children are very noisy, but let's go back for a little while." He glanced over at Drilgisa. "Do you care to join us?"

Drilgisa laughed. "No, thank you. I'll go and find a mule to kick me in the head. That would be less of a headache, I think."

Decebal grinned. "Understood." He turned to his son and steered him towards the celebration noise.

"Tata, may I ask you a question?" Cotiso asked as they walked.

"Of course. What is it?"

"What makes a great warrior? I have discussed this with my friends and everyone has a different answer."

"I see," Decebal nodded. "What do they say?"

"Some say courage, or fierceness. Some say physical strength is most important. Some say swordsmanship." Cotiso stopped walking and looked at this father. "I asked General Drilgisa today, but he told me to ask you instead."

Decebal heard the earnest tone in his son's voice. The boy was looking for a serious answer. He motioned Cotiso to a wooden bench by the stone path, and they sat facing each other.

"All those things are important, Son," Decebal said. "Without courage men run away. Without physical strength they are easily overpowered, and then they die. Without swordsmanship they are soon killed by a warrior who is more skilled."

"Yes, but which is most important?"

"What makes a great warrior is in the soul," Decebal replied. He raised an index finger and tapped Cotiso twice on the chest. "It starts here." He raised his finger higher and tapped him on the forehead. "And here."

The youngster paused. "Explain it to me, Tata."

"Why are Dacian warriors not afraid to die?"

"Because if we die in battle we immediately go to the heaven of Zamolxis," Cotiso said.

"Exactly. Death is nothing. Knowing that your soul is immortal gives you the courage to face any danger and fight any foe."

The boy nodded. "Yes, I understand."

"Courage comes from living in freedom, Cotiso. That is why we fight for Dacia, so we can be free." He paused and was gratified to see a look of calmness and determination on his son's face.

"And yet some men live in subjugation," Cotiso said.

"The man who lives in subjugation dies every day," Decebal said. "That shall never happen to me. Never, not for one single day."

"It will not happen to me either, Tata."

"Good. Grow stronger, and practice your swordsmanship and your archery every day. But always know this, my son, that in your soul you already are a great warrior."

"Yes, Tata. I will remember that."

Decebal clasped him on the shoulder, then stood up from the bench. "Come now, Cotiso. Family awaits."

Four days later Decebal was summoned to the living quarters of his Uncle Duras. The former King was in bed resting, as he did most days. He was an old man of sixty-seven, and few men lived to such an old age. His mind was as sharp as ever but he grew thinner and weaker every day.

A small crowd was gathered outside Duras' sleeping quarters. Queen Andrada, Decebal's older sister Dochia, his younger sister Tanidela, and half a dozen Dacian nobles were standing and talking among themselves. One look in Andrada's eyes told Decebal all he needed to know. This was King Duras' death watch.

Vezina sat in a chair by Duras' bedside. The two old friends looked to be deep in conversation.

"Hello, Uncle," Decebal greeted him. He leaned over the bed, picked up his Uncle's hand, and kissed the back of the hand. It was an ancient Dacian gesture of respect and deference for one's elders.

"Hello, Nephew," Duras replied, his eyes suddenly brighter and more alert. "Vezina and I have been talking. Join us."

"Of course, Uncle. What have you been discussing?"

Duras got a glint in his eye and managed a half smile. "My last days, Nephew. What else?"

Vezina laughed softly. "Also some old days as well. And also the days to come. We have been talking about you as well, Sire, and the future of Dacia."

"The future of Dacia is secure," Decebal declared. "You helped make it strong, Uncle."

Duras waved the comment away. "The future of Dacia is in peril." He looked from Decebal to Vezina, then back to the King. "You must make Dacia even stronger. We have been strong for hundreds of years. We have beaten back all enemies."

Decebal nodded. "Yes, Uncle. And we shall do so again."

Duras turned his head to the side and coughed, growing short of breath. He closed his eyes for a few moments to rest. When he opened them again they were watery but calm.

"Rome is a starving beast whose appetite has no limits," Duras continued. "They want to rule the world, enslave the world."

"No beast lives forever," Vezina said. "Any beast may be killed."

"Yes, that is true," Decebal agreed. "Twice Rome tried to invade us, and twice we bloodied them and beat them back."

Duras squeezed Decebal's hand, a grateful gesture. "Your military leadership made those victories possible." His eyes grew misty. "I never told you this, but I saw it in a dream."

"A dream, Uncle?"

"A week before the battle at Tapae, when we attacked General Fuscus, my brother Scorilo came to me in a dream. He showed me the great victory that was yet to come, and he advised me to give you the crown."

Decebal was astonished. He glanced at Vezina, who looked just as surprised as he was.

"My father advised you in a dream to make me king? Is this true, Uncle?"

Duras gave a sigh. "Perhaps it was Scorilo. And perhaps it was Zamolxis." He paused for a heartbeat, then gave Decebal a smile. "It does not matter, Nephew, because I already made that decision on my own. I knew that you were the strength of Dacia."

"Thank you, Uncle," Decebal said, deeply humbled. "I thank you for your trust in me. I would give my life to keep Dacia free."

Vezina leaned towards Duras. "It is comforting, my friend, to know that King Scorilo and Zamolxis approved of your decision. But then you always made the right decisions, it seems."

Duras looked at the two men, a solemn expression on his face. "Tell me, this treaty with Rome. Are the Romans arriving soon?"

"We expect their arrival any day now, Uncle."

"I see," Duras said. "And what do you hope to accomplish with this treaty?"

"An end to the fighting," Decebal answered. "We must rebuild our strength. So many thousands have died to defend Dacia."

Vezina nodded in agreement. "Yes, we must rebuild our forces. Domitian has enough troubles elsewhere at the moment, he does not want any more trouble with Dacia. It is the right time for a treaty."

"Good," Duras replied. "Make your treaty with Rome, but always remember this. The beast only makes peace when it is weak or wounded. Then it becomes the beast again."

"Yes, Uncle. I will remember. For now we make treaties because it suits our purpose. But I promise you this, Uncle. I promise you this. I will never forget that we are in a fight for survival with Rome."

Duras managed a smile. "Thank you, Nephew. And thank you my friend Vezina." His eyelids flickered and he suddenly looked very tired. He closed his eyes and was soon asleep.

Duras, the former king of Dacia, died quietly and peacefully in his sleep. He was mourned by the city for three days. The people dressed in funeral black. Many women stood or kneeled for hours in front of the royal palace, weeping and wailing as a way of expressing their grief. Duras was mourned as a fair and just king who devoted his life to his people.

On the third day King Duras was buried in a plot near the Holy Temple of Zamolxis. By tradition Dacians were buried in simple graves, with no headstones or statuary. He was buried wrapped in a shroud, with his face up, and his head pointing to the east. He was dressed in his finest clothes. His sword rested at his side.

A tall mound of freshly cut flowers was piled over his grave. These were placed there one by one by the people who came to pay their last respects. His funeral day was observed as a holy day of remembrance. In every temple the priests burned incense and sang hymns. As the sun set in the west a great pomana, the funeral feast, was given at the royal palace for all the citizens of Sarmizegetusa.

Chapter 17

You Would Call Us Barbarians

Sarmizegetusa, May 89 AD

ome's delegation arrived in Sarmizegetusa several days later. They were escorted by Dacian cavalry over the long mountain roads. Senator Paullus rode in his carriage, the other Romans on horse. It was too long a journey for a march.

Titus Lucullus came as a diplomat in Senator Paullus' travelling party. He was however first and foremost a soldier. He took notice of the many stone walled forts on the roads to the capital and knew it would be a difficult and bloody struggle to fight through all of them. Each would require a battle, and that would require transporting large numbers of siege artillery through the mountains. A campaign lasting several months would be required just to get through the mountain forts before reaching Sarmizegetusa.

The army of Tettius Julianus could not have accomplished that mission. They would have bogged down in the mountains in winter, starved, harried, and slowly depleted. Julianus had been right about one thing, however, and the thought of it made Lucullus smile. Titus made it to Sarmizegetusa first, but not in a fashion that either of them predicted. Titus came as a peacemaker.

The city of Sarmizegetusa was built on the edge of a steep cliff, and that by itself made it difficult to attack. As he approached the massive city gates Titus paused and looked up in wonder at the stone walls thirty feet high and nine feet thick. The walls were built with large blocks of stone. Wide ramparts on the top of the walls gave the defenders ample fighting room to repel an attack. The ramparts were made of limestone and andesite, a very hard volcanic rock. A number of the captured Roman scorpions and carrobalistae were placed on fighting platforms on top of the wall to cover the main road leading into the city.

Siege artillery would not break down Sarmizegetusa's massive walls, Lucullus judged. An invading army would have to go over the walls or dig underneath them. The rocky terrain made digging a very questionable proposition. The city would have to be sieged and starved out. That would most likely make it a very long siege.

On one side of the city was a steep mountain cliff that could not be climbed. Another side was built against the side of the mountain, and that too could not be accessed. Inside the walls, Titus saw as they rode through the streets, was a large sprawling city built on dozens of terraces that rose higher as they travelled deeper into the city.

The lower sections of the city were used for civilian housing. They also had room for granaries, water reservoirs, barns, grazing plots and animal pens, vegetable plots and fruit trees, and stores and workshops. Nearer to the top, the second-highest terrace held the royal palace. The highest terrace held the sacred areas and the Holy Temple of Zamolxis. This was a building designed in a round shape. It was held up by eight massive stone pillars that were, astonishingly, covered with a layer of gold.

The Roman delegation was given quarters in a building close to the royal palace. There were soldiers around, but the Romans did not appear to be under guard.

The Dacian spoken by the locals was surprisingly similar to Latin. Dacians and Romans found that they could routinely communicate with each other without the use of interpreters. Dacian traders and Roman traders negotiated terms and made agreements with each other without interpreters.

Titus was surprised to discover that Sarmizegetusa had running water. A sewer system was built underneath the city. The streets were kept very clean. Much cleaner, Titus had to admit, than Rome. To be fair Rome was a very ancient and very crowded city, but even so these Dacians made a point to keep their homes and their streets orderly and clean of all refuse.

The delegates were provided with a lavish meal including a variety of Dacian dishes. Most included vegetables with poultry, lamb, or fish, spiced to enhance the flavors but not overpower the ingredients. After weeks on the road eating porridge and other bland army food, the delegates feasted.

Diegis and Buri went to visit the delegates in the evening. They were accompanied by a young man dressed in the fine clothes of a Dacian noble. Titus knew both soldiers from their previous meeting at the camp of General Julianus.

"Greetings, Lucullus, we meet again," Diegis said with a friendly grin. "Welcome to Sarmizegetusa."

"Greeting, Diegis. Hello, Buri. Every time I see you two, peace soon follows. Or so it appears."

"And that is just how I like it," Buri said, surprising the Roman. "I fight when there is fighting to be done, but I am happier looking after my orchards of apples and pears."

"Of course, Buri. And I wish you many bountiful harvests," Titus said with a smile. He liked the big Dacian but knew he would not want to face him on a battlefield.

Diegis gestured at the young noble who came with them. "This young man is Osan. He will be your guide while you are in the city. Is there any place you would like to see, Titus?"

Lucullus gave an easy laugh. "After weeks on a horse, there is nothing I would like more than a nice Roman bathhouse. Do you have any in the city?"

"Not exactly," Diegis replied, "but we do have some nice Dacian bathhouses. You will not find them much different from the ones in Rome. Osan will show you to the nearest one."

"Excellent!" Titus said. "Young man, lead the way. I shall see you gentlemen at the treaty negotiations tomorrow."

"We shall see you then, Titus."

Senator Marcus Paullus considered it wise strategy to start talks with a bit of flattery. He gave Titus Lucullus a look that said, let me handle this. He turned to face King Decebal, sitting on his throne with the High Priest Vezina and Queen Andrada sitting in chairs on either side. Marcus stood tall and pitched his voice to the smooth oratory tone that he used in Senate debates. As a child and a young man he was schooled in the fine arts of oratory, as were all male children of the Roman nobility.

"The Emperor Domitian sends greetings. He salutes the proud history and the many riches of the Dacian nation." He paused very briefly for effect. "When Alexander rode through Dacia, some four hundred years ago, he called this the land of wheat and honey. Rich fields of grain as far as the eye could see, and a beekeeper in every village. Is that not so?"

Vezina gave him a pleasant smile. "Every child in Dacia knows the story of Alexander of Macedon. And yes, the wheat grows plentiful and our bees are as busy as ever."

Paullus cleared his throat and continued.

"The soil in Italy is ideal for growing vineyards, olive trees, and fruit orchards. We do not have the rich soil for the grain harvests that you enjoy, alas. For that reason we buy grain from other nations. We wish also to buy grain from Dacia."

Decebal leaned back in his throne. "You buy grain and take grain from Egypt, Sicily, Africa, and other places. Dacia will sell grain to Rome at fair prices."

"Thank you, Your Highness," Marcus continued. "The mountains of Dacia are filled with very large resources of iron, gold, silver, tin, copper, and rock salt. Dacian gold flows to all corners of the map. We wish to buy and trade for your mineral treasures as well, of course."

Decebal gave a small nod. "Very well. But come to your main point, Senator. Other than trade, what terms does Rome seek for a treaty with Dacia?"

"These endless wars are wasteful for both our nations," Marcus explained in a strong and sincere voice. "It is the wish of Caesar to have fair and just treaties with all barbarian nations, to the mutual benefit of all."

Andrada stirred irritably in her chair. "All barbarian nations?"

"Yes, Lady, all barbarian nations," Marcus continued, somewhat confused by her question. "By that I mean all nations that are not Rome."

"We are not barbarians, Senator," Andrada said in an even tone. "Our people have lived and prospered in this land for thousands of years, long before Rome was even a village."

Vezina gave a small smile. Decebal sat back and crossed one foot over his knee. He knew what was coming, and no one would censor the Queen.

Titus Lucullus took a conciliatory tone. "We mean no offense, Queen Andrada. It is only Roman custom to refer to other nations as barbarian nations."

"I will tell you what is barbarian," Andrada said, shifting her gaze from one Roman to the other. Her tone remained even but there was iron in her voice.

"In Rome a woman is considered the property of her father or her husband. He may do with her as he wishes, give her away in marriage against her will, even kill her if he wishes. If she has wealth she may do nothing with it without the consent of a male relative or guardian. In Dacia a woman is free to marry or not marry as she wishes, to use her wealth as she wishes, and to live as she wishes. Yet you would call us barbarians?"

"That is old Roman tradition," Marcus explained. "The killing of women is infrequent and disapproved of. And truthfully, Roman women do not object to our traditions."

"Perhaps they see no other alternatives, Senator! Caged birds raised in captivity do not dream of flying in open skies while they yet live behind bars."

Marcus gave an indifferent shrug. "Perhaps."

His nonchalance fueled Andrada's temper. "In Rome children are sold as slaves, and girls and boys are used for the sexual pleasures of perverse men. In Dacia we cherish and protect our children. Yet you would call us barbarians?"

Titus' face reddened. "Such behavior is not encouraged, Lady."

"Not encouraged," she repeated, "yet accepted. It is rumored that the Emperor himself keeps a harem of women and boys."

"Yes, it is rumored," Titus conceded.

"In Rome some of your poor and your old people live in gutters and starve to death. In Dacia we care for our elders and show them a proper reverence for old age. This we have done for as long as anyone remembers. And no one in Dacia lives in gutters or starves to death. Yet you would call us barbarians?"

Marcus Paullus was offended by this unfair comment. "The public grain dole has done much to prevent starvation, Lady. The Emperor's generosity provides free grain for the people of Rome."

Andrada scoffed. "The Emperor's generosity prevents food riots from the people of Rome. And that only in years when Egypt has a good harvest."

Both men looked at her in silence. Food riots were an occasional problem. Sometimes excessive floods or droughts on the Nile led to poor grain harvests, which then resulted in hunger in Rome.

Andrada was not finished. "In Rome you persecute and kill those who worship other gods. You crucify Christians and feed them to the lions and other wild beasts in your arenas to amuse the crowds." She looked towards Matei, the Christian minister, who stood nearby. He nodded in solemn agreement.

"You kill the Christians and Jews," the Queen continued. "In Dacia we worship Zamolxis as our greatest god. But Zamolxis is neither jealous nor afraid of other gods, and he does not command us to kill their followers. Yet you call us barbarians?"

Senator Paullus bristled. "We do not kill the Jews, we tax them with the Jewish tax. If they pay the tax they can worship their Jewish god. We kill the Christians because they reject the divinity of Caesar. They follow only their god Jesus. That is considered treason and they are a menace to Rome."

"And yet," Andrada said with exasperation, "here the Christians live freely among us and do us no harm. How is it that the Emperor believes they pose a threat to the might of the Roman Empire?"

"Caesar does what is best for all his people in the Empire," Paullus replied, growing more exasperated with having to explain things to this woman. "The Christians are subversive to the authority and the rule of Rome."

Andrada gave him an icy smile. "And that, Senator, might not be a bad thing. What Rome does best is to conquer and brutalize its neighbors, then justify it as the will of the gods. Perhaps the rule of Rome should be resisted."

Marcus stiffened at this insult but made no reply. Titus Lucullus seemed stunned by the brashness of her words. No one talked this way to Roman diplomats.

Andrada paused to catch her breath. "Well, Senator, hear this now. We will not be conquered or brutalized. We have no need for your barbaric and blood-thirsty gods. We have no use for Roman law. We are doing well for ourselves, and Rome would be best served to leave

Dacia in peace so that we may rule our own lives. Put that in your treaty, Senator."

The room was completely silent. Andrada stood up from her chair, her ire vented. She gave a small bow towards the King and the High Priest, then turned and calmly walked out of the throne room.

Marcus Paullus turned to look at Decebal, who watched the Queen leave with a half-smile on his face. The King simply shrugged his shoulders in response to the Roman's questioning look.

"Queen Andrada has a mind and she speaks it freely."

"She does indeed, King Decebal," Paullus said gruffly.

"Now then," Decebal straightened his posture on the throne, "let us discuss the terms of our treaty."

Treaty negotiations were concluded in one day. King Decebal agreed to be named a client king of Rome, a title that meant friend and ally. He would take no orders from Rome and Rome had no authority on Dacian soil. Dacia would not sacrifice its independence.

Concessions were heavily in Dacia's favor. Rome would provide Dacia with engineers and other skilled craftsmen to repair and build Dacian forts and roads. Most importantly, Rome would pay Dacia eight million sesterces per year for an indefinite period of time. This was a large sum of money and one that the Roman state treasury could ill afford.

Senator Paullus agreed to King Decebal's terms because Emperor Domitian felt pressured to make peace with Dacia and pacify them as a military threat. In effect he was paying Dacia to keep the peace.

The Emperor would also receive a letter from King Decebal to take to the Senate of Rome, indicating that Decebal was now a client king of Rome. This was a legitimate letter, not a fake letter as the Emperor had used on a previous occasion. Domitian would then declare this a great victory for Caesar and for Rome. That was how diplomacy and politics worked.

Vezina and Diegis stopped by to say their farewells as the Roman delegation prepared to leave. Senator Paullus was formal and stiff, wishing only to get on his way. Titus Lucullus was more friendly.

"Farewell, young man," Vezina said. "You seem like an honest and earnest Roman."

Titus laughed. "That is intended as a compliment to me, I take it? Or is it an insult to other Romans."

Vezina smiled. "I meant the first meaning, the compliment of you. I have not known so many Romans that I can insult all Romans."

"I agree with Vezina," Diegis added. "I knew that you were an honest Roman when we spoke outside the tent of General Julianus."

"I certainly recall that memorable meeting," Titus replied. "I would advise being a bit more cautious in the future, Diegis. Some Roman commanders would have had you gutted for your insolence."

Diegis gave a careless shrug. "I only spoke the truth."

"Truth can be a dangerous thing, at times." Lucullus turned to the High Priest. "You will not remember me, but we also spoke once."

Vezina raised an eyebrow. "We did? When was that? I would have remembered."

"I was the tribune for General Julianus at Tapae. You were the spokesman for the city standing on top of the wall. I rode up to the city gate to deliver the Roman ultimatum."

"I see," Vezina said, his mind drifting back to that unhappy time. "Yes, now I remember. You were on horse, at a distance, and wearing a helmet. I could not see your face."

"Indeed. But tell me, how did you escape the siege? The city was put to the sword."

Vezina's face darkened from recalling those painful memories. It was a grim reminder of why Rome remained the enemy.

"Magic, Titus. Magic," Vezina replied. "A puff of smoke, and poof, I was gone."

Lucullus gave Diegis a puzzled look.

Diegis laughed. "I keep asking him to teach me that trick but he always refuses. Stubborn and selfish, I call it."

Lucullus picked up his pack to deposit on the baggage wagon. "Are you satisfied with the terms of the treaty?" he casually asked the two men.

"If the King is satisfied then I am satisfied," Diegis replied. "And he seems satisfied."

"Will Emperor Domitian be satisfied with the treaty?" Vezina wondered.

Lucullus eyed him cautiously. "The Emperor wishes most of all to declare victory over Dacia. He will name King Decebal as client king and declare it a victory." He should not say any more, he thought. He was dealing with a master of information and political intrigue.

"And the Roman Senate?" Vezina asked.

Titus shook his head. "You will know what the Senate thinks about the treaty better than me."

Diegis smiled. "I would wager on that."

"Farewell, gentlemen," Lucullus said, summoning for his horse. "Perhaps we shall meet again. Rome's business with Dacia is far from done."

"Farewell, Titus," Vezina replied. "And in case you should wonder, the compliment still stands. You are an honest Roman."

Chapter 18

TRAVELERS

Rome, July 89 AD

Emperor Domitian and his chief poet Marcus Martialis enjoyed their afternoon wine in the royal garden sitting on marble benches underneath a shade tree. Usually Romans mixed their wine with equal parts water, but full bodied and undiluted wine made the poet more amusing and made the Emperor forget his troubles quicker.

The Emperor was in a good mood. He enjoyed the company of his poets, Martial and Statius, and was unfailingly generous with them. The goodwill and generosity was returned tenfold. He rewarded them, and they flattered him. Domitian believed that his legacy would be remembered for many generations to come by two things. His building projects would last through the ages, and so would the epic poetry of Martial and Statius.

Martial in particular was already admired for his many books of epigrams that he started publishing five years ago. The wealthiest Romans made it a habit to invite him to dinner or to send him gifts in order to win his favor. He heaped praise on those he favored, and scorn on those he disfavored. His most important patron, naturally, was Caesar himself.

"Recite something comic for me, Marcus," Domitian requested.

"Ah!" the poet replied with a smile. "I wrote a short poem about Acerra. Would Caesar care to hear it?"

Domitian raised an eyebrow. "Yes?"

Martial stood up and recited in a solemn voice. "Whoever believes that Acerra stinks from last night's wine, is mistaken. Acerra always drinks into the daylight."

"Hah!" Domitian burst out laughing and spilled some of his wine. "Stinks from this morning's wine! That is scandalous!"

"I am gratified that Caesar finds it amusing," the poet said with a curt bow. Acerra was not a supporter of Domitian, and Martial used his wit to create scorn as well as praise. He poured himself more wine and sat down.

"I must remember that and tell it at my next meeting with the Senate," Domitian chuckled.

"I would be deeply honored, my Lord and my God, if you did so." Martial bowed again. "And how goes the Senate?"

Domitian waved his hand dismissively. "Ah, you know how that goes. There is no end to their complaints. Mostly they complain about money, but in the end they give in and comply with my demands."

"I must say that your new villa looks magnificent, Caesar. Such lavish beauty! It will last through the ages as a monument to your brilliance and your divinity."

"Few Romans have the poetic soul to appreciate artistic beauty as you do, Marcus. The Senate only complains about the wretched costs." He frowned. "As you may know, some are petitioning me to bring Domitia Longina back to Rome."

"Truly? Hmm." The poet paused a moment to reflect. "The people might be happy if she was returned from exile, Caesar."

"Oh? You think so?"

Martial gave a careless shrug. "The common people are a simple and romantic lot."

"I shall consider it," Domitian said. "She could live in the palace, but not as my wife."

Martial kept silent. The Emperor's living arrangements with his niece Julia Flavia were not a secret. It remained a sensitive subject however, particularly now that Julia was with child. Domitian cared that the public should see him as a just and virtuous man.

"There are two more poems I wish for you to write," the Emperor announced.

"I am happily at your service, Caesar."

"You will write a magnificent poem praising my victory over the traitors living in Rome. I hear grumblings that there are too many exiles and executions."

"Of course, Caesar," Martial agreed. "The punishment of traitors is Caesar's justice, and the people should understand and approve the reasons why."

"There have been many exiles and executions and there will be more. It can't be helped," Domitian said. "There are some I simply cannot trust, so I exile them and take their wealth."

"That is understandable, Caesar. It is done in the service of Rome."

Confiscating the money and properties of exiled and executed men of wealth was an important source of revenue for the Roman treasury. This was not a practice that could be stopped anytime soon.

"You mentioned a second poem for me to write, Caesar?"

"Yes, Marcus. You will write a poem about my victory over Dacia and the capitulation of the barbarian king Decebalus."

Martial beamed. "With pleasure, Caesar. I have been meaning to do just that. Does this barbarian king wear smelly furs and eat raw meat, as people say?"

"I have summoned King Decebalus to Rome, Marcus. You can see him for yourself, in person."

Sarmizegetusa, July 89 AD

King Decebal summoned his senior council. They gathered around a large table in the throne room, the High Priest Vezina and the Queen sitting on either side of the King. Diegis, Drilgisa, Sinna, and Buri joined them. Buri found himself a little perplexed but nonetheless pleased to be invited to such a high level meeting.

"Emperor Domitian of Rome," Decebal announced, "has invited King Decebal of Dacia to travel to Rome." He paused to watch the surprised reactions on their faces.

"What is the purpose of this meeting in Rome?" Diegis asked.

Vezina gave a bemused smile. "Most likely to give the Emperor an opportunity to cut King Decebal's throat."

Nobody laughed. All knew that if Domitian had that opportunity he would take it.

Decebal continue. "The official invitation is for the King of Dacia to visit Rome and there receive his crown as a client king of Rome."

"The crown is only symbolic," Vezina explained, "but we should accept the invitation for purely diplomatic reasons."

Drilgisa was indignant. "What rubbish! You can't go to Rome!"

"Of course the King is not going to Rome," Andrada said. "They would have him arrested and thrown to the lions. Decebal is still a threat to Rome."

"Then who is going?" Diegis wanted to know.

Decebal gave him a grin. "You are going, Brother. You will be my envoy to Rome and will receive the crown from Domitian."

"Me?" Diegis was not pleased. "But I am to be married soon."

"The wedding will wait until you return. You are my brother and a prince of Dacia. That makes you the best representative."

"Anyone of lesser stature would be regarded as an insult to Rome," Vezina added. "That would be poor diplomacy."

Diegis leaned back in his chair in resignation, knowing that they were right. It was his duty as a member of the Dacian royal family to obey his king and serve the nation. He had to travel to Rome.

Andrada gave him a sympathetic smile. "I'm sure that Mirela will wait for you a few months longer. She understands royal duty."

"Yes, I will go," Diegis conceded. "As you command, My King."

"Good," Decebal proclaimed. "But you will not go alone. That is why I invited all of you here."

Now he had their full attention.

"Drilgisa, you will lead the diplomatic party as the senior man in the delegation. You are familiar with both the city and with Roman customs. Also you will discourage any acts of aggression against my brother."

For an instant a look of anger flashed across Drilgisa's eyes, then quickly faded. His anger was not triggered by Decebal but rather by his memories of Rome. He grew up as a slave in Rome until the age of twelve, when he was purchased out of slavery by a visiting Dacian trader. This man took him back to Dacia and raised him as part of his family. Drilgisa grew to love Dacia but he never forgot Rome.

"Yes, Sire," he replied, his voice even. "I will keep an eye on young Diegis here and make sure he stays out of trouble."

"Excellent," Vezina said. "You will be his guide as needed and a very able bodyguard."

Decebal noticed Buri looking at him intensely. "Yes, Buri, you also will make the trip. You will discourage trouble, but more importantly you will be the treasurer and carry the gold needed for expenses. Also, my friend, consider this a reward for your many years of service. It will be to your benefit to see the world."

"Yes, Sire," Buri said. "Thank you. The gold will be safe with me."

"I have one more suggestion, Sire," Vezina spoke up.

"Yes, Your Holiness?"

"It would be wise to also send a priest of Zamolxis to Rome."

Decebal considered the notion. "You are right, that is a good idea," he decided. "But that priest cannot be you, Vezina."

"No," Vezina smiled ruefully. "Not me. Zamolxis travelled the world as a young man and learned the knowledge of the world, but that is not my destiny. And besides, I am getting too old for such a long journey."

"Who, then?" Andrada asked.

"One of my younger priests. He comes from a noble family, and Diegis knows him. You are the same age and grew up together. His name is Mircea."

"Mircea?" Diegis asked, furrowing his brow. "Yes I know him, but not well. He trained to be a priest and I trained to be a soldier so we did not have much in common. He seems like a good man."

"He is a good man, and he has a good mind for diplomacy. He will represent Dacia well."

"So be it, then," Decebal concluded. "Diegis, Drilgisa, Buri, and Mircea. And you will need an escort. General Sinna?"

Sinna, the commander of cavalry, addressed the travelers. "You will take an escort of twenty cavalry. I will hand pick the men myself."

"Are we riding to Rome, then?" Diegis asked.

Decebal nodded to Vezina. The High Priest pulled out a map scroll from a sleeve pocket in his robes. Diegis and Drilgisa gathered around him for a look at the map.

"The travel route has been planned for you," Vezina said. "Half the trip will be by river, because it is faster, and half by horse. You will carry enough gold to pay for expenses and to purchase horses as you need them."

"Make preparations," Decebal told them. "You leave within the week. I want you back in Sarmizegetusa before the weather turns cold. And Diegis, you can rest easy that we will make all preparations for your wedding while you are gone. Just take care of this business in Rome."

The priest Mircea was a somewhat stocky man with short, wispy black hair and gray eyes. Dressed in his blue and silver priestly robes he looked like a younger, shorter, plumper version of Vezina. He did not have the confidence or poise of the High Priest but that was to be expected. Vezina had decades of learning and experience.

Even though they were the same age, Mircea had little in common with Diegis. They grew up with different interests, different friends, and very different types of training. Mircea was born into a wealthy family, but Diegis was born into a royal family with very different levels of expectations and responsibilities. Beyond that they were men of different character. Mircea was a diplomat, whereas Diegis was a warrior.

The priest was respectful and deferential towards his travelling companions. He seemed to be most comfortable with Buri. The big man had a natural curiosity about religious and scientific matters, and had ample time for long conversations with Mircea. On dark nights with a clear sky they studied the stars and Buri received an education in astronomy. Drilgisa on the other hand did not have much patience for priests. He spent his time with the cavalry troops and with Diegis.

The Dacian diplomatic party and their military escort travelled south across the Ister, then hired boats to travel further south on the Timis River. The land was flat, green, and fertile all along the Timis River valley. The river teemed with fish, which provided fast and easy meals roasted on a stick when they rested for the night. On the shores were flocks of geese, mallards, herons, and other water birds of all kinds.

"So much fertile land," Mircea observed as he watched the passing shoreline from the river boat. They were travelling south through Banat. "Why don't the Romans settle here, instead of coveting Dacia?"

Diegis was in a relaxed mood. "They don't want Dacia's land, Mircea. They want Dacia's women and children, and Dacia's gold."

"Yes, you are right," Drilgisa said. "They want slaves for the slave markets, but most of all they want Dacia's gold. The Romans are greedy bastards."

"A pox on them all," Buri growled. "They can't have our women or children, or our gold."

Diegis shook his head. "They won't have them, Buri. They attacked us twice with large armies and failed. Now we are invited to Rome to make peace." He turned to Drilgisa. "What should we expect when we reach Rome?"

Drilgisa spat over the side of the boat. "A smell such as you never smelled before."

Mircea gave him a funny, questioning look.

"That is not an insult, priest, it is simply a fact. You cannot know what a million people smell like crowded into one city until you go there. Most live in tall and crowded apartment buildings. They are built very close together and don't allow much of a breeze to flow through."

"But they have sewers, I hear," Mircea pointed out.

"Yes they have sewers, but the sewers do not cover the entire city. In the poor areas people throw their buckets of wastes into the street. Be careful where you step."

Buri looked doubtful. "I have pig pens at home. The smell won't bother me."

"We will be state guests of the Emperor and the Senate of Rome," Diegis said. "They will provide us with suitable accommodations, I am sure."

"And if they don't we'll pay for our own," Drilgisa said with a glance at Buri. Underneath his white woolen shirt and vest Buri wore a large leather money belt stuffed with Dacian gold coins. Dacian gold was highly valued because coins were minted with pure gold, not diluted with other metals. It would pay for horses, food, supplies, lodging, and anything else they might need.

They watched the land slowly drift by and prepared for many days of the same. None of them had ever made such a long trip before.

Rome, September 89 AD

Titus Lucullus always approached the Emperor's large and luxurious villa outside Rome with a feeling of unease. The villa was a palace, more richly appointed than the royal palace in the city. Domitian wanted an extravagant display of luxury and he got his wish. It was all built at state expense, of course, which earned him a great deal of resentment and hostility in the Senate. He was much better liked by the common people, who enjoyed the frequent gladiatorial games and chariot races that the Emperor provided for them.

Titus rode through the heavily guarded front gates to the main residence. He dismounted and handed the reins to a stable boy. Two Praetorian Guards in full armor led him inside the Emperor's waiting room. The room was filled with very fine statuary, and rich paintings covered the walls.

After a short wait he was led to Domitian's reception room. The Emperor sat on a couch, talking with Marcus Paullus and two other senators. Paullus saw Titus approaching and gave him a sour look. The two other senators bid farewell to the Emperor and walked out, barely acknowledging Titus' presence. Whatever Paullus might have said about him was likely not complimentary.

"Hail, Caesar!" Lucullus saluted smartly. He nodded a greeting to Marcus.

"Report," Domitian ordered. "What news of the travelling Dacian delegation?"

"Their party is approaching on the Via Flaminia, Caesar. They should arrive in Rome within a day."

"They are travelling with cavalry, I hear?" Domitian asked.

"An escort of twenty cavalry, Caesar," Lucullus said evenly. "They wish to discourage any trouble, I assume. After all they are escorting the brother of King Decebalus."

"I see," Domitian nodded. "These twenty cavalry will be stabled well outside the city walls."

"Yes, Caesar. Of course."

Paullus cut in. "They bring a priest with them?"

"Yes, Senator. Not Vezina, but one of his assistants. I am told his name is Mircea."

"And what does this heretical priest want in Rome?" The Emperor challenged. Any priest who did not worship the Roman gods was by definition a heretical priest.

"I do not know, Caesar."

"Spying for Vezina, most likely," Paullus sneered.

The Emperor frowned. He was by nature suspicious and Marcus Paullus knew how to feed that.

"Lucullus, you will personally escort these Dacians when they are in Rome."

"Yes, Caesar."

"You will keep an eye on this priest Mircea. If you see him spying, or plotting with any members of the Senate, arrest him."

"As you command, Caesar."

"This brother, Diegis," Domitian continued. "What is he like? I am told by Marcus that he did not have a strong voice when you two were negotiating our treaty in Sarmizegetusa."

Titus thought for a moment. "He is a general of infantry, Caesar. He is no diplomat. The only reason he is here is because he is the brother of Decebalus."

"He is a stooge," Paullus snorted.

"A pity the Queen did not come to Rome," Domitian said. "If she is as fierce as Marcus describes I would like to see her in the gladiator games."

"Alas, Caesar!" Marcus laughed.

"While the Dacians are in Rome, you two are my spies," Domitian instructed. "I want to know what they do, where they go, and who they see. Am I clear?"

"Perfectly clear, Caesar," Titus acknowledged.

"As you command, Caesar," Paullus replied with a bow.

Chapter 19

WHEN IN ROME

Rome, September 89 AD

*T*itus Lucullus met the Dacian delegation outside the city gate used by travelers from the northern provinces, the Porta Flaminia. He explained to them that the four main diplomats would be housed in a quality inn in the heart of the city. The twenty cavalry escorts, along with their horses and baggage wagons, would be quartered outside the city. This was the policy for all visitors to Rome, including royal visitors.

They entered through the city gate and walked south on the Via Flaminia, past the Field of Mars, into the heart of the city. Lucullus got the four delegates settled at their inn, then took pride in being their guide. He took them on a long and winding tour, pointing out the major historical sites in this, his city, the greatest city in the world.

"Rome is built on seven hills, gentlemen," he informed them. "In the valleys between the hills are the major roads, such as the one we are walking now, the Via Sacra."

"This is where the big parades go when Rome gives a triumph for an Emperor or a very distinguished general," Drilgisa added.

"Yes, you are right," Titus said. "Julius Caesar marched through here. Augustus Caesar marched through here."

"The Emperor Domitian marched through here," Drilgisa said, keeping a straight face.

"Yes he did," Titus said. He paused briefly, then added, "and will march again."

Buri turned to Drilgisa. "The smell isn't so bad once you get used to it."

"Wait until we get to the Subura, Buri. That's where the common folk live."

"There will be no cause to visit the Subura, gentlemen," Lucullus told them. "You will see the finest places in Rome, with me as your guide. You will dine at the house of Senator Marcus Paullus on the Palatine Hill, the finest neighborhood in Rome. You will be received by Emperor Domitian in the royal palace."

"Thank you, Titus," Mircea said with sincere appreciation. "This will be an education for us all."

Drilgisa grinned. "Perhaps you would like an education in one of Rome's brothels, Mircea?" The priest did not respond to the teasing, which only encouraged Drilgisa to continue. "There certainly are many to choose from. How many are there now, Titus? A hundred?"

"That, or more if you include the unofficial ones not licensed by Caesar," Lucullus replied evenly.

Mircea looked shocked. "Surely, one hundred brothels? Why does the Emperor allow such dens of immorality?"

Titus turned and patiently addressed him as if he spoke to a child. "Rome's brothels are not dens of immorality. They are a major source of tax revenue. Were the Emperor to close them, the state treasury would lose a great deal of money from taxes that were not collected from the brothels."

Diegis laughed easily. "There is part of your education about Rome, Mircea!"

The young priest remained silent. They approached a very large and magnificent stone arch that shined in the bright sunlight.

"This," Lucullus gestured up, "is the Arch of Titus. It was built of course by the Emperor Domitian to honor his brother the Emperor Titus. It celebrates the victory of Titus in conquering Jerusalem after the Jewish rebellion in Judea."

"It is very impressive," Diegis admitted. "Perhaps we should build one for King Decebal when we return to Dacia."

"Perhaps you should, you seem to have no shortage of marble," Lucullus allowed. "Over there, gentlemen, that circular temple is the Temple of Venus. This is where the Vestal Virgins keep the eternal flame of Rome burning. It is the sacred fire of Vesta and represents the life of Rome."

"I like this tradition better than the one hundred brothels," Mircea announced with a smile.

"Ah, now you are learning, priest," Drilgisa said. "Rome is a city of everything. It has everything you would want, and also everything you would not want."

Titus seemed pleased with the comment. "That is precisely true, General, from a philosophical perspective."

"It is also true from a practical perspective, Titus."

They came to a very large open space that was ringed all around by magnificent temples and marble faced public buildings.

Titus looked at it with pride. "This, gentlemen, is - "

"The Forum," Drilgisa cut in. He gestured to the left. "And in this direction is the Temple of Julius Caesar. You will surely be impressed by the very high, magnificent marble pillars with the statues of the Roman gods on top." He paused to let them take in the view, smiling because Buri was looking up at the highest pillar with his mouth slightly open. "The statue on the highest pillar is, of course, Jupiter. That raised platform in front of the temple is called the rostra. It is used for giving public speeches and for debates."

Lucullus looked at him, surprised. "You have visited Rome before, General Drilgisa?"

"I grew up here," Drilgisa replied, then walked ahead to end the conversation.

Titus looked at Diegis questioningly but got no answer. Buri and the priest Mircea seemed captivated by all the wonders surrounding them. Time to get his guests back to the inn, he decided. Rome was simply too big to be explored in one day.

The itinerary for the Dacian delegation on the second day called for them to be dinner guests at the house of Senator Marcus Paullus. The ceremony with Emperor Domitian, where the crown of the client king would be presented to Diegis, would occur on the third day. They would depart Rome a few days later.

On the way to their dinner engagement at the house of Paullus the Dacians took a tour through the Forum and its surroundings. Here they viewed some of the major sites in Rome. The temple of Jupiter Optimus Maximus left them in awe of its size and splendor. It made the Temple of Zamolxis in Sarmizegetusa look small by comparison.

Just outside the Curia, or Senate House, Diegis noticed that the crowd avoided a spot in the street that was paved with black marble. People walked around it, reverently, and went on their way.

"This spot," Titus Lucullus told them, "is a very ancient and very sacred location in Rome. It is called the Black Stone."

"Why is it sacred?" Buri asked curiously.

Titus turned to Drilgisa. "Do you wish to tell him?"

Drilgisa stared down at the street for a moment. He had not seen the Black Stone since he was a boy. Like all Roman children however he learned the story of the Black Stone at an early age.

"At this very spot, Buri, in ancient times, King Romulus vanished during a thunderstorm and was never seen again. Some people say that he turned into a god and flew away. Others say he was murdered here by those who were jealous of his power."

"King Romulus?" Buri asked. "Wasn't he one of the twins raised by a wolf?"

"He was," Titus explained. "He killed his twin brother Remus and became the first king of Rome."

"Roman kings appear to make a habit of killing their brothers," Diegis said wryly. "Luckily for me I am a Dacian."

Titus ignored the bait. Making jokes about the death of Emperor Titus, and the rumors of Domitian's involvement in it, cost men their heads.

"Come, follow me," Titus said. "The house of Senator Paullus is this way."

The house of Senator Marcus Paullus was a large mansion in one of the most exclusive neighborhoods in Rome. Only the wealthiest of the nobility lived here. Emperors built their mansions here. Paullus was one of the very oldest and noblest Roman families.

The Dacian party was greeted in the atrium by multiple servants who were superbly attentive to their every need. The servants were highly trained to follow every rule of etiquette to perfection. A failure on their part to follow even the most minor rule reflected badly on their master and earned them a whipping.

After wine and conversation in the library the guests were guided to a large dining room. The correct form for a Roman dinner party was nine people and three couches on which to recline. It made the dinner intimate enough but also lively. Besides the four Dacians and Titus Lucullus, Paullus had also invited two of his fellow senators, Publius Albinus and Catalus Bibulus. His wife Marcia also joined the dinner party.

Seating was assigned according to status. Diegis was seated on the right side of Paullus' couch, the place of honor. Drilgisa and Titus were seated with Senator Bibulus on the second couch. Mircea and Buri were seated with Senator Albinus on the third.

Marcus Paullus clapped his hands once and the servants brought in the first dish. The food was placed on low tables arranged in front of the couches on which the guests lounged comfortably.

"Lentil soup!" Marcia exclaimed to Diegis, who was seated next to her. "Rome adores it. We could not exist without it." She was a very pleasant, elegantly dressed, elegantly made up lady of the nobility.

"We like it in Dacia as well, Lady," Diegis replied with a pleasant smile. The soup was thick and delicious, flavored with subtle spices and warmed to just the right temperature. A harpist took her place on one side of the room and played soothing music to aid digestion.

The second course was a variety of seafood. Buri looked at it with suspicion because the fish and eels were prepared in sauces he had never seen before.

"Ah, the fish is safe!" Senator Albinus assured him. He was a gray haired man in his sixties with, it seemed, a perpetual twinkle in his eye. "Do try it, I'm certain you will enjoy it."

"Safe?" Buri asked, not sounding comforted.

"Safe indeed," Marcus Paullus interjected. "There is only one strict rule about fish in Rome, and it is never broken in my house." He paused, silently inviting his guests to inquire.

Diegis obliged him. "And what rule is that?"

"Never eat anything caught in the Tiber!" Publius Albinus said with a chuckle. Bibulus and Paullus joined in the laughter, and even Titus Lucullus cracked a smile.

Buri wondered why that was the case about the fish in the Tiber, but considered it wiser not to ask. He helped himself to some fish in a green sauce that was indeed very tasty. The meat course came next, hams and sausages served with roasted vegetables, and that was more to his liking. There was a dish with some kind of large bird legs that looked peculiar to him.

Marcia saw the puzzled look on Buri's face. She caught his eye and explained. "That is leg of ostrich boiled in sea water until very tender, then served in a mild pepper sauce. Do try some, it is very good."

Buri nodded pleasantly to acknowledge her explanation. No one in the Dacian party seemed interested in this exotic dish. Titus had no such reservations and eagerly helped himself to a bird leg.

Paullus noticed that none of his Dacian guests was drinking wine with their dinner. By Roman standards that was considered almost scandalous. "My friends, we have a selection of the very best wines. Falernian grapes from the slopes of Mount Falernus make red wine like nectar of the gods. We also have Picine, Sabine, Tiburtine, if you would like to sample?"

Mircea paused to take a sip of cool water from a silver goblet. "In truth, Senator, in Dacia we drink wine sparingly."

That took Marcia by surprise. "Oh, how sad! A good wine is quite essential for a good meal. Is that not so, Marcus?"

"Indeed so, my dear," Paullus agreed.

"Why, a meal without wine is positively uncivilized," Senator Bibulus declared. He was a portly man in his early forties. His florid cheeks and nose testified to his love for good wine of all varieties.

"Zamolxis discouraged its drinking when he walked the Earth," Mircea continued. "He preached that wine dulls men's senses."

"Nonsense!" Albinus protested. "Wine enhances men's senses."

"We do not prohibit wine drinking in Dacia," Diegis explained. "We simply discourage overindulgence."

Drilgisa turned to a servant standing nearby. "I will have some of the Falernian."

"At once, sir. Do you prefer it with cold or hot water?"

"Neither," Drilgisa replied. "I drink my wine undiluted."

"Oh, ho!" Senator Paullus cried enthusiastically. "Here is a man who lives life recklessly!"

"Not at all, Senator," Drilgisa smiled. "I simply like the taste of good wine and do not wish to diminish it." He took the goblet of wine the servant placed before him and heartily drained half of it. "This is excellent!"

"What have you seen in Rome thus far?" Paullus asked his guests. As the host it was his duty to spark conversation.

"On the walk here we saw the sacred Black Stone," Mircea said. "Its origin is quite intriguing."

"It is sacred indeed," Albinus joined in. "King Romulus became a god on that very spot."

"He vanished during a thunderstorm, they say," Mircea wondered. "Was he struck by lightning?"

"No one knows for certain," Senator Albinus replied. "It was very dark. One moment King Romulus was there, and the next moment he was not."

"This happened in the daytime," Marcus Paullus explained, "but it became very dark because a dark cloud descended and covered the King. When the cloud lifted, Romulus was gone. It is most likely that he ascended to heaven to join his divine father, the god Mars."

Mircea shuddered. "That was a very bad omen for Rome, then."

"How so?" Titus wondered. "Romans view it as a divine moment when Romulus became a god."

"Dacians do not fear death," Diegis began, "because our souls are immortal. The only thing we fear is the anger of the gods. The gods' anger is expressed by dark clouds, stormy weather, and lightning."

"How interesting," Marcia said. "The gods express themselves in mysterious ways. So you fear lightning, then?"

Drilgisa shook his head. "We do not fear lightning, Lady, but what it represents. It is a message from the gods that they are unhappy with us."

"It is considered a very bad omen," Mircea added. "Wars have been stopped due to such bad omens. Treaties have been rejected."

Marcus Paullus laughed at this barbarian nonsense. "Well then, thanks be to Mars that Romans always fight in fine weather, eh? We would never get anything done otherwise!"

"Battles are won or lost in all types of weather," Drilgisa replied drily. "As we have learned in the past few years in our wars with Rome."

"Indeed," Senator Bibulus said, and gave a very hearty belch.

Before dessert was served two female dancers entered the room to entertain the guests. They wore thin green and blue robes made from a translucent material that did little to hide their lithe figures. The dance was slow paced and beautifully choreographed for the role each of them played.

Dessert came in the form of honeyed mushrooms and a variety of cakes. Small cups with a thick, syrupy liquid were brought out. One of the cups was placed before each diner.

"You must try my special dessert wine, my friends!" Paullus told them with enthusiasm.

Senator Albinus raised an eyebrow. "What's in it, Marcus?"

"A sweet invention," Paullus replied. "Two parts honey, five parts wine, spiced with peppercorns and a dash of saffron. Try it!"

Diegis raised the cup to his lips and took a small sip. The drink was very sweet, sweeter than anything he had ever tasted. Mircea seemed to be enjoying his cup, sipping slowly. Drilgisa did not touch his, but signaled to a slave attendant to refill his wine goblet.

Senator Bibulus, on his second helping of honeyed mushrooms, suddenly made a gurgling sound. He signaled to a servant. The man calmly walked over and helped the senator to his feet, then guided Bibulus through a door that led to a patio. None of the Romans in the room appeared to be the least concerned.

Buri caught Titus Lucullus' eye. "Is he sick?"

Titus said nothing but gave a very small shake of his head. Buri's question was soon answered by the sound of retching from outside on the patio. That made Marcus Paullus look up and look around at his guests.

"Does anyone else wish to relieve themselves?" Paullus asked. "A servant will be happy to assist you."

Buri suddenly looked ill. The retching sounds from the patio made him uncomfortable. Drilgisa grinned at him.

"It is the custom here, Buri. When one eats and drinks too much, one relieves himself in the vomitorium. Then he eats and drinks some more."

"Yes," Paullus said, concerned about Buri's discomfort. "Do you wish to have a slave assist you?" he asked, gesturing helpfully towards the patio.

"No," Buri replied gruffly.

Senator Bibulus returned, resumed his seat with a polite smile, and resumed his drinking. "This is an excellent dessert wine, Marcus. I must teach my cook to make it for me."

Diegis put down his wine goblet and addressed their hosts. "We thank you for the food and for your kindness. However, we must leave now. Tomorrow we meet with Emperor Domitian."

"Caesar looks forward to seeing you," Paullus said, ever diplomatic even though he knew that it was not true. "He is eager to formalize our treaty and declare King Decebalus a client king of Rome."

The Dacian delegation smiled politely and took their leave.

Chapter 20

THE EMPEROR'S GAMES

Rome, September 89 AD

Conducting state business in his palace was convenient and much more pleasant than visiting the Senate House. On a fine, sunny day like today Domitian preferred to conduct business outdoors in his gardens. The palace garden was so large it was difficult to see from one end to the other. It was landscaped throughout with trees, flower beds, and fountains. Beautiful statuary decorated every path. Marble columns circled the outer perimeter of the garden.

The Senate of Rome was summoned to this state ceremony, along with important members of the Roman nobility and supporters of Emperor Domitian. Chairs were arranged in neat rows on the grass for the attendants' comfort. Domitian stood before the group in a toga that was bleached to a dazzling white. He was flanked by ten Praetorian Guards wearing armor shined to a very bright finish.

The Dacian delegation was seated to the side, separate from the Senate and the Roman nobility. For this occasion they were dressed in traditional Dacian clothing. White woolen shirts, tight woolen trousers with a leather belt, and shoes made from soft leather or deerskin. Diegis and Mircea wore the pilati on their heads, the lambs fur cap dyed black that was the symbol of Dacian nobility. Drilgisa and Buri were not nobility so they went bareheaded.

The Emperor Domitian addressed his talk to the Roman crowd, not the visitors. He described the two wars fought against Dacia and the victories won by General Cornelius Fuscus and General Tettius Julianus. These victories, as he described them, were directed by the Emperor himself. Every good thing that happened was planned and inspired by Caesar.

"Under the command of Caesar, who travelled to Moesia to lead the army in the tradition of Julius Caesar and Augustus Caesar," the Emperor lectured his audience, "General Cornelius Fuscus drove the Dacians out of Moesia and Banat."

His audience listened politely, including even Domitian's critics. Fuscus was well known to the nobility and had been well liked and respected for his long service to Rome.

Domitian continued. "The barbarians were routed! We drove them across the Danubius River back to Dacia. To this day, conscript fathers, the Dacians have not held another fort on Roman territory. Nor will they ever build another fort on our land again!" Domitian paused, smiled, and basked in the applause of his supporters.

"Obeying my orders, General Tettius Julianus won a great victory over the Dacians at Tapae. He trounced the Dacians on Dacian soil! During the sack of Tapae he put the city to the sword. That is the just and deserved fate for any barbarian nation that opposes the will of Rome!" Domitian shouted.

Diegis tensed, his face grim. It made his blood boil to remember the massacre of the civilians of Tapae. He took a sideways glance at Drilgisa, and to his great surprise saw that this fierce Dacian warrior looked relaxed and even amused. Drilgisa noticed Diegis looking at him. He gave him a casual smile and a wink.

Diegis understood and willed himself to calm down. This was a purely political speech intended to glorify the Emperor, and nothing more. Everyone in the crowd seemed to understand this. Domitian's supporters seated in the front rows looked pleased to acknowledge the greatness of Caesar, or at least they played the part. The other senators sat politely and quietly, not wishing to draw attention to themselves. Domitian would sing his own praises, they would have some wine and food, and this farce would be over.

The Dacians were there to also play their roles, which was to be polite and dutifully listen. They were only props in this performance. Drilgisa was barely paying attention. Buri found it more interesting to look around and admire the beautiful landscaping in the garden. Mircea watched the faces in the Roman crowd and tried to judge their political affiliations. Diegis, calmer now, waited patiently to be summoned to play his role in this pageant.

Domitian was nearing the end of his speech. "Decebalus, King of Dacia, now petitions Rome for a peace treaty. He understands with barbarian cunning, conscript fathers, that opposing Rome will lead to his destruction and the destruction of Dacia. He gives Rome solemn vows that he will cease all hostile actions towards Rome and the allies of Rome. He bends his overly proud neck and vows to serve as a client king of Rome."

The Emperor's supporters cheered to show their approval. After a short while Domitian raised his hand to silence them.

"Rome will grant this treaty to King Decebalus and Dacia. It is not Rome's wish to destroy Dacia, but rather to pacify Dacia. As Rome has pacified Britannia," the Emperor looked sternly at the crowd in the back, daring anyone to contradict him, "so we shall pacify Dacia."

No one challenged him. Caesar was Rome, and Rome was Caesar. Whatever Caesar wished for became law.

"King Decebalus is ill and feeble and could not make the journey to Rome himself to accept his crown as client king of Rome, so he sends his brother instead." Domitian gestured towards the Dacian delegation carelessly.

"Perhaps he is too afraid to come himself!" one of the Emperor's supporters shouted, which brought laugher from those around him.

The Emperor smiled at the man. It was a good note on which to end his speech. He turned and motioned to Titus Lucullus, who was standing with the Dacians.

Lucullus nodded to Diegis, and together they walked to the front of the audience to stand before the Emperor.

"Hail Caesar!" Titus greeted the Emperor in a loud voice and gave him the Roman salute. "I present before you Diegis, brother of King Decebalus of Dacia!"

Diegis gave him a small, formal bow. Domitian looked him up and down. He looked curiously at the lambs fur pilati, dyed black, unique to the Dacians. This man did not look impressive for a noble, not as regal in his appearance as a Roman nobleman in a proper toga.

"You will kneel before Caesar," Domitian informed him.

Diegis hesitated. Dacians did not kneel to anyone. Dacian nobility in particular did not kneel.

"You must kneel before Caesar," Lucullus addressed him in a low voice. When Diegis hesitated he reluctantly added, "It is necessary diplomatic protocol."

Not wishing to be undiplomatic, Diegis went down on his left knee. One knee would be good enough.

The Emperor smirked. He turned and gestured to a servant, who brought a silver tray upon which rested a thin headband made of gold. Domitian lifted the headband with both hands and held it up for his audience.

"Diegis, brother of Decebalus of Dacia! You humbly accept this golden diadem on behalf of the King of Dacia. King Decebalus will wear this crown to show his status as client king to Rome and to demonstrate his loyalty to Rome for all people to see!"

Domitian leaned down and gave the diadem to the Dacian. Diegis took it without a word. The ceremony was the message, words from him were not necessary.

"You may stand," Domitian told him.

Diegis stood up, gave the Emperor another small bow, and turned to walk back to the Dacian delegation. Titus Lucullus walked formally and stiffly by his side. Diegis held back the urge to laugh. He made this long trip to serve as a prop for one minute in Domitian's political show for the Senate.

The other Dacians were silent. Buri was irritated because he also considered it a waste of their time. Drilgisa gave Diegis an amused look, as if to say, what else did you expect?

"Now we stay for refreshments," Titus told them. He could not help but notice their sour mood. "Be friendly and polite, please. This is the Emperor's reception."

Servants streamed in carrying trays of drinks and light food. The senators and other guests gathered in small groups to talk. They all knew each other well and had no shortage of political and personal topics for discussion. The matter of Dacia was an unhappy subject and best left aside.

Diegis held up the slim golden headband. "Get me a sack for this, Titus?"

Lucullus gave him a look that pleaded for caution, hoping no one overheard them. "I will get you a box for it lined with silk. It is a royal gift and must be treated respectfully."

Drilgisa took a goblet of wine from a passing tray. "Give me a thick gold crown with jewels, and I'll treat it respectfully."

Mircea looked at the crowd of people milling around. "We should talk to some of the senators. The King and Vezina would no doubt like to hear what they have to say."

Lucullus turned to him with a look of alarm. "No, Mircea, that would be unwise. Who you talk to and what you say may very well put you in danger."

Mircea looked startled, but then understood. He gave Titus a nod of appreciation for the warning.

A servant approached and bowed respectfully. "Caesar wishes to speak with the Dacian delegation."

"Certainly," Diegis replied, and motioned to the others to follow the man.

Domitian was talking with a small group of supporters including Marcus Paullus and the court poets Martial and Statius. The poets were there to commemorate Caesar's diplomatic triumph. Martial said something that made the group laugh.

The Emperor turned to face his Dacian guests. "Are you enjoying your stay in Rome?" he asked, being polite.

"We are, Caesar," Diegis replied, also politely.

"It is enlightening, Caesar," Mircea added, and sincerely meant it. "Rome is very rich in culture and history."

"Indeed it is," Domitian agreed. "And we are making history at this very moment. Isn't that so, Statius?"

"Yes, Caesar," the poet agreed. "I am composing a paean to this occasion even as we speak."

Martial gestured to Diegis. "Your name, Diegis of Dacia, will be recorded for posterity along with the divine Caesar."

"How exciting," Diegis replied mildly.

"Have you been to the Colosseum?" Domitian asked.

"No, Caesar, they have not," Lucullus answered for them.

"Ah!" Domitian exclaimed, finally showing a spark of interest. "Tomorrow is the first day of my games. You must come!"

Diegis gave another small formal bow. "We would be honored to attend, Caesar. Who can visit Rome without seeing the Colosseum?"

Diegis glanced at Drilgisa to get confirmation. He was shocked to see that Drilgisa seemed in a daze, staring into the distance. He was still as a statue and oblivious to the conversation around him. He was looking at a group of three senators talking some distance away.

"We will see the games tomorrow, certainly," Diegis said. "Now if Caesar will excuse us we should say our farewell."

"Very well," Domitian said, and looked back to his poets.

Diegis turned to go and took Drilgisa by the upper arm to lead him away. Drilgisa snapped out of his trance and followed him. Titus Lucullus also noticed the unusual behavior but diplomatically did not say anything.

After walking to a comfortable distance where they could talk without being overheard, Diegis stopped. Very discreetly he directed Drilgisa's attention to the group of three senators who were still standing together and talking.

"Who are those men?" Diegis asked.

Drilgisa's face was tense. He gave a small dismissive shrug.

"I know one of them, and he is a very famous man," Lucullus said. "That distinguished looking elderly man, the tall and thin one, is Marcus Ciocceius Nerva. He is the leader of the Senate."

That got Mircea's attention. He turned to Titus. "I wonder, might it be possible to have a word?"

"No!" Lucullus said emphatically. "You must not approach him."

Diegis ignored them and turned back to Drilgisa. "Do you know Senator Nerva?"

"No," Drilgisa answered in an even tone.

Diegis knew his questions would go nowhere. He took one last glance at the Emperor, still basking in the attention of his admirers, then turned and headed for the exits. The others followed quietly.

Drilgisa was honest in admitting that he did not know Senator Marcus Nerva. What he could not say was that he knew one of the other men talking to Nerva. A middle-aged, stocky man of medium height, wearing the white toga with the broad red stripe of a Senator of Rome. A man with thinning blond hair and green eyes, slightly narrowed like cat's eyes. A man he had last seen when he was twelve years old.

The day of the Emperor's Games was another fine, sunny day. That was considered a good omen for the success of the games. Lucullus arrived at the inn in early morning to escort the Dacian guests to the Colosseum. It was an experience that most visitors to Rome looked forward to with eager anticipation.

Diegis, Buri, and Mircea walked out the inn door to meet their Roman guide. Mircea in particular looked excited to see the stadium, Rome's most famous structure.

"Where is General Drilgisa?" Titus asked.

Diegis shook his head. "He is not coming. He says that he saw the Colosseum before. And besides, he ate some bad food last night that disagrees with him this morning."

"That is unfortunate," Titus said, disappointed.

"Lead the way, Titus," Diegis gestured down the street. "Perhaps Drilgisa will join us later."

The way to the Colosseum was easy to find because all the crowds were going in that direction. It was a very impressive structure even from a distance, and grew even more impressive as one approached. The largest amphitheater in the world was started by the Emperor Vespasian, completed by his son Emperor Titus, and made a marvel of games and spectacles by Vespasian's youngest son Domitian. It was rightfully recognized as the pride of the Flavian dynasty.

Standing in front of the Colosseum was the largest statue in the world. This was the Colossus, a giant bronze statue of the sun god built by the Emperor Nero. The local people were used to seeing it, but visitors to the city invariably stood and gaped.

"This way to the better seats," Titus Lucullus instructed. "Nobles sit in front, the plebs sit in the back and in the higher seats. You are guests of Caesar so you will sit in the best seats."

Buri laughed. "Never been treated like nobility before. There is a first time for everything, eh?"

Mircea looked around at the crowds, feeling slightly disoriented. "There are so many entrances. How do people know where to go?"

"There are eighty different entrances," Titus explained. "People know where they belong."

They made their way to a row of seats not far from the stadium floor. The Emperor's box was higher up but not far away. More people crowded in. Vendors sold food on a stick.

Diegis looked up into the stands. "If all these people could fight they would give you about ten new legions," he joked to Lucullus.

Titus nodded. "You have a good eye, General. There are some fifty thousand Romans here, so yes about nine or ten legions." He paused and smiled. "If they were all gladiators they would be fearsome, which of course they are not."

"When do we see the gladiators?" Buri asked.

"Not until the afternoon," Titus said. "The morning is for beast fights and hunts. At noon there are executions of condemned men, criminals and traitors."

"What kinds of criminals?" Mircea wondered.

"All types," Lucullus replied. "Murderers. Heretics."

A trap door in the arena floor opened. A winching device below the surface brought up a platform on which stood a strange horse like creature, about the size of a pony, with large black and white stripes on its body.

"That is a zebra," Titus told them. "It comes from Africa."

The skittish animal walked around in a circle, looking for escape routes but finding none. It gave up and stood still, looking at the people in the stands who were shouting and yelling for what they wanted to see happen. Two more trap doors opened and another two platforms came up slowly. A lion stood on each platform, restless and impatient. As soon as the platforms reached the surface both lions made a loping run for the zebra. They had not been fed and they were hungry.

The zebra panicked and dashed away, running along the wall of the stadium. It was very fast and able to outrun the lions. Many in the crowd were on their feet, yelling excitedly. They cheered for the lions, Diegis noticed, not the zebra. They admired the strong predators and despised the weak prey.

The zebra had greater speed but the lions worked as a team. They took different pursuit angles, trying to trap the zebra against the wall. After much chasing they had the animal trapped and closed in for the kill. The zebra stood still, petrified with fear, then at the last possible instant bolted forward trying to escape between them.

Both lions lunged at it at the same time. One landed on the zebra's back but was quickly shaken off. The other swiped a huge paw across the zebra's hind leg, leaving deep bloody gashes. The zebra ran away to the far side of the stadium but now it was bleeding and limping. The crowd groaned at the escape, then began to cheer again as the lions followed and rapidly closed the distance.

"That is not a fair contest," Buri growled.

"Lions against zebras in a closed arena is not a contest," Diegis said. "It is an execution." He looked around at the crowd surrounding them. "That's what they came to see, an execution."

The lions closed in again. The zebra tried a dash along the wall but was now slowed by its injured leg. One lion leaped and sank its jaws into one of the zebra's rear legs. The other lunged and bit deeply into its throat. The crowd rose to its feet and cheered. The zebra went down quickly.

The lions were allowed to feast on their kill for a short while, then animal trainers carrying long poles and spears came out and steered them into cages on the platforms. The platforms were slowly lowered into the lower levels of the stadium. The crowd waited impatiently for the next show to begin.

The next few hours were filled with various kinds of animal hunts. The highlight was a giant boar hunted by men on horses. The boar proved very difficult to kill, eventually bringing down a horse and goring its rider to death before five other spearmen finally managed to kill it. The crowd cheered the killing of both the rider and the boar.

Titus Lucullus turned to the Dacians. "Watch now. This is the last show before the lunch break. It is usually something special."

A large platform came up from the ground in the middle of the stadium. On it was a large cage with thick iron bars. Inside the cage was a very large black bear. The crowd cheered.

"That is the biggest bear I have ever seen," Buri proclaimed.

"Seen a lot of bears, have you?" Titus asked.

"Of course, many," Buri replied matter-of-factly. "We live in the mountains. We hunt in the mountains."

"Buri hunts bears with his bare hands," Diegis joked.

Titus started to laugh, then stopped as he watched a second large cage rise up right next to the bear cage. Inside the second cage were four grey mountain wolves. The crowd cheered loudly. They knew what the wolves represented.

Diegis turned to Lucullus with a grin on his face. "Is the Emperor sending us a message, Titus?"

Titus gave a small embarrassed shrug. He could think of nothing to say. It was plain however that the Emperor was playing a game with his guests as well as entertaining the crowd.

The bars between the two cages were raised, allowing the animals access to each other. Trainers with long poles jabbed at the bear until it lumbered forward into the cage that held the wolves, then the bars to its cage were allowed to fall shut. All five animals were now trapped in the same cage.

The wolves snarled and bared their teeth at the intruder but kept a cautious distance. The bear went to a corner and sat still, facing the wolves. It was not aggressive but simply acted like it did not want to be bothered. Trainers wielding the long wooden poles began to poke all five animals through the cage bars.

The wolves ran around to escape the jabbing poles. One ran too close to the bear, which caused the bear to take a swipe at it. The bear's tremendous strength lifted the wolf off the floor of the cage and hurled it against the bars. The injured wolf yelped in pain, its back broken.

Two of the other wolves rushed at the bear, biting at its paws. The third wolf instinctively sprang for its throat. Now enraged, the bear roared with anger and swiped at the airborne wolf with a front paw. Its sharp claws caught the wolf in the stomach and gutted the animal. It was a short and unequal fight, like watching a grown man dispose of four little children. Its opponents dead or dying, the bear retreated back to its corner. The crowd yelled and screamed its approval.

"Were those mountain wolves from the Alps?" Mircea asked Titus, curious.

"Most likely."

"Ah," the priest said knowingly, "Dacian wolves would have put up a better fight."

Diegis laughed and slapped Mircea on the back. Buri gave him a big toothy grin.

Some spectators were standing and leaving for the lunch break. Lucullus stirred to get up, but Diegis motioned for him to wait.

"I want to see the Roman custom for executing criminals," Diegis explained.

"As you wish," Titus agreed.

Four men and two women were brought by guards and led to the center of the arena. They walked with a shuffle because they were chained together by iron manacles around their ankles. One man and one woman looked quite young, the others were middle aged. They looked ragged and dirty from their time spent in prison. None looked like a dangerous criminal.

The guards left them there and walked away. The six prisoners gathered in a small circle. The young woman turned to the younger man and clung to him in a very tight embrace. He spoke softly into her ear. She was shaking with fear. The prisoners then slowly sank to their knees, and appeared to bow their heads in prayer. One of the older men was leading the prayers.

"Who are they?" Diegis asked Lucullus.

"Christians," Titus replied evenly. "They are convicted of treason and sentenced to death."

"What is their crime, to be guilty of treason?" Mircea wanted to know.

"They will not accept the divinity of Caesar. They insist instead on worshiping their crucified god Jesus," Lucullus explained patiently.

"If only they would acknowledge Caesar as their god, they would be allowed to live freely in Rome."

Mircea shook his head. "They would live, but they would not be free."

"They would rather die, then?" Buri asked.

"So it appears," Titus said. "Yes, they usually go to their deaths docile as lambs."

Eight trap doors opened in the stadium floor around the group of prisoners. Eight metal cages slowly raised up to ground level. The crowd roared its approval. Inside each cage was a lion, looking around at their surroundings then quickly focusing on the people kneeling a short distance away. They knew from past experience what to expect next.

"This should be stopped," Buri growled, his anger rising.

"No, Buri," Lucullus frowned. "No one can stop it but Caesar, and they die on orders from Caesar."

At a signal animal attendants raised the front side of each cage, giving the lions a free path to the prisoners. A cheer swelled up from the stands as men, women, and children watched for the carnage to begin. None of the Christians moved, still as statues, lost in prayer.

"They are not afraid to die," Mircea observed.

"No, they are not," Diegis agreed. "We are not afraid to die, either. At least we hope to die in battle, but these people are helpless."

Diegis went silent as the lions charged the prisoners. The animals had not been fed for days to make sure they were hungry. All eight lions were on top of the Christians in seconds. One of the lions bit one of the men on the back of the neck and dragged him aside. The other people were crushed under a pile of lions hungrily tearing at them. Instinctively the lions ripped out throats as the fastest way to kill their prey. There were a few loud shrieks of pain, then the voices were silenced.

"Die, traitors! Die!" A woman sitting nearby yelled, her face red with anger. Her neighbors shouted and yelled with her. The Emperor

Domitian had told them many times that Christians were bringers of plagues and pestilence, sickness and bad luck, and even earthquakes. The sooner they were all put to death the better.

Diegis looked at the crowd around him, most of them cheering. It made him angry and disgusted. Who were these people? Barbarians, as Queen Andrada called them.

Titus looked away from the grisly scene. He did not usually stay to watch the executions. Buri stared down at the ground, looking sick. Mircea watched in silence. He was repulsed by the bloodletting, but was astounded by the courage of the victims in their last minutes of life. What kind of faith produced such courage?

Diegis looked up at the Emperor's box. Domitian and his group were gone. The Emperor had stayed to watch the killing, but had no interest in watching lions feed. The most important thing was that the Christians were put to death. They would serve as an example to others and a deterrent to future would be heretics and traitors.

"I am leaving," Diegis said to Titus, rising up from his seat. Buri and Mircea followed his lead and stood up to leave as well.

Titus looked disappointed. "Leave already? But you will miss the afternoon games. The gladiatorial fights are scheduled right after the lunch intermission."

"Thank you, but no," Diegis said, shaking his head. "I have killed many men in battle, but I do not wish to watch people slaughter each other for no purpose other than to entertain the crowd." He inclined his head towards the feeding lions in the arena. "You must know what our Queen would call that?"

Titus grimaced. The memory of that discussion several months ago in the throne room at Sarmizegetusa was still fresh in his memory. "Barbaric," he replied.

"Yes," Diegis agreed.

Lucullus changed the subject. "You are leaving in two days, then?"

"We are."

"I shall see you tomorrow, then, and make preparations. You will need to be supplied for your journey."

"Yes, thank you," Diegis nodded. "Farewell then."

The others bid their farewells, and they headed for the nearest Colosseum exit.

Buri had an excellent sense of direction and steered them on the path towards their inn. They did not need Titus or Drilgisa for guidance.

After walking for a few blocks Diegis looked around casually, then frowned. A furtive little man had been following them since they left the Colosseum. He was holding back at a discreet distance but was also careful not to lose sight of them in the human traffic.

"Come this way," Diegis said and turned right at the next corner. Mircea and Buri followed. As soon as they turned the corner Diegis stopped and motioned for them to keep silent.

It took only a few seconds before the stranger following them came walking fast around the corner. He almost bumped into Buri and stopped, surprise and confusion on his face.

Diegis grabbed the man by the front of his tunic and pushed him firmly against the wall. He was an older man, small in stature, with thinning hair graying around the temples.

"No trouble, friend," Diegis said to him in a low and calm voice, "but why are you following us?"

"I mean you no trouble, my Dacian friends," the man replied in a humble voice.

"How do you know we are Dacian?" Mircea asked.

The man swallowed. "Everyone knows the Dacian delegation is visiting Rome. And, Your Holiness," the man nodded at Mircea, "I recognize the robes of a priest of Zamolxis."

"Who are you?" Diegis demanded.

"My name is Rigozus," he replied in a rush of words. "I was born in Banat. Before I came to Rome I travelled to Dacia many times. I have lived in Rome for the past twenty-five years. I am a shoemaker."

Diegis let go of his tunic but did not allow him room to move away. "You still haven't answered my question. Why are you following us?"

"Are you a Roman spy?" Mircea asked, remembering the warning from Titus Lucullus.

Rigozus looked shocked by the question.

"No, sir, I am not a spy," he replied. His voice dropped down to a whisper. "I am a Christian."

It was Diegis' turn to be surprised. He relaxed and took a step back to give the old man some breathing room.

"And, sirs," Rigozus continued, looking around from one face to another, "I beg you to help my daughter."

Chapter 21

OLD SCORES AND NEW BEGINNINGS

Rome, September 89 AD

*D*rilgisa did not know his way around most of Rome, being taken away from the city when he was a child. However he vividly remembered the way from the Forum to the familiar house on the Palatine. The two story house with the yellow painted walls, the red tiled roof, and the bright red door. The house where he spent his early childhood. The house of Senator Rufus Mutilus.

After the others had left for the Colosseum and the Emperor's Games, Drilgisa promptly changed into a plain brown tunic. He put on a dark brown cape over it, which came with a hood for protection against rain or hot sun. He had purchased a pair of cheap, plain shoes such as would be worn by a clerk or a shopkeeper. He sharpened his knife to a razor's edge, and this he tucked inside his belt. He walked out carrying only a plain cloth sack. The sack contained his regular clothes.

Drilgisa walked from the inn to the Forum. The sun was very bright so he pulled up the hood of his cape to cover his head. He walked around some of the vendors stalls and looked at some of their merchandise. He purchased a loaf of bread, which he carried under his left arm. He was in no hurry, and had no wish to draw attention to himself.

Drilgisa left the Forum and walked casually up the street leading to the familiar neighborhood on the Palatine Hill. Old memories of houses, intersections, very old and tall trees came back to him as he made his way up the street. These were wealthy neighborhoods, filled with fine houses that did not often change owners over the years.

Although the sights looked familiar, somehow it all felt different to him. The neighborhood felt like a different place. Drilgisa slowly smiled to himself. No, the neighborhood had not changed much at all. He had changed. That little boy was gone forever.

Drilgisa turned a familiar corner and there it was, same as ever. The bright red door set into the yellow painted walls. He felt a sudden tightness in his stomach but did not stop walking at his leisurely pace. There, on the side of the house, growing in a narrow patch of dirt, was the walnut tree with the low branches that he had climbed so often as a boy. In autumn the walnuts ripened and fell to the ground. It was a feast for squirrels and for little children.

He walked past the front door which he knew would be locked. There were no sounds coming from inside the house. He walked past the house to the next intersection, and then stopped. Now all he could do was to wait and watch. Senator Mutilus might be home, or he might not. He might go out, or he might come back from some appointment. If he went to the Emperor's Games he might not return until sundown.

It made no difference. Drilgisa had patience. Now all he needed was a bit of luck. He broke the loaf of bread in two and ate one half for his breakfast. While he chewed his bread he thought. It would not be difficult to climb over some walls and find a way into the house, but that was not an option he could choose. Servants and slaves would be in the way and some would be hurt or killed.

In any case, if a Roman noble was killed inside his own house it was customary to put all the slaves and servants to death regardless of guilt or innocence in the murder. It discouraged slaves and other servants from harming their masters.

No, Drilgisa would have to catch Rufus outside his house. For that he needed a little luck. The street was busy in the daytime and people came and went from the houses along the street. Servants running errands. People making deliveries. Residents going and coming on various businesses. No one paid any attention to Drilgisa. He was just another figure on the street.

His luck finally turned in the late morning when the red door opened and a female servant walked out, then headed down the street towards the Forum. Drilgisa's disappointment was short lived, for only minutes later the door opened again and the man himself emerged. Rufus did not even look in his direction, but turned right and headed down the hill towards the Forum just as his servant had done.

Drilgisa waited for a few moments before he followed. Rufus was dressed casually in a light blue tunic, not a toga. Whatever the nature of his engagement, it was a casual and not a formal affair. So much the better. Walking downhill was faster and in no time Mutilus reached the Forum. Drilgisa followed casually behind him. Once in the Forum there was no shortage of people and physical structures to screen him, and he could follow at a shorter distance.

The senator skirted the Forum and turned into a narrow street that followed the valley floor. Mutilus was slumming it today in the low rent districts, it appeared. He was heading northeast, into the Subura. There were many reasons why a Roman noble would go into that crowded neighborhood, although few involved noble causes. The more shady businessmen operated out of the Subura. So did the more exotic brothels. Knowing Rufus, Drilgisa would wager that his destination was more likely an exotic brothel than an illegal trader of questionable merchandise.

The senator walked quickly, with a purpose. He knew where he was going and was eager to get there. Drilgisa felt himself getting excited over this fortunate turn of luck. His heart was beating a tick faster. He quickened his pace and closed the distance.

They were walking on a narrow street. Just ahead was an even narrower alley between two tall apartment buildings. Even on a bright day little light penetrated between those tall buildings, and at ground level the alley was in deep shadow.

By the time they reached the alley Rufus was within arm's reach. Drilgisa grabbed him by the shoulders with both hands and yanked him into the space between the buildings. Rufus gave out an alarmed yelp, then was stunned into silence as Drilgisa swiftly brought up his right forearm and hit him hard underneath the jaw. He would have slumped to the ground but Drilgisa kept him upright by holding on to the front of his tunic.

"My purse is on my belt," Rufus croaked hoarsely when he found his voice. "There is a good deal of money, take it."

"I don't want your money," Drilgisa spat and slammed Mutilus against the wall.

"What do you want?" Rufus asked, suddenly very afraid.

"I want justice," Drilgisa growled softly in his ear, "you low slimy piece of snail shit."

"What? Justice? What justice?" Rufus gasped.

"You don't remember me," Drilgisa said. "You did not recognize me at the Emperor's reception. But I recognized you, Senator Snail Shit." Drilgisa used his right hand to pull back the hood of his cape. His left hand pinned Rufus to the wall.

Mutilus stared at him in confusion. The man's cold voice filled him with terror. Then he recognized something in the eyes. The eyes.

"No," Rufus groaned. "Quintus? Quintus, is that you?"

Drilgisa slammed him against the wall again. Rufus was dazed and bleeding from the back of his scalp.

"I'm not Quintus anymore." The voice was eerily calm and cold. "But now you remember me, eh?"

Mutilus was in shock. He gasped for breath.

"I was always a good master to you, Quintus. You were always my favorite," he said with a groan that ended in a sob.

"You were always a coward," Drilgisa spat in his face. "But you were too strong for a little boy. All those days and nights when I begged you not to hurt me. Begged you to leave me alone. Were you a good master then?"

"I was your master!" Mutilus protested. "I had a legal right!"

"As do I," Drilgisa replied. His left arm pinned the senator hard against the wall. "This is my right," he said, and in a swift motion with his right hand brought the knife upward to plunge deep into the throat of Rufus Mutilus. The Roman gasped in shock and pain, his eyes rolling up in their sockets, then collapsed to the street as his knees gave away.

Drilgisa stepped aside to avoid the gushing blood, although some had sprayed on the right sleeve and the front of his tunic. Mutilus twitched at his feet, then went still. A woman carrying a pail of liquid turned the corner, walking towards them. She paused as she saw the murder scene, and for a fleeting instant she and Drilgisa locked eyes. Without uttering a sound the woman dropped her pail and hurried back in the direction from which she came.

Drilgisa walked down the alley in the opposite direction at a pace fast enough to create distance but not attract attention. When he was halfway down the alley he stopped, stripped off his bloodstained clothes, and put on the clean clothes that he carried in the sack. He used the old clothes to clean off the blood from his knife, then tucked the blade under his belt. He left the bloody clothes and sack behind and walked calmly to the next street. Down the alley rats were already scampering over the body of Rufus Mutilus.

Drilgisa reached the inn in the early afternoon. He was surprised to find Diegis and the rest of the Dacian group already returned from the games. None of them looked very happy.

"Why back so soon?" Drilgisa asked casually. "Did the Emperor's Games disappoint?"

Buri frowned. "A waste of time, that's what it was." He shook his head sadly. "Those poor people."

"Where were you?" Diegis asked. "This morning you were unwell, then we come back and you're gone."

"What poor people?" Drilgisa asked Buri.

"Christians," Mircea replied. "Six Christians, men and women both. Domitian fed them to the lions in the arena."

"It makes me sick to think about it," Buri said.

Diegis turned to Drilgisa again, curious. "My question remains unanswered."

Drilgisa gave a casual shrug. "I am well. I went for a stroll."

"A stroll?"

"Yes. I went for a stroll in the city." He smiled. "I ran into an old acquaintance. It turned into a fine morning."

"I see," Diegis said. "And it appears that during your morning stroll you got blood in your hair. Just above the right ear."

Drilgisa raised his hand and swiped his fingertips above his right ear. They came away lightly stained with blood that was not quite yet congealed. "Hah, look at that," he said with mild surprise. He did not offer any further explanation.

"What are we going to do about Rigozus?" Mircea asked, sounding worried.

"Who?"

"Sit down, Drilgisa," Diegis said patiently. "There is a matter we need to discuss."

It was decided that Buri would stay behind at the inn with the money belt and the gold. If the others were arrested he would need to bribe or threaten, as became necessary, to set them free. They also needed to be discreet, and due to his size Buri always drew attention.

They met Rigozus shortly after sunset near a fountain off a street leading to the Subura. The diminutive Christian looked very nervous, but was overjoyed to see them.

"My friends, thank God you are here," he greeted them, sounding anxious. He looked curiously at Drilgisa, the newcomer, but thought it better not to ask questions.

Diegis walked past him down the street. "Come on, lead the way. The less standing around and talking the better."

Rigozus took the lead. Drilgisa walked beside him, keeping watch. Diegis and Mircea followed.

They walked down a narrow and dark street. The streets of the Subura were empty after sunset.

"So this is the rough neighborhood?" Mircea wondered. He found that he was intrigued by Roman culture. "There is no one about."

Drilgisa glanced at him but kept on walking. "The Subura is best known for three things, Mircea. It is most famous for barber shops and prostitutes."

"Ah, I see. And barber shops don't work at night, I take it?" Mircea asked with a chuckle.

"Very good! You are learning, priest."

"And what is the third thing the Subura is known for? Besides barber shops and prostitutes."

"Murders," Drilgisa said evenly.

Mircea went silent. It was always best not to tempt fate.

"Please do not talk like that, my friend," Rigozus pleaded. "I am sick with worry already."

"Listen well, Rigozus," Drilgisa growled. "You are taking us into bad neighborhoods in the night. If you betray us you won't live five seconds longer. Do you understand?"

The Christian seemed embarrassed that his intentions should be doubted. "Don't worry, the only thing I want is your help."

"How far are we going?"

"Not far. A few more blocks."

They came to a dilapidated five-story apartment building. This was a low rent building in a low rent neighborhood. Rigozus led them up five flights of stairs to the top floor. Half the wooden stairs creaked but nobody complained.

On the top floor Rigozus led them down the narrow hallway to the last door on the right. He knocked softly, a secret code. A short pause, and the door was opened cautiously by a man in his early twenties with brown curly hair. He looked relieved to see Rigozus.

"Come inside, quickly," the man said, stepping aside to make room for them. Once they were inside he closed and then bolted the door behind them. The smell of fear was in the air.

They were in a stuffy room that was barely large enough to fit all of them. This was not a room to live in, Diegis thought. This was a place to hide.

A woman, about the same age as the young man, was sitting on a straw mattress in the corner. Rigozus gave her a warm smile and beckoned for her to stand. "Come, Zelma, greet our friends."

The young woman got up and stood next to the brown haired man, who evidently was her husband. She looked to be with child but not too advanced.

Diegis turned to Rigozus. "I take it that this is your daughter. Now explain yourself, fully."

Rigozus seemed overcome with emotion. He gathered himself.

"This is my daughter Zelma. Nicolae is her husband. They are in hiding because they are persecuted." He paused and swallowed hard. "Without your help they will perish."

"Why are you persecuted?" Drilgisa asked. He was standing guard by the door.

"Because we are Christians," Nicolae replied. "All Christians are persecuted in Rome."

"Emperor Domitian pays generous rewards to informers to report Christians," Zelma explained. "Many greedy people take advantage of these rewards. Our neighbor is one and she reported us. Then she told us what she had done, in order to mock us. So we ran." She paused and touched her swelling belly. "But we cannot run for long without help."

Rigozus looked at them, his eyes pleading. "This morning you were at the Colosseum. You saw what happens to Christians who get arrested."

"Yes, we saw," Mircea said grimly.

"What kind of help do you seek?" Diegis asked.

Zelma's hazel eyes grew brighter. "We want to go to Dacia, sir! We wish to go with you. We have no future here. And even if we did, I do not want my child to grow up in Rome."

Nicolae put his arm protectively around his wife. "It is a lot to ask, sir, but it would be our salvation." He paused, and then added with passion, "I can work. I will do whatever is needed to help."

Diegis gave Drilgisa a questioning look. Drilgisa shrugged, but he looked skeptical. Their mission did not call for taking civilians along.

"What kind of work do you do, Nicolae?" Diegis inquired.

"I am a cobbler, sir. I mend shoes and make new ones. This good man," he nodded to Rigozus, "has taught me my profession for the past five years."

Mircea smiled. "So he has given you a profession and a wife. A good man indeed!"

"We have a long journey ahead of us," Diegis mused. "A cobbler might come in very handy. And what do you do, Zelma?"

"I am a healer, sir," she replied humbly. "I know medicinal plants. And I am not a surgeon, but I can mend wounds if they are not too severe."

"A cobbler and a doctor, what could be better?" Diegis asked. He directed his question to Drilgisa, who had missed the slaughter at the Colosseum and was not as touched by the plight of the Christians as he and Mircea were. Drilgisa had no opinion.

"What are your thoughts, Mircea?"

Instead of answering the priest turned to the young woman. "Your name is Zelma, my child?"

"Yes, sir."

Mircea gave her a smile. "Would you tell General Diegis what your name means?"

She seemed a little surprised by the question, then cleared her throat and answered. "Zelma means protected by God."

Drilgisa laughed and shook his head with amusement. "Even the gods want you to make this trip! You are indeed blessed, young lady."

Diegis nodded. "So be it. Zelma and Nicolae, you will travel with us as my servants and thus will be under my protection. You will be our doctor and our cobbler. When we get to Dacia you will choose where to live."

Nicolae and Zelma held each other in a tight embrace, their lives suddenly given new hope. Rigozus stood silently, tears streaming down his face.

"And what will you do, Rigozus?" Mircea asked.

"I do this for my daughter, and for Nicolae, and for my unborn grandchild who I will never see," Rigozus said. "As for me, my life is here. My second wife is Roman. A good woman, but she would never leave Rome."

"How many more Christians are there in Rome being persecuted and facing arrest?" Mircea asked.

"Many," Nicolae answered. "We meet in secret, in small groups. We live in fear of discovery but our faith is stronger than our fear of the Romans."

"I see that, and I believe you," Mircea said. "A faith that strong cannot be conquered."

"No, our faith cannot be conquered," Zelma said. She put her arm around her husband's waist. "Not even by death."

Rigozus caught Diegis' eye. "Sir? About the other Christians."

Diegis shook his head. "We cannot take more people."

"No, sir, not that," the old man explained. "Please tell King Decebal about the Christians in Rome. They need a place to go if they decide to leave here."

"I understand," Diegis replied. "King Decebal and Queen Andrada are aware of the plight of the Christians here. Tell people that they are welcome in Dacia, but they must make their own way there."

"Thank you. I will tell them. One day Rome will fall and Christians will be free. God's justice will prevail."

"Amen," Nicolae and Zelma said together.

Titus Lucullus escorted the Dacian delegation to the Porta Flaminia and said his farewells there. Somehow Diegis found and hired two Romans to be his servants, a young couple who worked as a cobbler and a doctor. He did not make any inquiries beyond that. Neither of the two young people could ride a horse so they would travel sitting on cushions in one of the baggage carts. That was very appreciated in particular by the young woman who was in the middle stages of pregnancy.

Drilgisa inspected the cavalry escorts and their equipment. Every man was accounted for. No one had gotten into trouble, although being housed outside the city gates helped reduce temptations that could lead to trouble. The soldiers were bored with playing dice games and were eager to leave.

"Thank you for your hospitality and your assistance, Titus," Mircea said. "This trip has been an education for me. You are a most capable instructor."

"You are welcome, Mircea. Give my regards to the High Priest Vezina when you return home."

Mircea nodded. "I shall do that. He spoke well of you."

Titus laughed. "Yes, he called me an honest Roman, I remember."

"Farewell, Titus Lucullus," Diegis said amiably.

"Give my regards to your brother the King, and to Queen Andrada as well," Lucullus said. He looked Diegis straight in the eye. "You know that Rome wishes to keep the peace with Dacia. I trust that they know it as well and will honor the treaty between us."

"Indeed," Diegis replied. "Rome has suffered heavy losses and so has Dacia. A peace benefits us both."

"I wish you a pleasant trip, General."

Titus hoped the treaty would last. Privately he had doubts, which he kept to himself. His worry was not the Dacians, even though King Decebalus was very headstrong and independent. No, his main worry was the reaction of the Senate of Rome and other powerful Romans.

A great many were angry with the Emperor for the concessions he gave to Dacia, not the least of which was the large sum of money to be paid to Dacia every year. Behind Domitian's back they were calling his treaty the inglorious peace. How long would Romans tolerate such an insult?

With Drilgisa and the captain of cavalry in the lead, the travelling party formed a column and headed north on the Via Flaminia. Drilgisa seemed to be in a happier mood. Mircea travelled with the pleasant young Christian couple in the baggage cart so they could discuss Zamolxis and Jesus.

Both gods were gods of peace, it seemed, who preached tolerance and love towards one's fellow man. Mircea would never forget the courage of the Christians facing death in the arena. In a world full of violence and death that kind of courage was unique, and he wished to understand it better.

Like all good Roman roads the Via Flaminia was built straight and flat. Soon the great city of Rome was just a speck on the southern horizon. Weeks of travel lay ahead.

Chapter 22

THE WEDDING

Sarmizegetusa, October 89 AD

*K*ing Decebal was in search of his wife. He could have simply sent a servant to find her, however that seemed like a frivolous thing to do when it came to his own wife in his own living quarters.

Granted that Queen Andrada was somewhat less predictable in her moods now that she was pregnant again, and given to starting new projects with a passion, but she was still his wife. They always knew each other's whereabouts when they were at home.

Except that at the moment the Queen was nowhere to be found.

Their daughter Zia walked by. The girl was carrying a white kitten towards the kitchen and seemed to be in a hurry. She looked at her father's face in passing and guessed the reason for his frustration.

"She's in the throne room, Tata. So is Aunt Dochia and Aunt Tanidela." Two steps later she remembered something and looked back over her shoulder. "Oh, and also Mirela!"

"Thank you, Zia," Decebal called after her. Leave it to children to be aware of their mother's location at all times.

He walked down a long hallway that connected the living quarters to the throne room. Guards were posted at the throne room entrance at all times, and access to the living quarters was highly restricted. They bowed politely to the King as he walked by.

The women were gathered in the throne room because it had the best map of Dacia and the surrounding lands. The map was spread out on a large table. Andrada was bending over it and pointing out places on the map, and Decebal's younger sister Tanidela was writing notes with a stylus on a wax writing tablet.

"By what right do you commandeer the royal map?" Decebal asked them as he approached. Andrada and his sisters knew that he was teasing. Mirela, who was going to marry Diegis, was not as sure. She sat up quickly, a little startled.

"Commandeer, my foot," Andrada replied calmly, not taking her eyes off the map. "I'm the Queen and it's my map too."

Dochia put a hand on Mirela's shoulder. "The King only jests," she said with a smile.

"Of course," Mirela said. Being around the royal family was a new experience for her, and she was still uncomfortable in the presence of the King. Diegis was still not back from his trip to Rome, although he was expected to be home very soon.

"What are you searching for?" Decebal asked.

Tanidela showed him the writing tablet. "We have one hundred more wedding invitations to send out. And that's just within Dacia proper."

Andrada straightened up from bending over the map, and gave a low groan as she put a hand on her lower back. She would give birth in less than two months and was feeling the strain of her pregnancy.

"Also another hundred guests from beyond our borders. Diegis is royalty," the Queen added. She waved a hand at the large map. "Kings, nobles, and chiefs will take offense if they are not invited."

"Indeed," Decebal agreed. "Do not neglect the princes and high nobles of the Sarmatians, the Marcomanni, the Scythians, and the Bastarnae. How many invitations so far?"

"Five hundred. Two hundred more should take care of everyone."

"Will they all come?" Mirela asked worriedly.

"Three in five will come," Andrada replied. "The others will only send gifts, but even so they will be pleased to be invited."

"So many people!" the young woman exclaimed in wonder.

Decebal gave her a smile. "Your wedding to Diegis will be a great feast and celebration, of course. However it is also a state function and a diplomatic gathering of Dacia's allies. Welcome to the family, Mirela."

Tanidela turned to her with a grin. "Welcome to politics, Sister."

Diegis and the rest of the Dacian delegation to Rome returned to Sarmizegetusa on a windy and rainy day. The travelers were wet and fatigued from the trip. The soldiers promptly retired to their homes. Diegis went directly to the royal residence to report to the King.

"Welcome home, Brother!" Decebal clasped him on the shoulder, then invited him to sit at the table in the dining hall.

Diegis sat down and gratefully accepted a mug of hot water and lemon, sweetened with honey, that was brought to him by a servant.

"A very long trip," Diegis declared. "I have seen the world, and I am happy to be back in Dacia."

"The reports tell me you had a successful meeting with Domitian," Decebal said.

"Ah, it was not much of a meeting, and nothing was discussed," Diegis replied. "The Emperor only wanted us there to show off before the Senate." He nodded his greetings to Vezina and Andrada, who had just walked in and joined them.

"No different from what we expected," Vezina said. "Yet still, it was important that you were there to represent Dacia. The treaty with Rome benefits us as well as them."

"Thank the gods that you are back, safe and healthy," the Queen declared with relief.

"Thank you, Sister," Diegis replied. He reached under his shirt and pulled out a soft cloth bag. He pushed it across the table towards the King. "This is for you, Brother."

"Gifts from Rome?" Decebal smiled.

Vezina took the bag. "Allow me to check it first for any evidence of poison, Sire," he said jokingly. He untied the bag and pulled out the thin golden diadem. "How generous of the Emperor!" Vezina said with a laugh.

"Let's not be ungrateful, Vezina," Decebal urged. "We hear that the Emperor's treasury is low these days."

"That depends," Diegis said.

"Depends on what?" Andrada asked.

"Depends, My Queen, on how many wealthy Romans he executed on trumped up charges of treason and other crimes. Domitian kills or exiles them and confiscates their properties to pay for his games and for his villas."

"Oh! How dreadful for those people," she exclaimed.

"It is a custom of sorts in Rome, My Queen," Vezina explained. "Domitian is not the first ruler to use that strategy and he won't be the last."

Decebal picked up the diadem, examined it for a second, and tossed it back on the table. "That can go back in the bag. I have no use for it."

Vezina turned to Diegis. "Who are the people waiting outside with Mircea? They look tired and hungry."

"They are my guests," Diegis answered. "Our guests. Refugees from Rome."

"Oh, but why keep them waiting?" Andrada turned to a servant. "Bring our guests in to join us."

Nicolae and Zelma were shown in along with Mircea. They were shy and uncertain in approaching the royal party, understandably so. The young couple had no idea how they should behave in front of royalty.

Diegis did the introductions. "King Decebal and Queen Andrada, these are my guests from Rome. Nicolae and Zelma are husband and wife. They are Christians who were persecuted by Domitian and faced death had they remained in Rome."

Andrada noticed Zelma's pregnancy, at about the same stage as her own, and got up to greet her. "Come, my dear, and do sit down. Some hot soup will warm you up quickly."

Two servants heard her and quickly rushed towards the kitchen. The new arrivals crowded in on chairs around the table, bewildered at being asked to join royalty so casually.

Nicolae bowed his head to Decebal and Andrada. "Thank you, Your Highness. General Diegis gave us our lives. He saved us from death in the arena. God will bless all of you for this kindness."

"Welcome, Nicolae and Zelma," Decebal replied. "We have a small community of Christian refugees in Sarmizegetusa. You may join them if you wish."

"I have gotten to know these young people well on our journey," Mircea spoke up, his eyes gleaming. "They will both be very helpful to the city. Nicolae makes very good shoes. Zelma is skilled in healing and herbal medicine."

"Wonderful," Andrada exclaimed. "Zelma, you may assist me in my medical clinic. And also in my herb garden because tending it properly takes knowledge and skill." She gently touched her swollen belly and laughed. "After we both deliver our babies, of course."

Zelma looked at her husband and saw that he felt as overwhelmed as she did. What kind of royalty were these, so hospitable to common strangers?

"Thank you, Your Highness," Zelma said shyly. "I pray that I shall be worthy of your trust."

Trays were brought in with bowls of soup and loaves of bread. The travelers were all famished. Conversation slowed while they ate.

Andrada turned to Diegis. "When you have finished your meal there is a young lady who is eagerly waiting for you."

"Of course! I have been thinking of little else the entire trip back."

"The wedding is scheduled in two weeks from now, so your return is very timely," Decebal told him. "It was scheduled to give you time to travel and also provide travel time for our guests."

"But not too much time," Andrada said with a smile.

"Oh?" Diegis glanced at the Queen. "Was someone in a hurry?"

"We all were," Andrada replied. "Your betrothed in particular. Now stop talking and eat. She's waited for you long enough."

The wedding of Diegis, Prince of Dacia, and Mirela, daughter of Sorin, a wealthy Dacian nobleman, drew guests from as far away as Germania in the west and Scythia in the east. Four hundred guests joined the local population for the outdoor wedding, followed by the wedding feasts. Fortunately the weather had not yet turned cold.

The wedding ceremonies started early in the morning. Including the religious rituals, feasts, singing, and dancing, they did not end until the following morning.

Both the bride and groom were dressed in the traditional, colorful and richly embroidered wedding costumes. The dress for Mirela, and the trousers and shirt for Diegis, were made from a woolen fabric bleached to a bright white. They were decorated with embroidery of silk thread in a rainbow of colors. Her long light brown hair was plaited in the back and decorated with flowers. He wore the lambskin cap of Dacian nobility.

Vezina presided over the religious ceremony and the wedding rites to ensure that Zamolxis gave his blessings to the union. Priests chanted and burned incense. The couple was then serenaded with traditional wedding songs.

After the religious service the couple was led to the wedding bread. This was a very large loaf of bread, specially made to be many times the size of a regular loaf. The bride and groom each tore off a piece of the bread and ate it. This would ensure that the marriage would be prosperous and fertile. The rest of the loaf was cut into small pieces and distributed among the guests as a symbol of the couple's happiness and goodwill.

The wedding feast was a cornucopia of roasted meats and poultry, freshly caught fish, breads, vegetables, and fruits and nuts of all kinds. Deserts came from a wide variety of pastries and cakes. Dacian bakers were always well supplied and generous with butter, cream, honey, cheeses, and fruits.

Wine was consumed at wedding celebrations, more so than in daily life, but Dacians drank alcohol sparingly compared to their guests from neighboring tribes. The lessons of Zamolxis were still a strong influence in Dacian life. It was believed that excessive use dulled men's minds and degraded their character. Alcohol was to be used primarily to celebrate special occasions.

King Decebal and Queen Andrada watched the proceedings from the royal table, set on a wide platform raised two feet above the ground. Decebal's family, including his children and his sisters, sat at nearby tables on the platform.

Various nobles and foreign dignitaries stopped by to greet the royal couple and pay their respects. One of them was Davi, a prince of the Roxolani Sarmatian tribe. Over the years the Roxolani and the Dacians proved to be each other's most dependable allies in fighting against foreign invaders.

Davi was a handsome warrior dressed in woolen trousers, woolen shirt hanging down over his hips, and a dark blue mantle hanging over his shoulders. Traditional Sarmatian clothes were very similar to Dacian clothes. Unlike Dacians, Davi's arms were richly decorated with tattoos. Dacians did not wear tattoos.

"Greetings, King Decebal," Davi said with a broad smile. "Thank you for the invitation and for this splendid feast. A Dacian feast is worth the trip and I never leave disappointed."

"Welcome, my friend," Decebal said. "Thank you for making the long journey. It is good to see you."

"Greetings, Queen Andrada," Davi bowed respectfully, taking in Andrada's state of pregnancy. "I trust that you are in excellent health, My Lady?"

"I am very well, Davi, thank you," Andrada replied. "I am happy to see you. Are you enjoying the festivities?"

"Very much so." He took a glance at the wedding couple's table. "I must say I have never seen Diegis looking so happy."

Andrada laughed. "Yes, I think marriage will be good for him. And you, lord? Still unmarried?"

"Still unmarried," he replied. His eyes strayed to the next table where Tanidela was talking with other guests. She must have sensed Davi's presence because she shifted her eyes in his direction.

Andrada caught his look. "Yes, she is still unmarried. Perhaps she would enjoy the opportunity to talk with you? It is so rare to see you a guest here, unfortunately."

"Would I ever question your wisdom, Lady?" Davi replied with a smile. "Now please excuse me, I shall go and find out." He gave a curt bow to the King, then headed towards Tanidela's table.

Decebal turned to his wife. "Playing matchmaker now, are we?"

"Shush, there is nothing wrong with that," she replied pleasantly. "Tanidela would be happy to find someone well suited for her. Dochia too, for that matter."

"Perhaps not Dochia," Decebal said with sadness in his voice. Dochia was his older sister by two years. Her husband was killed in battle more than eight years ago. Then her only child, a ten year old son, went swimming in the river and drowned. His sister was sadly still in mourning for them both. She enjoyed taking care of children but showed no interest in marriage again.

Andrada heard his sadness and touched his arm. "I do not make light of it, Husband. Sometimes people change. One never knows. It is not good to live life in a state of sadness."

"I pray that you are right. And no, it is not good for my sister to live her life in perpetual mourning. But she is very proud and always follows her own mind."

"That appears to run in the family, Husband." Andrada paused in thought, then laughed. "I even see it in our daughters!"

"Indeed," Decebal smiled. "Your daughters as well as mine."

Buri walked by, his son Tarbus following a step behind. The ten year old boy shared his father's curly hair and pleasant disposition. He was big for his age but it was unlikely that he would ever grow as large as his father. Buri was a giant among men.

"Tarbus! Tarbus!" Adila and Zia called out and waved at the boy. He waved back.

The girls ran over to their parents' table. "Mama, can Tarbus sit with us?" Zia asked.

"Of course he can," she replied. "Perhaps you should ask Tarbus, and also his father?"

Tarbus glanced up expectantly at his father. Buri chuckled. "Go on, Son, it's all right. I will wait for you." He watched the kids run off happily and smiled.

"Were we this happy when we were that young?" Buri wondered.

"I cannot remember when I was that young," said Vezina, walking up and taking a seat near the King. The High Priest always had an invitation at the royal table.

"Were you ever young?" Decebal asked him lightly. "I remember that you were old when you were my childhood teacher."

Vezina sighed. "In truth, Sire, it is a blessing to be old. I enjoy it. Life teaches us so many lessons and I am ever an eager student."

"Ah!" the Queen cried. She looked at Decebal and Buri. "Listen well, you younger men, for this is what wisdom sounds like."

"Thank you, My Queen," Vezina smiled.

"I appreciate your wisdom, Vezina," Decebal said. "I depend on it. As did my uncle the king before me, and as did my father the king before him."

Buri turned to the High Priest with a grin. "And what does your wisdom tell us about the new type of pears that were brought in from Gaul? They are more round than our pears, and are still green when ripe, but they are very sweet."

"Wisdom says plant the seeds, Buri. Nature will teach you the rest."

"Buri, join us," Decebal said. "You can stop worrying for one day, your apple and pear trees will be fine. You had an excellent harvest this year."

"Yes, join us," Andrada invited him. "We have hardly seen you since you returned from Rome."

"Ah, Rome," Buri scowled as he found a seat. "How is the young Christian couple? Zelma and Nicolae?"

"They are well," Vezina replied. "Nicolae found work in a shop making shoes. Zelma is heavy with child and still resting from her journey from Rome. They are both embraced by the other Christians in the city."

"Diegis told me about the Christian prisoners and the lions in the arena," Decebal said. He shook his head. "That is terrible business."

"They would have been next, if not for Diegis," Buri told them. "He saved two lives that day in Rome."

"Three lives," Andrada corrected him. "Zelma and I will both be new mothers soon. Her first, my third."

Buri gave a nod. "Yes, My Queen, you are right. Three lives."

"Ah, look," Vezina observed. "The gift ceremony is about to begin. That will take them a while with four hundred guests, eh?"

"It will," Decebal agreed. "However, tradition will be observed."

The gift ceremony started in midafternoon. The wedding couple sat at a table and each guest in turn came up and presented them with a gift. Rich and poor, noble and peasant, every guest brought forward their gift. From gold and silver necklaces, to jewels, to fine horses, to simple household items any couple would need, each gift was graciously accepted.

At the very end of the gift ceremony Drilgisa walked up with a mangy donkey. This donkey had thin and skinny legs, and a skinny neck. Mirela was surprised and puzzled by this unusual gift. Diegis took one look, and then leaned back roaring with laughter. He looked over at the royal table, where King Decebal looked back and grinned at him.

Hanging from the donkey's neck was a sign that said "Emperor." Resting on top of the donkey's head was Domitian's golden diadem.

The wedding feast lasted all day and all night. Traditional songs were sung, then sung again even more boisterously. Musicians played flutes, drums, and string instruments. The most popular traditional wedding dance was the hora, a group dance that involved very large numbers of people holding hands and dancing in a circle. The dance was repeated many times as an expression of communal unity and joy. It was a dance that people never tired of.

In late evening the wedding couple left for their wedding bed. The rest of the revelers continued on until sunrise.

One month later Queen Andrada gave birth to a son. He had his mother's lustrous black hair and his father's dark brown eyes. They named him Dorin. The very next day Zelma gave birth to a daughter, whom they named Lia. She had her mother's brown hair and hazel eyes. Nicolae joyfully made tiny baby booties out of rabbit fur for both infants.

Zelma helped the Queen in her medical clinic and herbal garden, and so from an early age the two toddlers played together under their mothers' watchful eyes. They learned to crawl together, and to walk and talk together. To an outsider they seemed like fraternal twins. They grew up treating each other as brother and sister.

The peace treaty with Rome held. There were a few minor border skirmishes but no major battles. The Emperor was preoccupied with problems closer to home, not the least of which were his and Rome's persistent financial problems. Caesar's paranoia and resentments towards the Roman nobility led to harsher treatment for all those he did not trust. This greatly increased the Roman Senate's opposition to the Emperor as well as their scorn for him.

For the time being Domitian gave up plans for invading Dacia again. He still paid a large annual stipend to King Decebal in order to keep the peace. This showed that the Emperor was afraid of Dacia, his critics said. Although these payments were deeply resented by the Senate of Rome the senators had no choice but to go along. Defying Caesar openly meant exile or execution.

Decebal used the Roman engineers provided by Domitian under their treaty to strengthen Dacian forts and improve roads. He ordered the engineers to build more artillery to be used in defending the forts. He used the hundreds of Roman deserters from Tettius Julianus' army to train Dacian soldiers in countering Roman fighting techniques. When the Romans attacked again they would find that Dacia was better organized and better prepared than ever.

Chapter 23

ALLIANCES

*A*ulus Cotta was a leader among the conservative group of senators who followed the strict Stoic beliefs of the philosophers Tacitus and Pliny. The Stoics believed in living a just, frugal, and simple life. They were opposed to monarchy and rejected the idea of the divinity of Caesar, which automatically made them enemies of the Emperor. In particular they regarded the moral depravities and financial excesses of Domitian with revulsion.

The Stoics kept their opposition a secret from everyone except their small closed circle. Public opposition to the Emperor Domitian brought charges of treason. Men lost their property, and more and more frequently their lives. Rome lived in fear.

This evening Cotta invited three of his Senate colleagues to his house for dinner. They reclined on three couches, placed in a close circle. Cotta was thirty years old, on the thin side, and lively in his tone and physical gestures. Quintus Matius was sixty-eight. He was usually the oldest senator in the room and thus treated with the most deference. Publius Gabinius was a portly man in his forties. Marcus Rubrius was a quiet, thoughtful man in his late thirties. What made them trusted friends was their philosophy and their deep animosity towards Domitian.

True to their Stoic philosophy the men ate sparingly from a simple meal of bread, cheese, olives, and water. The servants had been sent away. In Rome the walls had ears.

When the meal ended Marcus Rubrius raised his water goblet in a very solemn toast. "To Helvidius. And Junius. And Herrenius." All raised their goblets silently and drank.

The subjects of the toast had been executed by Domitian for their Stoic beliefs and opposition to Caesar. Many of the relatives and friends of those men were also persecuted and sent into exile.

As was often the case when senators gathered, the conversation turned to money. "What is the state of the treasury, Quintus?" Cotta asked. "The real figures please, not the imperial lies."

Quintus Matius had his finger on the state's finances. Like other senators not closely aligned with Domitian, he was perpetually in a state of worry. The Emperor and his friends prospered at the expense of everyone else.

"We have just enough to pay the army. Caesar never forgets the importance of that," Quintus answered. "Our grain purchases will be reduced by a third. And Domitian once again wants more money for his games."

"More games!" Senator Cotta cried in indignation. "The man is a bigger waste of money than Nero!"

"Yes he is. And that is exactly the point," Publius Gabinius said.

"What is exactly the point?" Cotta wanted to know.

"Domitian admires Nero. In fact he wishes to surpass Nero in the number and garishness of his public entertainments."

"And bankrupt the state in the process," Matius said.

"If the gods are just, may he meet the same fate as Nero!" Rubrius said angrily.

"Careful, Marcus, such honest passion might cost you your neck," Quintus Matius warned. "Although not while you are among friends, of course."

The conversation came to a pause. They all shared Rubrius' hopes about the Emperor's demise, but there was nothing they could do. Domitian was the sole dictatorial power in Rome, and they were all at his mercy.

"What is to be done about this reign of terror?" Gabinius asked.

"Reign of terror is right," Cotta agreed. "Any one of us could follow next in the footsteps of Flavius Clemens."

The execution of Flavius Clemens the previous year shocked and scandalized all of Rome. Clemens had been Domitian's cousin and his co-consul several years ago. Since Domitian was childless, he had designated Clemens' twin sons as his heirs.

At some point and for unknown reasons the Emperor began to suspect Clemens and his wife of "drifting into Jewish ways." That was taken by Domitian to mean that they did not accept Caesar's divinity, and that made them guilty of treason. Flavius was then executed. His wife Domitilla, who was also Domitian's cousin, was sent into exile. Their sons, Domitian's heirs, disappeared and were presumed killed.

Since this shocking scandal happened no Roman could feel safe, not even Domitian's friends and supporters. The senseless execution of Flavius Clemens started comparisons of Domitian's reign to Nero's madness.

Quintus Matius broke the silence, his voice calm and reasoned. "The only way to change things is for us to grow stronger, my friends. We need more allies in the Senate. We need allies in the army."

"And most importantly we need allies in the Praetorian Guard," Aulus Cotta added. Without help from inside the Praetorian Guard no person with ill intent could get close to Domitian.

"Is it time to approach Marcus, I wonder?" Gabinius asked.

No one needed to ask which Marcus he was referring to. Marcus Ciocceius Nerva was the elder statesman of the Senate of Rome. He was admired by the people. He had support in the Senate and also had connections in the Praetorian Guard. No one dared speak his name in connection to any opposition to Domitian however, because they knew it would place his life at risk.

Quintus Matius took a breath and let it out slowly. "It must be done. I will speak with Marcus. We will follow his guidance." He looked around at the three men. "Nothing reckless. Nothing rash."

Marcus Rubrius nodded. "Of course not. We are not reckless men, but we must be men of action."

"Exactly so. The future of Rome rests on our shoulders," Aulus Cotta declared, saying aloud what they all believed. They were now committed to action even at the risk of their lives. Change could only happen through action.

Sarmizegetusa, Summer 96 AD

The promise that King Decebal made to King Duras at his uncle's deathbed remained a key part of Dacia's strategy to fight off Roman invasion. In the seven years since then King Decebal formed alliances with dozens of tribes that suffered from past Roman aggression or feared future aggression.

Decebal's victories against Roman armies greatly increased his prestige in the region. That made alliance building much easier. Most importantly he strengthened Dacia's alliances with the Roxolani, the most powerful Sarmatian tribe, and the Germanic Bastarnae and Marcomanni tribes. Treaties were also made with the Celtic tribes west of Dacia, and the tribes of Scythia that lived northeast of Dacia.

The strategy meeting in King Decebal's throne room included his brother Diegis, the High Priest Vezina, and some important tribal allies. Prince Davi of the Roxolani was the same age as Diegis and had the same defiant warrior temperament. Fynn, a Bastarnae chief even as a young man, was a big burly warrior. Attalu was a chief of the Marcomanni, a large Suebi tribe in Germania who were forever a thorn in the side of the Roman Empire.

"Are Roman patrols active in Moesia?" King Decebal asked Davi.

"They stay in their forts for the most part," Davi said. "Very light patrols and they never approach our troops."

"They remember the beating you gave them in Banat four years ago," Diegis said with a grin. In the last major battle with Roman troops, a coalition of Roxolani and some Dacian forces beat back the Roman troops and inflicted massive casualties on a Roman legion. The legion was then disbanded rather than rebuilt.

King Decebal brought the conversation back to present concerns. "The Romans are docile in Moesia and Banat because they are in a defensive position. Domitian is not eager to be aggressive there." He turned to the Marcomanni chief. "What is the situation with General Trajan, Attalu?"

Attalu gave a small shrug. "He is not giving us trouble. Right now he has his hands full fighting the Chatti." The Chatti were one of the major Germanic tribes that had repeatedly clashed with Domitian's armies over the years.

"General Trajan is ambitious. Keep your eye on the Romans and be prepared for aggression," Decebal said. "At this time Emperor Domitian is not ambitious, but that could change."

"That is very true, Sire," Vezina said. "And if there comes a time when Emperor Domitian becomes ambitious, General Trajan will be the instrument to carry out his ambitions."

"I agree, Vezina. So, as I said Attalu, best to keep an eye on him."

"I understand," Attalu said. "However what I don't understand is this. How can you Dacians talk and talk, and not a single drop of ale or wine?"

"I was thinking the same thing," Fynn said with a laugh.

Diegis laughed with them. "We don't brew ale, but I'll show you where the best wine is."

"And on that note our talk is done," Decebal said. "Prince Davi, stay for a moment?"

"Of course, Your Highness."

As the others left Decebal turned to the prince. "I am informed that my sister is expecting to see you?"

"Indeed, so she is. The Lady Tanidela invited me to join the royal family for your evening meal. With your approval of course."

Decebal led him towards the doorway. "You have my approval and my welcome. Come now, we should not keep a lady waiting."

Rome, August 96 AD

The Empress Domitia Longina was returned to Rome after Julia, the Emperor's niece, had died suddenly and unexpectedly at a young age. The common people mourned Julia and welcomed back Domitia. She was well liked and admired for her beauty and grace.

Domitia was given living quarters in the palace, but separate from the Emperor's quarters. This was to her liking as well as his. They each had their own servants and schedules and it was not necessary to be together.

Stephanus, the Empress' steward, entered her dining room just as servants cleared away the breakfast dishes. He was a former slave of Domitilla. After being freed by her he found employment on the staff of the Empress. Stephanus was forty years old, a man of medium height and slim build. He was completely devoted to Domitia, to her safety and wellbeing. He was also the go-between between Caesar and the Empress when there was a need for communication.

"Did you sleep well, My Lady?" Stephanus asked politely.

"Well enough, Stephanus." She waited until the servants left the room. "Will you accompany me for a walk in the gardens?"

"Of course, My Lady. It's a lovely morning for a walk."

Domitia wanted to get outdoors where she could find privacy to talk. It was not safe for anyone to talk openly about sensitive matters in the palace. Anything that might offend the Emperor had to be treated as a sensitive matter.

The mood in Rome was despair. Five more wealthy patricians were executed the previous week. They were charged under the laws of majestas, or treason, but no one believed those charges to be true. Wealthy Roman citizens were murdered so that Domitian could take their lands and wealth.

Domitia and Stephanus walked to a quiet and open space near a marble fountain. Water gurgled gently as it flowed into the fountain basin from the mouths of two fish made of concrete. Bright morning sunshine shimmered on the water's surface.

Domitia looked off into the distance, lost in thought. Then a sad expression crossed her face. "I heard a dreadful rumor yesterday."

"What rumor, My Lady?"

"It concern Julia. Do you know how the poor girl died?"

Stephanus looked into her sad green eyes but said nothing.

"I am told," Domitia continued softly, "that she died in a failed abortion. I am also told that it was not her first abortion since she took to Caesar's bed."

Stephanus' face colored. "I do not know for certain if those rumors are true, My Lady, but people talk of them."

The Empress turned away. "That poor girl," she said in a voice barely above a whisper. "So much death in this palace."

Stephanus looked straight ahead to a spot down the garden path. He still remembered vividly the torture and execution of Paris, the actor. Domitia's former lover had been killed not too far from where they were sitting now. Stephanus was a servant in the company of Domitilla then, an audience to Caesar's revenge.

Domitia pushed her sadness away and hardened her face. There were more critical matters to think about. She turned to Stephanus and resumed her casual tone.

"Have you spoken with Petronius?"

"I have, My Lady," Stephanus replied just as casually, as if they were discussing the weather. "He is alarmed by the book, as you knew he would be."

Petronius Secundus was one of the two prefects of the Praetorian Guard. The existence of the "pillow-book" was revealed secretly to Domitia by Caesar's valet, Parthenius. This was a scroll kept under Domitian's pillow, and it listed all the names of the many people the Emperor suspected of disloyalty. These were the people who would be killed as occasions developed. Due to Domitian's paranoia it was a long list, and it kept growing longer. The Empress' name was one of the names on the list.

"Petronius has reason for concern," Domitia said evenly. "His name is in the book. As is yours, Stephanus. "

"I understand, My Lady," he replied grimly. "Petronius agrees and is in sympathy with you. He also, of course, understands the role of the Praetorian Guard."

"I trust that he does. It is a key role," Domitia said. She turned to look Stephanus in the eye. "But the less we talk of these things the better. Do what must be done, Stephanus."

"I will, My Lady," he promised. "You need say no more."

Stephanus gave her a small respectful bow and left. The Empress knew that she was trusting him with her life, but what choice was left to her? If Stephanus was suspected and arrested he would give her name under torture. If she did nothing she would eventually likely be executed like so many others. Better to fight for her life than to go like a lamb to the slaughter.

Domitia started a leisurely stroll towards the next fountain down the path. That one had a variety of colorful fish, many imported from Africa. On a sunny day their scales glimmered and dazzled in the crystal clear water.

A voice from behind her sent icy chills down her spine.

"Lovely day for a walk, my dear."

She turned to face Domitian, who caught up to her in a few quick steps. She had not heard him approaching.

"Indeed it is, Caesar."

The Emperor looked to be in a good mood. He flashed her a smile.

"Come, let's walk! I think better when I walk. Was that Stephanus you were speaking to back there?"

Domitia kept her face composed even as her heart beat faster. "Yes, that was Stephanus. He is reviewing my accounts."

"Be careful of that one. One hears rumors," Domitian shot her a quick glance, "that he embezzles funds now and then."

The Empress looked him in the eye. She was Domitia Longina, proud daughter of former general and consul Gnaeus Corbulo, and nobody played her for a fool. Not even Caesar.

"I thank you for the advice, Caesar, but you know that I command my servants efficiently." Her eyes flashed confidence and assurance, no hint of fear.

Her reply made Domitian smile. Even after her exile the Empress was still as spirited and beautiful as ever.

"Stephanus is a politician at heart, Domitia. He is good at talking to people and telling lies. Does he say much to you of how the winds are blowing in the Senate?"

"Nothing more than the usual, Caesar. Of which you know more than I."

Domitian frowned. "They always blame me. If something is not to their liking, I get the blame."

She nodded her understanding. "That is unfair treatment, Caesar, but unfortunately all too common."

"If I move legions from Britannia to fight in Dacia, they accuse me of giving away Britannia! If I move legions from Moesia to fight the traitor Saturninus in Germania, they accuse me of weakening Moesia and allowing the Sarmatians to take advantage! If I make a treaty with Dacia, they accuse me of paying crippling subsidies to Dacia! Crippling subsidies, imagine that! Those fools have no notion of what it would cost to keep five legions on Dacia's doorstep to keep an eye on Decebalus!"

The Empress looked at him sideways. "They might be in a more conciliatory mood, Caesar, if..."

"If what?" he asked impatiently.

She tried to find the right words. "If you didn't kill so many of them, perhaps."

Domitian was not amused. "Only you could say that to me and still keep your pretty little head."

"My apologies, Caesar. I do not wish to sound as though I question your wisdom. It was simply a thought."

Domitian's face darkened. "How am I to practice leniency when they question my decisions? How do I forgive treason? Never! How do I ignore these conspiracies against me?"

Domitia felt another cold chill down her spine but maintained her composure. "What conspiracies, Caesar?"

"Conspiracies against my crown! Against my life! What other kind of conspiracies matter, you foolish woman?"

The Empress flinched inside. "If plots are uncovered, Caesar, then surely heads will roll."

"Oh, heads will indeed roll," Domitian declared. "It seems that for now nobody believes the rumors are true. But tell me this, do you know why emperors are necessarily wretched men?"

"No, Caesar. I do not."

Domitian looked the Empress in the face and gave her a mirthless smile. "Because only their assassination can convince the public that the conspiracies against their lives are real."

Chapter 24

A DEATH IN ROME

Sarmizegetusa, September 18, 96 AD

*I*n Dacia, September 18 was the date of the major Autumn Festival for the god Zamolxis and the goddess Bendis. Zamolxis was the most important god of the Dacians, but not the only one. Bendis was a very ancient goddess of the moon, forests, and magic. Young women adored Bendis and prayed to her to provide them with healthy children.

In the morning the High Priest Vezina visited the living quarters of the royal family to review plans for the day with King Decebal. They were distracted by the loud commotion of children fussing over being dressed in their holiday clothes. The clothes designed to be worn on important holidays were made of soft white woolen cloth and embroidered with threads of different colors. The children sensed the special occasion and were naturally excited.

Queen Andrada was coordinating with her assistant Zelma to dress the "twins," six-year-olds Dorin and Lia. Diegis and his wife Mirela were preparing their five-year-old daughter, Ana, for her first holiday appearance in public. Ana had her mother's light brown hair and amber-brown eyes. She always listened to her mother, but when feeling anxious always sought comfort from her father.

The princess Adila was eleven and a veteran of these formal events. She took on the big sister role with all the younger children, giving instructions here one moment and encouragement there the next. The princess Zia sat off to one side. She was thirteen years old and no longer considered herself a child. Within a few more years she expected to be a mother herself.

Decebal did not mind the noisy family commotion. He treasured his family time when he was in Sarmizegetusa, the more noisy and lively the better. On this occasion however he needed to be able to hear and be heard. He steered Vezina to another room where they could talk, then closed the door behind them.

"Children get excitable for holidays, Sire," Vezina laughed softly. "Especially the younger ones."

"They do," Decebal agreed. "And they grow up fast. I can't believe that little Ana is already five."

"Yes," Vezina nodded. "The girl has made Diegis a changed man. More at peace with himself, I think."

"So the ceremony starts at noon?" the King asked, getting to the matter at hand.

"Yes, Sire. I will begin the religious service at noon, which lasts for one hour. Then we retire to the public feast. Before the feast begins you will address the people. For as long as you deem wise, Sire."

"Hungry people are never in a mood for long speeches, so I'll keep it short."

Vezina smiled. "A very wise policy."

"Before you leave," Decebal inquired as he walked the High Priest towards the door, "how goes the war in Pannonia? Will the Suebi ask for military assistance?"

Vezina gave the matter quick thought. The Suebi were a Germanic tribe whose treaties with Rome seemed to never last very long. On the other hand Dacia had been strengthening her treaties with tribes in Germania and neighboring regions.

"Rome's campaign in Pannonia is directed by Trajan. From what I hear his campaign goes well. The man has a gift for military tactics," Vezina said. "As for the Suebi, the Germans have not requested our assistance and I expect they will not. They take great pride in giving Rome trouble all by themselves."

"I expect that you're right. Keep me informed on Pannonia."

"As always, Sire. Now let us go and pay homage to Zamolxis and Bendis."

Pannonia, September 18, 96 AD

In the late morning General Trajan met with a small group of officers in his tent to review strategy. The legions had been fighting a series of skirmishes. The German tribes showed no signs of preparing for a major battle. This would make the campaign take longer, but he was certain that in time Rome would prevail.

"Is today not the 18th of September, Marcus?" asked General Gnaeus Pompeius Longinus, a playful smile on his face. The older man had long served as Trajan's close friend and mentor.

"So it is," Trajan replied, knowing exactly where Gnaeus was going with the question.

"Why then, it's your birthday!" Longinus exclaimed. That got the attention of the other officers standing nearby.

"It is indeed," Trajan said. "Not that I wish to make an event of it."

Longinus would not be put off. "Remind me, which birthday is it then? Thirty-seven? Thirty-eight?"

Trajan laughed. "It is my fortieth birthday, as you already know. Now you will tell me that I am getting old?"

"Not at all, not at all," the fifty-one year old Gnaeus protested. "Why, when I was forty I could march all day, drink all night, and fight ten long-haired Gauls in the morning. All that before breakfast, mind you."

"Of course," Trajan replied good-naturedly. "I shall try to keep up with you, Gnaeus."

Officers walked up to shake Trajan's hand and offer him birthday greetings. Birthdays were celebrated by the men who faced death as part of their daily routine. To a man, the soldiers felt fortunate to be serving under Marcus Ulpius Trajanus. Trajan was respected and admired, and they were happy to tie their fortunes to his.

Rome, September 18, 96 AD

In Rome the day began like any other. The Emperor Domitian met with a small group of supporters. He took his noonday meal in the gardens and listened to soothing music on the lyre as he sipped his best Falernian vintage. He drank only the best wines, and grapes from the slopes of Mount Falernus made wine like nectar of the gods. After the music and wine he would take his usual afternoon nap, then enjoy some "bed wrestling" with his favorite concubine.

Cassius Norbanus, the Praetorian Prefect along with Petronius Secundus, toured and inspected Caesar's sleeping quarters before the Emperor would arrive. Everything looked to be in order. Parthenius, Domitian's long-time valet, was preparing the royal bed with the help of a female slave. Fresh silk sheets and numerous pillows were put in place. Seeing Norbanus arrive, Parthenius sent the slave away.

"Everything in readiness?" Norbanus asked calmly.

"Yes," Parthenius answered softly. He was usually a nervous man, and today he seemed to struggle even more to control his nerves.

"Good. Simply do as you were told."

"Yes, sir," Parthenius answered. He stole a quick glance at the large silk pillow resting at the head of the Emperor's bed. Domitian always kept a sword underneath that pillow.

The valet's nervousness amused Norbanus and he put a calming hand on Parthenius' shoulder. "Everything is well, Parthenius. Simply do your part."

Parthenius gave a nod. How did these Praetorian officers stay so calm? Ice in their veins. It was beyond his understanding.

The Emperor Domitian came into the bedroom looking a bit drowsy from too much wine. He was accompanied by Saturninus

Saturius, his imperial chamberlain. Saturius gave Parthenius a glance, then looked away. They knew each other well from their many years of service to Domitian. Saturius' job was to aid the Emperor in preparing for bed.

Parthenius walked out into the hallway, past the four Praetorian Guards standing outside the door. There was a small crowd of half a dozen nobles, petitioners waiting for an audience with Caesar. One of them was the young Senator Aulus Cotta, who was petitioning Caesar on a matter of land holdings in Campania.

The petitioner who immediately stepped forward was Stephanus, a servant of the Empress Domitia. The man looked miserable due to his injured left arm. The arm was still heavily wrapped in a thick bandage a week after he had injured it.

"Parthenius, a quick word with Caesar?" Stephanus inquired. They were standing close enough to the door for the Praetorian Guards to hear their conversation.

"If it concerns financial matters it can wait, Stephanus."

Stephanus shook his head. "No, this is not about money. It is an urgent matter concerning Caesar. Urgent!"

"What is urgent?"

Stephanus lowered his voice. "Names, Parthenius. Highly placed names of conspirators. Caesar will be grateful to you if you grant me this audience."

Parthenius seemed to relent. "Wait here," he said, and went back into the royal sleeping chambers. He found Domitian sitting on the edge of the bed, dressed in a light sleeping tunic. The Emperor stretched his arms and yawned lazily.

"Caesar, Stephanus begs an audience. He says that he has names of conspirators. Highly placed names."

Domitian scowled. "The only thing that rascal is good for is spreading rumors. That, and stealing money."

Parthenius pressed on. "He insists that it is urgent, that men are conspiring."

Domitian waved his hand impatiently. "Show him in. Tell him that I will hear him if he has information worth hearing. And if he doesn't," Domitian smiled, "tell him that I will break his other arm."

"I will do so immediately, Caesar."

Stephanus was checked for weapons by the Praetorian Guard, then allowed into the royal bedchamber. As he approached the bed he was holding his bandaged left arm. It was wrapped from the wrist to the elbow. The look in his eyes, Domitian thought, was not pain. It was something else.

"Your arm is still not healed, Stephanus? You've had it bandaged for days now."

"A bad sprain, Caesar." Stephanus said. "I was careless and a horse threw me."

"You should be more careful then. Parthenius tells me you have names. What names?"

Stephanus walked a few steps closer to the bed. "It grieves me to tell you, Caesar, because they are dear to you."

"Don't speak in riddles!" the Emperor complained, irritated. "Tell me plain."

"I made a list for you. Here," Stephanus said, reaching under his thick bandage as he approached to stand in front of Domitian.

What Stephanus pulled from underneath his bandage was not a parchment with a list of names, but a long and thin knife. Domitian's eyes widened in alarm and he quickly moved backwards on the silk sheets covering the bed. Stephanus made a quick lunge with the knife for the Emperor's belly. Domitian twisted away to escape and the knife plunged deep into his groin. The Emperor screamed in pain.

"Guards! Assassins! Help!" Domitian screamed and slid across the bed towards his pile of pillows and his hidden sword, blood already spreading on the silk sheets. He searched frantically under the large pillow where he kept his sword for just such emergencies. His hand came out holding only the sword hilt. To his astonishment, the sword blade had been removed.

The Emperor looked frantically to Parthenius for help and was again astonished to see Parthenius quietly standing nearby, just watching the attack. Parthenius had betrayed him. He had removed the blade from his sword and left him defenseless.

Stephanus lunged forward with the knife again and stabbed him in the upper leg. Domitian screamed again.

"Guards! Guards!" the Emperor yelled again for help. Stephanus grabbed one of his feet and dragged him across the silky sheets to the floor. Domitian made a desperate lunge for Stephanus' legs and brought him down on the floor with him. He fought and clawed for the knife but could not wrest it away.

The doors to the royal sleeping chamber burst open. The four men who rushed in were not Praetorian Guards, but four of the Roman nobles who had been waiting in the hallway. They carried knives of their own. Aulus Cotta pulled Domitian away from Stephanus, and the four men fell savagely on the Emperor with their knives.

Caesar Titus Flavius Domitianus screamed with terror and pain until his mouth filled with blood, and then he screamed no more.

The five assassins barely finished their work when, to their big surprise, they were suddenly attacked by half a dozen palace servants. The servants were brought there by the screams of the Emperor, and they came running carrying kitchen knives and cleavers. A skirmish quickly broke out between them and the assassins.

"Stop!" Parthenius shouted at the servants, waving his arms to get their attention. "Don't fight! Stop!"

In the excitement and confusion he was not heard or was simply ignored. As Stephanus was fighting off one of the servants another one plunged a sharp kitchen knife into the side of his neck. He fell and joined Domitian on the floor in a spreading pool of blood. The servants were being held off by the assassins. Finally, seeing that the Emperor was dead, the servants ran away.

No Praetorian Guards came to Caesar's rescue. Once the attack on Domitian was underway they were held back by their officer Cassius

Norbanus, who would later report that the Praetorian Guard had been tricked and was not able to prevent the attack. The Guard did not join in on the assassination, but neither did they intervene to stop it. In the long tradition of the Praetorian Guard they once again played a key role in the transition of power in Rome.

News of the Emperor Domitian's death spread quickly through the city. The plebeians were for the most part indifferent. They expected the next Caesar to carry on much the same as the last Caesar. The grain dole and the games would continue, and life would go on as usual. Politics in Rome were mostly the business of the nobility.

The reaction in the Senate of Rome was euphoria. The Senate quickly voted that every public statue and other images of Domitian were to be destroyed. His statues made from precious metals would be added as bullion to the state treasury. His name would be erased from all public inscriptions and removed from public records. They would try and do everything in their power to remove the memory of the Emperor Domitian from Rome's history.

The Empress Domitia Longina retired to her quarters in the royal palace, attended by her servants. She was in no danger of harm from Domitian's enemies, and the people of the city still admired and loved her. She thought it best to keep out of the public eye for a period of time until things calmed down.

Publically Domitia would play the role of Caesar's widow in mourning. Privately she felt relieved and thankful to be able to live in peace without fear for her life. She had survived Domitian's madness and his cruelty. Although there would be rumors of her involvement in the plot against the Emperor, no one accused her publically and no evidence was ever produced.

In the early evening on September 18, the day of the assassination, Petronius Secundus went to the house of Senator Marcus Ciocceius Nerva. Parthenius went with him. Secundus, the other Prefect of the

Praetorian Guard, was there for official recognition. Parthenius was there for personal reassurance.

A house servant ushered them inside and showed them to Nerva's study, where the senator was calmly sitting and reading a book. He was not surprised to see them.

"You know the reason we are here," Secundus said after greetings were exchanged. "You are chosen to be the new Caesar, Marcus. You have the support of the Senate, the Praetorian Guard, and the army. You are well known and admired even by the plebs."

Nerva acknowledged the compliment with a polite nod. Instead of replying to Secundus however he turned to Parthenius.

"Is the Emperor really dead, Parthenius?"

"Yes, Senator. Emperor Domitian is dead. I was there to see it happen, and afterwards I examined the body myself."

Nerva breathed a sigh of relief. "Rome is better for it. I feared that I would not live long enough to see this day."

"We are all happy to see that you are alive and well on this day," Petronius continued. "Now Rome needs your leadership. You are the choice for princeps. Will you accept, Marcus?"

Nerva smiled. "I am the compromise choice, you mean. Come, we can be honest, Petronius. Before Domitian was killed how many men did you ask who turned you down before you came to me?"

Secundus shook his head. "That makes no difference. I did not take you for a vain man, Marcus."

Nerva laughed softly. "I am not a vain man! I am simply curious."

"You are the best choice possible," Petronius insisted. "You must accept the honor, Senator."

"Please, if I might have a word," Parthenius interjected. "Prefect Secundus is right. Rome needs your calm wisdom and your selfless service, Senator Nerva. There is no Roman who is a better choice."

"Then I hope that I am worthy of your trust, Parthenius." Nerva stood up from his chair. "Come, gentlemen. Let us go and speak with the Senate."

That evening the Senate of Rome voted, by acclamation, the title of Caesar to Marcus Nerva. He thus became the new princeps, the first citizen among equals, a tradition established by Augustus Caesar.

Emperor Nerva immediately changed the atmosphere of fear and terror in Rome. He promised that he would not rule as a tyrant, and it was very clear to everyone what he meant by that. He would not be Domitian. There would be no revenge or retribution against the old supporters of Domitian. He would not persecute his political rivals or enemies. There would be an end to exiles and murder of nobles, and to confiscation of their property. Those who were unfairly exiled would be summoned back to Rome.

The new Emperor promised to keep all military commanders in place, which made the army happy. He guaranteed that he would continue the high pay and elite status of the Praetorian Guard. He promised to reduce the very high taxes that had been imposed on the wealthiest Romans by Domitian.

To benefit the common people, Emperor Nerva announced plans to increase the grain supply in order to prevent food shortages. In a new spirit of freedom and reform, he even promised to restore the theater and pantomime shows that were not allowed during the reign of Domitian.

It was soon clear to everyone that Emperor Nerva was no Emperor Domitian. Domitian's reign of terror was over at last.

Chapter 25

IN THE HANDS OF THE GODS

Sarmizegetusa, Spring 97 AD

*K*ing Decebal presided over the meeting of his senior council in the throne room. Vezina, Diegis, and Drilgisa always attended. Military matters on Dacia's western border needed attention. Political developments in Rome needed to be discussed and strategy planned.

The news of Domitian's assassination had reached Dacia in late October and created some initial uncertainty. Not much was known in detail about Senator Nerva, now Emperor Nerva. The new Caesar eased any doubts by quickly sending a messenger to King Decebal to inform him that Rome would continue to honor its treaty with Dacia.

Vezina was responsible for collecting information from travelers, envoys, and paid informants. He began by giving the senior council a summary briefing.

"Emperor Nerva is keeping the peace in Rome so far," Vezina said. "The transition of power was remarkably smooth and peaceful by Roman standards. Usually they slaughter each other to determine who becomes the new Caesar."

"The killing of Emperor Domitian was no palace revolt, that much is clear," Decebal said. "It was planned in advance by those who rule Rome. That means the Senate, the army, and the Praetorian Guard must have agreed on Nerva as their choice."

"But why Nerva?" Diegis asked. "Drilgisa and I saw him briefly during our visit to Rome, although we were not allowed to speak with him. He did not look like an impressive figure."

"And that might be precisely the reason why he became their choice," Vezina said.

"How do you mean, Vezina? He looks like someone's nice old grandfather."

"Exactly the point!" Vezina exclaimed. "Senator Nerva was not seen as a threat to any of the parties involved. That is why we saw no conflicts and no bloodshed."

"Not yet," Drilgisa said with a wry grin, "but give them time."

Decebal turned to Vezina. "How old is this new emperor?"

"He is past sixty. And from what I hear, not in the best of health."

Decebal leaned back in his chair. "Nerva is a temporary fix for Rome. He is not a threat to us. The threat to Dacia, I am sure, will be the emperor who follows Nerva."

"Very true," Drilgisa said. "And who is that likely to be?"

All eyes turned to Vezina. He slowly shook his head.

"It is much too early to tell. We need more information from Rome, and we need to watch closely as events develop there."

"Watch the Praetorian Guard," Drilgisa advised. "Those bastards are usually behind changes in power."

"Ah!" Vezina said with a knowing smile. "Those bastards, as you call them, have already started."

The King raised an eyebrow. "What do you mean?"

"There was a rebellion among some of the troops of the Praetorian Guard, those who were supporters of Domitian. They felt betrayed by their officers, who stood by and allowed the assassination to happen."

"How did Nerva deal with this rebellion?" Decebal wondered. "He is no Domitian."

"He dismissed the old prefects, as the rebels demanded. He then replaced them with one Casperius Aelianus. He was a former prefect under Domitian and was favored by those protesting."

Drilgisa frowned. "That is not what I would have done. Rewarding rebellion leads to further rebellion." He turned to Decebal. "Is that not so?"

"True enough, Drilgisa. Which is why," the King added jokingly, "I don't allow you to get away with anything."

Drilgisa laughed. "You have no cause for worry about me. Anyone starts any trouble against you, I'll gut him."

"Nerva acted as the peacemaker," Vezina said. "That is what he was chosen to do."

"He showed a serious weakness," Drilgisa insisted.

Vezina waved the comment away. "Let Emperor Nerva deal with the problems in Rome. For now they don't concern us. Domitian lost his appetite for fighting Dacia and Nerva is not likely to be any more aggressive."

"Not unless he is pushed into it," Decebal added. "There are many in Rome who wish to end their treaty with Dacia. They view it as an injury and an insult to them."

"Yes," Vezina said. "Not only an insult to Rome's pride but also a burden on their state treasury."

King Decebal changed the subject. "How are the Germans faring in Pannonia?"

"They are giving the Romans a good fight," Drilgisa reported. He had contacts with the Chatti and other Germanic tribes. "However, General Trajan is driving them further west. He wants to push them out of Pannonia entirely."

"Invite Chief Fynn here to talk with us," Decebal instructed. "I want to know what the Bastarnae are planning."

"Yes, Sire. I will send an envoy today," Drilgisa said.

"Good. That is all for now," the King said, ending the meeting. He turned to his brother. "Diegis, a moment?"

"What is it" Diegis asked when the others left.

"You look troubled, Brother. Is something wrong?"

Pain flashed across Diegis' eyes. "Family matters," he said.

"What family matters? Is Ana well?"

"Ana is thriving, she is growing like a weed. It's Mirela that I'm worried about."

"How so?"

"She is getting very thin, and she is always tired."

"I see," Decebal said. He clasped Diegis on the shoulder. "Send her to talk to Andrada."

"She already has. But I will ask her to talk to her again."

"Good. Whatever can be done, Andrada will do it."

The medical clinic was located not far from the royal palace. Queen Andrada and her assistants provided advice on foods and herbal treatments for a wide variety of illnesses and ailments. They did not rely on magic or superstition. Food and herbal medicine was a form of medicine that went back to ancient times, and they relied on their knowledge and experience to guide their advice to patients.

King Decebal walked to the clinic as the sun was setting, turning the sky into a blaze of red and orange colors. Some assistants were still at work there, tidying up. He found Andrada and Zelma sitting on a couch placed against the wall, deep in conversation. Zelma stood up and bowed as the King approached.

Decebal motioned for her to sit. "You may stay, Zelma. I wish to speak with both of you."

Andrada saw the look in his eyes. "You talked to Diegis?"

"Yes, briefly. He tells me only that his wife is ill, but he is besides himself. Do you know more?"

"She is losing vitality much too quickly for a woman her age," the Queen began. "She is only..."

"Twenty-five years old," Zelma said when the Queen struggled to remember. "Much too young to be tired all day. Also she is losing weight and her pallor is not healthy."

Decebal frowned. "Do you have a diagnosis?"

Andrada shook her head. "We do not rush to judgment. She takes turmeric, ginger, and rosemary. Also tea made from holy basil."

"This will help with her blood and her energy," Zelma explained.

"Will she get better?"

"Time and patience are great healers," Andrada said. "Medicine may help, but the body heals itself."

Decebal knew that to be true. The body heals itself. Zamolxis taught that lesson to his people hundreds of years ago. All mortals can do is practice the habits for good health. The rest was in the hands of the gods.

"Then she will be well, if Zamolxis wills it." He glanced at Zelma. "Does your Christian god help in these matters?"

"Yes, Sire," the young woman replied. "I shall pray for the Lady Mirela's health."

By the time spring turned to summer neither medicine nor prayer were helping Mirela become healthier. She grew thinner and weaker, and the day came when she had to take to her bed. Diegis was very distraught and angry that he could not do more for her. He stayed by her side as much as he could. Their six year old daughter Ana was kept busy playing with the other children, but she was still acutely aware of her mother's sadness and her father's worry.

Ana walked into her parents' sleeping chamber to see her mother before she went out to play. This was an important part of her routine every morning and every evening. During the daytime her mother spent time with her father, and was busy being attended to by her servants. Aunt Andrada visited often.

Mirela always had a happy smile for her young daughter. "Come here, my darling girl. Give Mama a kiss."

Ana walked to her and kissed her cheek. "Are you feeling better today, Mama?"

"A little better, yes. Viviana is taking good care of me." Viviana was Mirela's attendant who stayed by her side, day and night. The elderly woman gave Ana a warm smile.

"That's good," Ana said. Her mother always looked so pale and that worried her.

"Zamolxis watches over me, so do not worry. Who are you going to play with today?"

"Lia is waiting for me outside. We are going to pick apples." Lia was Zelma's daughter and slightly older than Ana.

"That sounds wonderful, Ana. Bring back some nice apples for us."

"Yes, Mama. I will bring you the best apple in the orchard."

"That's my sweet girl. Now go and play," Mirela said.

Ana kissed her cheek again. "Goodbye, Mama."

In the afternoon Ana left the other children and went to talk with her Aunt Andrada. The Queen was patient with her and took the time to listen. Ana always felt better after one of their talks.

The little girl quickly came to what was on her mind. "Auntie, is Mama going to die soon?"

Ana understood what death was. Usually older people died, and they were buried and never came back. Often babies died soon after they were born if they got sick. One of her young friends died in the winter from a fever. Farm animals died all the time to provide food for people. Even at a young age she understood that in time all things die. The thought of her mother going away and never coming back, however, was too terrible to think about.

Andrada place a hand on her niece's arm, seeking to comfort with her touch. "Your mother is ill."

"I know that," the girl said with a sigh. "I want to know if Mama will die soon."

"I do not know, my child," the Queen replied tenderly. "It may be soon, it may be in a long time. We cannot know."

"It's not fair," Ana said, and tears came running down her cheeks.

Andrada pulled her close and held her in a tight hug. The little girl sobbed in her arms. "It's all right," the Queen whispered to her. "It will be all right."

"Why do people die?"

Andrada wiped the tears from the girl's cheeks. "Death is a part of life, Ana. We are born, we live, and we die. It is the will of the gods." Andrada paused to wipe away a tear from her own cheek. "It is a sad part of life."

"Where will Mama go?" Ana asked. "After she dies?"

Andrada held the girl's hand and looked into her eyes.

"Your beautiful Mama will go to the kingdom of Zamolxis. That is where all the Dacian people go. She will be happy there. And one day, when we die, we will go there too and we will see her again."

Ana smiled a sad smile. "Then I will see Mama again?"

Andrada touched her softly on the cheek. "Yes, of course you will see her again."

Ana's tears stopped, and she fell silent for a few moments. "I still feel sad," she said.

"Yes, I know. I feel sad too." The Queen paused and looked into her eyes again. "Listen now, here is what I want you to do."

"What, Auntie?"

"Two things."

"What two things?"

"Next week is the Messenger ceremony. That is the time when we send our prayers to Zamolxis. Do you understand?"

"I think so," Ana said. She was too young to remember the last Messenger ceremony, which took place five years ago, but she had learned about it as did all Dacian children.

"Good," said Andrada. "I want you to give the Messenger a prayer for Zamolxis. Ask Zamolxis to make your Mama healthy again."

"Okay, I will," Ana said. Her face became a little brighter.

"And the other thing is, I want you to go home now and tell Mama that you love her very much. Will you do that?"

"Yes, Auntie."

"Good." She gave Ana a goodbye kiss on the forehead. "Cotiso is practicing his archery outside. Ask him to walk you home." Cotiso was Ana's grown-up cousin.

"All right. Goodbye, Auntie."

After Ana left the Queen sat down on the couch, lost in a wave of sadness and frustration. Mirela had the illness some called the spider crab, because people grew tumors inside their bodies that looked like large spiders or crabs. And she was helpless to help them. Utterly helpless.

She could offer people herbal medicines and advice, and often that helped. Beyond that it was all the will of the gods. Sometimes the gods listened. She hoped that was true.

Cotiso and his friend Petipor competed fiercely against each other in the Messenger competition. Both were mature young warriors, strong and athletic. Both had keen, sharp minds and were of the highest character. Both were handsome of face and had unblemished skin. All these things were important because the man selected to be the Messenger to Zamolxis was required to be the most perfect of all Dacians.

Since ancient times, every five years Dacia selected a young man to carry their highest wishes and hopes to Zamolxis. Most often the god accepted the gift from his people, and their wishes were granted. More rarely the gift was not accepted, which was then taken as a very bad omen.

Young warriors competed for the honor of being chosen to be the Messenger. It was a path to immortality. The contests included races on foot and on horse, feats of strength, spear throwing, knife skills, archery, and horse archery. The most deserving warrior was chosen by the temple priests of Zamolxis on the basis of athletic skills and physical appearance.

King Decebal and the High Priest Vezina watched from the side of the athletic field as the top five remaining competitors finished an archery contest. Petipor was the best athlete of the group, easily the fastest runner and best horseman. Cotiso was the superior archer, on foot and on horseback. Both were equally well liked by the young women of the city. The other three finalists knew that their own chances were slim but continued to compete due to dedication and simple pride.

"Cotiso has mastered the bow," Vezina said as another of the young man's arrows found the middle of the target.

Decebal grinned. "He is a better bowman than a swordsman. To his credit, he spends hours each day practicing his archery skills."

"I do credit him, Sire. He is a fine young man."

"Who do you favor, then? Him or Petipor? Or one of the others?"

Vezina became thoughtful for a moment. "Today, I do not favor any of them. Tomorrow, Zamolxis will provide guidance."

Decebal nodded, satisfied with the honest answer. Tomorrow the Messenger to Zamolxis would be chosen by Vezina and his priests. His son Cotiso would be chosen, or he would not. It was in the hands of the gods.

The following day the skies were clear and bright. Vezina declared it a very good omen. Dark skies showed the gods' displeasure, bright skies were a sign of their approval. It was a good day to choose the Messenger.

The five eager competitors stood before the Temple of Zamolxis, facing a very large crowd gathered to watch the ceremony. They wore their best clothes and were perfectly groomed for the occasion. Their faces were calm, hiding the emotions and the tensions within.

Queen Andrada stood beside the King and squeezed his hand. She was nervous.

"Who will Vezina choose?" she wondered.

"All the priests together make the choice," Decebal said.

"Yes, I know that," she replied impatiently. "However Vezina is the one who announces the choice."

Vezina and fifty more of the Priests of Zamolxis, all wearing their blue robes trimmed with silver thread, walked out of the Temple and lined up behind the five young men. Vezina walked out in front. The crowd grew silent, respectful of the solemn occasion.

"Look at Cotiso, he looks so calm," Andrada said in a soft voice. "I don't know if I could be that calm."

Decebal was lost in thought and barely heard her. He took a deep breath and let it out slowly.

The High Priest walked in front of the five warriors. Cotiso and Petipor stood side by side in the middle of the line. Vezina looked at each of them for a moment, then reached out with his right hand and placed it on the shoulder of Petipor. He guided the young man out of the line and led him to the front of the crowd. Petipor's face was filled with joy.

Cotiso's face did not show any emotion. His disappointment was tempered by happiness for his friend. He understood how sacred and solemn this moment was and maintained his poise as Vezina spoke to the assembled crowd. He caught the eye of his father, the King, but could not read his expression. The Queen looked at him with a gentle smile on her face.

For the next three days Petipor, the chosen Messenger to Zamolxis, stood in the Temple and received a stream of visitors of his fellow Dacians. He listened patiently to the wishes, hopes, and prayers of each person. One of them was a six year old girl named Ana, the niece of the King, who prayed that Zamolxis would make her mother whole again. He promised her that Zamolxis would hear her message.

It was the noble and most sacred duty of the Messenger to carry the people's wishes to Zamolxis. He was the gift of his people to their god. The perfect warrior, a gift worthy of a god. No Dacian could hope for a greater honor.

On the fourth day the sacred Messenger to Zamolxis ceremony was performed. Again a large crowd gathered in front of the Temple, even greater than before. A long wooden stage, raised to the height of a man, was erected in front. King Decebal, Queen Andrada, Cotiso, and the rest of the royal family were seated near the side of the stage. People in the crowd talked quietly among themselves as they waited for the priests and the Messenger to arrive.

High Priest Vezina led the Messenger out of the Temple, with Mircea and a long line of priests following in their wake. Vezina walked Petipor up the steps to the top of the stage. Four Dacian men waited for them, dressed in colorful ceremonial clothes.

Petipor walked to the front of the stage and looked out over the crowd, his blue eyes glistening with emotion. Just below him, on the ground in front of the stage, he saw three warriors standing and waiting. Each carried a very long spear.

The young man turned toward Vezina and smiled. This was the fate chosen for him by Zamolxis and he accepted it gladly. The High Priest touched him on the forehead and gave him a long and heartfelt blessing. Then Petipor lowered himself to the stage floor and stretched out on his back. He crossed his arms over his chest, and closed his eyes. He was at peace.

At a signal from Vezina the four men on the stage each took hold of one of Petipor's arms or legs. They lifted him off the stage floor and up to waist level. Below them, on the ground, the three warriors with the long spears readied themselves.

The Dacians on the stage tossed the Messenger high up in the air and over the edge of the stage. The warriors on the ground positioned themselves so that the falling body landed directly on the tips of their spears. All three spears penetrated the torso of Petipor. Some people in the crowd gasped.

The three spearmen slowly and gracefully lowered the body to the ground. Mircea knelt over Petipor for a few moments, then checked for a sign of breath. He looked up at Vezina at the top of the stage and gave a solemn nod. The Messenger was no longer breathing.

The High Priest turned to face the crowd, raised both arms to the sky, and said a prayer. Zamolxis had accepted their gift and all would be well.

Two months later, on a gloomy and rainy day, Mirela lost her battle with her long illness. She was mourned by the royal family and the entire city. Most of all she was mourned by her husband Diegis and her daughter Ana. She was buried two days later in her finest dress, along with her jewelry and a few prized possessions.

Mirela was buried near the grave of King Duras. She was laid in her grave wrapped in a shroud, face up, with her head pointing to the east. The people mourned her as they had mourned King Duras. Their grief was even more intense because the beloved Mirela died so young. The pain of loss is always greater when life ends too soon.

Chapter 26

THE TRUE POWER

Rome, August 97 AD

Caesar Nerva was reviewing design plans with his main architect when the Praetorian Guard came to arrest him. He promptly dismissed the frightened architect, along with the plans for new granaries in the Port of Rome. The man took his drawings and left in a rush.

Casperius Aelianus himself, the restored prefect of the Praetorian Guard, led a group of twenty soldiers into Nerva's quarters inside the imperial palace. They were in armor and armed with swords, as was the exclusive right of the Guard in the royal residences.

"What is the meaning of this? I did not summon you!" Nerva said crossly to Aelianus.

Aelianus walked up to the Emperor, cool but very determined. "We come of our own accord, Caesar. We do not require a summons. The Praetorian Guard demands justice for the assassination of noble Emperor Domitian. Until justice is delivered, Caesar, you will be in the custody of the Guard."

Nerva went red in the face. "I am Caesar! You will not dare arrest me! I order you to leave! You will return to your quarters!"

The Prefect remained insistent. "We do not wish your detention, only your cooperation in arresting and punishing the assassins of the

Emperor Domitian." He gestured to one of his lieutenants, who walked up to Caesar and presented him with a scroll.

"What is this?" Nerva asked indignantly. He knew that he was in danger, but was also deeply offended to be dictated to by men who should be groveling at his feet and obeying his every command.

Aelianus was very direct. "That is a list of names of the traitors and assassins who were implicated in the assassination of Domitian. You will have them brought to us, here, immediately. The Guard will then deliver justice."

Nerva quickly scanned the names on the list. Parthenius, the valet of Domitian who disarmed the Emperor and arranged for Stephanus to enter the bedchamber. Petronius Secundus and Cassius Norbanus, the former prefects of the Praetorian Guard who were complicit in allowing the assassination to happen. Saturninus Saturius, imperial chamberlain who conspired with Parthenius. Senator Aulus Cotta and three other Roman nobles who stabbed Domitian to death along with Stephanus.

The Emperor threw the parchment down to the ground. "Never!" he shouted.

Prefect Aelianus picked up the list and handed it back to Nerva. "You will order these men to be brought here. Immediately, Caesar. You will then sentence them to death for the crime of treason. The Guard seeks justice, not murder, and we will execute these criminals under the authority of Caesar."

"I will not have these men executed," Nerva declared forcefully. "I would rather die first."

"Be reasonable, Caesar. We wish only your help, not your death. Until you deliver these men and we deliver justice," Aelianus gave the Emperor a hard look, "you are not permitted to go anywhere and no one is permitted to see you. These are the requests of the Praetorian Guard."

"These are the demands of the Praetorian Guard!" Nerva spat. "I named you to be prefect of the Guard, Aelianus. The prefect follows orders! He does not give orders to Caesar!"

Aelianus stood firm. "Give the necessary orders, Caesar, or we sit here and wait until you do."

"Then we wait," the Emperor stubbornly declared.

After two days of waiting, and thinking, the Emperor Nerva knew that he was beaten and his position was hopeless. The men who were sworn to protect him had turned against him. There were no powers in Rome strong enough to defy the Praetorian Guard. There was no army that would march on Rome to rescue him.

Accepting humiliation, Nerva reluctantly gave the orders to have the men on the list arrested and brought to the imperial palace. The ex-prefect Norbanus and Senator Cotta could not be located. The rest were dragged in, one by one, some with multiple bruises and cuts on their faces.

Prefect Aelianus had them brought to the royal garden, which was what Domitian would have done. Parthenius, Secundus, Saturius, and three nobles were lined up in front of Nerva and Aelianus with their hands tied behind their backs. They were forced to kneel. All except Secundus had the sad and resigned look of doomed men on their faces.

"Give the order, Caesar," Aelianus urged.

Nerva looked at the helpless prisoners and slowly shook his head to show his reluctance and displeasure. Parthenius gazed up at him with an abject look of confusion and fear in his eyes. Secundus gave his captors an angry and defiant look.

"Does Caesar take orders from a prefect of the Guard?" Secundus asked scornfully. "That never happened under my watch."

Aelianus sneered. "The Emperor was killed under your watch! You failed in your most sacred duty, you traitor. Now you will be punished for your crime."

Nerva turned on him. "It is the duty of Roman courts and judges to determine criminal guilt and give out punishment. It is also in the power of Caesar. You, Prefect Aelianus, do not have this right!"

Aelianus held firm. "And yet here we are. You must give the order Caesar, as we agreed. The Guard will not rest until justice is served to these criminals."

The Emperor looked up at the sky, as if seeking answers there. The gods remained silent. He looked back to the prisoners, some of whom were pleading for mercy with their eyes. He gritted his teeth and shook his head in disgust but could see no way out.

"I sentence these prisoners to death for the crime of treason," Nerva finally declared. "They are guilty of the murder of Caesar Titus Flavius Domitianus."

Petronius Secundus spat on the ground to show his disgust with these proceedings. Aelianus smiled cruelly and moved towards him, drawing his sword as he walked.

"Petronius Secundus, you betrayed your sacred oath to protect Caesar and you betrayed your brothers in the Guard. You deserve a traitor's shameful death, but as a brother in the Guard I shall allow you a small mercy."

Petronius refused to look at him and stared hard at the ground. Aelianus raised his gladius high with both hands, then brought it down very hard against the back of Secundus' exposed neck. The blade cut through the spine and Secundus died instantly. His body slumped and fell to the right, blood gushing to soak Parthenius' leg. Parthenius was too petrified with fear to move.

Aelianus turned to him. "And you, Parthenius. You are a special kind of villain. You conspired against Caesar with his enemies. You allowed an assassin past the guards to attack Caesar. And finally and most cowardly, you robbed Caesar of his sword so that he could not defend himself. What punishment is just for you?"

Parthenius was shaking like a leaf. He had no answer.

"With Petronius I was merciful. With you, Parthenius, I shall be harsh," the Prefect continued. He turned to the two guards standing by the prisoner. "Strip him."

The men drew knives and cut and tore away Parthenius' tunic, then his undergarments. He was made to stand before Aelianus in complete humiliation. The Prefect looked at him with disgust.

"Castrate him," he ordered in a cold tone.

Parthenius screamed as one of the guards used his knife to carry out the order. Nerva turned his head away in disgust. Parthenius only stopped screaming when the other guard standing behind him wrapped both hands around his neck and squeezed hard. Parthenius was choked to death slowly, his face turning purple, then fell to the ground in a heap.

"Enough of this barbarity!" Nerva shouted. "This is not justice, it is savagery!"

"Now we shall do executions," Aelianus said. He nodded to the other guards, and one by one the other prisoners were dispatched with a gladius through the belly or throat.

When the killings were finally over Emperor Nerva glared at the man he had appointed as his Praetorian Prefect. That was an action he deeply regretted now, but what was done was done.

"Are you now satisfied with your justice, Aelianus?"

The Prefect smiled the content smile of a conqueror. "We are not quite finished, Caesar. There is one more thing for you to do for the Guard."

Later that same day the Emperor Nerva stood on the steps of the Senate House addressing a large crowd gathered before him. Behind him stood Casperius Aelianus and the twenty other members of the Praetorian Guard execution squad. Many senators and other nobles had known Nerva for decades and knew him very well. It was clear to them that Emperor Nerva was speaking under duress. Caesar was not the one in power this day. No one dared speak out in protest.

"These men standing with me are the finest, the most noble men of the Praetorian Guard," Nerva began in a loud voice. "They are the best of Rome. Today they avenged the murder of Emperor Domitian by executing those most wicked and sinful men who assassinated Caesar!"

There were a few murmurs in the crowd but no one reacted with any passion. People stood in silence and watched. Casperius did not care how the crowd reacted, but he wanted them to hear the next part. He was doing his duty and protecting the Guard.

Nerva continued. "These men acted on the orders of Caesar. I wish to thank these brave men for their devotion to honor and justice. All citizens of Rome must thank them! These men are heroes of Rome!"

His humiliation utter and complete, Emperor Nerva turned and walked away. It was a sad and lonely walk back to the imperial palace. He was escorted on the way by the Praetorian Guard, the men sworn to serve and protect him.

One week later Senator Quintus Matius, seventy years old and one of the few men in the Senate older than Nerva, was enjoying his after dinner wine with the Emperor. Their friendship in the Senate went back more than forty years.

Quintus knew well that his old friend was deeply troubled by the recent power struggle with the Praetorian Guard. The Emperor's public humiliation was worse, a deep wound to the pride of a very proud man from a very old and noble family.

After a period of quiet reflection Nerva asked the question that was uppermost in his mind. "Do you think I ought to abdicate my crown, Quintus?"

Matius paused to consider the very serious question. "No, Marcus. I do not."

"And why not? They showed to everyone the limits of Caesar's power. In a most humbling and humiliating fashion, no less."

Matius shook his head. "It is too soon. If you give up the purple now it would lead to chaos. Rome still needs you. Also, and I tell you this because it is very important for the future of Rome, you must leave a strong legacy, Marcus."

Nerva shrugged. "I have no heir. What legacy can I leave?"

Matius persisted. He knew that he was in the right and that made him as stubborn as a dog with a bone. "If you were to abdicate now your legacy will be that you quit and left Rome in chaos. That would be a terrible legacy. Certainly no legacy worthy of you."

Nerva became silent again, deep in thought. Matius could always be counted on to be the voice of reason. "Very well, Quintus. You are right once again. My legacy is that, before I die, I shall steer Rome in a new direction. I will not let her drift into ruin."

"Good," Matius said with a satisfied smile. "I hoped you would reach that conclusion, Caesar." The senator paused briefly and his face darkened. "And what of Casperius Aelianus and his cronies?"

Nerva raised his brows. "What of them?"

"Their treatment of Caesar was a grave injustice. They should be punished."

The Emperor smiled sadly. "The world is full of injustice, my friend." He paused to take a sip of wine. "Casperius showed us that the Praetorian Guard is more powerful than Caesar. I cannot punish him because there is no one in Rome who can carry out my order and punish him."

"May the gods punish him then," Quintus said with bitterness. "This injustice cannot stand. Caesar and the Senate of Rome must rule Rome, not the Praetorian Guard."

Nerva raised his wine goblet in a toast and gave Matius a wry smile. "May the gods punish him, then."

In October Emperor Nerva received a letter from Pannonia, from General Marcus Trajan. Included with the letter was a laurel wreath for Caesar, to celebrate the victory of driving out the Germanic tribes. Pannonia was now secure as a Roman province.

Nerva went to the Forum Romanum and mounted the rostra, the raised stage from which important public announcements were made. A very large crowd soon gathered including the Senate of Rome. Word spread quickly that important news from Caesar was expected.

Emperor Nerva, wearing his laurel wreath, proudly described the great victories won by General Marcus Trajan in Pannonia. He read the letter from the general, which made it very clear that Trajan also credited Caesar Nerva for his leadership in the military campaign. The crowd was in a happy and celebrating mood.

Nerva finished his speech about Pannonia, then raised his voice so that everyone would hear him well and made a final announcement. "May good success always attend the Roman Senate and people and myself. I hereby adopt Marcus Ulpius Nerva Trajan."

With that, Nerva left the rostra and headed back to the imperial palace. Senators gathered and talked in small groups. Quintus Matius sat quietly and smiled to himself. His good friend, Marcus Nerva, had just cemented his legacy and set the course for the future of Rome.

Moguntiacum, Germania, November 97 AD

General Marcus Trajan was back at his base in Germania when news reached him of his adoption by Emperor Nerva. Nerva's strategically picked choice of messenger with the news was twenty-one year old Hadrian, Trajan's former ward. Trajan became one of Hadrian's two guardians following the death of the boy's father. Hadrian was only ten years old at the time, and afterwards he grew up in Trajan's household.

Hadrian found Trajan with his old friend and mentor, Gnaeus Pompeius Longinus. He greeted Trajan warmly and saluted General Longinus formally.

"Who is this young Hercules come to visit?" Longinus asked in good humor. Even as a young man Hadrian was tall and powerfully built. He had a full head of curly hair and a curly beard cut short in the Greek fashion. His intelligent and lively eyes reflected his amusement at life.

"Gnaeus, you remember my ward Publius Hadrianus. We call him Hadrian."

"I remember a young boy who was always running after his Greek tutor to teach him more Greek philosophy and poetry," Gnaeus said. "Look at you now!"

"Generals," Hadrian addressed them respectfully, "I am sent by Caesar Nerva with news from Rome." He took the large leather pouch from underneath his arm and handed it to Trajan. "From Caesar, General."

"We're family, Hadrian. In my tent you may call me Marcus."

Trajan took the leather pouch and carried it to a table. He took out a very large diamond ring, looked at it briefly, then put it aside. Then he took out a long letter written on a parchment scroll and began to read silently.

Longinus turned to Hadrian. "You two are cousins, as I recall?"

"My father and Marcus were cousins. That makes me some kind of distant relative, I suppose," Hadrian smiled.

Trajan laughed at something he was reading. He put the letter down and gave Longinus a somber look.

"I am named the adopted son of Emperor Nerva. He gives me the titles of Caesar and Imperator."

Longinus whistled softly. "This is momentous news, indeed. He names you his successor!"

"Exactly," Hadrian agreed with enthusiasm. "Caesar announced it publically, in full voice, from the rostra!"

"What was the reaction from the crowd? And the Senate?" Trajan asked. For all his humble outward appearance, the man burned with a fierce inner pride.

"At first very surprised because it was completely unexpected. Then very positive. Everyone thinks you are the excellent choice, Marcus. There is no dissent in Rome."

"None?" Trajan asked, not convinced. There were always warring factions when it came to transitions of power.

"None!" Hadrian said emphatically.

Trajan gestured at the letter. "Caesar writes of trouble with the Praetorian Guard. Is there a problem still?"

Hadrian shook his head. "No, Marcus. There was one unpleasant incident where Caesar was forced to order the execution of Emperor Domitian's killers. Once you were named Caesar's heir however the Praetorians became more docile."

"Bastards!" Trajan spat.

Longinus cut in. "Never mind the Praetorians. History is being made here, gentlemen."

"Perhaps so," Trajan allowed.

"Who is considered to be the greatest emperor in the history of Rome?" Longinus asked. He turned to Hadrian. "You're a well-educated young man, you should know the answer."

"The Divine Augustus," Hadrian replied. It was the standard textbook answer.

"Correct. And what," Longinus continued, "was the very first step in the rise of the Divine Augustus to power?"

Hadrian shook his head, not having an answer.

"When he was adopted by Julius Caesar," Trajan answered.

"Precisely! We are at that point in history again. I am certain of it."

Trajan laughed. "Marcus Nerva is no Julius Caesar."

"No he is not," Longinus said. "But you can be another Augustus."

Chapter 27

Trajan's Justice

Sarmizegetusa, February 98 AD

Vezina entered the dining room of King Decebal and Queen Andrada at a brisk walk. "News from Rome. The Emperor Nerva is dead. He died last month. He was in poor health for some time, I am told."

"As you predicted, Vezina," Decebal said, unsurprised. "He did not last very long as the new Caesar."

"As you also predicted, Sire." Vezina pulled up a chair at the table. "Nerva was a safe choice for them until they could decide on a new emperor for the longer term."

"And who is their new emperor?" Andrada asked.

"The Spanish general, Trajan. He is serving as governor of Upper Germania. Or was serving as governor, to be accurate. He is now Emperor Trajan."

"He is a very effective military leader," Decebal added. "He wore down the Germans and drove them out of Pannonia."

"Will this change things between Dacia and Rome?" Andrada asked. "I rather liked the years of peace since the last war against Domitian and Julianus."

"That is yet to be determined, my dear," Decebal replied. "What will this Trajan be like as the emperor, Vezina?"

"I have been asking many people that question, Sire. He seems like a simple man, and also a complicated one."

"What man isn't?" Andrada quipped, glancing at Decebal. She laughed and turned back to Vezina. "Forgive me for interrupting, Your Holiness. Do continue."

"He is said to be not very well educated, but very intelligent. For certain no one questions his military intelligence. He is a soldier, not a scholar. He has the common touch with people. His soldiers are very loyal to him."

"Is he ambitious?" Decebal asked.

"Oh, no doubt," Vezina replied. "He comes from humble family beginnings, not some ancient patrician family. He is from Hispania, not Rome and not even Italia. And yet today he calls himself Caesar. What extraordinary ambition that must have required!"

Decebal nodded in agreement. "I see your point. My question is, where does his ambition lead him?"

"Does it lead to Dacia?" Andrada asked.

"In time, I think yes," Vezina replied. "Our wars with Rome are not over, My Queen."

The King sat back in his chair, gathering his thoughts. "We should send an envoy and extend our well wishes to him. Who can we send?"

All three grew quiet. The best choice would have been Diegis, a high ranking member of the royal family. The death of his wife Mirela the previous summer left him devastated however. After a period of mourning he left Sarmizegetusa to inspect the forts and troops along the Ister frontier. His daughter Ana was practically adopted into the family of Decebal and Andrada. She had the loving attention there of her aunts, Dochia and Tanidela, the sisters of Diegis. She also had the company of Lia, Zelma's daughter. The two of them quickly became inseparable playmates.

Vezina broke the silence. "Let us wait, Sire, and see what develops. We don't yet know when Trajan will be travelling to Rome."

"Very well," Decebal agreed. "But keep a close eye on Germania and what the new Emperor Trajan is doing. He is no Nerva. Nor a Domitian, for that matter."

Moguntiacum, Germania, July 98 AD

Five months later Emperor Trajan was still in camp in Germania. There was a great deal of work to be done in strengthening defenses along the Rhine and the Danubius. In any case he was in no hurry to travel to Rome. When he finally arrived in Rome all things would be in order, as he planned them.

Trajan was re-organizing his staff in charge of the armies in the provinces of Germania, Banat, and Moesia. Gnaeus Longinus would leave soon to command an army in Banat protecting the Danubius frontier with Dacia. The Emperor was interested in strengthening defenses there as much as on the German borders.

Trajan was training Hadrian for a command position. The young man was very bright and learned quickly. He also had Trajan's gift for the common touch with his soldiers. He marched with them, ate their simple food along with them, and slept outdoors when they did.

Hadrian still carried some Hellenic ways about him, but Trajan blamed that on his wife Plotina. While he was away on campaign the majority of the time, Plotina took an interest in Hadrian's education. He developed an unhealthy interest, in Trajan's opinion, in poetry, philosophy, and architecture. Some of the officers were calling him "the Greek." Coming from a Roman, it was not a compliment.

"Tell me about your views on Dacia," Trajan said to Longinus.

"Sooner or later we must deal with them and with Decebalus," Longinus replied. "After the Germans they are our second biggest problem. Decebalus has a strong army. They are well organized. And he has put together a strong coalition of other tribes in the region."

"True enough," Trajan agreed. He smiled. "And less us not forget, they have a great deal more gold and silver than the Germans."

"A great deal more gold and silver, Marcus. Their mountains are very rich in both."

Trajan poured himself more wine. He had a passion for good wine and always made sure that his supply was well stocked.

"Tell me, Gnaeus, in your honest estimate, why did Domitian's campaigns against Decebalus fare so badly?"

"Many reasons, some of which we already discussed. Domitian was arrogant and possessed a poor military mind. He appointed commanders like Cornelius Fuscus because they were loyal to him."

"Tettius Julianus is a very capable army commander."

"True. However the campaign was delayed too long, and Julianus was undermanned."

"Undermanned! Undermanned, you say?" Trajan asked and shook his head incredulously. "Julianus had nine legions!"

Longinus gave a shrug. "Nine legions were not enough, evidently. Decebalus bogged him down in the mountains of Dacia. Julianus was forced to retreat to Moesia for the winter."

Trajan shook his head. "We will not make the same mistakes."

"Certainly not. Decebalus is a superior military mind and he uses our own tactics against us, so we must change our tactics. We must also modify our armor and weapons."

At that moment Hadrian walked into the tent. He looked tired, hot, and dusty.

"Ah!" Longinus cried. "Young Hercules returns."

"Welcome, Hadrian," Trajan greeted him. "How was your trip?"

"The same as every long trip in the summer, Caesar," Hadrian said wearily. "Hot and dusty."

"Indeed. Come, have some water. Or perhaps wine?"

"Water would be fine, thank you." He poured himself a large cup and downed it thirstily. "I shall provide a report of my tour of the Danubius frontier, Marcus. But first I need a bath and a good meal."

"Of course. Gnaeus and I were discussing Dacia. "

"I was saying," Longinus continued, "that we must make some changes to the legionnaire's armor. Our men lose too many arms and legs, and sometimes their necks, far too easily to the Dacian falx."

Trajan nodded. "I have thought the same."

"The falx is the long sword built like a scythe?" Hadrian wondered.

"It is not a sword, exactly. But yes it is designed on the principle of the scythe. And it is lethal against our armor in its current design."

"Changes will be made," Trajan declared.

"I have read about Cornelius Fuscus at Tapae," Hadrian said. "Rome lost four legions and their standards to King Decebalus."

"The loss will be avenged," Trajan said with conviction. He cleared his throat. "Did the Praetorians arrive with you?"

"Yes, Marcus. They are here, as you ordered. They travelled from Rome and I met them on the road to Moguntiacum. I sent a scout ahead to inform you."

"Well done. I have been waiting for them." The Emperor turned to Longinus. "Well, Gnaeus. Shall we go see our loyal Guards?"

Casperius Aelianus, prefect of the Praetorian Guard, and five of his top officers were sitting under a large shade tree. They were tired from their long ride in the hot weather, but were still waiting to be summoned by Caesar. Trajan was not travelling to Rome yet so he ordered these leaders of the Guard to travel to Germania instead.

Prefect Aelianus had no worries. As a young man he had served with Domitian's father, Vespasian, in Judea. The Emperor Trajan's father had also served there, and the two men had known each other well. Aelianus considered himself a friend of both the Flavian family and the Trajanus family. The two families had always been allies. The Emperor Trajan, when he was younger, had served Domitian well as an able general and as governor of Upper Germany.

Attius Suburanus, one of Trajan's officers, brought servants with water and wine for the waiting men. He knew Aelianus casually from his time in Rome. He joined the men for a cup of wine.

"When does Caesar plan on travelling to Rome?" the Prefect asked. "The people are eager to see him and honor him."

Suburanus gave a shrug. "Caesar plans out everything in detail. He will first put things in order here along the Rhine. Then we will do the same along the Danubius in Banat and Moesia. How long that will take, who knows?"

"I would not have that kind of patience," Aelianus said. "I would be in Rome enjoying the adulation of the people and keeping the Senate in line."

"You are not Caesar," Attius said evenly. "Emperor Trajan plans to do great things, and great things are not done in a rush."

"Here comes Caesar now," Aelianus said and got up on his feet. His men did the same.

Trajan, Longinus, Hadrian, and twenty of the Emperor's guards approached them at a brisk walk. This was a surprise. Other men went to see Caesar, not the other way around.

"Hail, Caesar!" Aelianus saluted. His men followed suit.

Emperor Trajan seemed very somber as he looked over the officers from the Praetorian Guard.

"Prefect Aelianus! Do you know why you are summoned here?"

"No, Caesar. I thought rather that Caesar wished to re-appoint us as his officers of the Praetorian Guard." Aelianus paused and gave Trajan a small bow. "If Caesar would grant us that honor."

Trajan's face darkened. "Do you believe that you are fit to serve as the officers of the Praetorian Guard?"

That took Aelianus by surprise. "Indeed, Caesar, I do. I have been a loyal friend of the Flavian family and the Trajanus family since I served with your father in Judea."

"You men," Trajan gestured at the Praetorians angrily, "usurped the authority of Caesar when you were sworn to protect Caesar!"

Aelianus took a deep breath. This was not something any of them anticipated.

"We sought justice against the murderers of Emperor Domitian," Aelianus explained. "Justice was delivered to the assassins. No harm came to Emperor Nerva."

Trajan exploded. "No harm, he says! You challenged the authority of Caesar! You diminished the dignity and honor of Caesar! You very publically humiliated Emperor Nerva, my adoptive father! And you call that no harm?"

Aelianus stood stiffly at attention in the face of Trajan's blistering attack. "No harm was intended, Caesar. We sought only justice for a murdered Emperor."

The Emperor looked up at the sky impatiently, then looked at the faces of each Praetorian in turn. "You were not summoned here to be reappointed to your positions. I would not take a nest of snakes to my bosom."

Aelianus swallowed hard. "As you wish, Caesar."

"You were all summoned here to be punished for your crimes." Trajan paused to let the message sink in. "Your crime is treason against Caesar and the people of Rome."

General Longinus nodded to the guards who surrounded the Praetorians. "Place them under arrest," he ordered.

As Trajan's guards seized him and took away his sword, Aelianus noticed that six soldiers produced long ropes with hanging nooses at one end. They threw the ropes over two of the large branches on the shade tree. This was to be their hanging tree.

"The penalty for treason is death," Emperor Trajan announced in a loud firm voice. "I sentence these men of the Praetorian Guard to death by hanging."

The execution was carried out swiftly and efficiently. There was no protest nor resistance. Casperius Aelianus had nothing more to say and accepted his fate with dignity. He kept his eyes fixed on the sky as the hangman's noose snuffed out his life.

Trajan watched the men die, and then calmly walked back to his tent. He was joined by Longinus, Hadrian, and Attius Suburanus. The Emperor ordered some of his best wine and used it to give a toast.

"We made a small bit of history here today, gentlemen. And we shall make a great deal more before we are done."

"Hail Caesar!" Attius saluted. "Justice is done and Emperor Nerva is avenged."

Trajan turned to Hadrian. "I want news to reach Rome quickly, and you Hadrianus will be my messenger."

"I am honored, Caesar," Hadrian said. "I can't wait to see the faces of some people back in Rome!"

"No gloating," Trajan ordered. "Keep it honest and simple. Oh, and Attius will travel with you. In Rome he will assume responsibility as the new Prefect of the Praetorian Guard."

Suburanus gave Hadrian a smile. Everything had been arranged of course, per the Emperor's planning. The only one not involved in the planning was Hadrian himself.

"The message about what we did here today will be received very clearly in Rome, young Hercules, so do not worry about what to say," General Longinus advised. "Do you know what that message is?"

Hadrian thought for a moment. "That Caesar has a strong sense of loyalty and justice. That he has an iron will and takes decisive action." He paused and turned to Trajan to gage his reaction. "And that those who are not loyal or do injustice will pay with their lives."

Trajan laughed and put his arm around Hadrian's shoulders. "Well said, Hadrian! We'll make a statesman out of you yet!"

Chapter 28

AN UNEASY PEACE

Sarmizegetusa, August 99 AD

*T*he very large bonfire sent showers of red embers floating up into the dark night. Dacians burned large piles of wood because they loved the light and hated darkness. Light was a symbol of the god's presence. Darkness was a symbol of evil and death.

King Decebal and guests sat watching a very lively young people's dance. Twenty dancers between fifteen and twenty years old flew through the air, going through fast-paced and intricate dance steps. The large crowd around them kept up the rhythm with clapping, whistling, and chanting.

Sitting to Decebal's right were two Germanic tribal chiefs, Fynn of the Bastarnae tribe and Attalu of the Marcomanni tribe. Both had been strong allies of King Decebal for many years.

To the King's left, on the other side of Queen Andrada, Prince Davi of the Roxolani Sarmatian tribe sat with his wife Tanidela. He and Decebal's sister married three years ago. The Roxolani had long been Dacia's closest and most dependable allies in their wars against Rome. The marriage of Davi and Tanidela made the alliance even stronger.

Everyone drank chilled wine in the heat of the bonfire. The two Germans pushed aside the wine goblets and brought out their own drinking horns. Usually these were used for ale but they worked just as well for wine. Both of the chiefs were large and burly men who were used to heavy drinking.

Attalu took a big swallow from his drinking horn and smiled with appreciation. He leaned his bearded head in Decebal's direction to be heard better above the loud music. "When I leave I will take a few amphorae of this wine in my baggage cart. We don't grow grapes like these on my land."

"Of course, my friend," Decebal said. "Take as much as you like."

Attalu saluted him with his drinking horn, then quickly pulled back as a twirling female dancer passed too close. He splashed some wine on his shirt and laughed it off.

"I will do the same," Fynn said. He was feeling the wine and his eyes twinkled. "Your Dacian dancing girls are lovely, Decebal. Maybe I will take one home as my wife, eh?"

"If they are willing, then they are yours." Decebal pointed to a very pretty seventeen year old female dancer with long black hair and striking blue eyes. "That one, Fynn, is not for you to take!"

The Chief feigned outrage. "Oh? And why not?"

Decebal gave him a wry smile. "Because she is my daughter Zia, and if you touch her I will have to kill you."

Fynn leaned back and laughed. He reached out with his drinking horn to have it re-filled.

The young dancers built up to a frenzied finale, then all stopped at the same instant after the final step of the dance. Faces glistening with perspiration, they turned as one to face the royal family and bowed in unison. The crowd cheered and shouted their approval. Zia glanced at her parents for a moment then ran off to join Adila and their friends.

Tanidela leaned over to the Queen. "Zia has blossomed since I saw her last, which was three years ago at my wedding. My little niece is a woman now!"

"Yes she is," Andrada replied. "She is looking forward to her own marriage soon."

"Oh! How exciting for her."

Andrada looked at Prince Davi with a smile. "You will come to the wedding, of course."

"Of course, My Lady," he smiled back. "Nothing could prevent us from making that trip." The lands of the Roxolani Sarmatians were a good distance away, to the east of Dacia and north of Moesia. They were a people that bred horses and were superb riders, and were able to travel quickly anywhere they chose to go.

Diegis walked up holding the hand of his daughter, eight year old Ana. The girl had the light brown hair and amber-brown eyes of her mother Mirela, who was now in Zamolxis' heaven. She walked quickly to her Aunt Andrada's side and gave the Queen a hug. Andrada hugged her back and kissed her cheek.

"Did you have enough to eat, Ana?" she asked.

"Yes, Auntie. It was delicious."

"Oh, she eats very well," Diegis said. "It's her sleep I'm worried about. She wakes up with nightmares almost half the nights."

Andrada turned to the girl, calmly. "So you have nightmares, do you? What kinds of nightmares?"

Ana looked shyly at the ground.

"She wakes up crying and frightened about strigoi in the room," Diegis answered for her. Strigoi were the evil spirits of dead people that roamed in the dark.

Andrada took Ana gently by the shoulders. "My brave girl, do not be afraid. The spirits will not harm you. You father will talk to a priest and get some holy water with basil." She looked up at Diegis. "That will keep the strigoi away from your bedroom, your Tata knows this."

Diegis laughed. "That's why we are here! I was looking for Mircea or one of the other priests."

"Tut, tut, my boy! Only ask for the best," a familiar voice said, and Vezina joined them. He looked kindly at Ana, who always seemed a little awed by the sight of the High Priest in his blue robe stitched with silver and gold. "Ana, do you know who is the greatest strigoi chaser in Dacia?"

The girl silently shook her head.

"Why, me, of course!" Vezina cried, which made Ana smile. "And do you know, Ana, how many strigoi have ever tried to attack me in all my years?"

"How many?"

"Not a one! Not a single one. And do you know why?"

Ana's smile became brighter. "Because they are afraid of you."

"Exactly! They are afraid of me. I am not afraid of them." Vezina turned to Diegis. "I will come by your quarters later this evening. I will bring the best potion there is to scare the strigoi away."

"Thank you, Your Holiness," Diegis grinned. "Does that sound all right, Ana?"

"Yes, Tata," she said calmly. "We will scare the strigoi away."

"High Priest Vezina has very powerful magic, Ana. Why, a long time ago, he escaped from a Roman army by using his magic. A puff of smoke and, poof! He was gone."

Vezina chuckled. "Those were a different breed of strigoi."

"Good, the problem is solved!" the Queen declared. "Ana, Dorin is over there. See that big tree? He is training Toma not to herd people. Would you like to go and help him?"

"Yes, Auntie!" Dorin was Andrada's son and Ana's cousin, just one year older than her. Toma was Dorin's new sheep dog puppy. The puppy was following its natural herding instincts, but lacking any animals to herd it was trying to herd people instead. Many sheep dog puppies had to be trained to not do that.

Diegis watched his daughter run to her cousin and his puppy. "That is just what she needed. Thank you, Sister."

"Don't worry, she will be fine," Andrada said. She smiled brightly at them. "Lucky girl! She has a brave father and the best strigoi chaser in the kingdom on her side!"

Early the next morning King Decebal and his guests went to watch the Dacian infantry train. Drilgisa and Diegis accompanied them. Besides sharing manpower the allies also shared training routines and military strategy. When they had to fight together it was best to do so as a coordinated army, not as independent tribes.

The infantry soldiers faced off in pairs. Some were armed with spears, some with falxes, some with sicas, and some with axes. Most carried the round or oval Dacian shield, oak wood with a copper outer shell. More than a few soldiers wore Roman plate armor, carried the large Roman shield called the scutum, and fought with a gladius.

Fynn of the Bastarnae had a question for Drilgisa, the general of infantry. "Are the Romans very useful for you?"

"Yes they are," Drilgisa replied. About three hundred legionnaires had deserted the Roman army and joined the Dacian side. Many of them were now employed as trainers of Dacian troops. "It is not so much that they teach our boys how to attack, Dacian soldiers attack using Dacian tactics. They are most helpful in teaching our soldiers how to defend against Roman tactics."

"That is smart strategy," Attalu said. He turned to the King. "Might we borrow a few of them for a while?"

"Certainly," Decebal said. "They can be as helpful to you as they are to us. How many do you need?"

"About fifty should be enough."

Decebal turned to Fynn. "And you, Fynn?"

"Yes, I like the idea. About fifty for us as well."

"And you, Davi?" Decebal asked.

Prince Davi shook his head and laughed. "My men fight from horseback. What the Romans could teach Sarmatians about fighting on horse, my troops have already mastered by the time they are twelve years old."

"Of course," Decebal grinned. "I was only asking to be polite." He turned towards one of the senior Romans. "Danillo!"

Cassius Danillo walked over quickly and saluted the King and his group. "Sir!" The former centurion had gray around the temples but still kept himself fit for military service. He was a soldier for life.

"Danillo, tomorrow Chief Attalu of the Marcomanni and Chief Fynn of the Bastarnae will be returning home. You will pick fifty trainers for each of them to travel with them."

"Yes, sir," Cassius said. "Might I ask for how long the men will be assigned to their new locations?"

"Ah, that is a good question," Decebal said. He turned to the two Germans. "Most of these men have Dacian wives and families here. They will want to know how long they will be away. Is six months' time sufficient?"

"Yes, six months," Fynn said, and shot a glance at Attalu. The other man nodded agreement.

"Very well then, six months. Carry on, Danillo."

"Sir!" Cassius saluted, then turned and briskly walked away.

"You treat your Romans very well," Attalu remarked.

"I do, and so should you, Chief," Decebal said. "When these men came to our side they stopped being Romans. If they ever fall back in Roman hands again they will be executed."

"Are there any spies among them, do you think?" Davi asked.

"That is very highly unlikely," said Diegis. "Most have been here for ten or twelve years. If any leave without permission and without a very good reason, we catch them and kill them."

King Decebal turned to his visitors. "These Romans here are not our enemies. Our enemies, gentlemen, are the Roman legions in Moesia, Banat, Pannonia, and Germania. Those are the legions that will attack us when Rome becomes aggressive."

"Of course," Davi said. "For now the legions in Moesia are building up their strength. They are building more roads and forts. Emperor Trajan toured the area with his staff and left detailed orders for his generals."

"The same in Banat along the Ister, and before that in Germania," Fynn added.

"Trajan is a master strategist," Attalu said. "That makes him more dangerous. It also means that he will not attack until he feels ready."

"I agree," Decebal said. "He's had plenty of military success in Germania and Pannonia. He inspires loyalty and confidence in his men. That makes him a dangerous military leader."

"As are you, Sire," Drilgisa said.

Decebal waved the comment away.

"No matter. The battle is not between Trajan and me." He looked around at the face of each man. "The battle is between Rome and all the rest of us."

"Then let the bastards come!" Fynn said. "My men will be ready."

"So will the Marcomanni," Attalu said.

"I will talk to the other Sarmatian chiefs," Davi said. "They know the danger of Rome and they will unite."

"Yes, they will," Decebal acknowledged.

"We must be clear on one thing, King Decebal," Davi continued. "Dacia must lead. You, King Decebal, must lead, because the tribes north of the Ister all place their hopes in you."

"Dacia will lead, and Dacia will fight," Decebal said forcefully. "And I vow this, before all of you. For as long as my heart beats, and for as long as Zamolxis blesses me with the wisdom and the strength to lead men into battle, I will never stop fighting."

Rome, October 99 AD

The Emperor Trajan finally travelled to Rome, almost two years after being made Caesar following the death of Emperor Nerva. By the time he reached the city it was clear to all citizens of Rome, from the wealthiest noble to the lowest pleb, that this was a different kind of emperor. Unlike the arrogant Domitian who took what he wanted and evicted people from their homes during his travels, Trajan paid for lodging for his staff and for supplies needed. Tales of his modesty and dignity reached the people of Rome long before the royal party neared the city.

Caesar Trajan entered Rome on foot via the Porta Flaminia, the approach to the city from the north provinces. As was the custom for Caesar he was preceded by twelve lictors who carried fasces wreathed with laurels. There was no parade or any other formal procession, but the Emperor was greeted everywhere by ecstatic crowds who lined the streets and filled the plazas. Little children were hoisted on their parents' shoulders so they could catch a glimpse of the new Emperor. Medical patients left their sickbeds so they could do the same.

Trajan first went to greet the assembly of senators, knights, and other nobles who were enthusiastically on his side. He spoke about the history and grandeur of Rome, and the glory of things yet to come. He made a public vow that he would not practice tyranny. He made a promise to the Senate of Rome that no senators would ever again be executed without due process in the courts.

The city's old unhappy moods, of fear under Emperor Domitian and uncertainty under Emperor Nerva, were gone. Those were now replaced by a new air of security and optimism. Rome was now ruled by a very different kind of emperor.

Trajan was escorted to the Temple of Jupiter, where he made the traditional sacrifice at the altar. He made sacrifices at other altars in the city, all part of the religious ceremonies required of a new Caesar.

Finally, late in the day, the Emperor Trajan and Empress Pompeia Plotina retired to the Imperial Palace. Pompeia was just as modest and unassuming as Trajan, with no putting on airs of privilege or demanding special treatment. They arrived at the palace without any fanfare, no different than any ordinary citizen coming home.

It was a new day for Rome. It was a new day for the world.

Historical Note

The story of Dacia and Rome continues in the second novel in the series titled *Decebal and Trajan*. The story concludes in the third novel titled *Decebal Defiant: Siege at Sarmizegetusa*.

This is a novel, not a history book. Even so the author has made good faith efforts to present events and historical figures from that ancient era as accurately and fairly as possible. Ancient sources were taken into account as well as modern historical retrospectives.

Original historical accounts from that era (85 - 99 AD) are scarce. They are spotty and sometimes contradictory from the Roman side, and almost non-existent from the Dacian side. The author reserves the right of poetic license to fill in the gaps where history is silent or uncertain, and to create a meaningful and entertaining narrative for this novel.

The history of ancient Dacia is preserved mostly in folk tales and songs. No written accounts survived written by Dacian historians to tell the Dacian side of the story. Due to religious beliefs and cultural traditions they did not build statues to glorify their leaders, heroes, and gods, as the Romans excelled at doing. Unfortunately posterity is worse off for it. Although the Dacian culture was a very ancient and complex culture, it is barely recognized, much less mythologized, in history or the arts.

This series of novels examine the wars between ancient Dacia and ancient Rome between the years 85 AD and 107 AD. They do so in large part via a portrayal of the life of King Decebal of Dacia. He is an important historical figure who curiously has not received proper due in either history or historical fiction.

Decebal was without question a highly influential figure during that historical period. He very ably led a wealthy and powerful nation in Dacia, galvanized the resistance to Roman expansion in Eastern Europe, and gave Rome fits for twenty years. He was widely regarded and respected in his time as a military genius, even by the Roman historians of the time and by Roman leaders such as Emperor Trajan.

Although very little is known of his personal life, Decebal's actions show him to be a fierce protector of his people. He was a fighter for freedom and independence. He showed many of the qualities that, in modern culture, are associated with people we call heroes. He was most certainly a charismatic and complex figure to have had such a profound impact on his world during his lifetime. Today he is commemorated as a national hero by the descendants of the ancient Dacians in modern day Romania.

The story of King Decebal cannot be told without also telling the stories of two Roman emperors, Domitian and Trajan. Most people with an interest in ancient history are familiar with the wars between Decebal and Trajan. These are depicted on Trajan's Column and in some histories of the time.

Most people are much less familiar with the reign of Domitian, when Dacia routinely inflicted serious military defeats on Roman armies. Dacia's humiliation of Rome during the reign of Domitian was a large determining factor in what prompted Trajan's revenge tour in 101 AD.

The apologists for Roman myths (and they are legion) will portray the conflicts between Decebal and Domitian as evenly fought, if not outright Roman victories. The facts on the ground prove otherwise. Domitian gave up on trying to fight Dacia in 89 AD and paid Dacia large sums of money annually to keep the peace. Who was honestly and objectively the winner in that negotiated peace, which was known to contemporary Romans as "Domitian's inglorious peace"? Even the ancient Romans of that era knew the score.

Some might conclude that this novel portrays Emperor Domitian in a decidedly negative light. The author asserts that the historical facts almost demand it. Domitian was considered one of the lesser and most hated emperors of Rome, and with good reason. We don't need the ancient historians, such as Suetonius or Cassius Dio, to tell us that Domitian was a vile character. A simple objective look at his known behavior tells us that he was a vile character.

In sharp contrast Emperor Trajan is considered by many to be the *optimus princeps*, the greatest of all emperors of Rome. As a military strategist he was at least the equal of Decebal. As Emperor he was a much more complex and interesting figure than Domitian.

Trajan spent the first three years of his reign as Caesar preparing for what he knew would be the inevitable conflict with Dacia. At that time Dacia was the third strongest military power in Europe behind Rome and Germany. When he was fully prepared Trajan attacked Dacia with the largest army in the history of Rome. The outcome of those wars profoundly changed the history of Dacia and also Rome.

On a more general note the author acknowledges that some of the views regarding ancient Rome that are portrayed in these novels do not fit the standard stereotypes about life in ancient Rome that are so prevalent in novels and movies. This is entirely intentional, and let the facts (and opinions) fall where they may.

Many people are familiar with Napoleon's famous dictum that "history is written by the winners." Fewer people are perhaps familiar with another Napoleonic dictum, namely that "history is fiction agreed upon." The second dictum is just as accurate and meaningful as the first, and in fact is inseparable from it. Napoleon was an astute judge of history as well as of human character. History is biased and is best viewed with a critical eye. This is the opposite of accepting dogma and stereotype.

The history of the Roman Empire is of course better documented than the history of ancient Dacia. It is also heavily prejudiced to the

Roman point of view and told primarily from the Roman perspective. The sources of Roman history either were actually Roman or were sympathetic to the Roman Empire. In this "sympathetic" column we could well include 90% of historians, novelists, playwrights, poets, and moviemakers. From Suetonius to Shakespeare to Ridley Scott and *Gladiator*, everyone knew the drill.

The Hollywood myths about ancient Rome, of bloody gladiator fights, military conquests, and palace assassinations, are what feels true for most people because those stories and images are so familiar. Yet they represent only a small slice of life in those ancient days, and typically a slice of life that is greatly exaggerated for theatrical effect. Shakespeare knew that it made good entertainment long before the producers of Hollywood movies.

The popular and mythologized view of the Roman Empire is that of conquerors who spread culture and civilization to much of their known world. This is the "fiction agreed upon" in Western culture. The historical reality is somewhat more complicated.

It is estimated that the Roman gladius killed more people than any other weapon in the history of the human race. Going beyond accepted dogma, another view of the Roman Empire might be that of a highly successful imperialistic military power that butchered and enslaved tens of millions of people. Did anyone stop to ask those millions of people how they felt about being "civilized" by Rome?

Decebal Triumphant is a novel that asks the question from the point of view of the people of ancient Dacia. This is certainly the road less travelled both in history and in historical fiction.

The Dacians were not hoping to be "civilized" by Rome – they were already civilized.

ABOUT THE AUTHOR

Peter Jaksa, Ph.D. is an author living in Chicago, Illinois. He is a lifetime student of European history during the era of the Roman Empire. In particular he is a student of the history and culture of ancient Dacia.

Books by Peter Jaksa

Historical Fiction:
Decebal Triumphant
Decebal and Trajan
Decebal Defiant: Siege At Sarmizegetusa

Psychology and Self-Help:
Life With ADHD
Real People, Real ADHD

www.addcenters.com

Made in the USA
Coppell, TX
08 April 2021